THE WOLVES

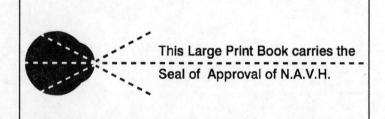

THE WOLVES

ALEX BERENSON

WHEELER PUBLISHING
A part of Gale, Cengage Learning

GALE
CENGAGE Learning·

Farmington Hills, Mich • San Francisco • New York • Waterville, Maine
Meriden, Conn • Mason, Ohio • Chicago

GALE
CENGAGE Learning·

LIBRARY OF CONGRESS CATALOGING-IN-PUBLICATION DATA

Names: Berenson, Alex, author.
Title: The wolves / Alex Berenson.
Description: Large print edition. | Waterville, Maine : Wheeler Publishing Large Print, 2016. | © 2016 | Series: A John Wells novel | Wheeler Publishing Large Print hardcover
Identifiers: LCCN 2015048923| ISBN 9781410484871 (hardback) | ISBN 1410484874 (hardcover)
Subjects: LCSH: Large type books. | BISAC: FICTION / Thrillers. | GSAFD: Suspense fiction.
Classification: LCC PS3602.E75146 W65 2016 | DDC 813/.6—dc23
LC record available at http://lccn.loc.gov/2015048923

Published in 2016 by arrangement with G. P. Putnam's Sons, an imprint of Penguin Publishing Group, a division of Penguin Random House LLC

Printed in the United States of America
1 2 3 4 5 6 7 20 19 18 17 16

For Ezra — batter up!

I didn't know what was going to happen next, and that is the feeling that every player lives for. Centuries of players, of brothers in arms, have felt the same.

— THE BALLAD OF A SMALL PLAYER,
Lawrence Osborne

PROLOGUE

WASHINGTON, D.C.

The President wanted to see John Wells.

The feeling wasn't mutual.

Wells sat in the emergency room at the Virginia Hospital Center in Arlington, waiting for a doctor to set the foot he'd broken a day before on another continent, when his phone buzzed. A blocked number.

"Mr. Wells?"

"If you say so."

"Steve Lipsher at the White House. The President would like to invite you to a meeting in the Oval Office. Four p.m."

"Shafer gonna be there?" Ellis Shafer, a CIA lifer and Wells's closest friend. Currently stuck inside a federal jail not five miles from this hospital, his reward for helping stop a war.

"Just you, the President, and Ms. Green." Donna Green, the National Security Advisor.

"Then no. I can't."

The silence that followed suggested that no one had ever turned Lipsher down before.

"Someone will call you," Lipsher finally said, and hung up.

Wells was tempted to turn off the phone. Five minutes later, it buzzed again. "John. It's Donna Green. Justice is drafting the release order, but we have to find a judge, and it's Sunday, remember?"

"You locked him up easy enough."

"We'll get it done. Promise."

"What about the senator? He coming, too?" Wells meant Vinny Duto, the former CIA director, now senator from Pennsylvania. For the last month, Wells, Shafer, and Duto had secretly worked together against a billionaire casino mogul named Aaron Duberman who'd tried to trick the United States into invading Iran. Duberman's plan had nearly succeeded. Shown false evidence that Iran wanted to smuggle a nuclear weapon into the United States, the President had set a deadline for Iran to open its borders or face invasion.

But barely twelve hours before, Wells and Duto had delivered proof of Duberman's plot to Green, forcing the President to back down. In a midnight speech from the Oval

Office, he called off the attack.

Wells had expected that the President's next move would be to punish Duberman for what he'd done. Expected and hoped. Green's tone, simultaneously wary and pleading, suggested otherwise.

"No Duto," Green said now. "And that's not negotiable."

Wells wasn't surprised. Green and the President had forced Duto out of the CIA two years before. Now Duto had the upper hand. He could destroy the President simply by revealing the truth, that Duberman had suckered the United States. Though Duto had already hinted to Wells that he had another agenda. As a price for his silence, he would make the White House help him in the next presidential election. A straight power play, standard operating procedure for Duto, whom Wells imagined kept a shrine to Nixon in the basement of his mansion.

"Fine," Wells said. If Green didn't know that Wells disliked Duto almost as much as she did, Wells saw no reason to enlighten her. "I'll see you at six. Give you time to get Ellis out, me to get my foot set."

"You're picking the time for a meeting with the President?"

"Come to an emergency room without

11

hundred-dollar bills taped to your forehead, see how long it takes them to fix you."

At 5:45 p.m., Wells offered his driver's license to the White House gate guards and limped toward the West Wing entrance. The worst of the winter was over. Wells wore only jeans and a bright red T-shirt that read *Chicago Homicide: Our Day Starts When Your Day Ends.* Hardly appropriate for meeting the President. But he couldn't make himself care.

As Wells passed through the metal detectors, he knew he should feel good. He and Duto and Shafer had kept the United States out of war. Yet Duberman was still in his fortified mansion in Tel Aviv. Meanwhile, the President's back-and-forth had damaged the United States already. An hour after the President's announcement, Iran's Ayatollah Khamenei made his own speech. He thanked Allah for "defeating the Zionist-American crusaders" and promised that "American lies will not stop our mighty Islamic Republic from using its nuclear facilities *as it sees fit.*" The last four words were new. In the past, Iran had insisted it would develop its nuclear program only for peaceful purposes.

Then Russia and China said they would

lift all economic sanctions against Iran. "The United States must learn not to meddle with other nations," Russia's Foreign Minister said, in a finger-wagging lecture that was more than slightly ironic, given his own country's recent adventures in the Ukraine.

The White House confined itself to repeating the points the President had made the night before. *We will fully review the evidence that Iran was trying to smuggle weapons-grade uranium into the United States. The ultimatum for an invasion no longer serves either side.* The Pentagon had already leaked plans to bring home the troops it had just flown to Turkey and Afghanistan. A *New York Post* headline summed up the popular view: "THANKS, MR. PRESIDENT. WE JUST LOST A WAR WE DIDN'T EVEN FIGHT!"

So Wells wasn't surprised that the mood inside the White House was grim. Though it was Sunday, the West Wing was crowded. Presidential aides trudged along the narrow hallways, staring at their phones for bad news. In the Oval Office anteroom, Wells found Shafer. He was freshly scrubbed and in his best suit, but the bags under his eyes suggested he hadn't enjoyed his time in jail. Or maybe Wells had just forgotten how old Shafer was. They had first met when Shafer was in his late forties. Wells supposed part of him still saw Shafer that way, thick curly hair and a cynic's smile. Now Shafer's hair had become a white horseshoe at the fringes of his skull. His shoulders were bent and narrow from too many years in front of a computer.

He still had the smile, though, the one that warped the edges of his lips. He gave it to Wells. "Chicago Homicide? I'm the one who goes for pointless acts of rebellion."

"Learned it from you, Dad. So don't I get a hug? Or you got enough man-to-man contact the last few days?" Wells couldn't talk to anyone else on earth this way.

"I was in there, no way of knowing what was happening, this siren came on like they were evacuating the place, then the intercom, a voice I'd never heard, *We have decided to broadcast the President's speech tonight because of its importance.* Five words in, I knew you won."

"*We* won, Ellis."

"Lucky us. Now we're here for our prize."

The door to the Oval Office opened. "Gentlemen," Donna Green said.

The President was in his mid-fifties, nearly as tall as Wells, though not nearly as muscled. He wore a tailored blue suit and white

14

shirt. No tie. He extended his hand and looked Wells over. His eyes were resigned, like Wells was an unwanted suitor marrying his daughter. *No idea what she sees in you, but I guess we're stuck with you.* Still, he radiated command and power, the arrogance of the man who always had the last word. Beside him, Green was small and frumpy, in a wrinkled blue sweater and a shapeless gray skirt. Like Shafer, she seemed almost aggressively unfashionable.

"Please." The President indicated the twin yellow couches in the center of the room. "Anyone need a drink?" *Nothing formal, just a friendly chat.*

Wells and Shafer shook their heads.

"I could ask about your foot," the President said to Wells. "Offer to sign that cast. But I have a feeling you're not in the mood."

"Let's just stipulate that we've had the small talk," Shafer said. "You were charming."

"As always. I want to apologize to you, Mr. Shafer. It goes without saying that we should never have detained you —"

"But I'm guilty. I leaked that information, sir."

The President's smile didn't waver. "You've both done a great service."

"You're taking this well. Considering Ladbrokes is making book on when you'll re-sign."

"Good for them. I can't say I was happy when Donna came to me last night. But I'm not angry at *you*. We failed. We shouldn't have needed you. But we did. And for that, I thank you. At some point, I'd love to hear the story, how you did it, start to finish."

Wells found himself impressed with the man's apparent sincerity. Then he heard Shafer. "Very good, sir." A parody of an English servant's accent. "Very, very good." *Veddy veddy guhd.* He golf-clapped. Twice.

Until now, Wells hadn't realized the depth of Shafer's anger. He wondered how far Shafer would push. How much the President would take.

"You're so happy, how come you didn't tell the country the truth? You lied your ass off last night. Now you're about to ask us to keep our mouths shut like good little sol-diers. After we tell you the story, of course. Guys like you *always* want to hear what happened. From your bulletproof offices. Why don't you ask my man here" — Shafer nodded at Wells — "about the nightmares he gets. You think you want the truth, but you don't even want the truth's second cousin, what it's like out there."

"Ellis —" Wells said.

16

"You think because we gave you an enema with the facts last night and you had no choice but to back off your war, everything's cool, we'll keep our mouths shut. And in return we get a secret medal we look at for five minutes before you lock it in a safe and promise that our grandchildren get it fifty years after we're dead? Shiny and gold? Heroic Workers of the Revolution? Tractor on it?"

"Mr. Shafer —"

"I'm not finished. *Sir.* What about Duto? All he wants is your job and you can't give it to him right now, not unless you've secretly rewritten the Constitution. But I bet you promised him you'll make it happen as best you can. Which would be a disaster, in case you don't know. But you don't care. All you want is to stay in here."

Shafer wiped his forehead. "Now I'm finished."

A flush climbed the President's neck like an infection. He reached for the pitcher of water on the table between the couches, poured a glass, drank it down. Wells figured he was buying time to cool off. Yet when he spoke, his voice was even.

"I had that coming. I lied like a rug to the whole country. About Duberman, all of it. Didn't see a choice."

"The truth is always a choice —"

"My turn. I let you talk. Should I have told the world that one man, a civilian, hired a couple of dozen operatives, almost faked us into a war? Would that have made us look better? Everyone's blaming me. Let 'em. Let them say I was bluffing, the Iranians beat me. I know this stains my record forever. I'll take that. Better than the alternative."

The President rattled off the sentences quickly and with an almost unnatural precision. Wells wondered if he'd slept at all the night before, if he'd taken a little helper this morning to stay awake.

"You want to know what I want," the President said. "I am not telling you to keep your mouths shut. Not threatening you. Not implicitly, explicitly, in any way. You want to call *The New York Times,* go ahead. Tell 'em everything. We won't deny it. We won't split hairs about what you told us and when. You want the truth out, you can have it. My only request. Please tell me in advance, so I can be ready."

"To resign?"

The President poured himself a fresh glass of water, looked into it as if it might hold the answer. For a man with no leverage, he was making a decent case, Wells thought.

18

Neither threatening nor begging. Treating them as equals, telling them the choice was theirs.

"Probably how it shakes out."

The bald, liver-spotted truth. They could make him quit, if they chose. Wells wondered if he could substitute his judgment for that of 320 million Americans. Though if the voters knew the truth, would they keep this man in power?

"But you'd rather we didn't." Shafer spoke quietly now.

The President didn't bother to answer.

Shafer looked at Wells. "I said my piece. You?"

The question meant Shafer hadn't decided. Otherwise, he would have forced the issue, dragged Wells along. Wells looked at Green. "You've been quiet."

"I've been listening. Like I should have last week."

"Can he survive? Or is he ruined?"

Green's eyebrows rose. "You're asking me to tell you if I think he should quit? In front of him? And you expect an honest answer."

"I do, too," the President said.

"And if I say it's time?"

"Donna, if I've lost you, then I've lost everyone."

"All right, then," Green said to Wells.

19

"The truth? We're better off with him. As badly as we screwed the pooch, you want to air all this?"

"Suppose we don't air it. He quits in a couple weeks, gives whatever reason he likes." Talking about the man like he wasn't in the room with them.

"That's worse. And either way, the Veep is not the guy for this job. He wants to be liked too much. Talks too much." Green leaned toward Wells. "I know we made a huge mistake. But in the end, you showed us the proof, we listened. No war. Now give us the chance to fix the damage we've done. If we can't, you can go public anytime."

Wells had spent the last dozen years making life-and-death decisions, but he felt unequipped for this one. He looked at the President. "If I agree — and I'm not saying I am — you flush the CIA. Hebley, all his guys. And Ellis gets to stay as long as he likes. He's ninety and drooling, doesn't matter."

"Ninety and drooling?" Shafer said.

"Protection for my son, my ex-wife. I ask, the Secret Service watches them. Forever."

"Not a problem," the President said.

Wells had the uncomfortable feeling that the President had expected his demands exactly. He decided to shake the tree. "And

20

I'll need ten million dollars."

The others, even Shafer, sat up straighter.

"Excuse me?" The President's voice was tight. Offended. The reaction Wells had hoped to provoke. "I didn't think you were in this for the money."

"I'm not."

"So this is, what, a tip?"

"Not that you need to know. But half to an animal shelter in New Hampshire. Long winter up there for strays." Wells thought of Tonka, the mutt he'd found years before, in his ex-girlfriend Anne's keeping now.

"The other five, yours to keep."

"Now that I'm freelance, I don't have someone to call at Langley if I need a plane or a dozen guys with guns. My winning smile only goes so far. I usually find I need to offer cash, too. I had a couple of million from the Saudis, but I spent it. So, a refill."

The President nodded. Wells sensed he was looking for a reason to say no but couldn't find one. "Fine. Tell Donna where to send the money and we'll get to you Monday. Anything else? Your own aircraft carrier?"

"Stay out of the way while I take care of Duberman."

The President shook his head.

"Then forget it." Wells stood.

"John —"

"Please don't call me John. We don't know each other that well." What he needed to say came to him all at once, a speech brewing for years. "You know what's always the same? The top guys always skate. We never touch them. American, Saudi, whatever, they make their messes and everybody else cleans up. I don't mean to sound naïve, but I've had enough compromises for the greater good. Duberman, we can take him. Nobody's protecting him."

The President nodded. "Somebody spends two hundred million dollars to get you reelected" — as Duberman had done for this President — "he's not just a donor. He's a friend. He's been in this room. Then he tries to fake the United States into a war? Fake *me*? You think I don't want him to pay?"

"Then let me do something about it."

"Not you. We're going to do this the right way, even if it takes time. We have to take him out in a way that doesn't blow back on us —"

"On you —"

"Me and the country, yes. You can have everything else. But not Duberman. You don't like it, call the papers." The President reached into his inside suit pocket, came out with an iPhone. "Secret Service lets me keep it as long as I'm in here and can't lose it."

He pressed his thumb to the home button to unlock it, tossed it to Wells. Then sat back on the sofa, as studiously casual as a poker player who had shoved all his chips into the middle of the table. *Over to you. Call or fold.*

This guy. He'd humiliated himself and the country. Yet he still acted like he was in charge. Like sheer force of personality would see him through. The world's best bluffer.

Wells saw the irony. He complained no one ever held the men in charge accountable. Now he had the chance to make the most powerful man in the world pay. Only he couldn't do it. He handed the phone back. "You promise me, I stay out of it, you'll get him."

"I will do everything possible. Understand, that doesn't mean blowing up his mansion or his plane with his family on it. No collective punishment. No civilians and especially not his wife and kids. Him only, and maybe that one bodyguard, the one who's always with him —"

"Gideon." Wells wouldn't forget Gideon Etra's name soon. Or ever.

"Yes. Gideon's a legitimate target. So? Will

23

you give me a chance?"

"One condition. Get him out of Israel. Within a week."

The President shook his head in confusion.

"Tel Aviv's the hardest place to kill him. The Mossad and Shin Bet will know the second you bring in a team. He can hole up in his mansion. And he probably figures you won't come after him if he has his family around. Flush him, make him move, maybe he makes a mistake. Goes to that island he owns, nice fat target."

"They won't kick him out without a good reason," Green said. "We'll have to tell Shalom" — Yitzhak Shalom, the Israeli Prime Minister — "the whole story."

What Wells wanted. The more people knew, the more pressure to act the President would face.

The President and Green whispered briefly.

"Okay," the President said. "But he winds up in some underground compound in Moscow where we can't touch him, don't blame me."

Wells looked at Shafer. "What do you think, Ellis?"

"I'd like to know what Duto wants."

"Nothing you wouldn't expect," the President said. "Carte blanche in naming the new DCI. All my donor files, plus all the oppo research we have on every potential candidate, both parties."

"You told him no to that?"

"I told him yes to everything."

"You gave him your dirt."

"It isn't that juicy. Politicians are boring these days."

"What are you going to do when he tells you he wants you to endorse him?"

"Truth is, that would barely move the needle. Even in the primary. Nobody cares what I think. I'm the past. The past can't sign bills. The only way I can guarantee he gets the job would be to make the Veep resign, name Duto Veep, then resign myself. That would be a constitutional crisis in a can. I'd rather have it all come out."

"Plus you'd be out, anyway," Shafer said.

"Correct. So that's not happening."

"Just don't underestimate him."

"Lesson learned. So? You on board?"

Shafer tapped Wells on the leg. "Good enough for him, good enough for me."

"And vice versa," Wells said. "For a while."

"How long?" Green said.

"Time limits only cause trouble." An unsubtle reference to the President's failed deadline. "Last thing. I don't want anyone on me. I find out you're watching, it's off."

"Fine."

Then they had nothing else to say. Green gave Wells and Shafer cards without names, just numbers on the front and back. "Cell and home. Call anytime."

"Let's go to Shirley's," Shafer said, when they were finally off the White House grounds. A run-down bar in northeast D.C., left over from the District's bad old days as the Murder Capital. It sold two-dollar shots of no-name booze, and its bathroom sent customers to the back alley. The perfect place for a defeat celebration.

"Your wife won't mind?"

"My wife is just happy I'm out of jail."

"Drinkers wanted — inquire inside" read the sign taped to Shirley's front door. The room inside it was dirtier than ever. Like going down-market was a strategy. Wells wanted to summon some nostalgia for the place, irritation for the eight-dollar-a-beer gastropub that would replace it as Washington's gentrification spread ever farther east. He couldn't. It could have been cheap and local and still have had pride.

Wells ordered a Budweiser and didn't drink it. Shafer ordered whiskey and did. One shot, a second, a third. Shafer wasn't a big drinker, and the shots added up. A rheumy film blanked his eyes. After his fourth shot, he poked Wells in the side, his finger hardly denting the muscle over Wells's ribs. "I ever tell you about Orson Nye? My first COS?" Chief of station. "In Congo? That first posting in Africa, back in the day, I had the worst case of Nile fever."

"West Nile?"

Shafer smirked. "No, like Potomac fever." Washington residents used the term to describe the naïve excitement that young arrivals to the city displayed over their proximity to power. *That intern's got Potomac fever so bad, we could have him research the weather service budget for a month and he'd love it.*

"Hard to imagine." Wells peeled the label from his Budweiser and sloshed the liquid inside back and forth. Muslims didn't drink. He was Muslim. Thus, he didn't drink. The rules were the rules.

He missed beer, though.

"Oh, but I did. Loved it, all of it. The embassy parties. Chartering a plane so some twenty-year-old could fly me into the jungle for a meeting with the Angolan rebels. The weekly briefings in the secure room. The safe with the gas masks and the nines and the grenades. All the coms protocols we had to use, back then it wasn't just some encrypted phone. Our secretaries practically needed Ph.D.s. Checking out the surveillance photos we had of the KGB residents, knowing that they had the same photos of us. Spy versus spy. So glamorous."

"I'm waiting for the *but.*"

"But. Took me maybe a year to figure out that everything we did was for show. Mobutu was all that mattered in Congo." Mobutu Sese Seko, the country's president for thirty-two years, until just before his death in 1997. "And all he cared about was money. Carter talked a good game about human rights, but he kept the man's palms greased. Reagan didn't even pretend to care."

Shafer raised his glass and the bartender shuffled over.

"One more?" The guy looked like he belonged in a nursing home, not a bar.

"At least. Your name's Ed, right?"

"Depends who's asking."

"You'll never guess where we were today, Ed."

"Got that right." The bartender filled Shafer's glass, swiped a pair of dollar bills from the counter, walked away.

"Gonna miss this place," Shafer said.

"Makes one of us. Mobutu?"

"Back then, nobody worried about terrorism; the COS and the ambassador threw parties all the time. Open bar, wide open. One night, I'm drunk, I start spouting to Orson, the people of Congo are starving, Mobutu's stealing with both hands. We're standing by, letting him; why don't we do something about it? He's drunk, too, big guy, old-school agency, country-club type. Pretty wife. He puts his hands on my shoulders, leans in — he smelled great, by the way —"

"I'm not sure what to make of the fact you remember that."

"I can't say a man smells good? And he said, 'Look, you want me to send a cable, *Time to get rid of MSS*? We'll go to the secure room, do it right now. Just promise me one thing.' And I said, 'What?' And he said, 'Whoever comes next will be better. At least Mobutu's greedy first and a sadist second. At least I can go over to the palace, ask him to lay off the fingernail pulling and leg breaking when it gets too bad.' "

Shafer had delivered this monologue in a Jimmy Cagney–esque voice that apparently was meant to be Nye's. He raised his glass. "Here's to you, Orson. You shut me up good. You know what I said back to him? *Zip-a-dee-doo-dah, zip-a-dee-ay, my oh my* —"

29

Wells didn't like seeing Shafer drunk. "Had to have been guys who were better."

"And worse. We couldn't tell 'em apart. Whoever we picked would say the right things until he took over. Then maybe we'd find out the truth. And plenty of broken glass along the way. Plenty plenty. Even after only a year over there, I was sure of that."

"So Mobutu stayed in power for another twenty years, almost, and destroyed Congo."

"Sure did. Hasn't improved since he died, though."

"How come you never quit, Ellis?"

"I have a good marriage, right?"

"I don't know much about marriage, but it looks that way."

"Great family. All the drama I didn't have in my personal life, it went to the agency. I always thought of the CIA as a woman. A beautiful woman. She cheats, she fights, she lies, but you get addicted to the drama. Of course I only went out with three women in my life, so what do I know?" Shafer downed what was left of shot number five and reached for the bottle in front of Wells. "May I?"

"Please don't."

Shafer took a pull, belched. "Nectar of the gods. Though not Allah."

"You think we did the right thing by letting him skate? The President, I mean."

"Heck if I know, John. I know you weren't ready to do it, and I wasn't, either. Let's see what happens. Donna Green was right about one thing. We can always change our minds."

Wells was done with this crusty bar. And with Shafer. "Let's get a cab."

"One more."

"No more." Wells lifted Shafer off the stool. He was light as an empty sack and Wells wondered if he might be sick.

Not that. Not Shafer, too.

"You want to stay over?"

"So you can watch me sleep, report my nightmares to the President?"

"It happened."

"*Once.* You poured it on thick enough."

Outside, Wells led Shafer south and west until they found a taxi.

"Get out of this town," Shafer said, as he slid inside. "It doesn't agree with you. Sort out your love life. If you can't do that, at least go see your kid. Give our fearless leader a chance to keep his word."

"He can't get away with this." Wells wasn't sure whether he was talking about Duberman or the President.

"You'll know when it's time. We all will."

31

Shafer hauled the door shut. He didn't look back as the cab rolled away.

PART ONE

1

HONG KONG

Aaron Duberman owned estates all over the world. But since marrying Orli Akilov, an Israeli supermodel, he had spent more and more time in Israel. After the President's speech, he was glad he had. Since its very beginnings, Israel had been a haven for Jews who faced persecution. A "law of return" gave all Jews the right to gain Israeli citizenship. Duberman wondered if he should take advantage.

At the least, he planned to stay inside Israel indefinitely. The United States would hesitate to kill him here without telling the Israeli government of its plans. And Duberman doubted the government would let another country kill a Jew inside Israel. Especially him, especially under these circumstances. The Prime Minister would surely see that Duberman had done what he'd done to protect Israel from Iran.

Five days after the President's speech, Duberman learned how wrong he was. He was eating dinner with Orli and their twin sons at the mansion when his gate guard called.

"Yaakov Ayalon is here." The guard's voice carried unmistakable respect. Ayalon headed the Israeli Security Agency, the famous Shin Bet, Israel's FBI. "He asks you meet him at the gate."

"Tell him I'll be glad to see him inside."

The response came back seconds later. "He asks you meet him at the gate."

"I have to go," Duberman said to Orli.

"At dinner?" She treated dinners with the twins as close to sacred. Even on nights when they ate out, they often had a first meal at home. Duberman had joked she wanted him to become bulimic. *Just like your friends in the business.*

He kissed her and the boys, wondering if he'd ever see them again, stepped through his cavernous mansion, past the Jeff Koons balloon-animal sculptures and the Keith Haring paintings. Fifty million dollars' worth of modern art in the front gallery alone. Barely a rounding error in his thirty-billion-dollar fortune.

What good was any of it now?

Outside, the night was calm, the air fresh and clean. Three Ford Mondeos sat nose to tail, two men in each. Ayalon waited by the gate. He was a bantam of a man, with black nerd-chic glasses, a neatly tailored suit, close-cropped gray hair. He looked like a psychiatrist with a rich clientele.

"Your phone, please."

Duberman handed it over. Ayalon turned it off, tucked it in his pocket.

"You can come with me."

Surely the Israelis wouldn't pluck him from dinner to put a bullet in his head. But then what exactly was the protocol for an assassination?

Ayalon led him to the middle Ford. "I know it's less fancy than what you're used to." Within minutes, they were on Highway 1, headed southeast, toward Jerusalem. Whenever Duberman made this drive, he was struck by how small Israel was. Jerusalem and Tel Aviv were barely forty miles apart. The whole country was about the same size as New Jersey, though longer and narrower, less strategically defensible. When the Muslims threatened to push the Jews into the sea, they weren't speaking rhetorically.

Yet the hills outside Jerusalem were beautiful, even in the dark. For one short stretch, the highway coursed through a canyon that offered the illusion of being wild country.

37

Then it turned and rose toward the glowing lights that marked the newest western tendrils of the ancient city.

Minutes later, they turned onto the road that led up the hill that was home to Israel's central government complex. "Knesset?" Duberman said, the name of the Israeli parliament. Ayalon didn't answer.

Instead, they turned into the parking lot of the Israel Museum, a low cluster of modern buildings that occupied prime real estate near the parliament. A loading bay big enough for a tractor-trailer was open. The lead and chase cars waited outside as the Ford carrying Duberman drove to the back of the bay. Duberman reached for the door.

"We wait inside," Ayalon said. Fifteen minutes later, a five-car convoy sped into the bay, an armored Cadillac limousine in the center.

"Out."

Duberman stepped out as the Caddy stopped beside the Ford. A burly bodyguard emerged from the right back door. "Fine," he said, and a tall man unfolded himself from the back seat. Yitzhak Shalom. Ayalon and the guards walked away, leaving Shalom with Duberman. The two men were about the same height, but Shalom was painfully thin. His breath carried the oily smell of grape leaves. They'd met dozens of times. Duberman had donated millions of dollars to Shalom's political party. But Shalom's face suggested that neither the money nor their friendship nor Duberman's marriage to Orli would help him.

"Mr. Prime Minister —"

"I've spoken to your President." A slight emphasis on *your,* a reminder that Duberman was American, not Israeli. "You need to leave."

"But Tel Aviv is just getting nice."

"You *joke*?"

"The right of return."

"Doesn't apply to murderers."

"If you've spoken to the President, you know I only aimed at Israel's enemies."

"What about the Americans your people killed?"

Duberman couldn't deny the accusation. As part of the plot, his operatives had killed a CIA station chief and his bodyguards, hoping Iran would be blamed.

"When he told me what you'd done, I nearly offered to solve the problem myself." Shalom lifted his head and huffed, a single short exhale, like a witch casting a spell. This close, Duberman smelled his stomach bile. "Please don't think about begging your right-wing friends for help. Yaakov and I are only ones who know the truth. If that changes, you won't benefit."

"Don't you see that what I did, I did for Israel?"

"If you think that, you're an even greater fool than I thought. You have forty-eight hours. Of course you can keep your properties here, but you can never come back."

Me and Moses. Banished from the Promised Land. Duberman feared the Prime Minister wouldn't appreciate the comparison. "What about Orli?"

"Did she know?"

"Of course not."

"Then she can stay. The children, too." Shalom turned away. Just before he stepped into his limousine, he looked back. "Two days, Aaron. Don't make the Shin Bet come again. They won't be so polite."

Ayalon didn't ride with him back to Tel Aviv. Duberman had the Ford to himself. The highway rolled by as he considered his next move. If Israel was closed to him, Europe was out, too, and of course the United States. Isolating himself on his island would only make him an easier target. *A mysterious early-morning explosion has destroyed the mansion belonging to casino billionaire Aaron Duberman on his private island of Gamma Key. Duberman is missing and presumed dead in the explosion . . .*

Presumed dead. What about faking his death, taking off with a few million dollars? Duberman doubted he could stay hidden for long, even with plastic surgery to disguise his features. He was too well known, and facial reconstruction wasn't effective for people in their sixties. Like the people inside them, faces turned grooved and worn, their features difficult to change. Even if the surgery succeeded, where could he go? Besides English and Hebrew, he spoke a little Spanish, nothing else. Would he move to a village in the Peruvian jungle and act the part of an overaged hippie interested in the local shamans?

No matter where he went, he'd have no contact with Orli or his children. The CIA and NSA would watch them forever. He'd have no friends, no possibility of making any. He'd have no way of spending his millions without attracting attention that he couldn't survive. He'd be in an open-air prison of his own design, waiting for the day when a hit team knocked on his door.

He had to have a better choice.

China. The country that had saved his

parents from certain death. They had escaped the Holocaust by fleeing from Vienna to Shanghai after Hitler's troops crossed the Austrian border in 1938. Almost eighty years later, maybe China could do the same for him. He had a mansion on Hong Kong Island, near the top of Victoria Peak. The President had told Israel the truth, but he wouldn't want to show the same weakness to the Chinese. If the United States decided to come after him in Hong Kong, it would do so on its own, without Chinese help. Of course, the President still might try, but the risks were even bigger than they'd be in Tel Aviv. Hong Kong was as densely populated as any city in the world, and the Chinese wouldn't look kindly on an attack that killed their citizens.

Plus Duberman had a good excuse to live in Hong Kong for a while. His casinos in Macao, forty miles west of Hong Kong across the Pearl River Delta, were the heart of his company. He would add even more security guards to convince the President that killing him wouldn't be worth the trouble. Maybe in a few months, tempers would cool. Maybe he could secretly offer to donate his fortune to the President's favorite charity, buy himself penance.

Maybe, maybe, maybe. Duberman knew

the odds were long. But he knew, too, that he had no choice. For the first time, he understood in his bones why gamblers stayed at his tables long after they should have left. Why they reached for the last credit card in their wallets, the one they had promised themselves never to touch, the one for the groceries. Whatever the odds, they were in too deep to leave. Once you'd lost everything, why not hope for a miracle?

As he walked through the mansion toward his bedroom, he found himself hoping Orli would be asleep. Or even out. Anything to avoid having to explain what had happened tonight.

Duberman had been a legendary playboy. He'd long since lost track of how many women he'd bedded. A thousand, at least. As he'd neared sixty, he realized he wanted to leave something besides casinos and stained sheets behind. He wanted children, and to him children meant a wife. Orli wanted kids, too, and she'd figured out rock stars might not be her best bet. She was cynical enough to understand the deal they were making, smart enough to stick to it, to know that he wouldn't tolerate her stepping out.

Despite the age difference, they got along.

Like him, she was fundamentally unpretentious, street-smart rather than bookish, and a hard worker, even if her work consisted of two-hour Pilates regimens. They even had a solid sex life. Duberman couldn't perform like a twenty-something anymore, but he was still in shape, and what he lacked in vigor he made up in experience. With the help of a drug called Clomid — beloved of steroid cheats and fertility doctors — Orli was soon pregnant with twins.

The pride Duberman felt surprised him slightly. Orli's offer to take a DNA test didn't. He'd made her sign a prenuptial agreement. If they divorced, she would receive tens of millions of dollars. But they both knew that money was a fraction of his wealth. She wanted him to have no question about his paternity, so that he would leave everything to her and their children without hesitation. He agreed to the test. Why not? He didn't think she was bluffing, but he saw no reason to take the chance. Sure enough, the children were his.

Orli was a better mother than Duberman had expected. She threw herself into the dirty details of being a parent, changing diapers and mashing food. He was embarrassed he'd ever questioned her motives for having them. In a way, he envied her. He loved the twins, but on a minute-by-minute basis he wasn't much interested in their pooping or their squirming or the mushy noises that they made.

He stepped into their bedroom and found her awake and in bed, typing on her laptop. She flipped it shut, stared at him. Even furious, she was distractingly beautiful. Every part of her fit together perfectly, and she had the natural grace of a gymnast.

"The head of Shin Bet?"

"It's complicated."

"Tell me the truth."

"The truth is, better if I don't."

"Then I leave. The boys with me." She slid from the bed, picked black yoga pants up off the floor. "You think I need your protection, Aaron? I'm beautiful, I must be stupid. Did I ever tell you how I lost my virginity?"

He knew her secrets. Even some she thought belonged only to her. Not this one. "I assumed it was to me."

No one was smiling at his jokes tonight.

"I was fifteen, I went to Paris, my first big round of shows, Dior picked me to walk. A big deal, Dior. My agent, Nicholas was his name, he said he needed to stop at his office before he dropped me at my hotel. We get there at six-thirty, you know, France, nobody works past five, the place is empty. He takes me into his office, says, 'Let's have glass of wine to celebrate. Your first big score.' I said, 'No'; he said, 'One glass.' "

"Wasn't Natalia with you?" Her mother.

"At the hotel. Anyway, he gives me the wine, and it tastes a little funny, but I don't know anything about wine. I drink it. Five minutes later, I don't feel so well. Five minutes after that, the room is spinning, I pass out. When I wake up, I'm on the floor of his office, and he's inside me. Blood all over the floor, and it *hurts.* No one tells you that, how much it hurts. I screamed. I begged him to stop. He told me I'd get used to it, next time I'd like it better —"

She rubbed her hand across her mouth, closed her eyes, fifteen again and back in Paris.

"Finally, he's done. A virgin, he says. Didn't think those existed anymore. I tell him he'd better kill me, I'm telling my mother when I get back to the hotel, I'm calling the police. He says go ahead. He holds up my wineglass, says I was drinking, no one will believe me, everyone knows models are little whores. Anyway, if I do, I'll never get another job, not in Paris or any-where."

"So you didn't tell your mother?"

46

Orli laughed, small and bitter. "I did. The very minute I came to our room."

Duberman sat beside her. She edged away.

"She told me I'd get over it. You know, good money, and there was something else, too. Mothers and daughters, I don't think men can understand, my mother was pretty enough, but forty-seven, her looks were fading, and I was —"

"This."

"She told me I would remember for the rest of my life, the way men really are. That being beautiful makes you a target. She said I shouldn't think anyone would believe me. Understand, I was still bleeding, bruises on my legs."

"I'm sorry, Orli." The only words he had, however inadequate.

"She asked me, was I *sure* I hadn't invited him. We were in a little hotel on the Left Bank, the sixth floor. Our room had a balcony, and I walked outside and looked down and the pavement called to me. But then I decided, no, I won't give them the pleasure, not my mother, none of them. You think I don't know the world?" She reached over, took his hand, squeezed once. "You'd better tell me."

He didn't answer. She let go of him, pulled on her shoes, went to the bedroom door, long, sure strides. "I'll take the boys to Sam's." Her younger sister, whose given name was Shasa, but whom Orli always called Sam. "Don't fight me for custody. I'll take the prenup."

"Orli —"

"Then *let me judge.*"

He should have stayed silent and let her go. Kept her away, kept her safe. But he couldn't face losing her, much less the boys. So he told her. Not everything, but enough.

"You tried to fool the United States into invading Iran," she said, when he was done. She sat beside him on the bed, touched his neck gently, a nurse calming a feverish patient.

"It must seem —" Another sentence he couldn't finish. "I promise it's true."

"But the CIA found out the truth."

"Not exactly." He understood her confusion. "This man Wells who used to work for them, and two others. One a senator named Duto."

"The ones who came to the mansion?"

"Right." In the desperate days before the President's deadline, Wells and Duto had come directly to Tel Aviv to confront Duberman. "The third one still works at the agency — Ellis Shafer is his name. They figured it out together and went to the

48

President."

"Here I thought I had the best story of the night. And the President doesn't tell the truth because he thinks it'll make him look guilty, too. Because of all the money you gave to his reelection."

"Exactly. People will believe he knew what I was doing. Even though he didn't."

"So why did Mr. Shin Bet come?"

"The President won't say anything in public, but he told the Prime Minister the truth, what really happened. He asked the Israelis to make me leave —"

"Why?"

"Probably because they think I'll be an easier target outside Israel. And Shalom agreed. You and the boys can stay. I have forty-eight hours to get out."

"You can't change his mind?"

"He practically threatened to pull the trigger himself."

"Where will you go? Somewhere in Africa they don't have electricity, they don't know you. Tibet, a monk. After all your women." She laughed, with a mocking edge.

"Hong Kong."

"You think the Chinese love your casinos so much they'll protect you?"

"The President will be too embarrassed to tell them. Maybe I can wait it out. Best case, he doesn't do anything for the rest of his term, he's too busy hoping not to be impeached. When he's done, the next guy doesn't know anything about it."

"What about this man Wells?"

A good question. "I don't know. He might come after me, too, or he might decide it's enough, he stopped the invasion, let the President deal with me."

She tilted his face toward hers. He didn't think she'd ever looked at him so carefully before.

"One last look before you leave?"

"You know why I chose you, Aaron?" She smiled. Her teeth were not quite perfect, with a tiny space between the top two in front. Somehow models were allowed to have gapped teeth, the only imperfection the arbiters of beauty permitted.

His face must have betrayed his surprise.

"Don't tell me you thought *you* chose *me*?"

But, yes, he had. Even with the age difference. "I thought my offer was compelling." He raised his hands to the mansion around them.

"You weren't my first billionaire."

Something else he hadn't known.

"I looked at you, how hard you worked, the engine never stopped —"

"You knew I would be too busy to bother you much."

"I thought, this guy's the same now as he was when he was twenty, didn't have a penny. He just wants to win."

"And that was appealing?"

"You can't imagine how *lazy* rock stars are. Half the reason they wind up as junkies is that heroin is the world's best excuse to do nothing. So you went after me, you swept me up, maybe it was a little bit cheesy, over-the-top, the million-dollar ring —"

"Four —"

"Like you couldn't even imagine I'd say no. How you've lived your whole life. Now, finally, you went too far." She cocked her head, looked at him critically. "Tell me again why you did this? Aside from proving that you could?"

He pointed to the Tel Aviv skyline through their window, the apartment buildings glowing along the beach. "It all looks solid. But a nuclear bomb —" He snapped his fingers. "It's gone. And the problem is no one believes it can happen until it does. It seems like madness. But mad things happen."

She twined her fingers in his. "You really think you can get out of this?"

"It's possible."

"Then I'm coming with you."

"Orli —"

"No one thinks I had anything to do with it, right? If everyone knows I'm innocent, who's going to touch me?"

"The longer you stay, the more my guilt becomes yours."

"But not right away."

"No. The Americans will assume you don't know. And even if they start to suspect you, they would probably warn you first."

"Then I'm not going to worry about that. Promise me, from now on we're partners."

"Yes. Partners."

Forty-six hours later, they were on Duberman's personal Boeing 787 Dreamliner, bound for Hong Kong. The mansion on Victoria Peak was fully furnished. Even so, they were carrying dozens of trunks of clothes and jewelry, along with their personal chef and Orli's trainer. The travails of the super-rich.

As they flew, Duberman wondered whether the United States would pluck them out of the sky, force them to land in an American ally like Tajikistan, and from there bring him back to American soil for trial. But the hours and the countries passed and then they were in Chinese airspace and he knew they were safe. Their arrival at the

VIP terminal in Hong Kong was a strange anticlimax. They cleared immigration without a hitch, convoyed up to the mansion on the Peak, and unpacked. In other words, told the people who worked for them to unpack.

The days turned into weeks. They settled into a routine of sorts. Orli worked. She even left Hong Kong sometimes for photo shoots. Duberman encouraged her. He didn't want her to feel she was stuck. And his absence from the public eye would be less notable if she went out.

Meanwhile, Duberman spent most of his time in the mansion. He left only to visit his casinos in Macao, a fifteen-minute helicopter ride. He always flew at night and made sure he was never the only passenger by asking big Hong Kong gamblers to ride with him. They viewed the chance to ride with him as an honor. No doubt they would have felt differently if they'd known he was using them as human shields, insurance against the risk that the United States would blow his helicopter out of the sky above the South China Sea.

He watched CNN International and the BBC religiously, wondering when his role in the plot would leak. But the White House seemed concerned mostly with damage control. In interviews, the President and his advisors blamed the CIA, saying it had misinterpreted Iran's intentions. A month after his failed deadline, the President fired Scott Hebley, the DCI that he himself had put in place. On the cable news shows, talking heads joked that the President might not have pulled off an invasion of Iran, but he had sure ravaged Langley.

Congressional leaders demanded the President and his aides fully explain what had happened. The White House refused, on the grounds of national security and executive privilege. Some members of Congress threatened to impeach him, but the idea didn't gain traction. After all, the United States *hadn't* gone to war. Polls showed most Americans believed the President had been bluffing all along, hoping an invasion threat would force Iran to end its nuclear program. They were upset the move had failed. But a majority of them also thought that second-guessing it would weaken the United States. As far as Duberman could tell, the political stalemate worked to his advantage.

Duberman received more good news with the return of his top bodyguard, Gideon Etra. During his confrontation with Duberman in Tel Aviv, Wells had cut Gideon's left

Achilles tendon, literally hobbling him. Surgeons in Israel had stitched the fibers in the heel back together, and Gideon had spent months in rehabilitation. He was almost healed, though he still couldn't run. Duberman trusted Gideon more than anyone else in the world, even more than Orli. A decade before, Duberman had spent millions of dollars on an experimental bone-marrow treatment that saved the life of Gideon's son Tal. *Kill for you,* Gideon had told him, when the oncologists pronounced Tal free of leukemia. *Or die for you.*

Duberman started to let himself believe the President might leave him alone. He asked Geoffrey Crandall, his local lawyer, to look into whether he and his family could become permanent residents of Hong Kong. A *yes* came back quickly. The territory had strict immigration laws, but it was as eager for billionaires as everywhere else. Once again, Duberman had cheated the odds. Yet along with Duberman's elation came fresh anger.

At John Wells.

Wells had ruined his plans. If Wells hadn't gotten involved, the United States would already have attacked Iran. Instead, the country was a bigger threat than ever.

Tehran knew the United States would never invade. It could build a bomb at its leisure. Sooner or later, the world would have to let it join the nuclear club.

Wells was to blame.

Plus Duberman would never be safe while Wells was alive. Wells had killed a dozen of Duberman's operatives. He was surely furious that Duberman had escaped what he would call justice. Duberman guessed the President had promised Wells he would act and asked Wells to stay away. But with each passing week, Wells would trust that promise less, move closer to coming after Duberman on his own.

On a humid Wednesday, thunderclouds swirling over Hong Kong's magnificent harbor, Duberman brought Gideon into his office. "How's your ankle?"

"Better every day."

"As long as you don't tear it again."

"I didn't tear it the first time."

The perfect segue.

"I want to take care of him," Duberman said.

"Stir this up. Now? Whatever calculation the President's making, if you kill Wells, the truce will be off. He'll have to hit you back."

"What if Wells comes after *me*? Here, to Hong Kong, tries to attack me, kill me, in the house where I live with my family —"

"Self-defense."

"Wells is a problem for him, too." Him, in this case, meaning the President. "Maybe he thanks me for taking care of this."

Gideon sat on the couch across from Duberman's desk, rubbed his wounded ankle. He was a trim man in his mid-fifties who still carried himself like the soldier he had once been. Not just a soldier, a sniper, with thirty-six confirmed kills during Israel's 1982 invasion of Lebanon. His nickname was Chai-chai — *chai* being a Hebrew word that meant "life" and also "eighteen." Duberman sometimes wondered what Gideon felt about all those kills. Were the details still sharp, or had time blurred the edges of his memories? Could you forget killing a man?

"So, what, you invite Wells over?"

"The expansion opens in two months." Duberman was adding a hundred-and-ten-story tower to 88 Gamma Macao. Its two top levels, almost eighteen hundred feet above the South China Sea, would be open only to the highest rollers. The Sky Casino, atop the Sky Tower. The tables would take minimum bets of one hundred thousand Hong Kong dollars, the equivalent of $14,000 U.S. *The world's highest casino,* 88

57

Gamma promised in press releases. *For the world's greatest gamblers. The Sky has no limits!* "I'll give interviews. Talk about how I'll be there. How much I love living in Hong Kong, how I might spend the rest of my life here."

"You think he'll be watching."

"He put a gun to my head and I *laughed* at him. He's watching."

"He'll figure a trap."

"Doesn't matter. He can't stop himself. It'll make him crazy."

"That's what you want? Maybe keep your head down, count your blessings."

The pushback surprised Duberman. He'd figured Gideon would want a chance for revenge. "I thought he cut your ankle, *Chai.* Not your balls."

Gideon cursed under his breath.

"It's like this. If I'm going to live, I want him dead. And if I'm going to die, I want him dead, too."

"So he comes. Then what? Not like we can ask the police for help."

"We put men down in the city, watch the main MTR stations. He can't hide here."

"Seven million people in Hong Kong."

"How many look like him? The city's too small and there aren't enough ways up here.

Sooner or later, we'll see him. Then he's ours."

2

SAN DIEGO

Evan Wells at the three-point line . . . jab-steps left at the basket . . . pulls back, elevates —

John Wells put up his hands and lunged at his son. No chance. Evan twisted away, extended his arms, let go of the basketball at the apex of his jump, the rock spinning off his fingertips, textbook. *Over the defender . . .* He lifted his arms over his head and grinned. *Bingo!*

Wells looked over his shoulder just as the ball split the net. Evan wasn't just running Wells ragged, he was offering real-time commentary with every dribble. If he didn't make the NBA, he had a future on ESPN.

Wells leaned over, hands on hips, sucked the cool gym air into his burning lungs. Chasing Evan for forty-five minutes had exhausted him. Worse than two hours of weights. At least he knew his broken foot was healed.

Evan collected the ball, flicked it smoothly between his legs. "Take a break, John?"

"Don't go easy on me." Wells slapped for the ball, found only air. "Make me feel old."

"You are old. Starting to wonder how you make it out there."

Out there, I have a gun. Out there, there's no court and no rules. Wells shuffled to the water fountain, drank deep. Like everything else in the gym, the fountain was brand-new, a tribute to San Diego State's nationally ranked men's basketball team, the Aztecs. Theoretically, the court was open to any student. But everyone knew the team had dibs.

Evan played shooting guard for the Aztecs, though he wasn't a starter. Of course, as he liked to tell Wells, his chances would have been better if Wells hadn't made him disappear for a month during the season. The fact that Wells had been trying to save his son's life cut no ice.

Three more Aztecs stepped into the gym. All wore white T-shirts with SAN DIEGO BASKETBALL printed in block letters across their chests. Like the entire campus didn't know who they were. College sports had changed since Wells played linebacker at

Dartmouth. These kids were basically un-paid pros. They had strength coaches and hot tubs and massage therapists. They had nicknames on *SportsCenter* and fifty thousand followers on Twitter.

Lamenting the good old days. Another sign of middle age. Still, Wells noticed a difference in his son. Evan had always been confident. Now he seemed almost arrogant. Adulation was a drug as dangerous as any other.

"Two on two?" Evan yelled across the court. For him, the last forty-five minutes had been only a warm-up. To Wells, he muttered, "No problem, right, Pops?"

Wells wanted to be upset his son was ditching him so blithely, but his legs told him he was lucky to avoid more punishment. "Call me tonight. We can grab dinner. If you want."

"It's Friday." Evan's way of saying he would have other plans.

Wells had been in San Diego for a month, making up for lost time. Trying to, anyway. He and Evan's mother, Heather, had divorced in the late nineties, when Evan was an infant. Back then Wells had just joined the Central Intelligence Agency. He spent much of the next decade in Afghanistan and

Pakistan, an undercover operative infiltrating al-Qaeda. Along the way, he converted to Islam. Over the years, lots of people had asked him why. His answers never seemed to satisfy them. Wells supposed that even he couldn't claim to understand his decision completely. He only knew that Islam's tenets fit him better than Christianity's, rested more easily on his head and in his heart.

While Wells was undercover, Heather remarried and took Evan back to western Montana, where she and Wells had grown up. Even after Wells returned to the United States, Heather kept him from Evan. She said random visits from Wells would be hard on the boy. She never mentioned his conversion, though Wells thought it troubled her. She viewed it as an affectation, a cheap way for him to distance himself from the person he'd been. And from her.

But Wells could hardly argue with Heather's insistence on keeping him away, whatever her reasons. He officially quit the agency a few years after coming home, but he remained addicted to undercover work. He missed Evan's adolescence as completely as he had the boy's childhood. Another man raised his son.

His failure to be part of Evan's life

gnawed, an ulcer that wouldn't heal. When Evan turned eighteen, Wells told Heather that he planned to approach the boy directly, with or without her approval. Their first meeting was a disaster. Evan knew that Wells had worked for the CIA. He saw Wells less as a person than a walking symbol of Guantánamo Bay and all the other compromises and mistakes the United States had made during its war on terror. Wells left Montana thinking he would never see his son again.

Then a kidnapping forced Evan to ask Wells for help, dangerous help, help that Wells had provided without complaint. Now they were more than strangers, less than father and son. Evan seemed happy enough to have Wells in San Diego. They met for breakfast every day, played basketball most afternoons. They even had dinner when Evan didn't have a better offer. Evan introduced Wells to his friends as "my biological father." When they were alone, he mostly called Wells John or Pops, the last word delivered with a soft irony that perfectly fit their relationship.

Their physical resemblance helped. They were both tall, with brown hair, brown eyes, a hint of tan in their skin from Wells's Lebanese grandmother. Wells had grown up on hunting and football. He was rawboned and muscled, bigger than his son. Evan was lean and slippery, with a basketball player's glide. Even at his fastest, Wells couldn't have matched Evan's first step. Now, past forty, he had no chance. He chased his son around the court as hopelessly as a bull charging a matador. And loved every minute. Wells had told himself before this trip that he would be satisfied with whatever relationship Evan wanted.

Evan even slipped sometimes and called him Dad.

Still, Wells knew he hadn't sorted out his life. A psychiatrist would surely ask him why he focused so hard on Evan, a relationship where he would always be a substitute, instead of working to understand why the women who loved him — first Heather, then Exley, now Anne — always left.

The shrink would no doubt also tell him to accept that he would need to leave the field soon. His body didn't forgive mistakes as it once had. Three months before, Wells had broken his foot jumping off a wall in South Africa. The injury had nearly gotten him killed. The psychiatrist would probably tell him to forget about Duberman, too. The billionaire was the President's problem now.

Why Wells didn't talk to shrinks.

Evan knew that Wells had ended Duberman's plot to try to fake the United States into war. So far, he hadn't asked for details. The story wasn't exactly the elephant in the room, more like a shiny new Ferrari in the driveway, at once cool and absurdly showy. *Aside from stopping a war, how you been, Pops?*

Wells wondered if Evan was also trying to figure out how he felt about the killing that was an inextricable part of Wells's life. Over and over, Wells had broken the most basic law, the one that undergirded all the others. *Thou shalt not kill.* At that first meeting in Missoula, Evan had called Wells a psychopath. Now Evan was studying military history and strategy. Wells wondered if his son was considering following him into the Rangers and ultimately the agency.

Wells knew the cost of the path he'd taken better than anyone. A wall, unseen and unbreakable, split him from the civilian world. He could pretend, but he would never belong. He wasn't sure what he would say if Evan questioned him straight out for advice about joining. He found himself hoping Evan wouldn't ask. What kind of father did that make him?

The dream-blue California sky bubbled over Wells as he bicycled back to the apartment he'd rented a mile from campus. He'd imagined San Diego State as a playground by the ocean. In fact, the University of California–San Diego had the prime real estate. SDSU was ten miles inland, bordered by an interstate instead of the beach. Still, Wells found his apartment pleasant enough. It was a two-room white box in a complex with a pool, a gym, and even a tennis court.

San Diego's halcyon weather made doing nothing easy. Too easy. Downtown and the beaches were filled with guys who spent their days hanging out, though they were too old to be students and too young to be retired. They had streaked blond hair and sun-faded tattoos and girlfriends just out of high school. They lingered in packs in coffeehouses, talking about surfing in Hawaii and camping in Joshua Tree. They made Wells want to get a job, any job.

Instead he hung out with Evan, waiting to stop waiting. The President had obviously decided that he wouldn't go after Duberman unless he had a perfect shot at making the death look accidental. Duberman was too canny to give him that opportunity. Wells felt the pressure inside himself building, real as a blocked pipe.

Even so, Wells couldn't quite make himself move. He needed to be sure he was ready for another mission that would put blood on his hands. Going after Duberman was a choice, and Wells wanted the choice taken from him. He wanted a *summons.*

Wells had come to San Diego after two months of riding buses. The day after his meeting with the President, he had bought a backpack and an e-reader and his first Greyhound ticket. Washington to Atlanta. Atlanta to Jacksonville to New Orleans. New Orleans to Houston to Dallas to El Paso. El Paso for a while. He stayed in shape with pull-ups and push-ups and sit-ups. His foot healed and he sawed off the cast and started to run again, rebuilding his endurance mile by mile.

He slept in motels with leaky showers and busted air conditioners and doors patched with plywood. He grew a beard. Days went by when he hardly spoke. He carried a phone, but only to call Evan. He spent his days tunneling into the Civil War a word at a time.

El Paso to Albuquerque, Albuquerque to Denver, Denver to Salt Lake, Salt Lake to Phoenix. West and north and south, but mainly west. He disappeared into the American underbelly, bus stations and cracked concrete, diesel fumes and crumpled trash. The land outside his windows changed like a cheap green-screen backdrop, swamp to flatland to mountain. But the buses were always the same, rattling beasts with lumpy seats that made sleep difficult and dreams impossible. Their cabins stank of greasy fries and unwashed men. Not everyone on them was desperate. Wells sat beside college kids on road trips, soldiers visiting girlfriends, a librarian on her way to a romance writers' conference in Phoenix. Some of the Greyhounds even came with Wi-Fi and reserved seats. Yet the desperation they carried was inescapable. They were public housing on four wheels. People with a choice didn't ride them.

Even the librarian was newly divorced and nearly broke. She'd budgeted precisely two hundred and forty dollars for the three-day conference. *Figured I could either drive and sleep in my car or ride this and have money for a motel,* she said. She was in her late twenties, dark blond hair, with a round, pretty face and a soft, heavy body. She warmed up to Wells in a hurry. After an hour, she let her fingers graze his thigh. He made the mistake of asking what kind of romance she wrote. *Hardcore stuff,* she said. *My ex wasn't into that, but I am. What about you?* She squeezed his leg, and Wells felt himself stir. He hadn't been with a woman since his cruise with Anne, before he'd ever heard of Aaron Duberman. He'd forgotten how quickly and easily men and women could join when their bodies wanted to meet.

Maybe they could do each other some good.

But he didn't want complications, even the uncomplicated kind. He picked up her hand, put it back in her lap. *Probably more like your ex,* he said. *Too bad,* she said. At the next rest stop, Wells walked the parking lot to stretch his legs. When he got back on, he found the librarian two rows up, next to a Marine. She winked, and he felt a ridiculous surge of jealousy that she'd be joining the twelve-foot-high club with someone else.

Every city had mosques, usually near the bus stations. For a while, Wells prayed in them. But he felt unwelcome. He knew why. In spite of, or maybe because of, his flawless Arabic and his new beard, he looked too much like an FBI agent trying to pose as a Muslim. Eventually, he stopped going. He didn't want trouble of any kind. He wanted to float as aimlessly as a branch on a river. But aimlessness didn't come easy for him.

He tried not to think about the meeting with the President, or to question whether he'd made the right choice. But he did. Every day. He tried not to think about the women who'd left him. But he did. Every day. He didn't find peace. He didn't find much of anything. Near the end, he stopped looking. He wasn't sure if he was wasting his time. Maybe wasting time was the point.

Phoenix to Las Vegas to Reno to Seattle to San Francisco. In Vegas, Wells wandered the Strip, walked through Duberman's palaces, ignoring the security guards, who found him wherever he went. He expected to hate the casinos, but he couldn't. They seemed silly, a place for people who had too much time, too much money, too little imagination.

He checked on Duberman every few days. About three weeks into his trip, he found a post on a fashion blog reporting that "Orli Akilov has made a splash in Hong Kong, where she and her mega-billionaire husband have moved for the spring — and maybe longer! 'I think it's important that our sons live all over,' the Israeli beauty told reporters at a party sponsored by Cîroc vodka. 'I want them to be world citizens.' "

At least the President had made good on his promise to force Duberman from Israel. Wells awaited the news that Duberman had died in a plane crash or from a sudden bout of pneumonia. It didn't come.

Instead, Wells read that Vinny Duto had formed a presidential exploratory committee. Then the governor of California, a potential primary opponent for Duto, said he wouldn't run. He didn't explain. Maybe the President's files had better dirt than he'd said.

Wells wanted to vent his anger to Shafer. He called Evan instead. *Finally made it to Cali. Mind if I come see you?*

Anytime, Pops.

One final ride, San Francisco to San Diego. Five hundred miles and twelve hours for sixty-nine dollars. At a rest stop outside Los Angles, Wells shaved his beard. He knew his son would see it as a mountain-man pose. *The Grizzly Adams hipster look is so 2015!*

Wells stepped out in San Diego with an aching back and something like nostalgia. He wouldn't miss the buses. But he would miss their connection to a simpler era, when Americans could still disappear inside the country's vastness. Before license-plate-

72

scanning cameras and GPS trackers, biometric identification and metadata collection. When people still could hope to outrun their bad luck. Frederick Jackson Turner was wrong. The frontier had stayed open for a while after 1890. But it was closed now.

At first Wells thought the knock on his apartment door was a mistake. Only Evan knew where he was staying, and as Evan had pointed out at the gym that afternoon, it was Friday. The kid's sufferance of Wells didn't extend to weekend nights.

Wells looked up from *Homage to Catalonia,* George Orwell's dispatches from the front lines of the Spanish Civil War, as brilliant as everything else Orwell wrote. "Yes?"

"Pops?"

At the door, Evan had a liquored gleam in his eyes and his phone in his hand. "Check it out."

The phone's browser was open to an article about Aaron Duberman. *Fortune* magazine. "He's opening a new casino in Macao. Says he's going to preside over a day of celebration."

Wells skimmed the article: *world's tallest casino-hotel, $4 billion investment, et cetera . . .*

"How'd you see this so fast?" The article

was less than an hour old.

"I have a Google Alert for him."

"Why would you do that?"

"Because I want to know what he's up to. Obviously."

"Obviously."

"He's trolling you with this, John. Trying to get under your skin. You know that, right?"

"More likely he's just seeing what he can get away with." But Wells wondered if his son was right, if Duberman's move was directed at him personally.

Evan plopped on Wells's couch, twisted open a beer. "You never told me what happened at the end."

"You never asked."

"I am now."

Wells told him everything, those manic last days, how he and Shafer and Duto found Rand Witwans and delivered him to Washington. How the President convinced Wells and Shafer to let him take care of Duberman, a promise that he apparently didn't plan to keep.

"You should tell somebody," Evan said, when Wells was done. *"The New York Times."*

"Making the President resign. I can't do it."

"He was going to start a *war.*"

"Duberman fooled him, too."

"But he doesn't care. The President of the United States looked you in the eye and *lied.*"

Wells could only laugh. The bigger the stakes, the bigger the lies.

"What?"

"Sometimes I forget how young you are."

"Duberman is sticking your face in it, too, and you don't care. He wanted to have you killed, he tried to get us to invade another country —"

"I thought you believed in the law, Evan."

"The law has nothing to do with this. This is power."

There they were, the words that Wells had run from for three months. The words he knew were true. "You do understand I could easily get killed going after him."

"You didn't last time." Evan spoke with foolish confidence. Another reminder of his youth.

"I was lucky last time."

"I don't believe you."

Because you don't know what you're talking about.

"Good." Evan stood. "You're going to kill Duberman, and I'm going to get laid."

"You do that, my boy." Wells followed his son to the door. "One favor. Take real classes, stuff that challenges you —"

"Of course —"

"No. *Listen.*" Wells felt his anger at his son's too-easy assurance leaking out. "Your team, it's a gravy train. Not a lot of people on this campus are going to talk back to you. But try to remember how lucky you are. Don't be an asshole."

Evan's head jerked like Wells had slapped him. Wells wondered if he'd pushed too far. Then Evan stopped, turned. "Could be I had that coming. Can I ask you something, John?"

Wells knew this was the question he didn't want to hear.

"This morning, I wanted to know about the agency, how you joined, you got all squirrely, you didn't want to talk about it."

"That's years away. And what if you go pro?" Wells filibustering now.

"One white spot-up shooter makes the NBA a year, and it's not gonna be me. Point is —"

Evan paused, and Wells saw that he feared asking the question as much as Wells feared hearing it. Why? Because Evan feared Wells would judge him too weak and say no? Or because he wasn't sure he wanted to join and feared Wells would say yes?

"Point is, would you want me to go your way?"

"Yes." The word escaped before Wells could stop himself. "I would."

3

SAN DIEGO

In the morning, Wells called Shafer. "Ellis."

"He is risen."

"Funny."

"I didn't know you'd take my advice so seriously." Though Shafer's unsurprised tone suggested otherwise. "Where you been?"

"Hanging out with Evan. Before that, some of the country's finest bus terminals."

"Fun times."

"Beats D.C."

"What doesn't?"

"We should have known he wouldn't do anything."

"I think we did."

"I'm going to Hong Kong."

"No doubt they'll roll out the red carpet. Planning on telling our fearless leader?"

"No."

"He'll find out, anyway."

"Good," Wells said. "He wants to invite me back to the Oval Office for another chat, tell me I'm messing up his plan for world peace, great."

But Wells didn't think the President would try to stop him from going after Duberman. At this point, the White House couldn't be sure who might talk if Wells vanished or died. Plus the President had practically invited Wells to freelance by failing to deal with Duberman himself. Wells wondered if the President was cynical enough to hope that Wells would take the bait and get himself killed in the attempt.

"This is where you tell me I'm making a mistake, right, Ellis?"

"No. You've given him enough time. I'm just wondering if you have any idea how you get to our friend once you're there?"

"Not yet. You?"

"Not a one. Never stopped us before."

The *us* made Wells smile. "How's Vinny?"

"Last time I saw him, happier than a pig eating crackers."

A pig eating crackers? A classic Shaferism, an expression that sounded vaguely down-home, but in fact existed nowhere outside Shafer's mind. Wells never knew whether Shafer meant them as homage or parody.

"You know they basically gave him back

the agency," Shafer went on.

"Even riding the bus, I figured that much out."

Twenty-seven days after his failed deadline, the President had fired Hebley and his top aides. He made the announcement late Friday afternoon, when governments and companies dumped bad news, with Duto beside him.

We now know the CIA misunderstood Iran's intentions and perhaps even its ability to produce highly enriched uranium. I do not blame General Hebley alone for these mistakes, but they highlight a need for a new direction at Langley. However, I do not want to cripple our intelligence agencies at a time when America faces serious threats. As the agency's former director, Senator Duto is uniquely positioned to help me fix this crisis. The President nodded to Duto, implicitly acknowledging him as an equal. *The senator believes the CIA's new director should be familiar with its strengths and weaknesses, rather than another outsider. After careful consideration, I have agreed.*

After a bit more throat-clearing, the President named a seventeen-year agency veteran named Peter Ludlow as acting DCI. Ludlow had been section head of the Directorate of Operations for East Asia, overseeing intel-gathering and covert ops against China and North Korea. He was a favorite of Duto's, and his promotion proved Duto's power.

"You know Ludlow?" Wells said now.

"Some. He's smart, but I hear he's nervous about this. Getting jumped about five steps. He'll be in no hurry to prove he's his own man."

Duto once again proving his canniness, choosing someone who would depend on him. "How is it there these days, Ellis?"

"Weird even by the usual standards. Everybody knows something, but nobody knows the whole story. The people who do are afraid to talk. They're worried about blowback, maybe Congress gets serious, starts papering the place." *Paper* meaning "subpoenas." "Plus nobody is sure how long Ludlow will last, what deal the President and Vinny made. Mostly, people are keeping their heads down, waiting to see how it shakes out."

"What about you?"

"What about me? People tiptoeing around me, asking sideways questions." Shafer laughed hollowly. "When I needed them three months ago, they were hiding under their desks. I'm not doing anybody any favors. Mostly, I'm spending my time on cleanup. Seeing whether Duberman had any connections here that we didn't find before. Answer seems to be no. Which we can both agree is good news. Also, I checked everything we have on him. Less than I would have hoped. I think we stayed away because he donated all that money to the President, we didn't want to get involved. But I did find satellite shots of that mansion of his in Hong Kong. Two years ago, he put a mantrap inside the perimeter wall. In case you were planning on paying a visit."

"Hard target."

"Ron Jeremy hard. I'll send you the pictures. It's way up near the top of Victoria Peak."

"How nice for him."

"You won't want to hear this, but you should call Duto. Tell him to make Ludlow help you out over there. You're gonna need it."

Shafer was right. Wells didn't want to call Duto. "He's not going to help." If Wells killed Duberman, Duto would lose his best leverage over the President.

"Don't be so sure. Maybe he thinks he's squeezed the White House for all he can. Now he figures he gets the real story public, looks like a hero for stopping the war. Plus when it comes to Vinny, never discount sheer perversity as a motive. Especially when he's running good."

Shafer was right on that score, too. "So that's it?"

"Yep. How's Evan?"

Wells hesitated. "He was talking about signing up."

"Family business. He ask your advice?"

Wells let the question hang.

"Whatever you told him, remember, ultimately he has to decide for himself, John."

"If something happened —"

"Something happens to all of us."

"You think that's profound, but it doesn't even qualify as glib."

"I only mean you aren't responsible."

Wells hung up, angry now with Shafer and himself for mentioning Evan. He pushed the thought aside, called Duto.

"Senator."

"John Wells. Miss me?"

"Like herpes. Campaign's going well, I see."

"We can always use volunteers. Interested?"

Wells was sick of this joust already. "Why is our friend still alive, Vinny?"

"Blame me for anything, but not that. Not

my choice. As you know."

"Tell me the agency's watching him, at least."

"Watching, yes. I can tell you he spends most of his time in his mansion, but he's helicoptered to his casinos in Macao a few times. Always with passengers."

"Smart man. How about in Macao?"

"Far as we can tell, he stays inside his casino complex. Which is huge."

Far as we can tell. What Duto was really saying was that the CIA hadn't put anyone on the ground to watch Duberman, much less tried to turn anyone in his inner circle or bugged his offices or mansion. It was sticking to zero-risk satellite and drone surveillance.

"And before you ask, no finding," Duto said.

A finding was a legal excuse for murder. As an American citizen, Duberman had Constitutional protections giving him the right to due process, including a trial. If the United States wanted to ignore those rights and assassinate him, the President had to sign a special order, officially called a "memorandum of notification" but generally referred to as a "finding."

Findings were controversial. But Presidents had used them before, notably in the case of Anwar al-Awlaki. Al-Awlaki was a Yemeni-American cleric with ties to al-Qaeda. In 2010, the Justice Department issued a secret forty-one-page opinion that the government could legally kill him. The opinion said his role in al-Qaeda made his assassination legal as part of the broader American war against the group. With the legal opinion protecting him, President Obama signed a finding. A year later, a Predator drone blew up his car with a Hellfire missile.

"Al-Awlaki doesn't cover it?" Wells said.

"No." Duto explained that the White House counsel, without naming Duberman, had asked the Justice Department if it could apply the al-Awlaki opinion against an American citizen who wasn't a member of al-Qaeda. Justice turned him down, saying the President needed a fresh opinion.

But Duberman's case had little in common with al-Awlaki's, and not just because of Duberman's wealth. He had never been charged or even publicly identified as a suspect in any crime. He had never called for terrorist attacks on the United States. He lived in Hong Kong rather than the Arabian Desert. The United States could easily ask Hong Kong to extradite him.

Even the most eager-to-please lawyer at Justice would have a hard time explaining why he ought to be assassinated instead of arrested and sent home for a trial.

Of course, the President could still sign a finding on his own, without the opinion from Justice backing him up. "He won't do it himself?"

"Doesn't look like it. Too risky."

The President had boxed himself, Wells saw. He feared public blowback too much to prosecute Duberman legally. But he feared his own legal liability too much to order a killing. "And there's no way around it?" Wells knew the answer before he asked. Nods and whispers wouldn't do. Without a presidential order, the CIA wouldn't target an American citizen, especially not Aaron Duberman.

"I think he'd rather have Duberman alive and scared than dead, anyway."

"Tell the truth, Vinny" — Wells was conscious of the absurdity of the words even as he spoke them — "you like him alive, too. This way you can beat up the President with him anytime."

"I don't care. You want him, have at him."

Wells heard it now, a tiny slur in Duto's voice. Wells had seen Duto's liquor collection, hundreds of bottles of small-batch bourbon and single-malt scotch. It was past noon on the East Coast, and for the first time, Wells wondered if Duto was a weekend alcoholic, hiding his thirst as pretension. *I'm not drunk. It was a taste test. Eight kinds of bourbon, see?* Drink suited Duto's personality. It would drop his inhibitions without touching the meanness at his core.

Or maybe Duto just loved the idea of having a ringside seat as Wells battled Duberman. Wells choked out four unpleasant words: "I need a favor."

"Do tell."

"I'm going to Hong Kong. Promise me the agency won't get in the way."

"That's a question for the DCI."

Duto playing games, pretending he wasn't running Ludlow.

"Keep jerking me around, maybe I'll broadside the honey wagon. Take it all public."

"I care why?"

"Might make people wonder how come you didn't tell anyone three months ago."

"I seriously doubt that'll be the first question that comes up. Nonetheless. Don't get huffy. You really want this? You haven't had enough of this guy?"

Wells let the question hang until Duto sighed.

"Fine. I'll tell Ludlow."

"COS HK will play ball?" Chief of station, Hong Kong. Technically, the station in Hong Kong should have been called a base. By long-standing tradition, the CIA had only one station in every country, usually in the capital, Beijing in the case of the People's Republic. But because Hong Kong had been a British territory independent of China before 1987, its CIA outpost had historically been called a station. The title had survived the handover.

"Of course. Garry Wright's his name. Used to work for Ludlow. Matter of fact, maybe we can go one better. Under the circumstances, the station can't offer active help. Personnel, I mean. But technical support, yes."

For a change, Wells wouldn't have to sneak his gear through customs, or buy a pistol in a parking lot. "You'd do that for me, Vinny?"

"You're welcome. Give me some time to make the calls."

"A day."

"You wasted three months on vacation, now you're in a rush?"

Wells told himself he hadn't wasted three months. He'd spent time with Evan. He'd healed physically and mentally. He'd given the President a chance to keep his word.

Now recess was over.

Wells brewed himself a pot of coffee, sat with his laptop, reading everything he could about Duberman, looking over the photos Shafer had sent of Duberman's mansion on Victoria Peak, checking maps of Hong Kong and Macao. No doubt Shafer had done the same work in Langley, but Shafer wouldn't be on the ground. Wells wanted to think the situation through for himself.

He read, made notes, read some more. Wells had met Duberman once, at his mansion in Tel Aviv. He knew firsthand that Duberman had superb security, former Israeli soldiers and Mossad operatives. In Hong Kong, he lived in what was basically a castle. The photos showed a mansion high on Victoria Peak, the 1,800-foot mountain that was the highest point on Hong Kong Island. The Peak rose almost straight out of Hong Kong's harbor. A concrete-and-steel maze of apartment towers, skyscrapers, and boulevards covered its lower half. Then the sprawl ended. The top half of the Peak was steep, forested, and surprisingly undeveloped. Only a few dozen astronomically expensive homes and apartment buildings lined its narrow roads.

The topography offered Duberman amazing protection. An approaching sniper would have nowhere to hide except in the slopes of the Peak itself, where he would leave an obvious heat trail. The way the mansion hung off from the mountain meant that even a world-class marksman would have a tough time finding an angle on Duberman. Further, the surveillance photos revealed that the mansion's windows were made of thick ballistic glass, the kind used in armored vehicles, which would stop everything up to a .50 caliber Barrett round.

Wells wasn't interested in humping a sniper rifle up Victoria Peak as the Hong Kong police chased him. In truth, he didn't love snipers. The ones he'd met took a little too much pleasure in killing people unawares. He didn't see any avenues for a quick hit. He would need time, probably a couple of weeks, to probe for a hole in Duberman's defenses, do the on-the-ground work that the CIA had avoided. He wanted a safe house that had a clear line of sight to Duberman's mansion. Along the way he would need to keep himself off Duberman's radar as long as he could.

As a rule, Wells didn't favor disguises like wigs and colored contacts. They only worked in movies. And even the most expertly applied masks couldn't beat biometric tools, which measured features like retinal pigmentation that couldn't be changed. Of course, Wells had successfully infiltrated al-Qaeda. But the jihadis had known he was American. Wells had not hidden his identity as much as subsumed it. He had convinced them, and maybe even himself, that he was one of them.

Hong Kong had more than fifty thousand white residents, mostly bankers, lawyers, and executives. Wells decided his best bet would be to pose as a rich investor new to the territory. If he were lucky, he might find an apartment on the Peak itself, close to the mansion. If not, he would settle for an apartment on the top floors of one of the fifty- and sixty-story buildings that rose from its lower slopes, an area called the mid-levels.

Even the closest of those apartments would be a mile or more from Duberman. But if Duto kept his promise of gear, Wells could set up long-lensed cameras to monitor the mansion. He would learn Duberman's patterns. What hours did he keep? Did he ever drive to the city below? The slopes of the Peak were too steep for helicopters to land on the mansion's narrow lawn. So where was the helipad that Duberman used to commute to Macao? What roads did he take to it, and how big a convoy? Who visited the mansion, and for how long?

After he was settled in Hong Kong, Wells would consider traveling across the Pearl River Delta to Macao. He didn't think he could risk spending time in Duberman's casinos, but maybe he would throw around a couple hundred thousand dollars, talk to managers and staff at competing properties, find out what he could about 88 Gamma.

Wells couldn't be sure what bit of information would open the door to a clean kill. But he knew that the more string he gathered, the better chance he would have. He also knew his plan had holes. To say the least. In reality, it was not a plan as much as an idea for a plan: *I'll go to Hong Kong, see what happens.*

He was sure of one thing, anyway: He would need money. The President hadn't kept his promise on Duberman, but he'd sent the ten million dollars on schedule. At a Chase near his apartment, Wells withdrew two hundred thousand dollars in cash, twenty neat packets of hundred-dollar bills that formed two solid bricks.

He stuffed the money into his backpack

and found his way to the nearest big mall, where a Bloomingdale's awaited. He would need new clothes to play this part. A blonde with bored blue eyes waited at the personal shopper counter. "Sir? May I help you?" Her lips hardly moved, as if she'd decided Wells wasn't even worth the energy to shoo away.

"I need five good lightweight suits. Ten button-down shirts and ties. Four pairs of shoes, two dress and two casual. Also jeans and casual shirts."

"I'm sorry, can you repeat that?"

"It should be expensive. Smart-looking."

"You mean like Hugo Boss?"

"What would a hedge fund manager wear?"

"You're a hedge fund manager?"

"I want to dress like one."

She smiled. "You're cute. Diane sent you, right? She keeps threatening to set me up —"

Wells handed her a credit card. "Check the limit."

She disappeared through a door marked associates only, returned a minute later. "Let's go shopping."

"Just so you know, I don't know anything about this stuff. I hope you have good taste."

She laid a hand on his arm. "The best."

Four hours, twenty-three thousand dollars, and some flirting later, Wells had exactly the clothes that a fortyish banker would wear. *I'm going on a trip,* he'd said, when she asked why he needed the suits so fast, no time for tailoring or alterations. She hadn't prodded him.

"We'll deliver everything this afternoon," she said. "Will I see you again?"

"Anything's possible."

"So no."

Wells tilted his head to concede the point. "Good luck, then. With whatever you have planned."

"At least I'll know I'll look sharp."

As he stepped out of the store into the California sunshine, his phone buzzed. Duto.

"Garry Wright knows you're coming. I'm sending you his number. He says get a clean phone when you get there, text him. I told him whatever you want, it's yours."

"Thanks, Vinny."

"I don't need to tell you this, but if it goes bad —"

"You're right. You don't need to tell me."

Wells hung up. He felt a surge in his chest, a feeling he didn't want to acknowledge. Excitement, raw and rank. He started to call Evan, but hung up before he finished dialing. They'd said what they needed to say the night before, and neither of them was a fan of tearful good-byes. Instead he thumbed in a text: *Off to Hong Kong. Stay cool.* Evan didn't need his advice on staying cool. He deleted the last two words, replaced them with *I love you.* Anything else? No.

He sent it. Even before he'd put the phone away, it buzzed with a response. *Love you, too, Pops. Knock 'em dead.*

Now he wanted to call Anne, to tell her where he was and where he was going. To tell her that at least he'd connected with Evan. He wanted to ask her about the spring in North Conway, whether the mud had dried and the trees blossomed at last, whether the red fox that hunted mice in their backyard had survived the winter, how Tonka was doing. Whether she'd had time to hike, whether the state police had finally scheduled her detective training.

But he'd quit his claim on her. He had no right to ask her for emotional support. Even less to offer her the same. He put away the phone and booked himself a flight to Hong Kong. Good-bye, San Diego.

4

MOSCOW

Mikhail Buvchenko sold death for a living. Proudly.

Buvchenko was the biggest arms dealer in Russia. For the right price, he could deliver 9-millimeter Makarov pistols or surplus T-54 tanks. Dictators and drug lords were welcome to his merchandise. He'd sold surface-to-air missiles to Bashar al-Assad of Syria and flamethrowers to rebels in the Congo. Flamethowers. *I leave the judgments to you American moralists,* he'd told *GQ* years before, his only published interview in English. *The ones who brought us napalm and Hiroshima.*

Buvchenko had even created a twelve-hundred-man militia of former Russian soldiers. They met at his estate twice a year for training. His very own National Guard. A year earlier, the Kremlin had paid him fourteen million dollars to send them into

Ukraine. In two months of fighting, they'd shot down four Ukrainian army helicopters and destroyed a dozen tanks. Buvchenko had cleared four million dollars in profit.

Not bad for a man who had grown up in a two-room apartment on the edge of Volgograd, the southwestern Russian city once called Stalingrad. By any name, the town was best known for its role as a human slaughterhouse during World War II. More than a million Germans and Russians had died in a terrible five-month battle for the city.

Volgograd hadn't changed much since. Buvchenko's childhood had been bad by Russian standards, which meant it was unimaginable by American. When he was twelve, his father bled to death from an alcohol-rotted stomach. His mother died three years later. They bequeathed him only one gift, uncanny size and strength.

In fall 1991, just as his mother received a diagnosis of lung cancer, the Soviet regime finally sputtered out. In Saint Petersburg, the intellectuals raised their glasses to the end of tyranny. In Moscow, the Communist elites plotted to steal Russia's incredible natural resources, their final revenge on the nation they'd ruined. But in hinterlands like

Volgograd, the state's collapse created a vacuum. Then winter came.

Buvchenko never spoke of that time. And never forgot it. A surgeon convinced his mother to spend the family's savings on an operation to remove the top lobe of her right lung. The surgery went badly, no surprise, considering that the surgeon was an alcoholic. His mother was left with a wound in her chest that wouldn't heal. Morphine and antibiotics at Volgograd Clinical Hospital No. 12 were reserved for patients who could pay. After watching his mother writhe for a week, Buvchenko brought his sister Dasha to the hospital.

"Tell Mamma good-bye," he told her. So she did. She was a year younger, an obedient, foolish girl. One of her school friends had given her a Bible months before. Now she read it each night. As if God had any use for their broken lives.

"We have to pray for her, Mikhail. Ask Jesus for help —"

"Leave the fairy tales, Dasha. Stand by the door and make sure no one's coming." Like anyone would bother. Her room had four cots, but the other three were empty. Most of the nurses had quit after months without pay. The good citizens of Volgograd preferred to die at home.

Buvchenko lifted his mother's head and pulled out her pillow, thin and flimsy inside its greasy case. Even a few months ago, she'd been heavy. Now she was a skeleton with lips. She stank of death, or something worse, her insides rotting through the hole in her breastbone. She'd been a decent enough mother, he supposed. Though she'd never saved him from his father's belt. The scars stippled his back.

Her eyes widened and she opened her mouth to speak. Before he could, he shoved the pillow on her face. She kicked and squirmed and clawed. Then, even faster than he expected, she sank into the bed.

"It's a sin," Dasha said. But she didn't try to stop him, or even raise her voice.

He felt something leave that room when his mother stopped kicking. Not her soul. Another fairy tale. No. A piece of *him.* He knew now the truth of the world's cruelty, and what he needed to do to survive it. The realization was equally frightening and freeing.

A week later, he told Dasha he was leaving Volgograd. She followed him like a dog as he packed up his canvas backpack with clothes and cigarettes and the two sharpest knives in their kitchen. *Please. Help me.* The very reason he had to go. She was too soft.

He couldn't save her. Even if he could, the price would be his own life. She trailed after him all the way to the train station, sobbing like the child she was: *Mikhail, what will I do?*

He knew the answer. In a year or two, she would be on the streets, finding out first-hand about sin. *You'll be all right,* he said. *In a few years, I'll find you and we'll live together in Moscow, a prince and princess.*

You promise, my brother?

I promise.

He never spoke to her again.

He lived on the streets of Moscow for a year, twelve cold and desperate months that finished what was left of his humanity. Then the Red Army took him. By eighteen, he had fought his way into the Spetsnaz, the *spetsialnogo naznacheniya,* the Russian army's Special Forces unit. He was nearly two meters tall, one hundred ten kilograms, a bundle of muscle and rage. He made even his commanders nervous. *We'll send you to Grozny* — the capital of Chechnya, where Russia was fighting a vicious war against Muslim separatists — *and you can kill all the rats you like.*

The same year, Buvchenko learned his sister had died of a heroin overdose. He got the news in a call from a police detective from Volgograd. *We can postpone the crema-tion if you want to come down, Sergeant.*

Burn her as soon as you can. Get her out of this world.

He spent four years in Chechnya. The rebels there were a vicious bunch, in every way the forerunners of ISIS, down to their snuff videos. They hated the Spetsnaz, and Buvchenko knew what they'd do to him if they caught him. He was equally merciless to the ones he captured. He came home with a dozen medals for combat bravery and a jar full of ears. Two sides of one coin.

Away from the front lines, the military's rules bored him senseless. He quit three months after his last deployment, went to the Democratic Republic of the Congo to work as a quote-unquote technical advisor. Unlike a lot of wannabe mercenaries, he had real experience. Within months, he was ferrying AKs and RPGs to the eastern Congo, where a half-dozen militias fought for the jungle's diamonds. He spent three years in Africa before coming back to Vol-gograd, where he had easier access to advanced weapons like helicopters. Year by year, his deals grew. To add to his profits he brought heroin and cocaine back into Rus-sia on the same jets that flew weapons out.

In the seventies and eighties, the legendary arms dealer Adnan Khashoggi had made billions of dollars brokering weapons sales to Saudi Arabia. Buvchenko would never be in that league. These days the biggest orders went country to country, making nine-figure skims impossible. Still, by his thirty-ninth birthday, Buvchenko had seventy million dollars in banks in Moscow, Geneva, and the Cayman Islands.

Buvchenko's line of work did have drawbacks. Two years before, a federal grand jury in Virginia had charged him in absentia with arms trafficking, supporting terrorism, and money laundering. He'd never sold a single weapon on American soil, or to a group like ISIS. He'd sell to everyone, but not those savages. Not after what he'd seen in Chechnya. No matter. The meddlers in the United States believed they ruled the entire world.

The warrant led Interpol to issue a Red Notice for him, asking its members to arrest him at their borders or if he passed through their airspace. Now he chose his destinations with care. Western Europe was out. He would land on the moon before he set foot in New York. But thanks to long-range jets and carefully edited flight manifests, he could still get to the Middle East, Africa, even South America.

But he spent most of his time on Russian soil, where the Americans couldn't touch him. And Russia was more than comfortable for him. Along with an apartment in Moscow, he had an estate outside Volgograd with a shooting range, a stable, and what might have been the best-equipped gym anywhere in Russia. Buvchenko's body was his only religion. He rose at dawn each day to lift weights and inject himself with a steroid regimen that three doctors had helped him design. Nearing forty, he had biceps bigger than most men's legs. His eyes were too small for his face and his neck too big, but he was handsome in a bruising way. He had no problem finding girlfriends, though he tired of them quickly.

As long as he kept himself too busy to think about the cruel pointlessness of existence, Buvchenko couldn't complain. Life was good.

Still, he had to keep Papa happy. Papa Putin, and the men around him. Without the Kremlin, Buvchenko didn't have a business. The Defense Ministry arranged the arms-transfer licenses he needed for open-market deals. For his *other* sales, the Foreign Ministry quietly orchestrated clearances so his cargo planes could fly to the Caspian Sea and then over Iran to the Gulf of Oman.

From there, the jets could travel all the way to the east coast of Africa over open water.

Buvchenko paid well for the help. He gave to Papa, too, always through a bagman, never directly, of course. He never asked for anything in return. Simply by taking the money, Putin confirmed Buvchenko's status as a friend. So Buvchenko didn't mind the fact that his fortune would have been three times as big if not for the bribes. Better to be part of the pack. Among the hunters, not the hunted.

And so the summons the night before had come as a deeply unpleasant surprise. Buvchenko was eating dinner with his newest girlfriend when his phone buzzed, a series of zeros filling its screen. The FSB used that code when it wanted to be known and answered.

Buvchenko waved the woman out, reached for his phone.

"Mikhail." The voice was slurred yet commanding, a particularly Russian combination. Like the speaker was too important to bother to speak clearly.

"Director Nemtsov?"

For five years, Oleg Nemtsov had been Director General of the FSB. He'd won the job the old-fashioned way, by destroying his rivals. One was now serving eighteen years in a Siberian prison for "anti-Russian activities." Another had died in an avalanche in Switzerland. *An avalanche!* Polonium poisoning was child's play compared to burying a target under a wall of snow in the Alps without hurting anyone else. Even the old KGB would have been impressed.

"I need to see you, Mikhail. Ten a.m. tomorrow. At Lubyanka." The FSB's headquarters, a stone fortress near the Kremlin.

Buvchenko rummaged his brain, wondering what he'd done. Nemtsov's tone suggested trouble, but Buvchenko had no thoughts of trying to flee. Nothing would anger the wolves more.

The next morning, Buvchenko arrived at Lubyanka's main entrance fifteen minutes early. He'd driven himself at dawn to the airport. He wore his best suit, handmade by an English tailor who visited Moscow to outfit wealthy Russian men who had what the tailor delicately called "border issues."

In the lobby, guards passed Buvchenko through a metal detector, took his phone and his Rolex, told him to wait. An hour passed before three unsmiling minders appeared. They brought Buvchenko to a windowless room that stank of the sour sweat that came with fear. The only furniture consisted of three chairs and a bare metal table. Beneath the table, brown stains circled a drain covered by a rusty grate. Buvchenko asked no questions. The men wouldn't have answered, anyway.

At least they hadn't handcuffed him.

The deadbolt slammed as they left. Without watch or phone, Buvchenko couldn't track how long he waited. Finally, the deadbolt slid back and Nemtsov appeared. The FSB chief was in his early fifties, medium height and trim. He wore his wavy gray hair combed back from his forehead. His face was ordinary except for his eyes, which were blue and absolutely without feeling. He sniffed as he walked in, like Buvchenko was a rotting piece of meat. He was alone, no bodyguards or aides, the day's first good sign. A thin manila folder was tucked under his arm.

"Director General —" Buvchenko stood.

"Sit." Like he was talking to a dog. "Do you know why you're here, Mikhail?"

"No, sir."

"You are so stupid." In fact, Nemtsov used the words *dolbo yeb,* a far more profane phrase. "A gorilla in a suit." He took a photo out of the folder, slid it across the table.

Buvchenko's turn to curse.

"John Wells."

"You know him."

"Three months ago, he came to me in Volgograd."

"Why? Not the story you told us then, the real one."

Buvchenko didn't consider lying. Not to this man, not in this building. "He asked me if I knew where he could buy a nuclear weapon, or the material to make one."

"Did he tell you why?"

"Because of Aaron Duberman. That Jew billionaire who owns casinos. He thought that Duberman was behind the uranium the United States found in Turkey. To be honest, I didn't believe him. But a woman I had dealt with before, Israeli —"

"Her name, please —"

"She called herself Salome."

"And how did you know this Salome?"

Buvchenko sensed Nemtsov knew the answer to every question he asked. "She'd bought weapons from me. I put her in touch with hackers. She paid well. This was years before."

"Did you know her real name at the time? Where her money came from?"

"She wouldn't tell me either one. I asked a few times and then dropped it."

"This is how you do business."

"I only met her on my terms, in Moscow or Volgograd. She wasn't a threat to me or Russia. The weapons she wanted were small. She was obviously setting up a cell of some kind. To be honest, I thought they were high-end thieves — jewel thieves, maybe. I hadn't spoken to her in a while and suddenly she called, brought up Wells."

"When?"

"Maybe ten days before he came. She said he might approach me and that if he did, I should play along, find out what he wanted, then call her. She said she would give me a million euros. I thought the whole thing was strange, but I said fine."

"Did she say why?"

"Only that he was causing trouble. I didn't know about the uranium or Duberman until Wells asked. As I said, I didn't believe any of it. It seemed impossible."

"Did you know Wells?"

"Only that he was former CIA. Never come across him before. He's tough, though."

"Spare me the *pedik* talk. Wells came. And you called this Salome as she asked."

"She told me to keep Wells at my mansion overnight. She had an idea for a way to take care of him. Tell the Volgo police he was

108

smuggling drugs. A kilo of heroin."

"Which you would provide from your stash."

"Yes."

"You didn't ask why she was so anxious to be rid of him. If maybe his story was true."

"I didn't see any advantage in knowing."

"And she agreed to this brilliant plan?" Nemtsov sarcastically emphasized the word *brilliant.*

"Sure. But it didn't work. Wells got rid of the heroin before the police came. I never did figure out how. When they couldn't find it, they put him on a plane to Moscow. Salome said I had to call up here and make sure Wells didn't leave the country. But she told me not to mention Duberman."

Buvchenko wondered if he was as stupid as Nemtsov said. How had he deluded himself into believing this episode would disappear?

"So you came up with another stroke of genius. Telling Colonel Fyodorov that Wells had come to you to buy weapons to smuggle to the jihadis in Syria."

"As I said, Salome —"

"I don't care what the Jewess told you. *You lied to us.* Take off your suit coat, gorilla. Lay it on the table."

Buchenko didn't ask why. When he was done, Nemtsov whistled, a single piercing screech. A big man stepped into the room, with a blue nylon bag a meter long. He unzipped it, pulled a dark wooden rod with a black leather strap wrapped around it.

A whip.

Nemtsov unrolled the leather lash from the whip's handle, and when he was done held up the tip to show Buvchenko the steel barbs studding the leather.

Now Buvchenko knew why the room had a drain.

"Will you take this like a man or does he have to stay?"

Buvchenko leaned forward, pressed his arms against the table, exposing his broad back. Suddenly he was ten years old, in Volgograd, his father staring with blank, furious eyes as he unbuckled his belt, angry because he was down to his last bottle of vodka. Because Buvchenko was home too late or too early. Or for no reason at all. Buvchenko begged for mercy while his mother and Dasha hid in the bathroom. He was as powerless now as he'd been then. He reminded himself to clench his jaw, press his tongue into his mouth, a trick he'd learned as a child.

Nemtsov circled behind him —

Buvchenko heard the snap of the whip and felt its sting at once. These barbs went deeper than his father's, into the meat of his back. Truly Buvchenko was glad for the pain. Otherwise, his rage might have overcome him, sent him for Nemtsov's throat.

"One."

The whip cracked again —

"Two."

Buvchenko choked back a howl. He wouldn't give this man the pleasure.

"Three." Each cut a centimeter or two from the next, rising toward his shoulders. Nemtsov an artist. Buvchenko wondered how many men he had lashed.

"Four. Five." Two quick ones, then a pause. As Nemtsov moved behind him, Buvchenko felt blood trickling down his back. He'd need a new shirt. This one had cost four hundred dollars. A grunt, half cough, half laugh, came from low in his throat. As an answer, Nemtsov cracked the whip five times more in quick succession, neatly scissoring the first cuts. The pain was a wet fire burning, promising scars red and rough and as thick as fingers. The metallic tang of blood filled the room.

Nemtsov came to the front of the room. "Sit up."

Buvchenko raised his head, made himself

look at Nemtsov.

"Beg me to stop."

Buvchenko shook his head. The motion set his back ablaze. Nemtsov raised the whip and snapped it past Buvchenko's face, so close that Buvchenko saw the barbs release their cargo of skin and muscle. His skin. His muscle.

"I can take out your eyes, if you like. Or if you want something else, put you in a coffin. Breathing air through a straw. Of course we'd have to build a big one for you, but it wouldn't take long. Or we could stuff you in a regular one, hope your heart doesn't stop. You think you won't beg for mercy?"

Buvchenko had seen the truth in Chechnya. Every man had a limit. The harder Buvchenko resisted, the harder Nemtsov would work to break him. Still, he wanted to fight. "Whatever you like."

He wanted for Nemtsov to raise the whip. Instead the FSB director looked at him with an almost clinical detachment. "I've read your Spetsnaz files. I know you're not afraid." Nemtsov's voice was suddenly gentle. He sat across the table from Buvchenko, reached over to squeeze his hand. "Not a traitor either. Otherwise, you'd be dead already. I promise I don't want to hurt you. You made a mistake. You looked at the money this woman offered, didn't see the consequence. You must know that you should have told us the truth about Wells from the start. Now say you're sorry so we can leave this behind."

Nemtsov had given Buvchenko permission to confess without cowardice. Better than a priest. An unexpected wave of gratitude filled Buvchenko's throat. He wanted to admit everything, suffocating his mother, stabbing those two *pediks* in Moscow who'd tried to grab him in Izmailovsky Park, the time in Grozny he'd killed the mother and father and three little girls —

He knew Nemtsov was playing him, breaking him with false kindness instead of real pain. But understanding the manipulation didn't lessen its power.

"You've wanted to say you're sorry for a long time. Probably since your sister died."

Of course Nemtsov knew. "I wish we'd had interrogators like you in Grozny," Buvchenko said.

Nemtsov smiled, maybe the first genuine expression Buvchenko had seen from him.

"I'm sorry, Director. I shouldn't have lied."

"Good." Nemtsov whistled again. This time, a medic entered, gauze and tape and tubes of ointment in his gloved hands. He sliced off the remains of Buvchenko's shirt and bandaged the wounds. Nemtsov left, returning as the medic finished. He held a bottle of water and two glasses. He set them down on the table but didn't pour.

"So. Finish the story. You sent Wells to us." Picking up just where he'd left off before the whipping.

"I did. Fyodorov told me you'd caught him at the airport, brought him here. I thought that would be the end of it, but the next day I heard you'd let him go. I didn't understand, but I didn't want to ask any more."

"He told a story, outsmarted his interrogator. Did you ever speak to him again?"

"No. He didn't contact me, nor I him. I promise you."

"What about Salome?"

"Only to tell her that we'd let Wells go. She was angry, even angrier when I reminded her about the money she'd promised. She said I hadn't kept my side, that Wells should never have gotten out of Russia. She told me not to call again. I told her I wasn't finished with her, but it turned out I was. We haven't spoken since."

"Then a few days later the President of the United States calls off the attack on

Iran, you didn't think you should tell us all this?"

"I swear, Director, I didn't realize the connection. The story the President told had nothing to do with Duberman. Just that he wasn't invading. I called Salome a few times, sent her emails, but she never answered. The months passed and the thing seemed to fade away."

"You didn't want to think about it."

"I suppose." Nemtsov was right, of course. Buvchenko saw now that he hadn't wanted to chase the truth, had feared the implications. He'd been worse than a fool.

He only hoped Nemtsov would give him a chance to redeem himself.

Nemtsov reached into his file, set two photos on the table. A woman, pretty, slightly mannish. Salome.

"That's her," Buvchenko said.

"Her real name is Adina Leffetz. Was. She was Israeli. She was shot in South Africa three months ago. Near Cape Town. Almost certainly by your friend John Wells."

"Did she work for Duberman?"

Nemtsov nodded.

"So Wells told me the truth about the uranium?"

"We aren't certain yet, but we think so."

"If Duberman tried to lure America into

war and failed, and the United States knows the truth, why is he still alive?"

"I imagine their President fears killing him might raise too many questions. And he's in Hong Kong now. Hard to hit."

Nemtsov poured two glasses of water. Buvchenko's mouth was dry, his throat a rasp. He wondered how much blood he'd lost. He reached for a glass, drank deep.

"You want to make matters right, Mikhail?"

"Of course."

"Then I have something for you to do."

Buvchenko nodded. *Yes. Anything.*

5

BETHESDA, MARYLAND

Trevor Robinson ducked his head, spread his legs, waggled his hips, dug his cleats into the manicured fourteenth fairway of the Congressional Country Club's Blue Course.

"Pretty," Vinny Duto said.

"Hush." Robinson took a couple of practice swings and then lifted his four-iron high, brought it down smooth, a perfect stroke that sent his ball exploding into the clear blue sky. He and Duto watched in silence as it arced to the green and bounced close to the flagstick.

"Ain't easy being this good. I almost feel sorry for you, Vinny."

"Shareholders know how much time you spend practicing?"

Robinson laughed. He was a seven handicap, a West Point graduate who had earned a major's golden oak leaf at twenty-nine. The Army marked its stars early, and it had

117

marked him. Instead he'd quit to join Lockheed Martin. Now he was chairman, the first black man to run a major defense contractor. The year before, he'd made twenty-three million dollars. His looks surely hadn't hurt his rise. He was tall and handsome, with dark skin and close-cropped salt-and-pepper hair. Easy to imagine four stars on his shoulders.

Duto, not so much. After years of 5 a.m. workouts, he remained as thick and stubby as the cigars he favored. He was bulky rather than fat, cocooned in the soft muscles of late middle age. Easy to imagine him wrapped in a towel in a Turkish bath. His face was a cross between Nixon's and LBJ's, jowly and sagging, a caricaturist's dream.

But Duto had learned politicians didn't have to be pretty. Tough worked fine, and he had no problem with tough. He had been the longest-serving CIA director in the agency's history. After the President forced him out, he won a senatorial race in Pennsylvania. He feared he would end his career as one of a hundred gasbags fighting for airtime. Then fate, in the form of a retired Colombian army officer named Juan Pablo Montoya, had intervened. Montoya, not to be confused with the Formula One driver, gave Duto a tip that ultimately led him and

Wells to the truth about Aaron Duberman.

Now Duto had the President in his pocket. The White House was a real possibility. Duto was a Christmas-and-Easter Catholic. He took Communion twice a year, mouthed down stale wafers and cheap red wine. He wanted to believe, but he knew he didn't. When he closed his eyes in church, he felt nothing but an urge to nap.

Too bad. He wished that when he ate dirt, he would have a chance to thank the big guy for the breaks that had come his way.

"Do my shareholders know? Hell, they pay for my lessons." Robinson's Darth Vader baritone brought Duto back to the Congressional. "Business development, Senator. Your shot. Your third shot, I may remind you. That second one barely rustled the ball, but it counts nonetheless."

"Rustled? Big word from a guy who makes bullets." Duto saw his caddie approaching. "Ross? That a five I see in your hand? You want me to lay up when Trevor's already on the green?"

"There's a tough bunker if you miss to the right."

"He's trying to tell you that I'm a better golfer than you," Robinson said.

Duto couldn't argue. His handicap was in

the mid-twenties. Maybe the high twenties, if he counted his extra tee shots. The low thirties. No matter. As far as he was concerned, the game's only fun lay in going for broke. "Gimme the four."

The caddie came back with the four. Duto grabbed it, waggled his hips in conscious imitation of Robinson, let loose with a vicious rip. He shocked himself by catching the ball flush, his best shot of the day by far. The Titleist traced a perfect arc, bounced at the edge of the green, stopped eighteen inches from the pin.

"Knew you had it in you," Robinson said.

Haven't shot that good since Bellville, Duto wanted to say. He felt twelve feet tall. Let his lefty buddies whine about golf, the Congressional's membership policies, the water it wasted to perfect its fairways. They would never understand the sunshine filling his veins.

"Now it's in you."

"Don't get too excited. Still have to make the putt." Robinson stepped close to Duto, spoke low. "Though the way things have been going for you, it shouldn't be a problem."

"Smart, Trev. Wait all day for me to hit a shot that puts a smile on my face, now you talk business."

Robinson grinned. "Governor Barnett. How about that? When everyone thought he was in." The California governor had called a surprise press conference the week before to announce he didn't want to subject his family to a presidential race and wouldn't seek the Democratic nomination. "Lucky for you."

"Better to be lucky than good." Duto set off down the fairway, Robinson a step behind.

"What's funny is that maybe two days before that press conference, I heard a crazy story about Barnett in Vegas."

"Doesn't sound like him." Barnett was an old-school liberal blowhard. Unions and environmental groups loved him. He would have made Duto's life tough during the primaries. Lots of Democrats were ready for a hard left turn.

"Yeah. I didn't believe it myself. Sanctimonious SOB. Doesn't care about all the manufacturing we do out there. A Democrat who makes me want to vote Republican." Robinson was one of the Democratic Party's biggest donors. *Democratic Presidents buy F-35s, too,* he'd once told Duto. *Besides, my company gives to Republicans 70-30. Best if I balance the scale.*

"Like that would ever happen. So what

was the Barnett story, anyway?"

"Keep pretending your people aren't the ones spreading it."

"Indulge me."

"Word was he wound up in an ER in North Las Vegas at four a.m. with chest pains."

"Lots of guys our age get chest pains, Trevor."

"Probably why no one noticed at the time. But somebody heard about it, got a look at his records, HIPAA and all. Good ol' Simon told his doc he'd been doing coke two days straight. Something about an HIV test, too, unprotected sex with multiple hookers."

"A good time was had by all," Duto said.

"Indeed."

"Anybody can start a rumor."

"The person who told me had seen a copy of the ER report. With all the details, the treating doc, even his insurance card. Lo and behold, two days later Barnett's out of the race."

"Guess he didn't want to debate the finer points of medical privacy laws."

"Guess not. That quick, your biggest worry from the left is gone. Meanwhile, the Veep's Colombia/Cuba mistake makes him a laughingstock all week." A recording of a meeting with the German Foreign Minister revealed the Vice President repeatedly mistaking the two countries.

"Overblown, you ask me."

"What I'm trying to figure out is where that tape came from," Robinson said.

"The Germans leaked it to get us back for pushing them on Ukraine."

"I asked Klaus" — Klaus Fischer, the German ambassador to the United States — "and he swears it's not so. And he wouldn't lie to me. Not about this, anyway. He says it came from the White House. I'm asking myself, why would the White House leak a story that makes the Veep look bad? Any ideas, Vinny?"

They were close to the green now. The caddies were well ahead, out of earshot. They knew when they weren't wanted. The Blue Course was beautifully designed, each hole masked from its neighbors, offering the illusion that every two- or foursome had the course to itself. Still, Duto heard the sharp pings as clubs struck balls, soft congratulations, an occasional curse.

If he were President, the course would belong to him alone.

And Robinson's words confirmed what Duto already knew. He was winning. Of course, not a single vote had been cast yet. But behind the scenes, Duto and his rivals were fighting over the big donors. To have any chance, a candidate had to raise tens of millions of dollars to hire staff, charter airplanes, rent hotel rooms, buy television ads. Most of the early money came from just a few thousand donors who wanted to join together around a candidate, avoid a nasty nomination fight that would give momentum to the other party.

What Robinson was really telling Duto was that he understood that Duto was clearing the field. And that he supported the play. Otherwise, he wouldn't have brought it up. Duto couldn't stop a grin. "I'm just trying to represent the good people of Pennsylvania."

Robinson stopped walking. "How long have we known each other, Vinny? Since I was selling helicopters to the Colombians and you were running missions that got them shot down. So don't blow smoke up my ass. I'm starting to believe the rumors."

"What rumors are those?" Time to tread lightly. Duto didn't want to burn the White House.

Yet.

"That you have the President's lady parts in a vise and he'll do whatever it takes to keep you happy."

"You could have figured that out watching CNN."

"That it's about Iran."

Duto waited for more, but that one word seemed to be all Robinson had. Robinson was one of the most connected guys in Washington. Duto would have expected him to be closer. Duto really was running good, the general crackdown on leaks working for him. Nobody at Langley wanted to risk a prison term for talking to a friend.

Duto still needed to be careful, though. A flat denial would be too obvious. Instead he offered a corner of the truth. "I warned Donna Green that our intel on Iran wasn't as good as what the agency was telling them. That she was going out on the ledge."

"You weren't the only one saying that. So why'd the President make you the crown prince *and* give you the entire community to run?" The intelligence community.

"Maybe he likes me."

Robinson smiled. "He hates your guts."

"People change."

"Biggest lie yet."

"Maybe I memorialized my warnings."

A satisfied rumble came from somewhere in Robinson's throat, the sound of one predator respecting another. "You put it in writing? If that HEU had turned out to be

125

Iranian, the White House would have crucified you."

"But it wasn't."

"How come you were so sure?"

Duto rested a hand on Robinson's arm. "Instinct. That's all I can say."

"Mmm-hmm." Robinson shook his head, letting Duto know he didn't believe a word. "Anyway, to the victor goes the spoils. And I'll make sure my friends know how I feel." A list that included hundreds of wealthy African Americans, and every top executive in the defense industry.

"That means a lot, Trevor."

Robinson waved over the caddies, his way of telling Duto he'd said what he needed to. As he lined up over his putt, Duto's phone buzzed. A Maryland number that he knew belonged to Donna Green. He sent the call to voice mail. The National Security Advisor could wait.

A moment later, the phone buzzed again.

"Putting here," Robinson said.

"Sorry. Gotta take it." Duto clicked through.

"The President and I need to see you this afternoon."

Duto figured they'd found out that Wells was heading for Hong Kong. He suspected they'd tracked Wells despite their promise to leave him alone. "Another three-way, Donna? Have some mercy."

"When can you be here?"

Duto had no plans to give up the last of his round. It was nearly three. Four holes, a shower, a cigar with Robinson on the back deck, traffic — "Say six."

"I know you're playing golf, Vinny."

"Fine, five." He'd forget the cigar.

At 5:15, he stepped into the Oval Office. The President and Green stared, unsmiling, at him from the couches in the middle of the room. Didn't they know their anger only fed him? They'd made this mess. Duto had no reason to help them. Truly he'd warned them.

Let them hate him.

"Glad you could spare a few minutes," the President said.

"My pleasure."

"Did you know Wells is going to Hong Kong?"

"You said you wouldn't track him." An answer that ignored the question.

"He made a reservation under his own name for a flight from L.A. tonight," Green said.

"Then I assume he wanted you to know he was going."

"Are you helping him?"

"John Wells doesn't need my help." Another non-answer.

"Are you helping him?"

"No." *Not directly. I mean, I'm not going over there.* Not a lie. Just a narrow interpretation of the truth.

"Because I'm about to ask the CIA to get him out of there —"

"Bad idea. Everyone in the DO" — the Directorate of Operations — "knows his name. It would make for questions you don't want to answer."

"You do it, then," Green said. "We've given you everything wanted."

"Why are you still here, Donna? Everybody knows he made you sign a resignation letter." Everybody didn't know. Duto was guessing.

But Green sat up like Duto had slapped her, and he knew he'd guessed right.

"He must figure you're still useful. Wish I knew why —"

"Enough," the President said. "You'll not speak to her that way. Not in here."

"He can speak to me however he likes," Green said. "I know what he is."

The words failed to sting. *What am I? No different than your boss. Or anyone who believes he has the right to sit in this room.*

*No different than anyone who's tasted power
and wants more.*

"Just so I'm clear," the President said.
"You won't tell the agency to help us."

"You're clear." The conversation was
probably being taped. Duto didn't care.

"You won't go to Wells, ask him to stay
out of this."

"You ought to know he won't listen to me.
As far as he's concerned, he gave you three
months to deal with Duberman, you didn't,
he's going to do it himself."

"We haven't had a shot."

"You haven't tried."

"We're just pulling ourselves out of this
ditch," the President said. "I've apologized
to the Brits, the Germans, the Turks, even
the Saudis. Donna's been to Iran twice,
productive conversations —"

"Productive because you're telling them
to do whatever they want."

"If something happens to Aaron Duberman, it'll all come undone."

*Don't you see it's come undone already?
You're lucky to have survived this long. I don't
know exactly how, who, when, but soon
enough somebody will smell your weakness
and jump it.* But Duto would let the President have his illusions. Every day, the man
helped him closer to the nomination. And

when the truth finally came out and the world asked him why he hadn't spoken earlier, he would have his answer ready: *The President asked for my silence. I agreed. I saw the harm he'd caused, and I wanted to give him a chance to undo it.*

The man sitting across from him would have no answer. Because Duto would be telling the truth.

"Who runs your errands if Duberman kills Wells?" Green said.

"You think that —" Duto broke off. "John's John. I can't control him and neither can anyone else. I suspect he's gonna eat a bullet one day, but that's his business."

"At least promise me that the station in Hong Kong won't help him. No missions."

No missions didn't mean no gear, so Duto was fine with that promise. "Okay. Otherwise, the agency stays out of it. You feel differently, call Langley yourself. Anything else? Because I have Nats tickets tonight and I don't want to miss the first pitch."

Duto pushed himself off the couch.

"We're done helping you, Vinny."

We'll see. "If there's nothing else, I'll show myself out."

When Duto was gone, Green sank back in

the couch, rubbing her arms. She felt as though she'd been flayed. "He's already measuring the drapes."

"It's a long road. His ego will run away with him, he'll make a mistake."

Then Green had a thought she didn't want. *Say you're right? How exactly will Vinny Duto's fall help you? Or me? Or the country, for that matter?* She'd served the President for nearly a decade, and *served* was the word. Eighty hours a week, fifty weeks a year, solving his problems. For her trouble, three months before, he'd pulled out his sword and made her fall on it. The worst night of her life. She wasn't sure what she hated more, the resignation letter or the fact that she still served in spite of it. Now she feared the President was mistaking his desire to stay in office for the interests of the nation he supposedly served. They were dancing like bears on a log and she wasn't sure why.

"You're sure it's all worth it?"

The President gave her the same hard eyes he'd just trained on Duto.

"You think I should walk out of here, Donna? Let that blowhard have it? Because I promise you that will never happen. You don't think I'm right for this job —" He inclined his head to the door.

She wanted to call his bluff. What was left of his credibility would collapse if she resigned. He wouldn't last a month. But she couldn't. The Veep was a genial joke. And Duto frightened her. She had felt his sulfurous anger up close, the joy he took in destroying his enemies. In destroying *her.*

Besides, after all the time she'd spent aboard the SS *President,* she had no choice but to go down with the ship. "How are we going to stop Duto if we can't even stop Wells?"

The President surprised her with a laugh. "Pathetic, isn't it? I'm not the first guy in this office who lost the CIA, but I suspect I'm the first who had it shoved down his throat by the former director."

"The fact you can still mock yourself makes me feel slightly better."

The President reached for the buzzer that called the Oval Office steward. "I don't know about you, but I need a drink."

Two minutes later, they were each sipping sour-mash whiskeys, doubles. The world seemed slightly more manageable. A welcome illusion. The President raised his glass. "To Vinny Duto. Maybe he'll have an accident on the way to the game."

"Choke to death on a hot dog. Which would still leave us dealing with Wells."

"Have to ruin the moment. Can we ask the Chinese to send him back at the airport?"

"They'll want to know a lot more than we can tell them."

"What about one of the other agencies? FBI, DIA, the Park Service? Ranger Rick. Stop, or I'll say stop again. Or is that the London bobbies?"

"Hey."

"Hey what?"

"You just gave me an idea."

She explained.

"Think they'll bite?" the President said.

"I think it's our best option. We'll tell 'em because Wells is ex-CIA, we don't want to get the agency involved —"

"True enough. Can they get guys in place before he lands?"

"If they want. If we ask nicely."

The President raised his glass, considered the whiskey inside. "I know what you think, Donna, but it's a long game."

"Is that meant to make me feel better?"

6

HONG KONG

Hong Kong lay fifteen time zones ahead of California, and more than seven thousand miles across the Pacific, a fifteen-and-a-half-hour flight. Wells's Cathay Pacific 747 went wheels up Saturday night, didn't land until Monday morning. The sun rose behind the jet, sailed past, set again. A day lost in the netherworld. If the nuclear apocalypse ever came, these long-haul flights would land in the radioactive rubble with what was left of humanity bleary-eyed and wondering why their phones weren't working.

Wells had spent more of his presidential ransom on a business-class ticket. Still, he slept fitfully, B movies rubbing his consciousness when he closed his eyes. He needed to quiet himself. Adrenaline bred sloppiness. Sloppiness bred mistakes. And Wells knew how dangerous Duberman could be. Not just because of his money. A lot of executive types ordered underlings into danger but wouldn't face it themselves. But in Tel Aviv Duberman had proven his courage. He hadn't blinked when Wells put a pistol to his head.

At Hong Kong International Airport, Wells offered his real passport to the immigration agent and stepped through unchallenged. No doubt he had just set off an alarm that the National Security Agency would pass to the White House. So be it. Wells had two more passports in different names, with credit cards to match. Plus the cash. John Wells wouldn't be appearing again in Hong Kong. With the agency not an option, the White House would need to call in the Chinese to track him. Wells didn't see the President taking that step.

Wells walked out of the air-conditioned arrivals hall, found himself in the subtropics. The late-morning sun glared down on the boxy red Toyota sedans that made up Hong Kong's cab fleet. As he stepped into the taxi line, Wells saw his error. He was used to traveling light. He could hardly run countersurveillance hauling a twenty-six-inch suitcase and a garment bag filled with brand-new suits. The idea itself was comic, out of a parody of a spy movie.

Wells doubted he was facing watchers.

Still, good tradecraft was good tradecraft. He handed the dispatcher a $100 HK note. "I need a driver who speaks English." The dispatcher stepped into the line of cabs, spoke to three drivers. At the fourth, he stopped, waved Wells over.

Wells stowed his bags in the trunk, slipped in front beside a chubby fiftyish man who wore oversized tinted glasses with black plastic frames. *Lin, Hong Xi Henry,* according to his hack license. Many Hong Kongers used both Chinese and English names.

"Where to, sir?" Henry sounded like he could be a host for the BBC.

"Peninsula." With its fleet of chauffeured black Rolls-Royces, the Peninsula was the most famous hotel in Hong Kong. It was actually located on the city's mainland or Kowloon side, not Hong Kong Island. If Hong Kong was the Asian version of New York City, the island played the role of Manhattan, and Kowloon the outer boroughs. Ferries, car tunnels, and subways connected the two districts, but they gave off very different vibes. The island was home to Hong Kong's tallest skyscrapers and priciest real estate. It was corporate and clean, filled with bankers and lawyers. But most of the city's population lived on the mainland side. Especially north of the harbor, Kowloon was overwhelmingly Chinese and chaotic. Its streets were narrow and crowded, littered with paper scraps and trampled bottles, redolent with the smells of tea and fish and diesel smoke. Hong Kong had a miserable shortage of affordable housing, and many Kowloon residents lived in apartments that could have passed for prison cells. If Wells had been Chinese, he could have disappeared into its most densely packed neighborhoods. But few white people lived in those districts, and Duberman's mansion was on the island, anyway. So Wells would have to spend a lot of his time on the island. But he planned to rent rooms on both sides.

"Beautiful hotel," Henry said.

Hong Kong had built its airport on an artificial island twenty miles west of downtown Kowloon. A relatively uncongested highway connected the airport with the mainland, giving Wells a chance to check for tails. He eyed the rearview mirror as they drove along a bridge bracketed by a hill on the right, gray water to the left, the eastern edge of the Pearl River Delta. Henry had the taxi pinned at the speed limit, 110 kilometers an hour, about seventy miles.

"Faster, please," Wells said. Henry didn't argue. The Toyota sped to 120 kilometers, tailgating a van in the passing lane — the right lane. Hong Kong followed British road rules. Vehicles drove on the left, and steering wheels were on the right.

The cabbie looked over: *Okay?* Wells turned his palms to face the ceiling, raised them, *up, up.* "I promise, we get stopped, I'll give you double the fine."

"In a hurry, sir?"

"Life is short."

"Especially if one has an RTA."

"RTA?"

"Road traffic accident."

Point, Henry. Still, he swerved into the center lane, cruised past the van to the open asphalt ahead. In the mirror, Wells saw a black sedan skimming through traffic, maybe a quarter mile back. A Mercedes a few years old, a C-Class with tinted windows. At this distance Wells couldn't be sure about the ethnicities of the men in front, or whether anyone was in back. He couldn't make the plate, either.

Wells wondered if he was looking at Duberman's guys, the agency's, maybe even the Chinese. Most likely Duberman's. But how could Duberman have found him so fast? Had he put full-time watchers at the airport? Someone inside immigration watching for Wells's passport in case Wells was dumb enough to enter using his real name?

Wells watched three seconds more, then tapped Henry's shoulder. "Great. Thank you."

Unless you're planning to run immediately, lay back as soon as you spot the tail. There's always a chance they won't realize you've seen them. Not a great chance, but it has happened, and why not give yourself every possible edge? The life you save may be your own. Advice from Guy Raviv, Wells's favorite trainer at the Farm, a surveillance expert from the days of KGB dead drops rather than ISIS death videos. Raviv was gone himself now. Lung cancer had stalked him as mercilessly as any jihadi. But his advice had saved Wells more than once.

They slowed, and Wells watched as the Mercedes closed to four cars behind. Not exactly subtle, but running surveillance was tough with a single vehicle. Anyway, subtlety wasn't always the point.

"Someone following us?" Henry reached for his phone. "Shall I call the police?"

"No."

"Sir?"

This guy might be too straitlaced for what Wells wanted. But he had to ask. "I want to hire you all day. Keep the meter running or we can set a rate."

Henry looked back at the Merc. "Those men —"

"I promise, they're only interested in me." *Though they might still hurt you.*

"Who are they?"

"What I need to find out."

Henry drummed his fingers on the steering wheel. Civilians in these spots were torn between fear and excitement, a once-in-a-lifetime chance for a break from routine.

"Why would they follow you?"

"Some people don't like me."

"What's your name?"

"John Wells." Wells saw no reason to be coy. The men in the Mercedes knew him.

"You're American."

"Just came from San Diego."

"California." Henry spoke the word with a wistfulness that Wells had heard before. *Callleee-fornee-a.* Outside the United States, people seemed to think of the state as an earthly paradise. Especially if they were older than fifty. "Friends with Snowden?" Henry grinned. Edward Snowden had fled to Hong Kong after leaking the National Security Agency's secrets to the world. Though he hadn't stayed long.

"Never met the man."

"Joke." Henry looked over. "For the day, five thousand HK." Seven hundred dollars.

Excitement had won. It usually did. Henry had no idea what he had just signed up to do, or the price he might pay. But Wells needed a driver too much to explain the truth. *Want a clean game, Evan? Stick to basketball.* He reached for his wallet, peeled off ten $500 HK notes.

"Change of plans. We're still going to the Peninsula. But when we get there, I'll leave my luggage with you. You park in the garage and wait."

The Peninsula had a shopping arcade that included exits at the back of the hotel, close to an entrance to the MTR, the Hong Kong subway system. Without luggage, Wells should quickly be able to disappear into the subway.

"No garage at the Peninsula. Valet only."

"Fine. I get out, you take off. Cruise for a while. Pick up a fare, do your job. After a half an hour, find a place to park and wait. When I'm ready, I'll call, tell you where to meet me."

Though Henry would wait a long time for that call. As in forever. Wells had everything he really needed, the money and the pass-ports, in the backpack on his lap. He could always buy new clothes.

"If they follow me —"

"They won't." Once Wells stepped out of

the cab, the men in the Mercedes would lock on Wells. Henry was clearly an innocent civilian. By the time they realized that Wells had ditched his luggage, Henry would be gone. So Wells hoped.

"And where do you go?"

"I'll work that out. But you'll have my bags, so I promise you'll hear from me. If you want extra money —"

"The price is the price. We agreed." Henry sounded almost offended, making Wells feel even more guilty for involving him.

The untouched hills of Lantau Island continued on their right for several kilometers. Wells would hardly have known that one of the world's most densely packed cities was only a few minutes away. Then they crossed a bridge and in the distance Wells saw Hong Kong itself. The island's skyscrapers jutted from the harbor. Behind them were the lush green slopes of Victoria Peak. Duberman was up there, looking down on the city. And the world. Wells felt an unexpected fury in his chest at the man's arrogance. Duberman was the ultimate one-percenter. He thought his fortune gave him license to do whatever he liked. Not only had he tried to dupe the United States into war, he was still dodging punishment. He had bet that not even the President could bring him to justice, and so far he'd won.

The airport highway merged into a narrower elevated road packed with trucks and taxis. Kowloon was all around them now, the island and Peak hidden. The cab sped past a complex of dozens of giant apartment towers, still more buildings rising around them. Then long blocks of older, lower buildings of dirty gray concrete, offering flashes of a hundred thousand lives, balconies stuffed with BMX bicycles and pigeon cages and what Wells could have sworn was a lime-green La-Z-Boy recliner warped in from the 1970s.

The Mercedes made no effort to close the gap. Wells suspected they'd picked up a second tail. Plenty of candidates lurked. The white Sprinter van three cars behind them, its sides suspiciously logo-free. The gray BMW 3 Series beside the Sprinter, two white guys up front.

Wells had assumed that Duberman wouldn't try to pick him off in the middle of Hong Kong, risk killing civilians. Neither the local police nor the Communist government in Beijing could ignore a gangland-style daylight murder of an American visitor. Shafer and Duto would make sure the Chinese knew where to look. Wells figured that Duberman instead would hole up in his mansion, wait for Wells to attack, then try to make him shark bait in the South China Sea.

But maybe Duberman figured he could manage the fallout from a killing. Even so, Wells made himself relax. Unless he planned to jump off the highway to the surface roads thirty feet below, he couldn't do anything about the tails, anyway.

"How far to the hotel?"

"Few minutes. Last exit before the tunnel."

"When you get close, stay in the middle lane, drive like you're going by, pull off at the last minute." An obvious move, but the only way to see for sure who else was on them. Wells waited for Henry to object, but the guy just nodded and squeezed the steering wheel tighter. He was into it now. Amazing how fast fear slid into excitement, and vice versa.

Despite the congestion the traffic moved smoothly, and after five minutes they reached a blue sign that announced 6A, Tsim Sha Tsui — Salisbury Road. Henry braked hard enough to throw Wells against his seat belt and jerked the steering wheel left. The Toyota slid across two lanes, nearly fishtailing into a minibus packed with teenagers. Behind them, a black Nissan sedan tried to follow but couldn't get by.

"Fantastic," Wells said.

They came off the ramp and were only a few hundred yards from the harbor. Hong Kong Island loomed across the water. Beside them, the expressway sank into the entrance to the Cross-Harbour Tunnel. Ahead, the ramp swung over the tunnel entrance to become Salisbury Road, the boulevard that ran along the central Kowloon harbor.

"Peninsula there." Henry pointed right.

Wells looked back. The Mercedes was coming hard after them. "Don't stop until you get there. Run the lights."

"Hong Kong taxis don't run lights."

"Make an exception."

Henry shook his head.

One day Wells would get himself a real wheelman. Though he'd still take Henry over the drunk who'd ferried him around Istanbul four months ago. He had been chasing Glenn Mason, a CIA officer turned traitor, that night. He'd felt then like he was near the end of his quest to stop the United States from being lured into war. In reality, he had hardly begun.

Fortunately, the lights favored them. Only three lay between them and the hotel, and all stayed green. Two minutes later, they turned into the Peninsula's entrance. The Mercedes tailed close, but made no effort to pull side by side.

The hotel was a U-shaped beige building that filled a block along Salisbury Road. Everything about it broadcast wealth, luxury, and power. Besides the Rolls-Royce fleet, two spit-polished Ferraris and a low-slung sports car that Wells didn't even recognize held pride of place in the front parking lot. Parking attendants in pressed uniforms watched the six-figure iron. Wells was glad he'd worn one of his new suits, even if the trans-Pacific ride had rumpled it. He was doubly glad that he was wearing Nikes and not dress shoes. He'd chosen sneakers to stay comfortable on the plane, but they would come in handy in the next few minutes.

A doorman hustled over.

"Checking in, sir?"

"Anything's possible." Wells stepped out, snapped the Toyota's door shut. Henry rolled away, and Wells trotted for the hotel. He thought about waiting in the lobby, confronting his pursuers. But he had no idea if they were holding. Plus he sensed that they, whoever they were, *wanted* a public scene. In lieu of attacking him directly, maybe they hoped to involve the police, put him on a flight back to the United States before he'd even unpacked, a cheap but effective way of keeping him from Duberman.

The lobby was as lavish as the cars outside. Wells hustled past the overstuffed couches where the hotel served high tea each afternoon and turned left into the arcade. He was trotting now, pants rubbing against his legs. This new Hugo Boss suit fit a little too well.

At the back exit, Wells checked over his shoulder. Two men were following him, one white, one Chinese, both with a lean, hungry, clipped look, foxhounds on two legs. They wore unbuttoned sport coats, loose enough to hide pistols. They ran toward Wells as he pushed his way out.

The entrance for the Tsim Sha Tsui MTR station was almost directly across Middle Road. Wells dodged a delivery van, hurtled down the escalator two steps at a time. He found himself at the intersection of brightly lit tunnels that stretched east, west, and north. Overhead signs indicated that the station's gates and platforms lay north. Wells ran that way, weaving through backpack-wearing students. He checked over his shoulder. His pursuers were still about a hundred feet back, and as far as he could tell their hands were empty.

As he neared the entrance gates, the passageway widened into a subterranean village, complete with coffee shops, fast-food restaurants, even clothing stores. The train platforms were another level down. Wells decided not to go for them. Buying a ticket would take too long, and he didn't want to risk arrest by jumping the gates. He felt more and more that his pursuers wanted him to make just that kind of mistake. Instead he turned right, down another long tunnel, this one even more crowded than the first. A teenager who had her nose in her phone nearly slammed into him, but he spun past her like a running back dodging a tackler and stayed upright.

After several hundred feet, the tunnel intersected at a sharp left with a narrower passageway. Overhead signs indicated that the new tunnel led to three exits. Wells took it. At the least he'd force his pursuers to guess which exit he'd taken. He ran up a set of stairs and found himself on a narrow pedestrian street crowded with restaurants and shops. He was sweating now, his face flushed, a spectacle to the Chinese around him.

Overhead, the street followed the same diagonal as the passageway underneath. Wells turned and doubled back, looking for a taxi. At Mody Road, he saw one. "Stop!" The driver looked at Wells, hesitated, pulled over. Before the guy could change his mind, Wells wrenched open the door and dove inside.

"Happy Valley racetrack." Wells had memorized twenty or so of the city's big landmarks so that he wouldn't have to waver in these moments. Hong Kong had two big tracks, Sha Tin on the mainland side and Happy Valley on the island. The driver looked at him, but the taxi didn't move.

"No race today."

Come on. Wells saw one of his pursuers, the white guy, come out of the exit, scan the street. The guy saw the cab and ran for it.

Wells pulled a $500 HK note from his suit pocket. "Go. Please."

The cab eased into traffic. Wells wondered if his pursuer would reach under his coat and start blasting, but instead he only grinned at Wells and pointed to his eyes. *Eye C U . . .* Wells didn't know what to make of the seemingly cavalier attitude. Hard to imagine Duberman's guys acting that way. But who else could they be?

■ ■ ■ ■

Happy Valley was closed, as the cabbie had warned. Wells paid him off and walked down to the Causeway Bay MTR stop, mopping the sweat from his face. After ninety minutes shuffling from train to train, simple countersurveillance, he found himself back in Kowloon's Mong Kok district. In a no-name electronics store Wells bought four low-end phones, Chinese brands with unfamiliar names, and a dozen SIM cards. He wondered if he should call Henry, but he couldn't take the chance that his pursuers had gotten the cab's plate and tracked him down. Instead he texted Garry Wright, the station chief. An answer came back in seconds. Wright had obviously been waiting. *Running late?*

Traffic problems, Wells wrote. *All clear now.*

U sure?

Yes.

A longer pause this time. Wells guessed that Wright was considering backing out. Then: *186 Hong Ling Street, #605. 1600.* They had arranged to use a simple code for their first meet. The street address would have an extra 1 in front, the room number would be one floor higher than the real room, the meeting time one hour later. So Wright wanted to meet in suite 505 of 86 Hong Ling at 1500, 3 p.m.

Forty-five minutes from now. Wells found a local map at a 7-Eleven. The stores were weirdly ubiquitous here. Hong Ling was only a few blocks away. Apparently, Wright liked Mong Kok for meetings, too.

The building was blocky and concrete and stuffed with massage parlors. Wells ignored the elevator and trudged up the fire stairs, which smelled faintly sweet, like they'd been sprayed months before with cheap perfume. The stairs and the fifth-floor hallway were empty. A pinhole camera was mounted above the door to 505, and its lock snapped open before Wells knocked.

Inside, Wells found himself in an apartment smaller than a one-car garage. A kitchenette with a hot plate and a pint-sized fridge occupied the wall to his right. The only window stared into a concrete airshaft. The ceiling fan dangled low enough to give Wells a haircut. Wright sat on a neon yellow couch that belonged in a home for the blind. A pistol sat on the table in front of him, a laptop beside it.

"Clean?"

"Yeah."

"Water in the fridge. Look like you could use it."

Wells grabbed a bottle of water and sat. Wright hadn't gotten the job on his looks. He was chubby and unhandsome. His eyes were pouchy, half-masted, his skin sallow, vaguely jaundiced. As if the years he'd spent in East Asia had seeped into his blood. He reminded Wells of Shafer, and Wells liked him straightaway.

Though he wasn't sure the feeling was mutual.

"Welcome to my happy home," Wright said.

"Trying to win a Guinness competition for World's Crappiest Safe House?"

"I wanted a place I could pay for out of petty cash. Only me and my DS" — director of security — "know it exists. Unless you messed it up. Did you?"

"I picked up a tail at the airport. Were they yours?"

"You wouldn't have seen ours."

"These guys wanted me to see them."

"Round or slant?"

Wells needed a moment to understand. *Eyes.*

"One each."

Wright grunted in surprise. "Can't have been the Chinese, then. They don't trust white folk enough to team up. And you think they meant you GBH?" Grievous bodily harm.

"Not sure. They had a chance. It would have been messy and public, but it was there. They didn't take it."

"Get the plate? We have access to the Hong Kong database and a lot of China, too."

Wells shook his head. "Could Duberman have an in at the airport?"

"The Macao casinos are connected at the top hotels here. If big players come to Hong Kong, they want to know. But I've never heard they have an in at HKIA. Maybe his guys leaned hard on somebody at an immigration counter."

But Wright sounded doubtful, and the theory seemed like a long shot to Wells, too.

"You know him well."

"Yes and no. After Gamma took off, this was about eight or nine years ago, we started paying attention. He bought the mansion seven years ago. Wanted something that would really impress the whales. You know much about gambling in Macao?"

"Just that it's huge."

"Correct. Hardly existed before 2001, a couple crummy casinos in downtown Macao. Now it's way bigger than Vegas. The biggest players come from the mainland. Guys betting a hundred thousand dollars a hand on baccarat. Or more. But they want a lot of hand-holding. One reason that Duberman's so big here is that he gives it. Even before he moved in this year, he was here glad-handing these guys two or three times a year."

"They like him?"

"Why wouldn't they? He's charming, hangs around with models, likes bling the way they do. Thing about China is that it's nouveau riche in a way you can hardly imagine. Some of the older guys remember the famines of the sixties. Imagine being afraid you'd starve to death when you were a kid, now you have billions of dollars."

"Whiplash."

"Yes. Plus they know they might lose it if they get sideways with whoever's in power. Upshot is they have this insane attitude toward money."

"They sound like Russians."

"Even richer. They literally come to an important meeting with a shopping bag full of Rolexes, one for everyone. Which sounds like a bribe, and it is, but it's something else, too."

"And Duberman played along."

"I don't know if he liked it, but he put up

with it. Spent time with them. Which isn't easy, because these guys are seriously insecure. The biggest guys, you can't even put them in the same room with each other, they get pissy if they don't think they have your full attention. Anyway, the reason I remember when he bought the mansion is that three months later, the COS told me to put together a file, go to him, ask for his help."

"As in spying on his customers?"

"A lot of these guys are high-ranking CCP" — Chinese Communist Party — "and most of the rest are in tight. They have to be. I set a meet with Duberman, low-key approach, the pitch was *We have dirt on the guys at your tables, you have dirt on the guys at your tables, maybe we should trade dirt, good for you, help you with credit risks, good for us, too.*"

"And?"

"Pfft. Shot down before we made it back to the office. Our customer relationships are sacrosanct, the lifeblood of our business, blah blah blah . . ."

"The usual."

"Worse. Langley actually reamed us out, had we followed the proper rules involved in approaching U.S. nationals, blah, blah. We got the message. He was way involved in politics back home, he didn't want us messing up his business, we better stay away. We didn't stop watching him entirely, he was too important, but we laid off. And we never went back to him."

"Then, three months ago, he moves here."

"Sure. Right after we decide not to invade Iran. Then the DCI gets fired and the President stops just short of bending over for Vinny Duto on national television. Now you show up and my new boss tells me to extend you every courtesy." Wright gave a smile that emphasized the lumpiness of his face. "I have all that right? That fact pattern?"

"I'd say you understand completely."

"Tell me something, then. Just us chickens. If Duberman did what I think he did, why are we not handling this officially? Why Muslim John?"

Muslim John? Wells let it slide. "Better ask the White House."

"We're *protecting* this guy? After he tried to jam us into a war."

"Looks that way."

"Were Hebley and the President working with him?"

Wells couldn't let that rumor spread, as much as he wanted to. "About a ninety-nine-point-nine-percent chance he duped them, too."

"Now POTUS thinks it's too messy to unwind."

"He claims he'll take care of it. In time."

"But you're tired of waiting."

"I'm more of a self-starter."

Wright snorted, a strange sound from his chubby little body.

"So I hear. Sounds like you have yourself a legitimate gripe, though."

Glad you agree. "What about Duberman's security?"

"So, in Macao, the casino has two heads of security. One is a former FBI agent from San Francisco. He's there to look good for Americans who come along chasing violations of the FCPA" — the Foreign Corrupt Practices Act — "or whatever."

"Is he clean?"

"Unclear. We've heard he's making a couple million a year." Giving him a couple million reasons not to ask questions. "Then there's a local, a guy they hired away from the Macao police. Not very nice. I wouldn't go over there unless you think you can get in and out without them seeing. Macao looks bright and shiny, but there are alligators in the basements. Much more than here."

"And who runs his security at the mansion?"

"Four years ago, he brought in an SAS guy" — the Special Air Service, the British equivalent of the Deltas.

"Don't suppose you know his name?"

"Figured you might ask, so I looked it up. William Roberts. But from what I can tell, he's mainly a caretaker."

"Yeah, the Mossad guys run the show."

"Anyway, that's about all I have. Before you ask, we haven't tried to get inside the mansion or recruit any of his guys. Nothing that needs verification."

Overseas stations had to ask Langley for formal approval — what the agency called plan verification — before targeting any American citizen for anything more than surveillance.

"Mainly drones, then?"

"Yeah. Not Predators, nothing like that. No way we can run those in this airspace. Souped-up versions of little commercial guys, just about this big" — Wright held his arms about three feet apart — "helicopter style, quad rotors. They don't have great optics, so they have to stay close. No weapons, either. But we like 'em because they have no markings, no way to prove they're ours. Even so, we've already lost two. Either he or the Chinese has some system that's frying their guts."

"But you've clocked him going to and from Macao."

"Yeah, with passengers every time. I gave the headlines to Vinny, but the details are on there." Wright nudged the laptop with his toe. "Have at it." Wright picked up the pistol, a snug 9-millimeter that would fit nicely in an inside waist holster, handed it to Wells. "Yours to keep. Spare magazines and a holster in the safe behind the fridge. Ka-Bar and a boot knife, too, if your tastes run that way. If you need something bigger, I can get it, leave it here." He fished a key from his pocket, tossed it to Wells. "No alarm or anything, just the door."

"You'd do that for me?"

"Now that I know the score, I might have even if I hadn't been told to. You have any thoughts, how to close the deal?"

"At this point, I'm mainly hoping to get a clear look at the mansion." Wells explained his plan to rent an apartment.

"Gonna be tough for you to take him if he knows you're coming."

"I didn't think I'd get made at the airport."

"But you did."

"Everybody makes mistakes."

159

"What if the family's in the way —"

"No. Clean only."

"You say so. I'll leave some long-lens gear here for you. Drones, too."

"I can fly them with no training?"

"They're pretty intuitive. Where's your stuff, by the way?"

"Left it in the cab. I'm a trusting soul."

"Do me one favor. No praying to Mecca in here. I'm not much of a Catholic, but I gotta draw the line somewhere."

Wells felt like he'd been ambushed. Almost literally. He found his hands at his throat, ready to stop a garrote. Then he saw Wright's smirk. "Tell me you're joking."

The smirk widened. "*Of course* I'm joking. True what they say about you, though, isn't it? A real believer."

I don't know why we're talking about this. I don't know what you're trying to prove. Maybe Wright wasn't trying to prove anything. Maybe he just couldn't keep himself from poking for sore spots. An occupational hazard.

"I'll tell Vinny how much help you've been." In other words: *Don't forget how high my connections run.* Wells didn't love playing that card, but after the Muslim John weirdness, he didn't see any choice.

"You do that. You need anything else, holler."

Then Wright was gone. Wells sat in silence for a minute, checked the room. The pistol was loaded, the knives and extra magazines and holster in the safe, as Wright had promised. Along with an unexpected bonus, a suppressor, what civilians called a silencer. Whatever he thought of Wells's faith, Wright had already come through. Still, the snide comments were a reminder that some people in the agency would forever suspect Wells for his conversion.

No matter. His new suits might be gone, but he had money, passports, and a pistol. Everything a good operative needed. He tossed the pistol and knives into his backpack and followed Wright out. Time to get to work.

7

MACAO, SPECIAL ADMINISTRATIVE REGION, PEOPLE'S REPUBLIC OF CHINA

The cat was orange and black and fat and sunning itself on a patch of weeds at the edge of the highway that connected Beijing with the capital's airport. General Cheung Han had plenty of time to notice it. His Mercedes limousine was barely moving, no surprise. Despite a massive road-building program, Beijing's traffic jams worsened every year.

As Cheung watched, the cat stood, stretched its legs, licked his big balls — and jumped into the traffic. *"Bai mu,"* Cheung said to his driver. The term literally meant "white-eyed" or "blind," but was slang for "stupid." The idiot cat was going to get himself killed.

They were in the middle lane, with the cat about twenty meters ahead. A delivery van in the right lane would surely squash the thing. But no. A second later, the cat poked his head out from under the van. He was moving deliberately. Almost mincing. Cheung saw what he wanted, a half-eaten piece of fried chicken lying between the right and center lanes.

He lowered his window. *"Gundan! Gundan, shagua!"* Scram! Scram, dummy!

The cat grabbed the chicken, a fat breast, almost too big for him to hold. It dragged on the pavement as he turned for the curb and dropped from his jaws.

"Greedy dummy!"

But the cat wouldn't give up. He picked it up again, a tighter grip this time. With the breast firmly in his jaws, he sauntered in front of a motorcycle, jumped to the curb, and straightaway tore into the chicken.

"Cheeky, isn't he?" the driver said.

"Lucky." *A good sign for me.* Cheung was on his way to the baccarat tables of Macao. He didn't need his favorite fortune-teller to know that the gods would be with him tonight.

At the airport, the limousine passed the civilian terminals and delivered Cheung to a nondescript two-story building used exclusively by senior leaders and generals. A

163

plain white jet waited fifty meters away, fueled and ready for the three-hour flight to Macao. The jet's exterior was indistinguishable from a Gulfstream V. In fact, it was a Chinese copy called the Smoothwind 10, assembled at a giant new factory west of Beijing.

Five years before, the generals of the People's Liberation Army Air Force had convinced the Chinese government to invest $42 billion in the civilian jet industry. They argued that the air force, which was struggling to match the American F-22 and F-35, would benefit from civil aviation research and development. The industry would also employ hundreds of thousands of Chinese in high-skill manufacturing and engineering jobs. The fact that the generals could steal a fortune along the way went unmentioned, though not unnoticed.

Despite all the bribes and kickbacks, the first Smoothwind rolled out of the new factory on schedule. Like the skyscrapers that sprang up overnight in Shanghai. Like the high-speed rail lines that soon enough would cover all of China. Like the factories around Shenzhen that churned out millions of mobile phones and laptops and tablets *every day.* Sometimes Cheung couldn't believe the progress his country had made.

He was fifty-four, old enough to have grown up in a village a thousand kilometers southwest of Beijing with seven hundred residents and no indoor toilets. Old enough to remember the unthinkable luxury of eating chicken on his fifth birthday and falling asleep with a full belly for once. Thanks to the hard work of a billion Chinese, the next generations would never be able to imagine that poverty.

Endless nights of studying took Cheung from Peking University to the Technische Universität Munich, where he studied operations research. Many Chinese students there found ways to stay in Germany or move to the United States. Cheung didn't see the appeal. The Western countries were rich. But they weren't his, and they never would be. Back home, he joined the air force. He learned to fly on balky J-7 fighters, flying coffins that killed two of his classmates in their first week of training. Cheung was comparatively lucky, surviving a failed takeoff caused by a blown hydraulic line. The accident shattered both his legs, effectively ending his flying career. He didn't complain. The J-7's problems showed him that even the bravest pilots couldn't overcome third-rate equipment. He joined the air force's research-and-development department. Twenty-five years later, he oversaw aerospace research for the entire People's Republic.

Along the way, he'd grown rich. He didn't see why the developers and bankers should be the only ones to make money. Why shouldn't the leaders who'd made the miracle possible with their foresight and hard work? Why shouldn't *he*? He had given far more to China than those pigs. For a quarter century, his legs had ached every day. For a quarter century, he'd walked with a limp. He deserved a share. Now he'd gotten it. And he hadn't stolen a single yuan. No. These were gifts. A property company bought up farmland that the air force needed for a new base and gave him one percent of its stock as a thanks for the tip he'd provided. The avionics company that made the Smoothwind's radar bought his son an apartment in Manhattan so the boy wouldn't have to live in a Columbia University dormitory. Cheung didn't even consider turning down the money. Who would have benefitted? The air force would build its base in any event. The radar worked as well as any other, certainly well enough to do its job.

The gifts added up quickly. Cheung had two hundred million dollars salted away in

Hong Kong and Switzerland. Money enough for his trips to Macao. He didn't apologize for those, either. Nothing like a night or two at the baccarat table to clear his head.

Ian Fleming made baccarat famous in *Casino Royale,* when Bond, James Bond, beat a Russian spy out of a fortune. But the game that Cheung would play was a pale cousin of Bond's. Where Bond battled other players, Cheung played the casino itself, under strict rules that gave the house a small but definite edge. For all its seeming complexity, baccarat was one of the most highly structured games that casinos offered. A ten-dollar blackjack player had more control over his fate than Cheung. Blackjack bettors controlled their hands, choosing whether to hit or stand. Baccarat players didn't.

In baccarat, a dealer laid out two hands of two cards each, one to the "player" and one to the "banker." The suits of the cards didn't matter, only their numerical values. Jacks, queens, and kings counted as zero, aces as one. The two cards were added to make the hand's value — but only the rightmost digit counted for the score. In other words, a hand of eight and six was worth four, not fourteen. A three and a seven equaled zero, not ten.

Zero was the worst possible score, nine the best. Any two-card eight or nine was called a "natural" and automatically won the hand.

If neither player nor banker was dealt a natural, both sides had one final chance to improve their hands. A player dealt five or less automatically received a third card. Then it was the banker's turn. After the last card was dealt, the hand closer to nine won. A tie was a tie, and neither side received any money.

Like blackjack, craps, and every other casino game, baccarat offered the house a hidden edge. Because the "banker" had looser rules governing when he could take a third card, he won about fifty-one percent of the hands. Bettors like Cheung chose to gamble on either the "banker" or the "player" side — the only decision they could make. If they chose the player side, they were paid even money when they won. If they chose the banker side, they paid a small commission, just enough to give the edge back to the casino. Either way, they were at a disadvantage of about one percent on every bet. The gap was small enough to be invisible to a casual bettor. A hot player could beat it for a night, a weekend, even a week.

But ultimately that one percent disadvantage couldn't be overcome. Card counting and bet sizing couldn't outsmart it. Joss sticks couldn't perfume its deadly math. In the long run, the house always won.

Cheung understood the odds. But he didn't care. He'd outwitted them often enough. In five years, he'd visited Macao twenty-six times. On nine trips, he'd left ahead, each time by at least ten million Hong Kong dollars. On one epic three-day visit he gambled for sixty hours and won one hundred and one million dollars. The general manager at 88 Gamma, Cheung's favored casino, gave him a twenty-four-karat gold plaque to commemorate his entry into the Hundred Million Club, players who had won that much money in a single trip.

Cheung remembered every delicious detail of those trips. As for the others, he'd lost, sure. Still, he thought he was close to even overall, even if he'd never precisely totaled his wins and losses. His great secret was that he knew when to shift between the player and the banker side. He'd once won eleven straight hands, flipping between player and banker five times along the way. It wasn't luck as much as intuition, as if the cards were speaking to him.

He was a very good gambler.

Only he wasn't.

In reality, Cheung suffered from a bad case of gambler's memory. His wins were big, but his losses were even bigger. In all, even counting his wins, Cheung had thrown away five hundred million Hong Kong dollars in five years at 88 Gamma. He was not the casino's biggest loser. That honor belonged to a property developer who had somehow lost two billion dollars. But he was in the top ten.

So Cheung's visits spurred a mix of awe, greed, and fear among the hosts and managers at 88 Gamma. Awe that a man could pour away money so stupidly. Greed because whales like Cheung translated into paychecks and bonuses for the people who served him. And fear . . . because Cheung's appetites extended past the baccarat tables. Sober, he was no more arrogant than the average Chinese plutocrat. But Cheung rarely stayed sober long. He drank to celebrate his wins and to drown his losses. The more he drank, the bolder his requests became. And Aaron Duberman had made clear how he expected his staff to treat

Cheung and his fellow whales. *Like kings. Whatever they want.*

To prove his point, Duberman himself regularly visited the ultra-high-roller VIP rooms. Whether the whales were winning or losing, shouting or calm, Duberman sat beside them and made happy promises. *If you need a break, please, share dinner with me. Foie gras? Bird's nest soup? Shark fin? Say the word, my chef will make it . . . We've made sure all your favorite hostesses are here, but if you're bored, let me know. More where they came from . . . I hope my manager told you we're hosting the welterweight Thai boxing championship. Front-row seats for you, naturally. But how would you like to watch the champ practice tonight? A private session, just you and his trainers.*

And, after fifteen or twenty minutes of watching, one last offer, this one whispered. *If you have any special requests, anything not on the menu, so to speak, Chou-Lai is the man to ask.* Chou-Lai Zhen held the deliberately vague title of Special Assistant/High Limit Operations. In reality, he was the house pimp and pusher. 88 Gamma was too careful to provide anything illegal itself. But Chou-Lai made sure that if a whale wanted companionship, female or male or both, or drugs, uppers or downers or anything in between, he'd have them.

Chou-Lai's services were available to only the biggest whales of all, men — and they were without exception men — who lost at least fifteen million Hong Kong dollars a year. They might not know exactly how much they were worth to 88 Gamma, but Duberman did.

Cheung spent the flight to Macao reading a classified briefing on the Snow Moth, a new fifteen-centimeter drone with an advanced self-guidance system. The Snow Moth was designed to be nimble enough to fly in the most crowded cities, small enough to sneak over hostile military bases. Its biggest problem was battery life. But a month before, air force engineers had redesigned its battery into tubes that could be embedded in its plastic skeleton. Now the Snow Moth could stay airborne for ten hours in smooth conditions, six in high winds. Production costs were estimated at seven thousand dollars each. For what the United States spent on a single fighter, China could build twenty thousand drones.

Another successful development program, another project that Cheung could recommend be moved to full production. China National Automated Aircraft Company would no doubt find a way to thank him. As the Smoothwind descended, he stuffed the report back in his briefcase and poured himself a taste of eighteen-year-old Glenfiddich. Only a taste, though. He wanted to be in top form tonight.

He landed at the Aeroporto Internacional de Macau just after 8 p.m. To the west, the sun set behind the mammoth casinos of Cotai — the artificial island that Macao had built to give the gambling industry room to expand. Two dozen casinos rose out of the landfill, with more coming. Duberman's 88 Gamma complex towered over the others. Its main casino was fifty stories of sleek black glass. Near that tower was the new skyscraper, which looked about ready to open. Cheung was already looking forward to opening night.

Technically, Chinese citizens needed visas to enter Macao. But for elite officials like Cheung, the border wasn't even a formality. A limousine waited for him on the tarmac, carried him through a gate beside the main terminal. No passport check, no record of his entry.

Ten minutes later, the limo rolled into a parking garage at 88 Gamma that was reserved for VIPs. Cheung's personal host Xiao, a dapper forty-something man in a

173

suit, bowed deeply as Cheung stepped out. "General." As a rule, Cheung preferred to be addressed only by his title, not his name. "So good to see you again."

Cheung merely nodded.

"Would you prefer to see your room, or directly to your table?"

Cheung felt the luck foaming inside him. "The table, I think."

Xiao nodded gravely and led Cheung to an elevator, where a tall Chinese woman waited. "General."

"What a pleasant surprise, Jian." A lie. She was always here for him. But he liked to pretend their meetings were coincidence, another form of luck. This part of the night was a show, one that the casino put on for him alone.

"I've missed you." Jian smiled shyly, leaned down, kissed his cheek. She wore a pale blue silk dress that draped her slim body perfectly.

Cheung wondered if he would bed her this trip. Probably not. She would no doubt agree if he asked. But he knew he could be rough. Inevitably, he grew angry at his conquests if they didn't do what he wanted. And ashamed of them if they did, especially if they seemed to like it. He preferred to see Jian as untouched and perfect.

Or maybe he just liked his women younger.

"To your table." Xiao pushed the button for the forty-eighth floor, reserved for the biggest whales. This particular elevator made only three stops: the garage, the main lobby, and forty-eight. As they rose, Cheung flipped open his gold cigarette case, another gift from 88 Gamma, and reached for a Dunhill. Macao banned smoking in its casinos, but the rule didn't apply to men like him.

The elevator door opened into a lobby whose glass north wall offered a stunning view of the nearby casinos and the city beyond. "I can't wait for the Sky Casino," Xiao said. "On a clear night we'll be able to see Hong Kong."

"As if the nights are ever clear around here." Cheung felt a pleasant impatience building. The cards were so close. He walked down the corridor that led to the VIP suites. At the far end, an open door beckoned.

Inside, Cheung found himself in a windowless room ten meters square, two baccarat tables side by side. The air was cool, with a faint jasmine scent. A painting of cherry blossoms by the Chinese master Qi Baishi adorned the back wall. Practically no one outside China knew Baishi's name, but he was a favorite of the new Chinese elite. The painting was worth at least fifty million dollars.

The tables were ready for play, dealers waiting, chips stacked high, cards shuffled and in the long plastic trays called shoes. Six decks in each shoe, three hundred and twelve cards in all, embossed with the 88 Gamma logo, a forest of skyscrapers growing out of a globe.

The dealers stood and bowed as Cheung entered. He chose the table on the right, the seat directly across from the dealer, a position that offered the best read on the cards.

"General. We've been waiting for you."

The dealer was a heavy man with a smoker's rasp. Lin. Cheung had gambled against him a dozen times. While the hosts and waitresses were uniformly deferential, the dealers had more freedom. Some seemed to root for Cheung and be upset if he lost. Others didn't hide their desire to beat him, as though the casino's money belonged to them. Lin belonged in the second category. Cheung would take pleasure in knocking him down tonight.

"Here I am." Cheung stubbed out his cigarette. "To begin, fifteen." As in million.

"Fifteen."

Cheung always bought in for fifteen, so the stacks were already counted. Lin tapped them for the security cameras before pushing them across the green baize. Four stacks of ten sky-blue chips, ten million dollars. Four stacks of ten orange chips, another four million. And two stacks of ten mint-green chips, the final million. Ten stacks in all, an even hundred chips. Lined up against the rail of the table they stretched not even fifty centimeters from edge to edge. Together, they were worth more money than the average American made in a lifetime. Cheung flipped two of the mint-green chips back.

"Ten thousands."

Lin tucked the chips into his drawer, slid back one more stack, ten yellow chips worth ten thousand Hong Kong dollars each. Cheung used those to tip the waitresses.

In the movies, high rollers like Cheung carried suitcases full of cash to fund their gambling. In reality, Cheung had brought only clothes. A week before, he had wired forty-one million Hong Kong dollars from a Credit Suisse account he controlled under a fake name to an equally anonymous Citibank account run by a Macao junket operator. The junket company kept seven hundred thousand dollars as a "travel and conversion fee" and sent the rest to 88 Gamma. Both the junket company and the casino knew the money was Cheung's. But his name was never attached to it, a prudent precaution. Cheung's gambling wasn't a secret, but the size of his wins and losses were. They might attract attention in Beijing. China's Ministry for State Security spied on Macao's casinos, looking for government officials and party leaders. But 88 Gamma guarded its VIP rooms to keep the ministry's operatives at bay.

Cheung took other precautions, too. On his first trips to Macao, he had brought friends. More recently, with his bets and his extracurricular appetites growing, he traveled alone. In any case, arriving by himself and with only a few dollars in his pockets added to the pleasure of the night. When he showed up this way, he could indulge the fantasy that the casino had *given* him the chips because it valued his company so highly. *We'll pay you to play with us.*

Usually, Cheung started small, betting a hundred thousand dollars a hand, and worked his way up. If he was winning, he increased his bet size gradually. If he wasn't, he might stay small for hours, then throw down a series of million-dollar bets, trying to shock the gods onto his side. But tonight he thought of the cat, its boldness on the highway. He decided to open fast. He pushed eight sky-blue chips into the box in front of him marked *Player*. A two-million-dollar bet.

"Two million." Lin's voice held a hint of surprise. "Starting with the maximum." Even 88 Gamma had limits. Two million per hand was the official maximum. In truth, the casino took bets as high as five million from regulars, gamblers whom the managers could be sure would return after a big win.

"Don't be scared! Deal the cards."

Lin pulled the first card of the night, the burn, from the shoe. He flipped the card up, showed it to Cheung. A king. A zero.

"A fine card. Let's go."

Lin pushed aside the burn, snapped out the first hand of the night. He passed the first and third cards to Cheung, placed the second and fourth on the spot on the table marked *Banker*. Cheung reached for his cards, leaned in close. No serious baccarat player turned over his hand too quickly. To do so was to invite the worst kind of luck. No, the cards had to be squeezed and pinched until they revealed their precious secrets. Cheung turned up the edge of the first card. In ultra-high-limit games, decks were never reused, so players could treat the cards as badly as they wanted.

A five of diamonds. An okay card, though hardly perfect. Eights and nines were the ideal starting cards, face cards the worst. Cheung flipped it over to show Lin.

"Let's see what you've dealt yourself."

Lin turned over the cards in the *Banker* space. Two fours. An eight. A natural eight. Lin smirked, not trying to hide his glee. Cheung's margin for error had vanished. He needed a four for his second card to win the hand, or a three to tie. Otherwise, he would lose to Lin without even the chance to better his hand.

"Two million," Lin said.

Cheung ignored him, leaned so close to the table that his cheek nearly touched it. He thought of the cat, fearless in traffic, only one goal. He turned up an edge — and found himself peeking at a four of spades.

Making nine. A natural nine. The best possible hand.

"Ta made niao," Your mother's dick. Cheung lifted the card high, spun it down. Security cameras caught everything in this room, so Cheung didn't worry about losing the hand if the card skipped off the table.

"Can you add that, or do you need my help?"

"Nine. Player wins. Two million." Lin picked out eight sky-blue chips and slid them across.

Cheung looked up, caught Jian's eye. She stood in her customary position beside the Baishi painting. Their proximity made both of them more beautiful. She came over and he reached up and wrapped an arm around her waist, leaned in to smell her honeysuckle perfume.

"Are you surprised, Jian?"

"Not for a second, General."

"A Johnnie Walker Blue. A double."

So went the night. Cheung's wins mounted hour by hour. He drank steadily until the room blurred into a single frame, the table and nothing more. Aside from the scotches, he neither ate nor drank. In fact, he didn't leave the table at all. His bladder ached, but he didn't want to risk disrupting the field of luck that had settled over him. Finally, he lost three straight hands and pushed himself from the table. He stumbled, nearly fell, but Xiao grabbed him. His mouth tasted of ash and whiskey and he could hardly see.

He steadied himself, looked at his watch. Nine a.m. He'd gambled through the night.

181

He looked at the chips — and the plaques beside them, coated with a deep black metallic sheen like the skin of a luxury car. Each plaque was worth one million Hong Kong dollars. He had four stacks of ten to go along with all his chips. How much had he won? Sixty million? More?

In twelve hours. Had anyone ever won like this?

He stumbled to the toilet and held himself upright as he pissed all over the floor. No matter. They'd clean it up. They'd do whatever he wanted to keep him happy so they could get their hands on the money he'd taken. Anything at all. He could squat like a monkey on the table and pull down his pants and open his bowels. Xiao would smile and move him to the other table so he could keep playing.

But no, he was done tonight. He had won all he could for now. To push further would be to spit at the gods. He would lose everything if he went back.

What he wanted was a woman. A girl. A little bird who would be properly impressed with *his* little bird, which, truth be told, was hardly bigger than his thumb. Years ago, in a hotel in Shanghai, a whore had laughed at it. He'd beaten her until her screams brought security to his door. He'd shown them his air force identification. They'd given her a clout, too, and taken her away.

Cheung didn't know why that memory came to him now. He hated it and yet some part of him enjoyed it, the way her face had changed when he'd stopped slapping and started punching, the fear in her eyes —

No. Enough. He would enjoy this night. This morning. Morning, yes. He laughed into the empty room, grinned at the skull in the mirror. He turned on the taps, buried his face in cold water until he was sober enough to know he could ask Chou-Lai for what he wanted, make his point without speaking too clearly. And he staggered back to his fortune.

8

Duberman was halfway through an hour on his elliptical trainer when his iPhone buzzed, a call from the casino. He didn't want to stop working out, but no one at 88 Gamma would call him on his personal phone without good reason.

"Sir? It's Malcolm." Malcolm Garten, who ran the ultra-high-limit rooms. "Are you all right? You sound out of breath." Years of kissing up to big players had given Garten a tendency to brown-nose.

"Get to it, Malcolm."

"It's about the general."

General Cheung Han. A great customer. He'd come in the night before. "He need a credit line? Not a problem. Whatever he wants." Unlike some whales, the general paid his chits quickly. Maybe he worried 88 Gamma would rat him out to the air force.

"No, sir, he's up. Sixty-two million."

184

Duberman whistled. No wonder Garten was upset. In truth, Duberman didn't mind. Cheung wasn't a hit-and-run player. Even if he hung on this trip, he'd be back soon enough. The math would grind him down. It always did. In the meantime, he'd remember this night. *Big wins breed bigger losses.*

"So what's he want? To up his bets to five million? You don't need to call for that, Malcolm. Keith can handle it." Keith Huang, the casino's executive director.

"No, sir, he seems to be done. In fact, he's passed out. But before he did, he had a special request for Chou, and I thought you should know about it."

Garten briefed Duberman on "special requests" from the whales, so Duberman knew that Cheung preferred Vietnamese women. And that they sometimes ended their sessions with him with bruises and black eyes. He wondered what Cheung could have said to upset Garten. He and Chou-Lai had heard plenty of unpleasant requests from the whales over the years. They understood the job.

Whatever it was, Duberman didn't want the NSA or the Chinese government to hear it.

"We'll talk face-to-face. Here. Figure an hour?" Duberman would have time to finish his workout and take a shower.

"Yes, sir."

Duberman hung up. He had just started to move again when Gideon appeared in the doorway, a sheet of paper in his hand.

"Not now —"

"You know those manifests from Hong Kong International —"

Duberman paused again. Gideon handed him the sheet.

The Chinese border authorities closely monitored the airport's real-time immigration records, and Duberman's guys hadn't found a way to see them. But every other week, the border-control desks sent a list of names and nationalities to the airport's management. HKIA kept its own meticulous records of how many foreign nationals had landed, mainly for marketing purposes. Gideon had found a local private security company that could provide the list for a mere ten thousand Hong Kong dollars a pop. Duberman assumed the list would be useless. It didn't contain photos or other biometric identification or even passport numbers, just names and countries. Wells wouldn't possibly fly in under his real name. But for ten thousand HK a pop, they could afford to take the chance. And there, halfway down the page —

John Wells. United States.

"Do we know when, exactly?"

"It's not sorted by date, but it has to be sometime in the last two weeks."

This morning was turning more interesting by the minute.

"Wonder why he used his real name."

"Not for us. Probably sending a message to the White House. He knew they'd see it."

"So the CIA knows he's here," Duberman said. "Are they helping him?"

"At the least, they aren't after him."

Not a happy prospect. Wells was lethal enough without help.

"You asked for it," Gideon said.

Duberman folded the note into a paper airplane, flicked it at the bulletproof glass that looked out on the city. Let Wells come. His luck couldn't last forever, especially now that Gideon's men knew he was here. "Now let's find him."

"I've already told our guys. If he's around, we will. Especially if he goes to Macao."

The surveillance cameras at Duberman's mansion in Tel Aviv had caught Wells clearly. Every security guard at the 88 Gamma Macao casino now carried photos of him, and the casino managers had promised a reward to anyone who spotted him. The casino's facial-recognition software was

187

looking for Wells, too. 88 Gamma had installed the system years before to spot card counters and chip thieves. It was nearly unbeatable. A month before, it had spotted a grifter whom 88 Gamma had banned the year before, even though the guy had gained twenty-five pounds and grown his hair long.

"Meantime, I put a second guard at the gate," Gideon said.

"Why's that?" The voice belonged to Orli. She stood in the doorway, a light sheen of sweat on her arms and legs. She'd added a daily hour of Krav Maga, the Israeli self-defense training that combined boxing and judo, to her workouts. The new muscle made her even more beautiful, as far as Duberman was concerned. He fetched the list for her.

"Take a look."

She scanned the list. "Wells? Good. I hope he comes by, so I can meet him."

"Chop chop?" Duberman raised his hands, a mock karate stance.

"No fancy moves for him. Just a bullet in his head." She turned for the doorway. "I'm taking a shower. When you're done in here, you should get wet, too."

"I have a meeting in an hour."

"Fifty-five minutes more than you'll need."

"Shameless," Gideon said.

Orli waved at him as she walked out.

"That she is," Duberman said. But he understood. Beauty conferred all manner of privileges, including the chance to express desire frankly. Put more bluntly, who didn't want to hear a supermodel talk dirty? He scurried after her to their private quarters.

An hour later and much relaxed, he greeted Malcolm Garten in a meeting room whose centerpiece was a meticulously designed six-foot-high model of the new Sky Tower. Garten didn't reach the top of the model. He was a small, carefully groomed man, his blue suit pressed and his hair tightly combed. His jittery eyes betrayed his tension.

"Malcolm."

"Mr. Duberman. Sir."

"Sit. You look tired."

Garten plopped down like all his muscles had given up at once. "I was up all night watching Cheung. Craziest run I've ever seen."

"How many drinks did he have?" Duberman knew that Garten was desperate to tell him what Cheung had wanted. Better to slow him down.

"Seven or eight, all doubles. Whiskey."

"Any drugs?"

"I don't think so, no. His thing's booze. After the fourth, I told the bartenders to water the next one down, but it didn't fool him. He tossed it over his shoulder like a pinch of salt, made us bring a new one. By the end, he was completely gone. Could hardly talk. Cursed at the dealer when he lost, grabbed for his chips when he won."

"He could still gamble, though." Duberman wasn't asking. They could always gamble. He'd once watched a poker player collapse onto the table during a hand. The guy insisted on finishing before admitting he was having a heart attack.

"Finally, he went to the bathroom. He was gone long enough that we wondered if we should send someone in. But he came out on his own. Talking about monkeys. It sounded like nonsense to me, and my Mandarin's pretty good. I double-checked with Chou-Lai, and he agreed. Gibberish. I asked Cheung if he wanted to play anymore. He said no and cursed at me, told me I was trying to steal his money. At that point, I cleared out the room so it was just him and Chou and me. We sat him down, got a couple of cups of coffee in him. It didn't sober him up, but it perked him up, if you see what I mean."

"Sure."

"Then he started talking about wanting a woman. Chou said fine. And Cheung grabbed him and said no, Chou needed to understand, the ones before were all too old. Way too old. And the thing is, his taste runs young, anyway."

"I know."

"But we didn't tell you, last time he was here, Chou took him where he goes when he's got to push the limits. He told me afterward, Cheung picked out the youngest in the whole shop, fifteen or sixteen maybe. She looked like a boy. So if that's way too old —"

Garten stared at the floor.

"I have four girls myself, sir. These guys, they want drugs, they want an orgy, they want dog meat with a side of shark fin, I'll chalk it up to human nature. Not pedophilia. Maybe Chou doesn't care, but I do."

"You're sure that's what he wanted."

"Yes, sir. Chou told him unripe fruit could make him sick and he said no, he didn't care, the smaller, the better. The more tender. I didn't know what to say. Thank God, he passed out."

"Where is he now?"

"We put him in his suite on forty-two. Guards outside. They'll text me if he tries to leave."

Duberman sat beside Garten, patted his shoulder. "Sounds like it was a tough situation and you handled it great."

"Thank you, sir. So now what?"

Duberman knew what he ought to say. *Cheung crossed the line. Sixteen is one thing, that's the age of consent lots of places. Even fifteen. But this, no. It's not just illegal. It's immoral. We'll make sure he never comes back to 88 Gamma.*

"Here's what I think. Based on how much he drank, he'll sleep all day, wake up with the worst headache of his life. He won't even remember what happened, and if he does, he'll be ashamed. When he wakes up, show him what he won. I'll bet he'll bank the winnings and go home."

"Do I tell him he's banned?"

"No, nothing like that. As far as I'm concerned he drank too much, made a mistake. We'll leave it there. We're not in the business of shaming our customers."

"So what happens next time?"

"I promise, we'll never help him with anything like that."

"Because he's going to ask again."

"Malcolm, I need to know you're on board."

Garten stared at Duberman, fear and

anger jostling in his eyes. Finally, he nodded. Duberman understood. He couldn't afford to quit. Not with four kids at home.

"Say it for me."

"I'm on board." The words choked out.

"It goes without saying, you keep this to yourself."

"Count on that." Garten couldn't keep the sarcasm out of his voice. Duberman let the insubordination pass. If and when Cheung came back, he would keep Garten away.

"Good. Go back to Macao. Get some sleep."

"Yessir." Garten stood, walked out with slow careful steps, like he was eighty and not forty. He didn't look back. When he was gone, Duberman sat alone staring at Hong Kong, thinking about the real source of his fortune, a dead wiseguy named Jimmy the Roller.

This was the early eighties. Las Vegas still felt like the frontier. Barely a half-million people lived in all of Clark County, huddled together against the heat and the scorpions. But for the first time, the FBI was putting pressure on the local Mob. Jimmy and his buddies were trying to move into legit businesses. Motels that rented by the hour.

Football hotlines promising winners for the low, low price of $4.99 a minute. *We are 8–1 this year on Monday night, best record anywhere, call now for this week's lock . . .*

Okay, maybe semi-legit.

The origins of Jimmy's nickname were lost to history. Depending on his mood, Jimmy claimed it came from the five-figure roll of cash he carried, to the late-night visits — *rolls* — he paid unlucky debtors, or to his forearms, sticks of solid muscle that indeed resembled oversized rolling pins. A trip to a pizzeria downtown had opened Jimmy's eyes to the nickname's possibilities. *Must have been '75, that idiot Ford was President, I'm at this joint on Fremont. The owner says "Hey, Roller," waves the pin at me. Hits me, I gotta carry one of those, it'd be perfect. Not just because it matches my name, unnerstan'? My business, I don't want to kill you because then how you gonna pay? I smack you with that thing it doesn't kill you, doesn't even put you in the hospital, it just hurts like a —*

No one argued the logic.

Duberman came to Jimmy with eyes open. He wasn't desperate in the conventional sense. He wasn't a degenerate gambler or a husband who needed to pay a pregnant stripper to leave town. He wanted to buy a casino. One-third of a casino, to be precise. A dump in Reno called the Sizzlin' Saloon. Two hundred and ninety-five rooms, sixteen blackjack tables. Duberman was a young manager at Flamingo Hilton, known for his hard work and his eye for showgirls.

He should have waited his turn at Hilton, worked his way up. But even by Vegas standards, he was ambitious and impatient. The Saloon was run-down and barely breaking even. But it had a great location, down the block from a new Harrah's. Duberman *knew* he could turn it around. At two and a half mil, it was a steal. Not even ten grand a room. He found two more guys at Hilton to take the chance with him, managers in their late forties whose careers had topped out. They had one question for him. Where would he get his share?

He told them not to worry.

To fight the Mob, Nevada had created a "black book," formally called the Gaming Control Board Excluded Person List: wiseguys, cardsharps, and assorted ne'er-do-wells barred from setting their steel-toed shoes in any casino in the state. Smarter than his buddies, Jimmy had stayed off the list. Nothing kept him from exercising his God-given right to throw chips on a table and pray for rain. Twice a month he stopped by the Flamingo for blackjack and craps. Despite his famous bankroll, he gabbed more than gambled. Duberman suspected that Jimmy was prospecting for business, guys who needed quick cash, and not hundreds of dollars but thousands or tens of thousands.

In his effort to go straight-ish, Jimmy had hooked up with Clark International Depository Trust. The bank's lofty name belied the fact that its branch network consisted of two dingy storefronts in North Las Vegas. Jimmy found borrowers to sign promissory notes with Clark at ruinous rates. He and his friends put up a third of the cash and made sure the loans didn't bust. In turn, they received half the profits, plus a chunk of the bank. A fine deal for all involved, long as Jimmy convinced his clients to repay their debts. Thus the rolling pin.

Jimmy was upfront with borrowers. *Won't look like this money comes from me. You can tell your wife it came from a real bank. Tell her it's a business loan, a new mortgage, whatever. But it's from me. You don't pay it back, I come for you. You see?*

They saw.

Duberman's bosses never admitted they knew Jimmy's game. Yet the Hilton gave Jimmy casino comps — freebies — normally reserved for bigger bettors. Duberman once asked why. *Keeping him happy is good business.* The Hilton's managers knew that the money Jimmy lent sloshed back to the tables soon enough. Anyone who wasn't willing to go a half step over the edge didn't last in Vegas. Duberman didn't mind the ambiguity. In truth, the town appealed to him for precisely that reason. He was not exactly amoral, but he liked to set his own limits.

Duberman flew Jimmy to Reno, explained why he wanted the Sizzlin' Saloon, saw Jimmy's eyes get big as saucers. The Roller had never made a loan for more than forty thousand. A deal this size would take him to another level. The risk was big, too. Jimmy and his guys would have to put up a six-figure chunk of cash.

Jimmy left Duberman in the dark for a week before he agreed. At a price. On top of the usual terms, Duberman had to give Jimmy half his share of the casino's profits. Forever. Duberman had no other options. He agreed, on one condition, that Jimmy and his partners stay away from Reno and let Duberman run the casino. Jimmy agreed. To Duberman's surprise, he kept the bargain.

For the next six years, Duberman worked harder than he could have imagined. Twelve-hour days, six and seven days a week, fifty-two weeks a year. His partners couldn't handle the strain, the constant round-trips between Reno and Vegas. They had families. Duberman didn't. After three years, he bought them out, putting himself even deeper in hock to Jimmy. Now he had full control. He dropped Sizzlin' from the casino's name, calling it only the Saloon. He put the waitresses in skirts that barely reached their thighs. He rented billboards across Reno promising to take any bet. He walked the floor every night, handing out trinkets to gamblers large and small. *I'm yer Saloonkeeper, and I promise you a good time. Even if it costs me!*

His hard work and salesmanship paid off. The Saloon filled up on Saturdays. Then Fridays. Then every day. The money started flowing, a little more each month. Six years after that first handshake deal, Duberman paid off Jimmy's original loans. A few months later, he took his next big step, opening two more Saloons in Las Vegas. Those were hits, too. Everything was working.

Everything except Jimmy. As far as the Roller was concerned, Duberman's promise of a fifty percent stake applied to the new casinos, not just the original.

Like we're married? Duberman said. *Till death do us part?*

Jimmy didn't smile. *Exactly.*

Duberman didn't think he'd made that deal. But Jimmy had the rolling pin. He put an auditor in the Saloon's offices to make sure Duberman didn't short him, and another auditor to watch the first. Every month, Duberman cut Jimmy a check. One hundred ten thousand. One hundred eighteen thousand. One hundred twenty-one thousand. Jimmy insisted that Duberman drop off the checks in person. He claimed he wanted to talk about business — *Who knows gambling better than me?* — but Duberman knew better. The Roller liked looking him in the eye once a month. Both to intimidate and for sheer pleasure.

Duberman started to wish he would make less money, so the Roller would get less, too. Worse, in the early nineties, other states started to legalize casinos. Duberman wanted to expand further, but he couldn't let licensing boards look at his finances. The Nevada gaming commission viewed him as a solid citizen and didn't poke too hard. But anyone who bothered to check his bank records would reach the obvious conclusion, that he had a secret partner. No casino regulator could ignore that red flag. Not only would he miss any chance at new markets, Nevada would close him down, too.

Duberman realized he needed to lose Jimmy, at any price. The Roller was now close to fifty. He spent his days hanging by the pool at his mansion in Henderson. A layer of fat encased his muscles. Still, he was used to violence, and to say this news would disappoint him was a hurricane-sized understatement. The thought of confronting him dried Duberman's mouth. Yet Duberman knew that some part of him *wanted* to stand up to Jimmy, the same reason kids peeked under the bed to make the monster vanish.

They met for dinner at Kokomo's, a surf-and-turf place at the Mirage, Steve Wynn's new palace on the Strip. The Mirage had cost $630 million, at the time the most expensive casino ever. Wynn had paid for it with junk bonds, Wall Street's version of Jimmy. The place had three thousand rooms and a tropical theme, a giant aquarium behind the registration desk, white tigers in the back. It had opened a couple months before, and it was packed in a way that made Duberman's teeth ache. The Mirage was the future. Women as well as men came to play, tourists along with hard-core gamblers, people who had never seen Vegas before. Duberman would never get to build anything like it with the Roller dragging him down.

At dinner, Jimmy wore a metallic gray suit that needed to be let out. Its shiny fabric rode his bulk like a topographic map. He was in a good mood. On the way to their table, Duberman had handed him the biggest monthly check yet, one hundred sixty-three thousand dollars.

Duberman waited for Jimmy to suck down his shrimp cocktail before he broke the bad news. "That's the second-to-last check I'm ever gonna give you, Roller."

Jimmy chortled, big laughs that strained his suit. The tourists at the other tables peeked at the spectacle.

"I'm serious."

"Something wrong? This your way of telling me you got cancer, a month to live? I'm sorry." Jimmy sounded genuinely upset. "I'll light a candle."

Duberman shook his head.

"You don't want to pay no more? Not how it works."

"I want to buy you out. Gimme a number, what you think's fair."

"Think I won't hurt you in here?" Jimmy cracked his knuckles, a snap like dry wood.

His hands were the size of dinner plates. "I won't put a steak knife in you?" He picked up his knife, wagged it at Duberman, put it down again. "Maybe not. Spoil dinner for these nice folks from Iowa. But outside. Tomorrow. The next day. You know it's coming. You don't sleep. A few weeks, nothing, you relax, nobody stays scared forever, then" — Jimmy put a finger pistol to his head and pulled the trigger.

"Jimmy. Listen." Duberman had rehearsed his speech a dozen times. *Fair's fair, neither of us ever thought I'd grow this way, that's not the deal we made, look at how much you made already, I'm not trying to cheat you . . .* But Duberman saw now that appealing to Jimmy's sense of decency was as pointless as telling Steve Wynn's tigers to stop eating meat.

Jimmy smirked. He thought he'd already won, Duberman saw.

Then Duberman knew what to say. "You don't take this offer, I quit." He realized as he spoke that he was telling the truth. "I'm not some stripper in your pocket. I'm not married, no kids, I'll get on a plane, you'll never see me again."

"You still have family."

"What, you're going to hit my seventy-year-old parents?" Duberman told himself

202

Jimmy had to be bluffing. "Roller, I'll give you and your boys five million dollars to go away."

"I'll make that in a couple years."

"Only you won't. Because I'll *walk*. Look at me, Jimmy. I'm not lying." Duberman leaned across the table, lowered his voice. "Something else. You been playing both sides, haven't you? Bet you told your partners on this I was giving up a quarter of the profits. Maybe a third. Never half. Why you were always good with keeping 'em out of the casino, make sure they never met me. So better for everybody, we keep this between us."

As he said the words, Duberman knew he was right. The Roller didn't answer, but his breathing slowed. He folded his arms, sat back. He reached into the envelope that Duberman had given him and mumbled to himself. Watching him do the math was painful. Duberman wanted to offer a calculator.

"A hundred of these. Sixteen-point-three million."

More money than Duberman had. To get it, he'd have to mortgage the two new casinos to the max. No matter. He wanted to jump on his chair and grab a bullhorn: *I'm free.* Only he knew if he agreed too fast, the Roller would jam him harder. "Can't swing it, Jimmy. Eight?"

"Sixteen-point-three."

"Ten."

"Sixteen flat. Take it or leave it."

"Where'm I gonna get sixteen million dollars?"

"The money you're making, a bank'll give it to you."

Duberman silently counted to five. "Fifteen million. That's the best I can do." He extended his hand. Jimmy let it float. "C'mon, shake my hand, Jimmy."

"Don't push it." But Jimmy shook.

"You made a great investment, you know. Too bad you can't get the *RJ* to write it up." The *Las Vegas Review-Journal,* the local paper.

Jimmy smiled. "Want to know the real reason I'm doing it? Places like this are gonna wipe the floor with you. You'll be out of business in five years."

Jimmy was wrong. Duberman rebranded the Saloons as sleek sci-fi-themed casinos he called 88 Gammas. His fortune grew every year and exploded after he opened in 2001 in Macao. Too bad the Roller hadn't been around to see Macao. He had died of a heart attack in 2000, high on coke and a stripper. Jimmy had always enjoyed life's simple pleasures. Duberman wondered what Jimmy would make of his problems now. *Boned like a porn star. Always had to prove you played by different rules. It comes back in the end.*

Or maybe not.

Back in the day, Duberman's friends would have told him he was a fool for even considering borrowing money from Jimmy the Roller. *Too dangerous. Get in bed with a guy like that, you never get out.* But if not for Jimmy, Duberman would have had to wait at least a decade longer to open his own casino. Maybe the chance would have vanished forever.

Instead Duberman had danced with the devil. And walked away without a streak of soot when the song ended. Now the orchestra was tuning up again. If what Garten said was true, and Duberman believed it was, General Cheung Han was a nasty piece of work. Under ordinary circumstances, Duberman would have banned him for life, forget the claptrap about shaming customers.

But these circumstances weren't ordinary. Every intelligence service in the world would want to know Cheung Han's secrets. He was a *chip.*

Right now, Duberman couldn't afford to
toss any of those away.

9

For his first week in Hong Kong, Wells watched Duberman's mansion with the drones from Wright. Controlling them was easy enough, and their cameras had decent resolution. The live feeds weren't hugely clear, because they uploaded through a satellite link that had limited bandwidth. But they also stored the video for Wells to play on his own computer later, a process no harder than popping in a DVD.

Still, as Wright had warned, the drones were vulnerable. Wells lost the first one on its third flight. After an hour looping around the mansion, it stopped responding to his commands, though its camera kept transmitting. Wells watched helplessly as it turned south and soared over the top of Victoria Peak. It flew another hour before running out of power and spiraling into the flat brown waters of the South China Sea. Wells couldn't help but think of Malaysia Airlines

Flight 370. He was almost certain that the problem was a Chinese air defense station on Victoria Peak. He cut the flights to thirty minutes, though he had no proof doing so would help.

Wells faced a second problem with the drones, one he hadn't expected. Once they got more than a couple hundred meters up, they were basically invisible. But on takeoff and landing, they were obvious. The CIA could launch them from the bay west of Hong Kong Island off a speedboat. Wells had to use the balcony of the apartment he'd rented on the lower slopes of the Peak. The day after meeting Wright, he'd found a two-bedroom with a clear sightline to Duberman's mansion. The place was made for a junior master of the universe, a thirty-something investment banker. It was sleek, modern, furnished with low metal tables and leather couches, a hundred shades of gray. On the midline between good taste and no taste at all. Much like the suits Wells had bought at Bloomingdale's, or the replacements he'd picked up at a mall in Kowloon. Not that the clothes or the apartment had done much good.

The apartment was fifty-two stories up. Still, Wells had plenty of neighbors to notice him sending drones off the balcony. On his fifth launch, he saw a Chinese kid in a nearby building waving at him. Wells quickly flew the drone around a corner and out of sight. Fortunately, the kid was tiny, five at most. His parents probably wouldn't believe him even if he told them. But eventually someone would see him and call the cops. In response, Wells restricted himself to one flight each morning, another in the afternoon, and two after dark.

After a week, Wells realized he needed another plan. The problem with the drones was both tactical and strategic. He was spending all day with them for two hours of surveillance. But even if he could have kept them airborne full-time, he doubted they would have helped. The video feed was mesmerizing. It showed him exactly where Duberman's guards were posted, the time of their shift changes, their weapons and armor. He'd seen Gideon outside, and caught Orli in a Bentley limousine on her way down the mountain. But he hadn't found any significant flaws in the security, and he hadn't even seen Duberman. The guy spent all his time inside. Even if Wells had happened to see him outside, the drones didn't have weapons.

Wells needed help from someone inside. But Gideon and Duberman's other personal bodyguards had come halfway around the world to protect him. Why would they betray him? Maybe Orli, if he could reach her without alerting the men who watched over her.

Then Wells realized. An option he should have considered before. He called Wright, burner to burner.

"Wondered if you went home," Wright said. They hadn't spoken since the safe house.

"Busy playing with the stuff you gave me."

"How's it working?"

"I'm thinking I may need a more direct approach. The guy who handles security at the house —"

"The Brit —"

"Yes, him." No names for this call. "Don't suppose you have a picture of him?"

"I do not."

"What about where he lives?"

Wright paused. "I can get that. You need it tonight?"

"Sooner's always better."

"Really think he'll talk?"

"Mamma always said it never hurts to ask."

Twenty-four hours passed, another day lost, before the address finally popped on his burner: *43 Tanner Road, Apartment 1604. Wife, kids.* Not so subtly warning Wells to be careful of innocent bystanders.

Thanks.

On the tab.

Wells looked up the address, found a tall apartment building with narrow, enclosed balconies. Thirty-eight stories and a parking garage. A real estate website showed that Apartment 2104, presumably the same apartment five floors up, had sold a month before for fifteen million Hong Kong dollars. Roberts wasn't taking care of a mortgage that size with his Special Air Service pension. Wells wondered how much Duberman was paying him. Maybe loyalty couldn't be bought, but it could be rented.

Wells reached for his pistol and holster, then stopped. Roberts almost surely didn't know the real reason why Wells was after his boss. Duberman could have told him anything. That Wells was a crazed gambler looking for revenge for losing everything. A Muslim convert who wanted to assassinate a billionaire Jew. If Wells expected Roberts to betray Duberman, he would need to build real rapport. Pulling a pistol on Roberts would hardly convince him of Wells's good intentions. Instead Wells picked out his passport, his real passport. He would have to knock on Roberts's door and hope the guy wasn't in a shooting mood.

It was nearly midnight. Wells could have waited for sunrise, but he didn't know how early Roberts went to work. Anyway, he was tired of waiting, tired of watching surveillance video on laptops. He jogged out of his building, dodged into an alley, hopped over a low wall into a pocket park. He came upon a teenage couple nestled together, making their own private world inside the city. A snatch of Springsteen came to him, *Newly discovered lovers of the Everglades / They take out a full-page ad in the trades . . .*

First time he'd thought of The Boss in a while. Anne hadn't liked Springsteen much. Wells had tried to take her to a concert the year before. *What? Three hours of hog calling?* She later confessed she'd seen the line on the Internet. A cheap shot, and it annoyed Wells, but he couldn't forget it. He had a hard time thinking of Bruce the same afterward.

The kissing teenagers disengaged, looked at Wells in annoyance. He left them to make out, got back to countersurveillance. Ten minutes later, he judged himself clean and turned downhill, toward the massive office towers closer to the harbor. Even at this hour, the air was thick and damp, in line with the forecasts, which promised heavy rain in the morning. Wells preferred the desert's oven heat or, even better, the clean, dry air of the high plains, easy winds carrying the smell of new-mown hay.

Montana.

An idea struck him as he passed a 7-Eleven. Convenience stores in Hong Kong sold liquor. Wells bought a bottle of Dewar's and a blank greeting card. *Mr. Roberts: You've heard things about me. I'd like to give you my side.*

Fifteen minutes later, a cab dropped him outside 43 Tanner. The building's lobby was trying-hard showy, an indoor koi pond and lots of marble. The doorman wore a blue blazer short in the arms and smiled insincerely as Wells walked in. Wells guessed this building didn't see many late-night visitors.

"I have a present for William Roberts in 1604." Wells held up the bottle.

"I call up —"

"Can I bring it to him?"

The doorman shook his head.

"How about you? I'll wait here, I promise."

Another shake. "What your name?"

Wells had hoped the bottle would lure Roberts downstairs before Wells had to give his name, keep Roberts from calling the mansion and getting backup until Wells had gotten a chance to speak to him. But the play had failed. At this point, the doorman would surely call Roberts if Wells walked out. And the security cameras had already caught him.

"John."

The doorman picked up the phone for a hushed conversation. When he was done, he pointed at a black leather couch. "Sit, please. He get dressed, come down."

Wells decided he'd give Roberts ten minutes. Even if Roberts called Duberman immediately, the guards at the mansion would need at least twice that long to drive down.

The elevators never moved. But after eight minutes, a man walked through the front doors. He was black, light-skinned, six feet tall, with a cruiserweight's sleek muscles and a touch of sweat that Wells guessed he had picked up running down the stairs. He wore a windbreaker, his right hand tucked inside the pocket, the pistol inside stretching the fabric.

"Mr. Roberts," the doorman said. Wells cursed himself for not realizing Roberts would take the fire stairs and circle around the building instead of simply taking the elevator. Wells would have done the same.

Roberts looked him over in a way that suggested that Duberman had told him Wells was the devil incarnate. "John Wells, then?" His accent that was London by way of the West Indies.

"Guilty."

Roberts didn't smile. "Raise your hands, stand. Nice and slow, please."

Wells did.

"Turn to the wall, place your palms on it."

Again Wells complied.

"Have a weapon?"

"No."

"You're lying, I'll shoot you right here, let the police decide if it was self-defense."

Roberts frisked Wells, edged the passport out of Wells's back pocket.

"Always carry your real passport?"

"Thought you might want to see it."

"Turn around, take off your shoes, kick 'em this way."

Wells did.

"Hugo Boss."

"I'm classy like that."

"Quiet."

You brought it up.

"Anthony said you have something for me."

"In the bag."

Roberts reached in, came out with the scotch and the card. "Dewar's, nice. And I've misunderstood you, have I?" He tossed Wells the bottle. "Take a drink. A good long one."

"It's for you."

"Take a drink."

Wells figured a religious argument wouldn't get him far. He uncapped the bottle, took a pull. He'd forgotten how liquor burned the throat. He gagged, kept it down. "Want some?"

"No thank you." Roberts sounded almost prim. "Put it down, let's have a walk."

Wells reached for his shoes.

"Those stay." Roberts proving he was a pro. Aside from handcuffs, the easiest way to control a prisoner was to take his shoes.

They left the building, Roberts two steps behind Wells. "Left here, left again" — up a concrete staircase that scraped at Wells's socked feet to a narrow wooded park that stretched along the hill behind Tanner Road.

"Braemar Park. Nice, innit?"

"If you say so." The scotch was settled now and gave the night a pleasant glow.

Roberts wagged his pistol at a wooden bench under a tall tree with smooth gray bark, an acacia. "Take a load off. Isn't that what you Americans say?"

Wells sat. "We snogging?"

"Only a .22, but this close it'll do." Roberts thumbed down the safety. "Give me one reason I shouldn't shoot you right now."

"If I'd wanted to hurt you, I would have brought a gun, not a bottle of scotch."

"That's one." Roberts lowered the pistol a fraction. "You wanted to talk. Talk."

"Thank you for not calling Duberman. For hearing me out." Wells aimed for a respectful soldier-to-soldier tone. "Mind if I ask, did he tell you why he's so nervous about me?"

"Like you don't know."

"Humor me."

"He told me everything. I don't blame you, she's a beautiful woman, but come on, man."

"Say again?"

"You're obsessed with Orli, and you're getting worse. It started with you going to her public events. Then you got her number, probably through your NSA buddies, and started calling her, texting."

"He told you I was ex-agency?"

"Of course. So Gideon called you, told you to cool it. You said no way, you were meant to be with her. Then in New York you crashed a photo shoot, scared her. She and Aaron went to Israel. But again you

217

found out where she was. You came to Tel
Aviv and they caught you there, too. So they
came here. Now here you are again."

Wells wanted to laugh. Of all the lies Duberman could have told, this one seemed
the silliest. Though he saw why Roberts
might go for it. Damsels in distress always
played. "You believed him?"

"Why wouldn't I? Orli's had stalkers
before. Though none as bad as you. They
showed me the footage, you at the mansion
in Tel Aviv. Plus she told me the same
thing."

Wells had always assumed that Orli was
an innocent, that Duberman had lied to her
and she had no idea about the false-flag
operation. That he'd made her come to
Hong Kong. But if Roberts was telling the
truth, Orli was playing along with Duberman's lies. Had she known all along? And if
not, why had she cast her lot with him now?

Thirty billion reasons . . .

"I've never even met Orli. I've seen your
boss once. He invited me to the mansion.
And Vinny Duto was there."

"So they're lying, Aaron and Orli and
Gideon, too." Roberts didn't hide his skepti-
cism.

"Start to finish. They tell you anything
about me besides that I was ex-agency?"

"Gideon said that his CIA contacts told him you've been having problems for years. Finally, they pushed you out. Quietly, because some people still remember that thing from Times Square way back when. He showed me your Wikipedia page."

Duberman had turned the real story almost exactly inside out. The public had briefly learned Wells's name years before, after he stopped a dirty bomb attack on Times Square. But he had asked the CIA and National Security Agency to scrub everything about him from public databases. Bit by bit, the agencies had done so. About the only trace of him left publicly was the Wikipedia page. Taking it down entirely would have attracted more attention than leaving it. But the entry was now only five paragraphs long and included just one picture, a slightly edited photo from Wells's high school yearbook.

Of course, Wells had carried out other missions since Times Square. But they'd all been classified, and his role in them had never leaked. The public had moved on. Almost no one outside the agency remembered him now. Wells knew the CIA had its own reasons for erasing him. By keeping his profile low, the agency could give friendlier operatives credit for his work. Still, Wells never questioned the trade-off. He much preferred to operate in secret.

Until now. He wished he could show Roberts some of what he'd done. "It's ludicrous."

"Then tell me why does he hate you so much?"

"I stopped him from starting a war."

Roberts lifted the pistol.

"I'm serious."

"Why you smiling, then?"

'Cause the truth is going to sound a lot crazier than the lie they're peddling.

"It's a long story."

"You get five minutes."

Wells offered the summary. Duberman had tried to fake the United States into attacking Iran. Wells, Duto, and Shafer stopped him. Roberts never lowered his pistol.

"After all that, why did he come here? Why not stay in Tel Aviv? He's Jewish, they'll look after him, yeah?" Roberts said when Wells was done.

"I asked the President to make the Israelis kick him out."

Roberts feathered his lips: *Pfft.* "The President. Of the United States. Of America. Dropped in on him, did you? Have a cuppa. I wish Aaron told me you were bonkers

220

besides being a stalker —"

Wells felt his temper rise. "I told him that if he didn't get Duberman out of Israel, Shafer and I would go public. I thought coming after him here would be easier than in Tel Aviv. So far, I've been wrong —"

"You can't think I'm enough of a knocker to believe that —"

"Look at the evidence. A week after the President calls off the invasion, Duberman moves here."

"That's not evidence, guv'nor. Not even a *coincidence.* That's like, a plane lands in New York, and a week later my wife gets pregnant. And a month after that, a dog barks."

"You don't believe me, let's call the chief of station here."

"Some random voice on the other end of the line. Buddy of yours who's equally crackers. I think not. You know Aaron's promised me a million quid if I bring you in. Time to make that call —"

With his left hand, Roberts fished a phone from his pocket. He kept the pistol steady on Wells. Wells wondered if he could reach Roberts before he got off a shot —

"Don't make me shoot you out here. Messy for everyone."

"Forget the COS. How about Vinny

Duto?" Having to ask Duto for help again chapped Wells, but he had no choice. If Roberts delivered him to Duberman, he was dead.

"The senator." Roberts looked at Wells with half-closed eyes, like he couldn't decide whether Wells was running a game or just nuts. "Why stop there? Let's call the President."

"It's noon in D.C. You want Duto or not?"

"Sure. Call him. Have him call me back from an official Senate number. Which I will check. Even then I won't believe you, but it's a start."

"Give me your number, I'll tell him."

Wells called Duto's BlackBerry. No answer. He called the emergency private number, the one Duto claimed he'd pick up anytime, anywhere. *I'm meeting the President in the Oval Office, I'll answer. So don't use it unless you have to.*

No answer. Roberts lifted his pistol. "Enough."

"One more time."

"All right, one more time, then we give up calling your boss and I call mine."

Ring. Ring. Ring. Ring —

"Hello?" Duto was breathing hard.

"I interrupt you with your secretary?"

"This best be good, John."

"Only if you care about me getting shot."
Wells explained what he needed.

"Tell him to give me five minutes to get
to a landline."

"Fast finish, huh?"

"Keep talking, maybe I don't get there at
all." Duto hung up.

"He says five minutes," Wells said to Roberts.

"Fine with me. Time for trivia."

Wells didn't ask what he meant.

Roberts's phone buzzed six minutes later.
Roberts held it up: 202-456-1414, the main
Congressional number. "Hello? Yes. Right
here. Telling tales out of school. Taking your
name in vain." A pause. "So it's true? Tell
me one thing, then. Let's say a second that
you're not pulling my leg. Why haven't your
people taken care of my boss already?"

A longer pause. "All right. I see. By the
way, three questions, Senator. Quick like a
bunny, so I know you're not Googling.
Where were you born? What's your middle
name? Your birthday?"

Roberts waited.

"Good. Good. Good. And a bonus. Your
ex-wife's name, please?"

Trivia.

"All right. You've given me a bit to think
about. If I call you back in an hour through

the switchboard, they'll put me through?"
One more pause. "I'll do that." Roberts
hung up, turned to Wells. "Whoever that
was told me to tell you that you need to
start standing on your own two feet. Also
that it wasn't his secretary when you called.
It was his secretary's wife."

Duto. All class. "I'm just glad he remembered his ex's name."

"Linda." Roberts tucked away the pistol.
"For now, let's say that I'm not calling
Aaron. Let's say that was Vinny Duto, and
he was telling the truth. What am I supposed to do with it?"

"I'm hoping for your help."

"To kill him?"

"No —"

"But yes. You won't ask me to pull the
trigger, you'll call it information about his
routine, his guards, what all. But either way,
you want help to find a way in for a clean
kill. And Orli, she on the menu now, too?"

"Of course not."

"Why *of course*, John? She must be at
least partway in it, if she's lying about you."

"You have my word. Call it chivalry."

Though chivalry hadn't stopped him from
shooting Salome in South Africa.

"Tell me something else. Why do I care?"

"Why do you *care*? He tried to start a war—"

"Didn't ask me to fight it. Man pays me well, treats me decent, maybe he's got some upstairs, downstairs in him, but if I had thirty billion dollars in the bank I'd have an ego, too. I've got three kids and a wife who doesn't work. So unless you're willing to write me checks for six thousand pounds a week —"

The answer Wells feared. "I hope you're banking most of it, because it's ending soon. Even if it's not me, someone's going to make him pay."

"Who? So he didn't want Iran to get the bomb. He's not exactly alone. Sounds to me like this is a matter for your President. He doesn't want to touch it, maybe you shouldn't, either."

"You were in the SAS, right?"

"Twelve years."

"What if the UK had gotten behind that invasion? Could have been your buddies over there, getting killed for a lie."

A soldier's sad tight smile crossed Roberts's face: *What else is new?* He turned away from Wells, toward the stairs that led down to Tanner Road. Wells felt the Dewar's curdling in his stomach. He'd worked up the courage to ask out his high school

225

crush, and she'd turned him down. Worst of all, he couldn't even blame her.

"Do me a favor," Roberts said over his shoulder. "When you come calling, keep me out of the crossfire."

"Don't forget. He lied to you, too."

"About what?"

"About me."

Wells saw he'd scored at least a minor point. "Give me your number."

Wells did. "Will you tell him you saw me?"

"Probably not. He'd want to know why I didn't call him right away, and I'm not sure I have the right answer. But I can promise you, he knows you're here."

"How's that?"

"They have the HKIA immigration lists."

Of course. "So they knew I was coming? They were waiting for me at the airport?"

Roberts shook his head. "Not exactly. They don't get real-time manifests. There's a delay."

"Because I was followed as soon as I landed."

"Wasn't us. I can tell you that."

So the airport chase remained a puzzle. Wells didn't like unanswered questions. They had a way of boomeranging.

"Anyway, I've got your number, you've got mine. I'm going to bed. Give me five minutes and then you can pick up those fancy shoes in the lobby. Next time, call before you come over. Better still, don't come at all."

Roberts disappeared. Wells followed five minutes later. His sneakers and the Dewar's waited on the doorman's desk.

Wells took the shoes, left the bottle. "Want it? I'm just going to throw it away."

The doorman shook his head. The perfect ending to a perfect night.

10

The midnight-blue BMW 550i sped up the side of the Peak, wipers fighting the tropical downpour to a draw, tires squealing on the wet pavement. The sedan fishtailed through a hairpin curve and closed on a Hyundai van until it was a hand's width from the van's back bumper.

"Trying to get inside his tailpipe," Mikhail Buvchenko said from the front passenger seat. Given the weather, Buvchenko preferred more brake, less gas. But complaining would have looked weak. He settled for a joke.

Buvchenko's driver, an FSB captain named Nikolai Vulov, answered by inching even closer to the Hyundai. Nikolai's driving style was perfectly Russian, mixing fatalism, impatience, hypermasculinity, and overconfidence. *We're all going to die, anyway. Now out of my way before I run you off the road!* Vodka often played a role, too,

though not today. All three men in the
BMW were stone sober.

Two minutes later, they reached a traffic
light at a ridge a hundred meters below the
top of the Peak. Here, the road from the
harbor intersected Lugard Road, a narrow
lane that encircled the summit. Duberman's
mansion lay three hundred meters west,
barely visible through the clouds. Nikolai
turned toward it.

"Easy here," Buvchenko said. "Let's have
a good look."

Normally, Lugard Road offered a billion-
dollar view of the city and Victoria Harbor.
Today, the rainclouds curtained the skyscrapers, and a high concrete wall along the
road hid most of Duberman's property.
Nikolai slowed to ten kilometers an hour.
Through the narrow gap in the mansion's
front gate, Buvchenko glimpsed a guard.
He wore a baseball hat and poncho to shield
himself from the rain and cradled a carbine,
an American M4. Beside him, a second man
sat on a motorcycle.

"I've seen prisons with less security,"
Nikolai said.

"He's worth more than all the prisoners
in Siberia put together."

"Thieving Jew."

"Always stealing, those Jews," said Sergei,

Nikolai's deputy, from the back seat. Sergei had sausage fingers and a bull's neck and the amazingly annoying habit of parroting Nikolai almost word for word. Nikolai and Sergei had picked Buvchenko up when he arrived in Hong Kong three days before. They'd driven him directly to the Russian consulate and locked him in a cell masquerading as a guest room. Finally, this afternoon, they'd come for him, told him they were taking him to Duberman. Buvchenko didn't mind Nikolai, but he was already sick of Sergei, a man who could make an expensive suit look cheap. Buvchenko had been the same way a decade before, before he learned to smooth his edges.

"Funny, I didn't know Duberman made anyone go to his casinos." Even as he said the words, Buvchenko wished he hadn't. He would win no arguments with these two.

"A Jew-lover. I wouldn't have guessed," Sergei said.

"Jew, gypsy, whatever, as long as he does what we want."

"That's the spirit," Nikolai said. "I'll loop around and then we'll say hello."

"No doubt he'll be thrilled to see us."

"For your sake, I hope he is."

"Right," Sergei said. "For your sake."

The road swung around the back of the

Peak. The south side of the island was exposed to the South China Sea, and the weather was notably worse. The wind whipped streaks of water sideways against the BMW's windshield, a giant open-air car wash. Nikolai pointed into the mist. "No skyscrapers down there. You'd hardly believe it's the same island."

"If you say so." Buvchenko was no expert on Hong Kong. He'd visited the city only once, a decade ago, before the American warrant for him and the Interpol Red Notice. But he'd had no problems on this trip. He'd flown Aeroflot nonstop from Moscow, under a Russian diplomatic passport in the name of Ivan Khorosho. Ivan was the Russian version of John and *khorosho* translated as "well."

A joke from his FSB masters. At least this one was painless. Unlike the whipping that Nemtsov had given him. A thin layer of skin and scar tissue now covered the wounds. Buvchenko changed his gauze dressing and dabbed on fresh antibiotic salve every other day. Still, the cuts stung like a thousand needles. Worse, at night they itched. Buvchenko needed all his willpower not to tear up the fresh skin. He could tolerate the pain as long as he was free of Lubyanka. Now he had to convince Duberman to take the

231

FSB's offer. No easy task, but if he failed, the stripes on his back would be only the beginning of his torture.

Five minutes later, the BMW rolled up to Duberman's mansion for the second time.

"Drive past the gate before you stop, so they know you don't plan to ram it," Buvchenko said. He opened his door as the BMW stopped. Sergei began to follow.

"Stay in the car," Buvchenko hissed. "You'll only mess this up."

"You're the boss." Sergei didn't hide the mockery in his voice. These two, and probably every FSB officer in Hong Kong, knew that Buvchenko had not come to them by choice. They'd seen his back. Nemtsov's cruelties were no secret.

Consider our station in Hong Kong your backup, Nemtsov had said in Lubyanka, after explaining his plan to Buvchenko. *They'll do what you tell them.* He hadn't spoken the next sentence, but Buvchenko heard it nonetheless: *As long as you do what I tell you.*

Buvchenko still wasn't sure why Nemtsov was using him to approach Duberman. Nemtsov claimed Duberman would pay special attention to Buvchenko because Buvchenko had met Wells. *He can't argue when you tell him that we know what he did to the Americans.*

Buvchenko suspected the real reason was that Nemtsov wanted to keep the FSB at a cousin's remove from the operation. If it went bad, Nemtsov would have Buvchenko killed without fear of political blowback. No one inside Lubyanka would stand up for Buvchenko. For all the bribes he'd paid over the years, he was an outsider, and the FSB saw outsiders as disposable.

Buvchenko put aside these curdled thoughts as he walked to the gate. Duberman had no way of knowing the truth. He would assume that Buvchenko had the FSB's full support.

A metal door beside the gate slid sideways as he approached, revealing the guard in the baseball cap. Up close, Buvchenko saw that the bulk of a Kevlar armor-plated vest stretched the guard's poncho. He trained his M4 on Buvchenko. "Hands high!" Like his weapon and his vest, his accent was American.

Buvchenko put his hands just above his shoulders, palms cupped in, the version of *hands up* that was almost satirical.

"On your knees."

Buvchenko wasn't kneeling for this man. He shook his head.

"I'll count three —"

"Shoot me, you'll regret it." Buvchenko would choose this American and his M4 over Nemtsov's whip for a thousand years.

"One — two —"

"Don't be stupid. I can help Mr. Duberman with his biggest problem."

"What's that again?"

"John Wells."

The guard cocked his head. "Your name?"

"Mikhail Buvchenko."

"Russian?"

"Very good. With the FSB. Heard of it? Now tell your boss before I get wetter."

A half hour later, Buvchenko stood in a garage filled with the most expensive cars he'd ever seen, including a black Bugatti Veyron. The Veyron had twelve hundred horsepower and could reach four hundred kilometers an hour, but it was so hard to handle that even professional racers had trouble with it. Bugatti had built fewer than five hundred. This one didn't look like anyone had ever sat inside it, much less driven it. Still, Buvchenko couldn't help but admire it for its raw power.

Putin had three, or so the rumors went.

Buvchenko was alone, Nikolai and Sergei waiting outside. As he preferred. Just inside the gate, the guard had patted Buvchenko down and wanded him with a metal detector and took his wallet, phone, even his belt. When he reached the garage, two more guards patted him down and wanded him again. Before leaving, they'd given him only one instruction: *Don't touch the cars.*

As he imagined for the hundredth time how he'd make his case, two men stepped through the door that connected the garage and the house. Buvchenko had seen photos of both, though he'd never met either. First came Duberman's chief bodyguard, Gideon Etra, a former Israeli soldier. Gideon was lean and hollow-eyed and seemed to favor his left leg. Buvchenko could have torn him apart in hand-to-hand combat. But the way that Gideon hung his fingers over the pistol on his hip suggested he wouldn't give Buvchenko the chance.

Behind Gideon was Aaron Duberman. A handsome man with an easy smile. The dossier that Nemtsov had given Buvchenko said that Duberman was in his sixties, but he looked a decade younger. "You're Mikhail Buvchenko?"

"I am."

Gideon stopped five meters from Buvchenko, the Bugatti between them. He said something under his breath to Duberman.

Hebrew, so Buvchenko couldn't understand it. He imagined it was a warning. Duberman kept walking.

"Nice of you to come all the way here to see me," Duberman said. "With the Red Notice and everything."

"I didn't think you'd tell. Since you have your own problems with the Americans."

"Fair enough. So did you come all the way up here to kill me? I warn you there's a line." Duberman laughed. His confidence surprised Buvchenko.

"I might be the only one who *doesn't* want to kill you."

"Gideon tells me I'm a fool for getting so close. I told him, 'No one who wanted to hurt me would have spent twenty minutes slobbering over my Bugatti.' "

Of course they'd watched him. "Beautiful car."

"My newest addition. I prefer the old red Ferraris with the ingénue eyes for headlights, but the Veyron has a certain appeal. Put wings on it, you could probably fly it."

"You've driven it?"

Duberman laughed again. "I'd crash it in a second. I've ridden in it, though. Nine kilometers in all. On a test track near Milan. They bring it in on a truck, you sit next to an F1 racer who drives three laps to prove it works, they put it back on the truck. So you're working for the FSB now? I thought you were freelance."

So much for Duberman believing Buvchenko spoke as a full FSB agent. "Every Russian works for the FSB, whether he knows it or not."

Duberman settled himself on a bench against the wall of the garage. "What's so important to the FSB to inspire this visit, then?"

"I knew the woman who worked for you, the one who called herself Salome. I supplied her. And I know John Wells, too."

"Lucky you." No surprise in Duberman's voice. So he knew the story, but wanted to hear Buvchenko's version.

"Back when the United States was threatening the invasion, Salome told me, look out for Wells. I told her he wouldn't call me, he's American and I don't do business with them. But she was right. He came to Russia, said he was looking for highly enriched uranium. Bomb-grade."

"Like the stuff that made the CIA think Iran had the bomb."

"Funny you'd mention it." Buvchenko smiled. *We understand each other.* "Yes, exactly like that. Wells and I had dinner, and that very night I called Salome. I could have killed Wells then, easily. He was at my house. Nothing he or anyone could have done. But she said, don't. Let him go, we'll set him up another way."

"Blame me," Duberman said. "I thought killing him would bring attention. And that Wells would never find what he was looking for, anyway. He was cleverer than I expected. I hope you didn't come all this way just to remind me of my stupidities."

"I came to tell you the Americans are going to kill you if Wells doesn't kill you first."

"If that's all you have to say, you've wasted your time."

"And that we can save you."

Duberman chuckled without a trace of humor. The noise echoed dully off the garage's concrete walls. "The FSB does favors now."

"Of course there's a price."

"You want my casinos? I doubt my shareholders would approve."

"Not the casinos. The people who gamble in them. And not only in Macao. Everywhere. Las Vegas, Monaco, the one you're trying to build in New York. The generals, the CEOs, politicians, bankers. Most of all, the top men from the People's Republic."

"Thousands of people."

"We'll give you a list of the most important. They lose too much, drink too much, use drugs, you tell us. Put them in rooms where we can see and hear."

Duberman didn't answer, the only sound the rain drumming the garage's concrete walls.

"So I'm clear," he finally said. "You want me to turn my entire company into a giant honey trap for the FSB and the Kremlin. Not for one target, one operation, but forever."

"Correct."

"I promise you, most of my players are nobodies. Say you find a couple every month to go after. Where do you recruit them? At the baccarat table? With their bodyguards watching? And the PLA security officers? Or, what, you send hookers to their rooms?"

"That's our problem. You provide the information, we do the rest."

"You have anyone specific in mind?"

"No one you couldn't guess."

"Probably a few Russians on there, too. Enemies of the state." Duberman laughed again, more life in him now. "Funny. The Americans came to me years ago. Less ambitious, but similar. 'You help us, we help you.'"

"You said no."

"Of course. It would have been suicide. The first whisper of this and I wouldn't have a business."

"They didn't argue?"

"I was in a slightly different position back then."

Duberman got up, walked around the Bugatti, once, twice, a third time, slowly, examining it from every angle. The way he circled suggested resignation to Buvchenko. *No matter where I go, I wind up back where I started.*

"So, Mikhail, what do I get in return for giving up what I've spent my whole life building? Aside from the pleasure of your company? All due respect, I have all the guards I need. In fact, I suspect having you around would make me an even bigger target."

They'd come to the crux of the offer. Buvchenko couldn't take credit for the idea. It was Nemtsov's.

"As soon as you prove your desire to cooperate by helping us with an operation, our ambassador to America will ask for a meeting with the National Security Advisor. He'll explain you fear for your safety, that you believe elements in the American intelligence community view you as a threat. You aren't sure why. You've asked for answers, haven't received them. You are now so worried that you've requested Russian citizenship and political asylum. The Kremlin expects to make a decision within a year. In the meantime, President Putin himself will be upset if anything happens to you. More than upset. Furious. Your well-being is now a matter of Russian national pride."

You'll know right away, Nemtsov had said. *If he doesn't say no right away, he'll say yes. Eventually.*

Duberman didn't say no right away. He pressed his hands together, considered the idea. "The Russian government will protect me. Make me a refugee? Like Snowden?"

"Exactly."

"So I'll be stuck in Moscow. Or somewhere even less pleasant."

"No. You'd have a Russian diplomatic passport. Your family, too. All the privileges of the Russian state, none of the winters."

"And when the United States says this is ridiculous, a farce, that I'm in no danger —"

"We would explain that you've provided specific information showing otherwise. If the United States disagrees, if it has information relevant to your asylum application, the Russian government will be glad to hear it. But such information would of course become public."

"You'd dare them to tell the truth."

"As of now, you face no criminal charges in the United States or anywhere. You're a businessman whose casinos employ tens of thousands of people around the world. A major charitable donor. A man Russia would be glad to have as a citizen."

Gideon said something in Hebrew to Duberman. The interruption seemed to annoy Duberman, but he answered and the two men had a back-and-forth. Finally, Duberman raised his hand — *Enough* — and turned back to Buvchenko.

"So I become Russian. Of course my assets will become the property of the state. Sooner or later."

Buvchenko shook his head. "Perhaps over time you'd donate to charities in Russia, groups for soldiers' widows and the like. But that would be your choice. Better for us if your casinos run normally." A lie, Buvchenko knew. The Kremlin's greed would be boundless.

"Widows and orphans. Good of me. And what would I tell my shareholders about my citizenship change?"

"What business is it of theirs? I'm sure all your lawyers could come up with an explanation, or a reason not to give one. You miss the forest, Aaron. You worry too much about your stock price, not enough about your heartbeat."

Another Hebrew interruption from Gideon.

"Quiet," Duberman snapped in English. But Gideon kept talking, and Duberman stepped around the Bugatti and put a finger in Gideon's chest. Buvchenko didn't need to know Hebrew to understand: *You work for me, and don't forget it.* Gideon listened and nodded and stepped back and pulled his Sig and pointed it at Buvchenko. Before Buvchenko even had time to be frightened, Gideon swung the pistol down and away and fired —

A pop that echoed in the garage —

The hiss of a leak of pressurized air —

And the Bugatti listed on its side.

The door from the house flew open. Two men ran in, rifles up, but Gideon and Duberman yelled to them in Hebrew. They backed slowly out, their eyes wide in shock.

Buvchenko understood their surprise. If one of his men had been insubordinate this way, Buvchenko would have broken his jaw to start, and gone from there. Duberman seemed stunned himself. He murmured and put out his hand. After a moment, Gideon laid the Sig in it and walked into the house.

Then Buvchenko and Duberman were alone.

Duberman tucked the Sig into his waistband. "Lucky me, he didn't mess up the body, only the tire." He rubbed a hand over the flattened rubber like he was patting a child on the head. "He thinks I should throw you off the side of the mountain. That no one ever wins a deal with the FSB."

"We'll be partners. You keep your side of the bargain, we'll keep ours." Buvchenko had no qualms about lying this way. He had his own masters to please. "May I ask you something? Gideon, you've known him a long time?"

"Before Orli gave me sons of my own, he was my truest family."

"Now you *do* have sons of your own. Maybe he doesn't like that."

Duberman didn't answer. Buvchenko knew he'd pushed too far, made the wrong play. He'd felt this way once in Grozny. He came around a corner, saw that he'd led his squad into a three-sided ambush. The feeling was not terror, but the sure knowledge of failure.

The terror came next.

"You need to leave, Mikhail."

"Sure. But remember, in the end, this house can't save you, your guards can't save you. Only a government can fight a government. You know it's true. It's why you tried to make America attack Iran in the first place." He handed Duberman a slip of paper. "My number. When you're ready, you call me."

Duberman leaned against the Bugatti. In his heart and his head, he knew the truth. This offer was poison. The FSB hadn't even bothered to send one of its own men. It had given him Buvchenko, a thug in an expensive suit who made his millions selling AKs to Africans.

Back in the day in Vegas, Duberman had seen this game. Guys started with second mortgages. Then pawnshops. Then Jimmy the Roller. For most, Jimmy was the last stop, the lowest rung. But some jumped off the ladder into the void. To pay Jimmy, they borrowed money from guys who didn't bother with nicknames. Miss one week of vig with those guys, you paid another way. You got in your car and drove a suitcase of heroin from Vegas to Chicago or New York. They sat in your house with your family as insurance against you taking off. If you messed up, got stopped, lost the drugs, they bailed you out. So they could bring you home. Then you watched them gangbang your wife before they shot you both in the head and dumped your corpses in the desert, a snack for the vultures.

Duberman had heard the stories enough times to know they were true. He'd always wondered, why didn't the losers just stop with Jimmy? Jimmy liked breaking bones. But he wasn't a psychopath. He preferred money to pain. He'd proven as much when he let Duberman buy him out of the Saloon.

For the first time, Duberman understood. The losers simply couldn't accept the reality that had already hammered them into submission. *This time, I'll turn it around.* Or else, maybe, they just wanted to buy whatever extra time they could, never mind the price.

Then again . . .

He wasn't one of those guys. He wasn't a cokehead who owed a loan shark a hundred grand. The FSB had come to him, not the other way around. And the plan had a certain crazy logic. The President had lied about Iran for months. The Russians would dare the President to come clean. He wouldn't. After that Duberman would be worth plenty to the Russians, and Buvchenko was right. They protected their assets.

Even better, Duberman already had a way

to prove his value. Cheung Han. A Chinese general with a taste for young girls. The Russians would certainly be interested in Cheung.

But who would he be then? A pimp, a procurer. In the service of Vladimir Putin.

He was pacing without even realizing, round and round the garage and the ridiculous cars. Decisiveness was his great secret. Lesser executives hesitated. Demanded more information. For forty years, Duberman had followed his gut. To Vegas, Reno, Macao. Everywhere he'd gone, he'd won. Until the last three months, he hadn't realized how simple his life had been. Strange to be past sixty and yet know so little about yourself.

Bill Gates and his other super-wealthy peers immersed themselves in the world's problems. Malaria. Women's rights. Not Duberman. He had cocooned himself away. Until, with Salome's help, he decided to start a war. Imperial ambition.

Even then, he would have won if not for Wells.

Of all the games in his casinos, he found roulette the stupidest, a white ball skidding over a spinning wheel, red to black and back. The players leaning close, believing they'd won, then shaking their heads as one last jump took everything away. Duberman felt like one of them now. Or the ball itself. He was sick of thinking, of being imprisoned in this nine-figure castle on a hill.

The door to the house swung open, and Gideon stepped through. This problem, at least, Duberman could handle. "Close the door, come here." He didn't speak again until he stood face-to-face with Gideon. "What was that?" Without waiting for an answer, Duberman swung, a straight right cross. He was past sixty, yes, but he worked out every day and had taken testosterone supplements for years. Gideon didn't try to protect himself. The punch caught him on the chin, knuckles on bone, sent him stumbling back.

"I'm sorry, Aaron. Truly. I lost control."

The only other time Duberman had seen Gideon so upset was when the doctors told him they were out of treatments for his son, that all he could do was enjoy the months Tal had left. *He's not dying,* Duberman had said. *I don't care what it costs, but we'll save him.*

Tal was alive today, married, three sons of his own.

"Quitting, Gideon? Too hot for you? Melted your promises?"

Gideon went to a knee like a knight before

a king. "Never. But you say no to this. You say no."

"*You* give *me* orders?"

"You can't dance with these people. You think you know, but you don't. You let them in, they destroy you. Destroy everything."

"So what, then, I wait here until Wells gets to me, or the President decides it's time?"

"The worst is that you'll lose your honor, too. You won't even recognize yourself."

"Why are you so sure I can't beat them?"

"What will you tell Orli?"

Gideon had a point there. Orli's parents were Russian émigrés. She hated the country, its government, everything about it. How would he explain to her that he was now working with the FSB? *For* the FSB?

He could wait, he supposed.

"If you'd done your job and taken care of Wells in Tel Aviv, none of this would ever have happened."

"Talk to Orli, at least. See what she says."

"You've made your speech and I'll think about it. Now out. Leave me."

11

After his failed effort to recruit Roberts, Wells trudged toward the skyscrapers that lined Victoria Harbor. The thought of going back to his apartment and trying again to spy on Duberman's mansion made him feel weirdly like the stalker that Duberman had said he was. *We're so perfect for each other. If you would only see.*

Past midnight, the island's central business district was mostly empty, the action on the other side of the harbor. Kowloon. Wells suddenly wanted crowds and noise. Let Duberman have the Peak. Wells would stay close to the ground, where he belonged.

The MTR was closed for the night. Wells hailed a cab and five minutes later was speeding through the Cross-Harbour Tunnel for the crash pad he had rented off Jordan Road. He'd found the place through Craigslist, a sublet from an American student going home after two semesters studying Chinese at the University of Hong Kong. *Looking to book flight ASAP! Any reasonable offer considered!* the ad said. Wells offered eighteen hundred dollars in cash for the month left on the lease. The guy agreed without even asking to see a passport.

"Had enough of Hong Kong?"

"It's an amazing city, but it grinds you down after a while."

"Aren't you worried I'm gonna trash the place? Cost you your security deposit?" A joke. The furniture consisted of a stained air mattress, a leaky refrigerator, and a chipped wooden desk.

"What are they going to do, sue me in Chicago?" The kid tossed Wells the keys. "Big for the front gate, little for the front door. Go nuts."

"I will."

Wells hadn't been back since. The place was even smaller than he remembered. Nine feet by ten at most. Dirtier, too. Stale cigarette smoke infused the walls. A single naked bulb dangled from the ceiling. The perfect safe house. No one in the world knew it was his. Though Wells wished he'd invested in a new air mattress. And a can of Lysol. He propped himself against a wall, fished out his newest burner.

One ring, then —

"That bad, huh?" Shafer's voice had roughened in the years that Wells had known him. Yet he still sounded permanently amused, cheered rather than frozen by his cynicism. Like a late-night sports talk radio host who proudly rooted for losers and would dump any team that became too good.

Wells didn't answer.

"Don't you want to ask me how I know?"

Not even a little.

"It's after midnight there. You don't call this late unless you have something good or you're desperate. And I know you don't have something good."

When Shafer was in these moods, talking to him was like arguing with the world's cleverest ten-year-old. "I always want to talk to you until I actually have to."

"What's the problem?"

"It's impenetrable. Might as well have a moat and ten thousand archers."

"You knew that from the first overhead."

"There's knowing, and then there's seeing. And I thought I'd catch him coming and going. Getting ready for the new opening. But he's locked up tight."

"Can't blame him. Any luck with the

channel changers?"

Channel changers, a/k/a remote controls, a/k/a drones. Shafer had nicely avoided using a word that would perk up any voice analysis software monitoring this call.

"If I had a team going over the wall, they might help. As it is, it's like a *National Geographic* feed. Watching lions sleep next to a watering hole." Wells decided not to explain that he couldn't keep the drones airborne for more than a couple hours a day. "I thought I had a move tonight. I talked to the guy who runs security up there. I don't mean Gideon or anyone from the personal detail. British. Ex-SAS. I figured maybe he'd help if he knew the real story."

"That was optimistic."

"Believe it or not, Duberman told him they needed all this security because I'm a stalker, I'm after Orli —"

"You do have your difficulties with women."

Wells could only laugh.

"He believed that?" Shafer said.

"She backed it up."

A pause as Shafer considered the implications. "Did she, now? I'll admit I'm surprised. But putting that aside. You told him the truth, now what? He gonna help?"

"He pretty much said it's not his fight."

"He going to narc?"

"I don't see him going that way, either. But he said Duberman already knows I'm here."

"So they *were* waiting for you at the airport?"

"He said no. That was somebody else."

Shafer stopped talking. But he was still there. Wells heard the slow rattle of his breathing. A good sound. It meant Shafer was circling the problem, trying to pop it open.

"You're all groping in the dark. Bunch of kids playing Spin the Bottle. If kids still play that anymore. Who knows? Everybody hoping somebody else screws up first. What about that new opening, the casino?"

"Haven't heard much. I think he was hoping I'd go to Macao and when I didn't bite —"

"Right. So he knows you're casing him. Meanwhile, he's doing the same, fishing, to find you while you're looking. You've got some help from us, he's got all he can buy, which is plenty, but neither of you wants the local constabulary involved."

"Tell me something I don't know, Ellis."

"Maybe if you had more active help from the station. Not just gear."

"No." Only Duto could open that door,

and Wells was done asking favors of Duto.

"You have any other ideas?"

"Nothing that's not terrible."

"Share with the group."

"Like, loading up the flying machines with C-4, dive-bombing them into the house." Wells had wondered if the drones could be converted into unmanned kamikazes.

"Tell me you didn't just say that."

"I said it was terrible."

"How about this? Get yourself a latex mask that looks like him, go up there, and knock on the gate. The guards get confused, let you in. Then he sees you in the mask and freaks. *If I'm not me, den who the hell am I?*" The last line spoken in a terrible Schwarzeneggerian accent.

"Ellis —"

"A race around the island. Ferrari versus motorcycle. You win, he turns himself in. He wins, you spend twenty years as a bathroom attendant in Macao, picking pubes out of urinal cakes."

"Ellis —"

"Duel at ten paces. Cliffside sumo match. One hand, one million dollars —"

Wells hung up. Called back five minutes later.

"Arm-wrestling."

"I'm glad you find this so funny."

255

"Nobody made you go over there." But Shafer had amused himself enough. He went quiet again, the good quiet. Five minutes passed, enough time for Wells to hear a mouse prowl inside the wall behind him, disappear, return.

"Still there or did you stroke out?"

"I have an idea. A way to shake the tree. Maybe. But it's not nice."

"Not her." Even if Orli had backed Duberman's lie about the stalking, Wells didn't see her as a target. Not yet. Not unless he could prove she knew about the original false-flag plot.

"No. You know the names of any of his bodyguards? The inner circle, I mean."

"Only Gideon."

"Would you recognize them?"

Aside from Gideon, Wells had seen Duberman's guys for only a few minutes at the mansion in Tel Aviv. "If I saw them on the street, probably. But if you're thinking you'll run pictures of ex-Mossad past me and I pick out the ones who work for him, it'd be a long shot."

"That's not what I'm thinking."

"You gonna tell me?"

"Go to sleep. I should know before you get up if I can make it work. Check your email then. And if you come up with any more terrible ideas —"

"I'll keep them to myself."

Wells folded up his two-thousand-dollar jacket for a pillow, unlaced his sneakers, stretched on the floor. He was asleep in minutes. He woke to a downpour, rain lashing the apartment's single window. It was afternoon. He'd slept twelve hours. Proof, not that he needed any, that rooms like this were his natural home.

The apartment had no computer, no Internet connection. Inconvenient but safe. Wells walked until he found the store he needed, a cubbyhole with tinted windows. The sign above promised *Gamers Paradise* in English. Inside, a dozen slack-faced teenagers hunched before wall-mounted televisions, muttering in Cantonese. Their hands crawled over keyboards as they destroyed the twenty-second century. A game of Spin the Bottle would have done them all good.

"I just need an Internet connection."

The guy behind the counter pointed to a battered Samsung laptop that sat in the corner like a rusted-out Pinto in a Mercedes showroom.

Wells logged on, found Shafer's emails. Individually each could have been innocent.

Collectively they were deadly as a smallpox vial.

First, old public pictures of Duberman. More important, his bodyguards. Wells recognized Gideon. He'd seen some of the others, too. He didn't know their names. But Shafer had figured out a way to identify at least two of them. His second email included photos from a decade earlier, headshots from a Pentagon database. The men had participated in joint American-Israeli seminars on fighting insurgencies at the Army War College. Uri Peretz and Avi Makiv. Captains in the Israel Defense Force. Trim, handsome men, both with dark, curly hair and brown eyes.

Wells wondered how Shafer connected the public bodyguard photos to the Pentagon identification shots. Probably through the facial-recognition software at the National Security Agency. Wells figured Duto had told the NSA to give Shafer what he wanted, as long as he didn't seem to target Duberman actively. Looking at former Israeli army officers would hardly raise eyebrows. Anyway, Wells didn't doubt the matches. Peretz and Makiv were exactly the kind of guys Duberman favored as bodyguards.

Wells wondered if the third set of emails would include immigration records or closed-circuit shots from Hong Kong International showing the men's arrival. That trick would have been impressive even for the NSA. Instead, the file included a year of credit card charges for Peretz and Makiv. The first few months were predictable, restaurants in Tel Aviv, gas stations in Jerusalem. Peretz had run up a week of bills in Rome. Makiv liked scuba diving.

After Duberman came to Hong Kong, the charges mostly stopped for a while, aside from recurring cable and phone bills. Peretz had a few charges at high-end Hong Kong hotels like the Peninsula. Less than fifty dollars each, so they weren't rooms. Wells imagined he'd stopped in for a drink or two. Makiv was a regular at a Nike store in Kowloon. He also had a charge in Macao at a place called the Grand Lisboa, which Wells thought was a casino.

Wells didn't know yet where Shafer was going with the credit cards. The relative lack of charges implied that Peretz and Makiv had holed up in the mansion since coming to Hong Kong. But the move was hardly a surprise. Duberman was keeping his bodyguards close.

Yet in the last two weeks, Peretz and Makiv had started using their cards again regularly. The same names came up over and over: Yung Kee Restaurant, Yat Lok Restaurant, Nha Trang Vietnamese Café . . . All restaurants, or so it seemed. The time stamps showed lunches and dinners, nothing too cheap or expensive, in the range of one to three hundred Hong Kong dollars, fifteen to forty U.S. Weirdly, the bills seemed to duplicate one another, each with the same amount on the same day. Wells wondered if Shafer had made a mistake, double-counted the receipts somehow. No. The men were eating together, splitting their checks.

Okay. So they were coming down from the Peak now. Why? Wells thought he knew. The fourth email confirmed the answer. It was the only one with a subject line: *I always feel like . . .* Shafer couldn't help his adolescent cleverness. *Somebody's Watching Me.* Wells remembered the song from his adolescence, a hit from the mid-eighties, the lyrics cute and creepy at once:

I wonder who's watching me now / Who? The IRS . . .

Wells looked up the lyrics online, discovered the song had belonged to a one-hit wonder named Rockwell. But unlike Rockwell, Wells knew exactly who was watching him. Now he knew where they were looking. The fourth email included street and satellite maps. Shafer had marked them with

260

the restaurants where Peretz and Makiv used their cards. They formed a rough semicircle around the southern exits of the Central MTR station, the subway stop nearest the roads that led to the Peak.

Duberman had sent his men down as pickets. He and Gideon hoped to catch Wells on his way to the mansion. Wells would bet that Peretz and Makiv weren't the only team, just the only one that Shafer had found so far. The move made sense. The area was crowded but compact. Wells was a head taller than the average Chinese man. He would stand out even if he tried to disguise himself.

But Wells had foiled the plan, mainly because he'd wasted so much time on the drones that he'd barely left his apartment since coming to Hong Kong. Meanwhile, Peretz and Makiv had their own problems. The Central MTR station was huge, more than a dozen exits, hundreds of thousands of commuters every day. The men couldn't set up in a van or car for more than a few minutes without blocking traffic and drawing police attention. Probably they were using an office as a static viewing post, splitting their time between it and the streets. Even so, the search would be boring and tiring.

Wells didn't doubt they were doing whatever they could to stay focused, keep their eyes up. They knew how dangerous Wells could be. Probably they were limiting their calls and emails to essentials, using burners instead of their usual phones. Otherwise, Shafer would have sent along a communications file, too. No doubt Duberman had used a shell company to rent the office they were using as their base, so Wells couldn't find them that way.

But they had made one mistake. A small mistake, sure. But fatal nonetheless.

They were rewarding themselves with lunch and dinner breaks. And paying with credit cards instead of cash. In doing so, they had given Wells what he needed to find them. He wouldn't need phone intercepts, much less anything fancy like the feeds from security cameras around the MTR station. Peretz and Makiv ate around the same time every day, and restaurants they had chosen were clustered within a few blocks, a diamond-shaped area near the heart of the central business district.

Tomorrow, or the day after, Wells would put himself close by. He wouldn't have to look for the men or guess where they might be eating. Shafer would simply have the NSA alert him the next time Peretz and

Makiv used their cards, and pass the name of the restaurant to Wells. Wells should have several minutes to reach it. The cards had to be swiped and authorized before a waiter brought the bills back to be signed. By the time the men paid and walked out, Wells would be waiting.

Not nice, Shafer had said, but Wells had no qualms. Unlike William Roberts, Peretz and Makiv knew why Wells wanted their boss. They could have quit. Instead they had come halfway across the world with Duberman. They were willing soldiers who would capture or kill Wells if they could.

This was not assassination, or even a sniping, but a slow-motion duel.

Wells printed the credit card receipts and the restaurant map, left the gamers to their virtual destruction while he walked up Jordan Road considering his own killing spree. He would need the pistol and suppressor he'd left in his apartment on the island, but he was in no rush. All around him the city buzzed, storekeepers shouting in Chinese, kids in school uniforms jostling. He felt more focused, at once adrenalized and relaxed. *Better.* Had he been born to hunt, or had all the hunting made him what he'd become? He supposed the answer hardly mattered anymore.

At a bookstore on Jordan, Wells bought detailed maps of Hong Kong. Back at his crash pad, he studied the area around the restaurants, trying to memorize every building and alley and intersection. Afternoon turned to evening, and Wells itched to recite the *maghrib,* the fourth of the five prayers Muslims were supposed to offer each day. He might not understand himself entirely, but he was sure that religion had nothing to do with his pursuit of Duberman. Over the years, most of the men he had killed had been Muslim. Should Duberman escape justice because he happened to be Jewish?

He had just finished his prayers when his phone buzzed.

"You understand what I sent? Or do you need turn-by-turn directions?"

All their missions together, Shafer still liked to pretend that Wells was dumb muscle.

"I was confused, but the guy at the next computer helped me out."

"Good of him."

"I assume you can set up an alert the next time they pay."

"Correct."

"And what's the delay?"

"One to three minutes. You might have to

264

jog, but you'll get there in time for an after-dinner mint."

"Any chance of a mousetrap?" Meaning had Peretz and Makiv intentionally used their cards to lure Wells into coming after them? An ambush within an ambush. But even as he asked the question, Wells knew the answer.

"That, what, they ate out for weeks to build this trail because they realized I'd find their names, trace the cards —"

"I get it."

"You will have the drop. I promise you. Up to you what you do with it."

They both knew what Wells would do with it. Two head shots. He would have to figure the Israelis for bullet-resistant vests, the police style that fit under clothes and could stop a medium-weight pistol round.

"Assuming I get away clear, what happens next?"

"Two of his guys go down. He has no idea how you found them, what went wrong."

"He's not the panicky type."

"Maybe not. But the British guy, I'll bet he quits right away. He doesn't need this. Maybe some core guys walk, too. Not Gideon, but the others, the ones I'm still trying to find. Even Orli, maybe she decides enough already, time to take the kiddos back to the promised land. What we really want. That would open things up nicely."

Probably a good read. "Hope you're right. Should I tell your coworker here about this?" Meaning Wright, the chief of station.

"I think he'll be happier not knowing."

Wells agreed on that score, too. "Anything else I need to know about my lunch dates?"

"They both spent some time in Lebanon, so I wouldn't underestimate them. But no."

"It was a neat trick, Ellis."

"What's that?"

"Figuring it out. Thank you."

"Thanks for noticing." Genuine pleasure in Shafer's voice. "You thinking tomorrow?"

Hitting fast was usually the right choice. Peretz and Makiv might stop using their credit cards, or disappear for a hundred other reasons. But lunch tomorrow was less than eighteen hours away, hardly time for Wells to gin up a viable escape plan. He worried less about live witnesses, who would barely have time to recognize what was happening before Wells vanished, than the public and private cameras that covered every block of the central business district. Having a wheelman would make the hit easier, but Wells didn't. Plus the forecasters were promising more rain tomorrow, making escape even more complicated.

"I think the day after."

Shafer's silence told Wells that he dis-agreed.

"Tell you what, Ellis, come over, we'll do it your way —"

"Fine. I hear anything new, I'll let you know. Otherwise, look for a text. Around one-thirty, based on the last few days. Happy hunting."

Then Shafer was gone. Leaving Wells with nothing but the echo of his last two words.

Wells waited in the Kowloon crash pad past midnight before he hailed a cab for the island. He spent the night's empty hours walking the area where the men ate each day. Topography and history had covered it with a jumble of streets that bumped into each other at odd angles and changed names almost at random. Wells didn't mind the maze. It would work to his advantage, letting him sneak up on Peretz and Makiv without warning and then disappear almost as fast.

Unfortunately, the video surveillance was as ubiquitous as Wells had feared. Cameras were mounted to the sides of buildings, over doorways, on traffic lights. At a minimum, Wells would need to hide his face with a Unabomber-style hood and oversized sunglasses. An actual Halloween mask would be better. But masks drew stares and camera phones. If he used one, Wells would have to discard it immediately in a blind spot without cameras.

Ultimately Wells decided the simplest solution was one he had used before, a motorcycle. Not just because bikes were far more maneuverable than cars. Motorcycles meant helmets. No one looked twice at a rider in a full-face shield. Even better, many of the skyscrapers nearby had underground parking garages open to the public. Instead of risking a chase, Wells would race for a garage a few blocks away. Inside, he would ditch the bike and his helmet and jacket. He would be back on the street before the police even reached the shooting. The plan wasn't foolproof, but no plan was.

Of course, ditching a motorcycle meant Wells needed one that couldn't be connected to him. He could try to steal one. Many older models had simple locks that could be broken open and turned with a screwdriver. Wells could also try Craigslist again, see if he could find another kid willing to trade keys for cash. But this time, going to the agency seemed simpler. Wright had already given him a pistol, after all. He could hardly object to providing a motorcycle.

Wells hoped.

It was nearly dawn. Wells decided to wait until morning to call Wright, ask the favor. Instead he stopped at his banker apartment to pick up the necessities: his pistol and suppressor, knife, a change of clothes. As he looked through his closet, he would have traded all the fancy suits for a pair of broken-in motorcycle boots. In retrospect, Wells felt dumb for thinking that he could disguise himself from Duberman, or fit into the world of the ultra-rich in Hong Kong, with a few expensive outfits.

The clean white sheets on the king-sized bed looked tempting. But as the night turned from black to gray, Wells left the luxury behind. If Duberman was looking for him on the island, he belonged in Kowloon.

The rain started just as he reached the crash pad. Wells catnapped for a couple of hours, then called Wright. Who got straight to business. "You talk to the man?" Meaning Roberts. Wells reminded himself that Wright was still a move behind.

"Yeah. Didn't get far."

"Now what?"

"Maybe I was calling to hear your voice."

"Ever deeper in the favor bank."

"Lucky I have good credit." Wells wondered about setting a face-to-face meet, decided not to waste the time. These burners were safe enough to risk asking straight out. "I need a motorcycle."

"Touring the countryside, are we?"

"Best if nobody can connect it to you."

"Tell me something I don't know."

"Today, if you can."

"You think I can just snap my fingers on something like that?"

Yes, as a matter of fact. It's a motorcycle. Not a Trident sub. Wells waited.

"Keys for you tonight," Wright finally said. "Back where we first met. Don't expect anything fancy."

"As long as it's not a moped."

"Don't give me any ideas."

Whatever Wright thought of Wells or this mission, he seemed to have decided that playing along was in his interest. The bike was a black Honda CB600F, a common sportbike, probably about a decade old, with a legal Hong Kong plate. The tires were worn but useable and the odometer read sixty-eight thousand kilometers. Wright had even thrown in a helmet with a tinted face shield.

By midnight the rain had blown through. For a change, the air felt clear and clean. Wells took the Honda for a run on the airport highway. If it was going to blow a cylinder or a tire, he preferred to find out now. And every bike had its own quirks. Some responded to only the lightest toe taps or throttle pulls, while others needed real pressure. *If you understood women half as well as motorcycles,* Anne had once told him . . .

Wells and the Honda got along fine. The bike was lighter than the one-thousand-cubic-centimeter monsters he favored but had plenty of pull. On the bridge to Lantau, he rolled the throttle and it surged to one hundred fifty kilometers an hour. It had more kick left, but Wells didn't press. The Honda handled nicely, too. Wells felt connected to the road in a way that he didn't on bigger machines. He leaned side to side, dancing over the rain-freshened asphalt, black and gleaming in the moonlight. After about three minutes, he forced himself to ease up. The bike might be legal, but he didn't have a local driver's license, much less a motorcycle endorsement. He rode slowly back to Kowloon, the engine's song buzzing in his head. If Wells could have found an excuse, he would have ridden all night. Instead he took the bike to the bottom level of a massive garage in Kowloon, four levels underground.

Wells had brought the pistol and suppressor with him on the ride. He walked to the back wall of the garage, looked for surveillance cameras. He didn't see any and fitted the long black tube to the end of the barrel. He aimed at a metal sign that read *PL 4* twenty feet away, squeezed the trigger. The pistol let out a soft wheeze, a weirdly human sound, and a single hole appeared inside the *P.* Good. Wright had done his job. Wells didn't doubt Shafer would do his.

The rest would be up to him.

In the morning, Wells picked up the Honda, took his place in the heavy commuter traffic making its way through the Cross-Harbour Tunnel, the bike burbling happily. He got to the island just past 10 a.m. Weirdly, he now faced the same problem as Peretz and Makiv. He couldn't hang around the Central MTR station without attracting attention. But he had to be sure he was no more than a couple minutes away when Shafer's text came.

He burned two hours with two slow loops around the island, countersurveillance if nothing else. Then he found a parking lot off Queen's Road East, barely a mile from the district where Peretz and Makiv usually ate. So far, he'd carried the pistol and suppressor in his backpack. Now he hid them inside a dark green nylon bag that he tucked between his legs.

At 12:45 — earlier than he'd expected — the burner phone buzzed. *Yung Kee.* A big restaurant on Wellington Street near D'Aguilar. Famous for its gold-painted exterior and its roasted goose. Not the name Wells had hoped to see. Wellington Street lay in the very heart of downtown, and Yung Kee was popular with tourists, increasing the crossfire risk. Still, Wells switched off the phone and rode out, down Queen's Road East to Queensway, surrounded by heavy midday traffic, buses and Bentleys and taxis. Ahead, a light turned yellow, but Wells accelerated through, then slowed as the nylon bag juggled between his legs. Just another messenger on a motorcycle, speeding between deliveries. Queensway became Queen's Road Central. Ahead Wells saw D'Aguilar Street.

He turned left on D'Aguilar, gave the bike more juice as he came up the hill. Wellington was not even a hundred yards up. Wells turned right and saw the big gold-colored façade of Yung Kee directly ahead. A dozen people milled outside. Wells edged the bike to the curb, kicked it into neutral. He was now twenty-five feet from the front door. He unzipped the bag, reached inside, wrapped his right hand around the pistol. No one gave him a second look.

With the traffic, he'd needed almost five minutes to reach Wellington. Too long. Peretz and Makiv might already have left. Unlikely but not impossible, depending on how quickly the NSA had picked up the card authorization and sent it to Shafer. He'd wait five minutes more and then go.

Three minutes passed before two white men stepped out of the restaurant's front door. Medium-height, the telltale bulk of bullet-resistant vests just visible under their sport coats. Brown-eyed and curly-haired. Peretz and Makiv. Side by side.

They turned right, toward D'Aguilar. Toward him.

Wells locked his hand around the pistol in the bag —

And *froze.*

He couldn't draw. The thought of shooting them on the street in cold blood, with a lunchtime crowd around them, tourists waiting their turn to eat roast goose —

Never. Never never never had this happened before.

They stepped toward him. Still, he couldn't move. Then Peretz tilted his head, and Wells saw the realization, knew almost before Peretz himself did that Peretz had recognized Wells from the way he was standing or the nylon bag or the tinted faceplate itself.

Peretz said something to Makiv and reached back under his coat, and Wells knew if he didn't move he would die, here on the street, rounds bursting through him —

Then, only, with the threat real, did the spell break —

Fill your hand, you son of a bitch —

As Peretz's right arm emerged, Wells pulled the pistol from the bag, squeezed the trigger easy and smooth, a perfect shot that gave Peretz a third eye and killed him instantly. He fell forward face-first, his nose crunching the concrete, a terrible sound —

As a middle-aged Chinese woman standing a few feet behind Peretz screamed, Wells turned the pistol onto Makiv, fired twice, forgetting the vest, automatically aiming center mass. The shots punched Makiv backward, but didn't him take down. He fired back wildly. Finally, Wells remembered to aim high. He pulled the trigger and Makiv's head jerked sideways like he'd been hit with the world's hardest right cross and gravity took the pistol from his nerveless hands and he toppled backward, dead before he hit the pavement.

Wells slid the pistol into the bag and kicked the motorcycle into gear and sped down Wellington. On the closed-circuit cameras, it would look like a perfect assassination. Seven seconds start to finish, two men dead.

Only Wells knew the truth, how close he'd come.

12

First the FSB. Now the Hong Kong police. Duberman was sick of uninvited guests.

Uninvited, but not unexpected. The bulletins about the killing of two men outside Yung Kee restaurant started around 1:30 p.m. *Shocking Daylight Shooting in Central — Police Seek Motorcycle Assassin,* the *South China Morning Post* reported on its website.

The biker had disappeared in the chaos after the shooting, the *Post* said. Police were searching the area and reviewing surveillance footage for clues to his identity, a spokesman said. He urged calm, saying that the murders appeared targeted and that neither victim was a Hong Kong resident.

Duberman and Gideon followed the reports from Duberman's study, both men as glumly silent as campaign volunteers watching their candidate lose on Election Night. Duberman tried to tell himself that Peretz and Makiv might not be the victims. *Sure, we lost New York, but Ohio could turn everything around.* But after two hours, he could no longer hide the truth from himself. Peretz and Makiv would have broken the no-calls rule if they were still alive.

"I can't believe it." Stupid words. The universe didn't care if he could believe what had happened. Doubly stupid because Duberman *could* believe. Once again, Wells had done what he did best. Culled the flock.

"You think Wells?"

"Who else?"

"Buvchenko, the FSB. To pressure you."

"You really hate them." Duberman considered. "No. This puts the police on me, and why would they want that? Also, one man on a motorcycle, that's Wells all the way."

"I don't know how he could have found them. Or even knew what they looked like."

"Let me ask you, Gideon. How can your men protect me when they can't even protect themselves?"

"He'll make a mistake."

A lame answer, but Duberman appreciated the effort. "And in the meantime?"

"We wait for the police. It shouldn't take long, since Uri and Avi listed this as their local address. Maybe they'll even catch him for us."

"The Hong Kong police? That's funny."

"He's not Superman."

"He's super-something."

"I'll talk to the gate guards, make sure they know what's going on."

"You mean you don't want to sit with me anymore."

Gideon offered an opaque smile and left Duberman to his thoughts. The afternoon passed bitterly slowly. Orli might have distracted him, but she was shooting a bikini ad on the Great Barrier Reef. Maybe he ought to be glad. He didn't want her to see him like this.

The call came from the front gate just before 6 p.m. "The police are here."

Ten minutes later, Gideon led two men into the study. They were older than Duberman had expected, in their fifties. Both wore pressed dark blue uniforms, with identical white shirts and black ties. They carried themselves with the quiet confidence of men who had legions of armed men at their disposal. Duberman knew at once they were very senior, and that their fast appearance meant trouble.

"Assistant Commissioner Tsang Tung-Kwok," the taller man said, his English slow and careful. "In charge of police on Hong

Kong Island."

"Deputy Assistant Commissioner Hargrove Lo, chief of detectives." Lo carried a manila envelope. His English was better than Tsang's. Duberman suspected he'd do the talking.

"Commissioners. How can I help you?"

"You don't know?" Lo shook his head. "You hear about the shooting today?"

"Of course."

"When you came to Hong Kong, fifteen men came with you. Bodyguards?"

"Mostly."

"Usually, you come with only three or four men. Why so many this time?"

"We knew we'd be staying longer." Duberman didn't want to tell the stalking story. He'd have to mention Wells, and he feared where that thread might lead.

"And you have," Lo said. "More than three months, leaving only for Macao. Usually you come only two, three weeks."

They'd obviously spent time checking his immigration records. Another bad sign. "The competition in Macao is brutal. My customers want to see me."

"Avi Makiv and Uri Peretz were two of your guards —"

"*Were?*" Duberman reminded himself not to overdo the surprise. "You mean —"

"I must regret to inform you that they were killed today." Lo offered a single nod that matched the strangely formal notification. "We need you for official ID."

"Of course."

Lo pulled two Polaroids from the envelope, handed the first to Duberman. "Uri Peretz?"

Peretz lay on his back, staring blankly at death through the hole between his eyebrows. Black-red blood dribbled out of his nose. The Polaroid's colors were flat, washed-out, and the image looked cheap. Posed, almost.

"Yes. That's him." Duberman felt the need to add more, a three-sentence eulogy. "He was a good guy. Funny. Liked the ladies." *He reminded me of myself.*

"Sorry." He didn't sound sorry.

"His nose." Duberman handed back the Polaroid. "Did someone hit him?"

"No, he fell after he was shot, it broke. We turn him over for the picture." Lo gave the second Polaroid to Duberman. "This one worse, I warn you."

An understatement. The bullet had split Makiv's skull, airing bone and brain matter. Duberman could put himself in Makiv's place only too easily. Three months ago, Wells had put a pistol to his head and

281

threatened to pull the trigger.

"Yes, Avi." Now Duberman didn't have to fake the tremor in his voice. "Their families live in Israel."

"Now we have ID, we ask police there to notify the parents." Lo stared at him. "Do you have any idea who did this, Mr. Duberman?"

JohnWellsJohnWellsJohnWells . . .

"No."

"Professional. Most likely meant as a message to you."

"I can see that's how it looks."

"You can't think of suspects? Not one?"

"These men worked for me for years. Protected me and my family. If I knew who'd done this, I would tell you."

"Maybe the killer waiting for you, expecting you to eat with them."

"I doubt it. I mean, I mostly eat here. If he'd been watching them, he would have known that."

"What they doing in Central?"

"I don't know." Duberman turned to Gideon. "Do you?"

"I think they had the day off."

The answer provoked a conversation in Chinese between the cops. Duberman wished he'd had the foresight to turn on the recording system in the study. He could have taped the men, had their words translated.

The men finished talking. Tsang looked at Duberman. "You have enemies."

"You don't get to thirty billion dollars without making enemies."

Tsang shook his head. *Wrong answer.*

"As soon as the Israelis tell us it's okay, they've told the parents, we will announce the names," Lo said. "And their connection with you. Many questions for you."

"I get it."

"You like Hong Kong?" Tsang said. "Feel safe?"

"Until today, more or less."

"What about your bodyguards?" Lo said.

"You'd have to ask them, but I think so."

"Yet these men were wearing vests."

"Vests?" Duberman knew they'd caught him.

"To stop bullets," Lo said. "Not normal, for men who have nothing to be scared of."

"I had no idea."

"Also carrying pistols."

"Well, yes. They were both in the Israel Defense Forces. Experienced with firearms."

"On their *day off.*"

Ouch.

As Duberman searched for an answer,

Tsang grabbed his arm. "They have permits?"

"I'm not sure. Gideon might know. Gideon?"

"I don't think they had Hong Kong permits."

"Right. No permits. What about other bodyguards?"

"I can check —"

"No need," Tsang said. "We check already. No one has permits. No more guns. We catch them, we arrest. Illegal. Illegal."

For a guy whose English wasn't great, Tsang got his points across.

"Commissioners, with respect, your concerns seem misplaced —"

"Hong Kong not Macao!" Tsang's voice rose. "Hong Kong safe. Safe for tourists, for business, for everyone. What happen today —" He shook his head vigorously.

Lo lifted a hand to Tsang. *Relax.* "We just want to solve this fast. We're hoping you can help us."

Despite the trouble he faced, Duberman had to fight a smile. Good cop, bad cop was universal.

"Your solicitors ask the government about citizenship," Lo said.

"I hope you're devoting as much energy to finding the killer as investigating me."

"This kind of violence, the territory has no interest. You understand?"

"I think so." *Looks like I'm wearing out my welcome all over.* "Can you tell me anything about the shooter? The reports say you have footage of the motorcycle. Have you gotten a look at his face?"

"So far, no. He was careful. The cameras at the Cross-Harbour show he came in from Kowloon this morning. But he was wearing the helmet. And the license plate hasn't triggered any alarms. He must have left it somewhere."

"What about the registration? Or was the plate stolen?"

"Motorcycle was legally registered by someone named Ha Jin more than a year ago in Mong Kok. We're looking for him, but he gave a false address. Probably fake name."

"The rider, do you think he was Chinese? Or white?"

Lo stared at Duberman for seconds that felt like minutes. "Until we see his face, we don't know. But most Chinese not that big. So probably white. Does that help?"

"Not really. In Macao, we've had problems with the Hung Hing triad."

Duberman was exaggerating. All the Macao triads demanded casino kickbacks. 88

285

Gamma handled them the way companies had always dealt with the Mob, by overpaying for messy but crucial services like garbage hauling. Hung Hing, the smallest of the major triads, was agitating for more business. Duberman's chief of security in Macao had assured him that he would handle the problem. *They'll see reason or we'll put them down.*

"No triad hires a round-eye for this," Lo said. "And even if he, the killer, was Chinese, have you had problems in Macao? Violence. Fires, workers beaten up, anything like that?"

"Not that I know of."

"Hung Hing starts with that. Not this. If we need to interview your bodyguards —"

"I'll make sure they cooperate. Some only speak Hebrew, so you'll need an interpreter."

Tsang's phone buzzed. He pulled up a text, showed it to Lo.

"We found the motorcycle," Lo said. "We must go." He shoved a business card on Duberman. "My mobile number and my office. Please call me if you think of anything."

"When," Tsang said. "When you think."

Lo, Jiang-Xi Hargrove, Deputy Assistant Commissioner, Chief of Detectives, Hong

Kong Police Force, the card read. Duberman wanted to tear it apart. He'd known the police wouldn't be happy with him, but he hadn't realized they would *blame* him for the disruption and bad publicity from the killings. They would force him out of Hong Kong if he didn't help them.

"Was that an interview or an interrogation?" He looked at Gideon. "And you. Day off? *Day off?*" Duberman knew the anger was counter-productive, but he couldn't stop himself.

"Did you want me to say they were chasing Orli's pretend stalker?"

"We have to give them something." Duberman, thinking out loud now. "What about a version of the stalker story? Without Wells. Say somebody's making threats. Anonymous letters, but serious. Worst of all, he always seems to know where she is."

"What about Roberts?"

Duberman needed a moment to remember. They had told William Roberts that John Wells was the man stalking Orli. They would have to convince him to sign on to this different version, unless —

"Tell Roberts to take a couple of weeks off. Paid. Starting immediately."

"He'll go for that?"

"Say we need to review our security after

what's happened. If he gives you too much grief, I'll order him myself. We don't have a choice. If they interview him, he'll mention Wells."

Gideon frowned. Duberman could read his mind. *Our lies don't even make sense anymore, for every leak we plug, two more spring . . .*

"I know what you're thinking," Gideon said. "The FSB."

Now I am. "Have a better idea?"

"At least promise me you'll tell Orli before you do anything."

Duberman stepped close enough to see the tiny flecks of gray stubble rising from Gideon's cheeks. "I don't want to keep having to say this. You're forgetting your place."

Gideon blinked, nodded. "I'm sorry."

"Talk to Roberts. Come back when you're done, we'll see if we can't come up with some story that doesn't sound idiotic for the cops."

"Yes. Boss." Gideon walked out.

The paper with Buvchenko's number was in Duberman's wallet. He'd carried it with him since the day in the garage. He must have known this moment would come, that Wells would keep coming and upset the equilibrium Duberman had managed to

288

create. He pulled out the wallet, battered brown leather, Orli's first present to him. He riffled through a wad of brightly colored Hong Kong banknotes, panicked briefly when he couldn't find it.

There. His fingers shook as he plucked it out. Gideon was wrong. The FSB needed him as much as he needed them. *Spy service seeks wealthy older gentleman for mutually beneficial arrangement . . .* He'd give them Cheung.

A pimp. Serving a pederast.

But what if there was another way? What if —

Maybe. If he could find a way to isolate Cheung. Maybe. Of course the FSB would have to do its part. But why wouldn't it?

Before Duberman could change his mind, he thumbed in the digits, pushed the green *call* icon. The phone was answered on the first ring. Like Buvchenko was expecting him.

"Mikhail? It's Aaron. We need to talk."

13

When the killing was done: Wells kicked the Honda into gear, twisted the throttle, leaned low over the handlebars, raced past the gape-mouthed tourists outside the restaurant. No one blocked his path or told him to stop. No one followed. Civilians never did.

For forty-eight seconds, Wells put the bike through its paces, a hundred and ten kilometers an hour on a crowded street, dodging traffic in both directions with the joy of a skier slaloming gate to gate, the engine's blessed roar drowning every thought. Then Wellington Street ended. He downshifted, slowed, crossed Queen's Road Central, and turned into the parking garage at Cosco Tower, a blocky fifty-story skyscraper with an ugly blue-black façade.

He ditched the Honda behind a column on the garage's second underground level. The police would still find it, but they might need an extra pass. He kept his gloves on as he pulled off his helmet and hooded gray sweatshirt and tucked them beside the bike. He didn't worry about leaving them. They were untraceable. He had bought the sweatshirt from a street vendor in Kowloon. It didn't even come with a label to cut off. Underneath it he wore a long-sleeved button-down blue shirt and a wide brown belt.

Next, Wells pulled a pair of brown Doc Martens and a folded H&M shopping bag from his backpack. He dropped the empty pack beside the helmet. Every movement precise and calculated. He laid the pistol and suppressor at the bottom of the H&M bag. He would keep them for now. A dangerous choice, but he needed a pistol, and he wasn't sure how quickly Wright could supply him a replacement. Finally, he pulled off his boots and gloves, laid them in the shopping bag over the pistol. He slid on the Docs, his transformation from assassin to paralegal complete.

He took the fire stairs to the street. Walking, not running. Five minutes had passed since he'd pulled the trigger. Even in New York, one of the few cities with a police force more sophisticated than Hong Kong's, officers needed eight minutes on average to respond to major crimes in progress. Of course, averages were only averages. A squad car might have been near Yung Kee. But even if the police had already reached the restaurant, their first priorities would be to triage the victims and make sure that they weren't facing an ambush. Only then would they try to track the shooter.

On the sidewalk, Wells saw that word of the killings had not yet followed him down Wellington. Men and women streamed out of Cosco and the skyscrapers around it, enjoying the sunshine on a pleasant post-monsoon day. On the other side of Queen's Road Central, sirens wailed, their volume increasing by the second. But the people around Wells were so far registering them mainly as an annoyance.

The entrance to the Sheung Wan MTR station lay a hundred meters west, an obvious escape route. Too obvious in a world of surveillance cams. When the cops found the motorcycle, they would canvass the footage around the parking garage. The fire exit wasn't covered, and Wells had protected himself by changing his clothes. They would know he was tall, and maybe that he was white. But Hong Kong's skyscraper district was filled with tall white guys, investment bankers who had rowed crew at Harvard.

The cops would have one great advantage, though. Thanks to the cameras at the garage entrance, they would know almost exactly when Wells had ditched the bike. They would focus on the minutes afterward, and especially the nearby MTR, looking for anyone rushing to leave the area. Wells did the opposite. He walked casually toward Central, on his lunch break like everyone else.

Minute by minute, the sirens howled louder, overlapping from every direction. A police helicopter circled low, swerving between skyscrapers, close enough for Wells to see the cameras mounted on its nose. A man a few steps ahead looked from his phone to the helicopter, then turned and broke into a trot. Behind him, a woman said, "Are you sure? Wellington?" In a city where everyone had a smartphone, news spread fast.

Fine by Wells. The commotion would cover his escape. He'd waited long enough. He needed to be gone before the police flooded the area. He doubted they would shut down the subway or set up roadblocks, but they might. They would almost certainly try random bag checks, a risk he couldn't take.

He hailed a cab. "North Point MTR." The

station was east of downtown, not far from William Roberts's apartment on Tanner Road. The driver pulled out, then braked as two police cars sped by.

"What's going on?"

The driver turned on his radio. Wells didn't understand a word, but the announcer's excitement was obvious.

"Shooting. Near here. Two men hurt. Maybe killed, the police don't say yet."

"They catch who did it?"

"Don't say that, either."

They drove east, leaving Central behind, as an armada of police cars came the other way. By the time the cab reached North Point, the sirens were only a whimper, and the city felt normal. No one paid Wells any attention as he rode across the harbor to eastern Kowloon.

At Yau Tong station, he transferred to the green line, which ran to the center of Kowloon, just a few blocks from his crash pad. He found an empty seat in the front corner of the first car and stuffed the bag between his legs. He was the only white face in the car, but he felt invisible. Without exception, the other riders craned over their phones, crashing cartoon birds into cartoon pigs, lining up rows of brightly colored jewels, reading texts in two languages, the train crowded and empty at once.

Wells folded his hands in his lap and tried to deconstruct those seconds when he *hadn't* pulled the trigger. But he stalled out quickly. He couldn't even pick the right word to describe how he'd felt. *Panicked?* He'd been calm. *Frozen?* Closer. But still not right. *Frozen* implied he hadn't made a conscious choice. If anything, Wells remembered the opposite. A single thought had gripped him, overwhelming a decision that should have been automatic. *Don't.* Had he feared he might kill a bystander? Or simply choked on the thought of cutting two more cords? Cousins, men in the business, men who were neither innocent nor guilty.

Even now he wasn't sure.

The fact that Wells hadn't entirely lost his survival instinct was cold comfort. When Peretz spotted him and drew, Wells gunned him down. But what if Peretz hadn't seen him, and walked by? Would Wells have let him go? Worse: What if Peretz *had* seen him, but walked past as if he hadn't, then finished Wells with a shot in the back of the head?

An operative who couldn't pull the trigger when he had the drop was worse than a rock climber afraid of heights, a danger not just to himself but to everyone around him. Wells's hesitation had given Makiv the chance to fire twice. Sheer luck that those rounds hadn't hit bystanders.

Strangely, Duto was the one who'd seen this crisis coming. He'd said so three months before, after they delivered proof of Duberman's plot to the White House. *You want it to be clean, John? You know that's impossible.*

At the time, Wells ignored the warning. A lecture from Duto on the dangers of conscience seemed the definition of irony. But maybe the man was right. Maybe Wells ought to buy a ticket on the next flight home. He'd sit in coach, where he belonged. He'd done enough for the cause. All the causes. More than enough. Too much. Let the great world spin while he watched, peaceful as an astronaut.

And Duberman would win. Wells would have killed Peretz and Makiv for nothing. He couldn't abide that. You couldn't make an omelet without cracking skulls. *Block that metaphor.* Wells choked a laugh down his throat. He closed his eyes and simmered as the train sped through the darkness, its destiny mapped, doomed to stop at the same stations, run the same tracks again and again. Until it was scrapped, replaced with a newer model.

This was the life he had told his son to

choose?

His phone buzzed just as he reached the crash pad, a text from Garry Wright.

That was you?

Sí.

Clean?

The question annoyed Wells. Wright should know better. *As a toilet seat.*

A pause. Then: *K. Anything else coming?*

Really want to know?

I do.

Not now. Wells would stay in Kowloon tonight, see how Duberman reacted, what the cops were saying, how much they had. Worst case, they would release a photo of him. He hoped Roberts would call, though he knew that the contact might be a trap. Roberts might decide that giving Wells to Duberman was his best hope to stay alive.

Might. Could. If. Then. The decision trees divided and divided again. Wells wanted distraction, but this room didn't offer much. No Internet, no television, not even a radio. So he prayed for forgiveness, for himself and the men he'd killed. The words came hard today, gritty as sand in his mouth. Yet when he was finished, he did feel more connected, more peaceful. *Fuller of peace?* It was not even 5 p.m., but he turned out the lights. His missions had taught him to bank sleep when he could. Odds were he'd need it soon enough.

A buzzing woke him. He'd dreamed of Anne, and for a moment he heard the crickets that filled the woods around their — her — house every spring. But when his eyes adjusted to the room's darkness he knew better. The burner, buzzing. A blocked number. Wright's flat midwestern voice.

"So you know. Police called us today, the consulate. They hooked the vics to your friend right away. Wanted to know what we knew about him. Seem to be blaming him. "Anything like this, a black mark on the territory, Beijing watches. Big pressure."

Both good and bad news. If Wells had made a mistake, the police would surely find it. But Duberman was already feeling heat. "They have anything?"

"They weren't in a sharing mood. But they did say that Duberman's lawyers requested citizenship for him a few weeks ago. They asked us if we knew, which of course we didn't. Anyway, they were fast-tracking it. Now it sounds like it's off the table unless he helps them."

An unequivocal positive. Duberman had no good plays. If he gave Wells's name to the police, he couldn't be sure where the investigation would lead. The stalker story wouldn't stand scrutiny. But if he refused to help, Hong Kong might revoke his visa, force him out. Where would he go? Maybe Macao. He could move into a suite at 88 Gamma, a casino's worth of protection.

But Macao, like Hong Kong, danced to Beijing's tune. It, too, would force him out sooner or later. And what about Orli? She might decide a casino wasn't the ideal family home, even if her husband owned it. Duberman's best move was still to make Wells disappear. At least then Wells wouldn't be around to knock down the stalking story.

"The cops? He won't help them," Wells said.

"Agree. You need anything, you know where to find me. BTW. Nice job."

If you only knew.

Wells hung up, flipped on the naked bulb overhead. He'd used this phone enough. He pulled its SIM card, laid down a hand towel to muffle the noise, smashed the case with a hammer he'd bought for just this purpose, five quick strikes that shattered the phone into shards of black plastic. A true no-regrets kill.

Nine p.m. The sun was down, but the city hardly seemed to notice. The streets of

Mong Kok were perfect for countersurveillance, narrow and alley-cut, easy for Wells to pick a jagged path north and west, quick turns to confound any watcher. When he was sure no one was on him, he dumped what was left of the phone in an open garbage bag. Three blocks later, he dropped the SIM card in a sewer.

On the way home — the crash pad, *home* — Wells stopped at a dim sum restaurant, bright fluorescent lights over a dozen narrow tables for two, but no couples inside. Just single men, spooning soup dumplings into their mouths like they were practicing for a competitive eating contest. Such a densely packed city and yet it felt so lonely to Wells, the most atomized place he'd ever seen. But then he trafficked in loneliness.

He hadn't realized how the day had emptied him until his first order arrived, dumplings stuffed with lamb, spiced cold noodles in peanut sauce. The tang of scallions and garlic. When his plates were clean, he ordered another course and another.

At least Peretz and Makiv had gone to their graves with their bellies full.

"Hungry, hungry," the waitress said. Wells nodded as his iPhone buzzed. A blocked number.

"That wasn't nice, what you did." William

Roberts. An odd opening, as though Roberts was taping the conversation and wanted Wells to confess.

Wells didn't answer.

"We should meet," Roberts said after a while.

"Outside the Star Ferry terminal, one hour from now, Kowloon side."

"Tomorrow at the Sha Tin track. Main concourse, north end of the betting windows, end of the first race. I'll give you a tip."

Wells didn't like the spot or the timing. The sooner they met, the less time Roberts had to set a trap, if he did mean one. And the Star Ferry plaza had multiple entrances and exits. Hard to cover, easy to escape. The track was the opposite. It lay several miles north of Kowloon, in an area called the New Territories. Highways fenced it on three sides, and the Shing Mun River on the fourth. Wells would have a hard time getting away, unless he stole a horse and forded the river.

"Tonight's better. What if I come over?"

"You will be met with lead." Roberts had all the leverage, as he knew. "End of the first, Sha Tin, or nothing. One chance, guvn'r."

"Give me your word you'll be alone."

"I'll be alone."

On his walk home, Wells mulled the situation. He didn't think Roberts had sold him out to Duberman. Yet the particulars of the meeting made no sense otherwise. He would have to bring the pistol, though a gunfight at the Sha Tin would be a disaster, even if no one was hurt. His face would be obvious on surveillance. He'd be the most wanted man in Hong Kong, no way to escape unless he could beg an exfil from Wright.

He decided to arrive at the track after the *second* race, about a half hour late. Standard operating procedure would be to come early, scope the site. But Roberts had proven on Tanner Road that he knew the usual tricks. Instead, Wells would make Roberts wait. Roberts wouldn't leave immediately after the deadline. He would wonder if Wells had made a mistake with the schedule. His watchers, if there were any, would be tense and irritable after an hour or more of looking for a man who wasn't there.

Of course they'd still have the numbers. The positions. And the advantage of knowing where he'd be and who he was.

Good. Then he shouldn't have any qualms

about shooting them.

That night Wells slept easily. In the morning, he showered, shaved, pulled on a clean white T-shirt and a pair of baggy khakis, plenty of room for his concealed-carry holster. He made sure his pistol had a full mag and a round in the chamber and then tucked it away.

He called Shafer, hoping to talk over what had happened on Wellington, what might happen today. Half therapy, half tactical rundown. But Shafer didn't answer. Morning in Hong Kong, night in D.C. Shafer was probably having dinner with his wife. Good for him. Anyway, Wells knew what he'd say:

Sure you want to walk into this?

I trust Roberts.

You met him once.

Yeah, and he could have given me to Duberman then if he wanted.

Wells hung up the imaginary phone. Maybe he wouldn't have convinced Shafer, but he'd convinced himself. As for his near-miss yesterday, he just needed to get back on the horse. And what better place to do that than a track? Ha.

Sha Tin's first race started around 12:45 p.m. At 1:15, Wells stepped off the MTR at the station directly across from the track. Conveniently enough, it was called "Racecourse." Not many people came with him. Only dilettantes showed up late.

Though it housed a thousand horses, Sha Tin was hardly pastoral. The opposite, in fact. Elevated walkways over Highway 9 connected the station with a wide concrete concourse outside the grandstand. A complex of fifty-story apartment buildings behind the MTR station loomed over the track. The grandstand itself stretched nearly a quarter mile, with room for eighty-five thousand spectators.

An oversized yellow horseshoe, the track's symbol, and brightly colored statues of horses marked the main entrance. As Wells came to it, he heard a muted roar, the crowd inside cheering. The cheer grew and grew and then abruptly cut out. The second race must be done. Wells fished in his pocket for a $10 HK coin, the grandstand admission charge, and hurried through the turnstiles. He was certain that Roberts would wait at least one race, but he didn't want to press the point.

Inside, Wells found the amalgam of carnival and desperation peculiar to racetracks. A disappointed hum, punctuated by a few joyous shouts, had replaced the cheers. A big favorite must have lost. A stick-thin Chinese man, body hunched by age, tore a ticket into pieces almost too small to be seen, then flicked his hands three times to scatter them and their bad luck, a ritual he had surely practiced before. Racing called itself the sport of kings. But at heart the tracks were just casinos, making paupers of their most fervent followers. *I'm having a great time, such a beautiful day at the races . . . and please please please let me win.*

Wells watched for Duberman's guards as he neared the betting windows, but he didn't see any. Nor anyone who matched their profile, no olive-skinned curly-haired men of fighting age. The crowd was heavily Chinese, a few white guys mixed in, so the Israelis would have stood out. A good sign, though proof of precisely nothing.

And there was Roberts, standing where he'd promised, hands in his pockets, relaxed.

Wrong. Wells was a half hour late. Roberts should have been tense. He wasn't, because he knew Wells was coming. He knew because a watcher had told him. Wells turned away just as Roberts spotted him. "John!"

Wells ran toward the entrance turnstiles, heard footsteps, Roberts and others angling from the front of the grandstand. Ahead of him, by the turnstiles, two more guys waited, one tall and beefy, the other small, wiry, his hand on his hip. Both white. Wells had never seen them before.

"Stop! Let's talk!" Roberts yelled behind him.

Wells had nowhere to go. If he drew, they'd shoot. Even if he killed them all and escaped, the police would run him down within the hour. And so he stopped. Turned. Raised his hands and knitted his fingers together on his head, a mute gesture of surrender.

"Thank you," Roberts said.

"Liar."

Roberts shrugged: *What'd you expect?* Another man joined him, a Chinese guy, face half hidden under a baseball cap. Wells recognized him, one of the men who'd tracked him from the airport. Wells didn't understand. If these were Duberman's guys, how come Roberts had insisted before that Duberman hadn't followed him that first day?

"Holding?" Roberts said.

Wells nodded.

"Mind if Kevin here relieves you of that burden?"

"I'd prefer he didn't."

Roberts looked to Kevin, deferring, *Your call, you're in charge.* A surprise.

"Long as you keep your hands where they are," Kevin said. "I'm confident that after you hear what we have to say, you'll come on your own."

"Are you, now?"

"Come on, let's talk on the grandstand. It's a beautiful day."

Roberts led the way as Kevin and another Brit fell in beside Wells. They were giving him a lot of credit. Or maybe the credit was going to the shooter behind him. The brief chase had attracted almost no attention. As they walked out of the concourse to the grandstand, Wells saw why. The third race was approaching. The crowd focused on the jockeys loading their horses into the starting gate, across the track on the backstretch. One of the horses, a big roan, didn't want to enter. He was rearing, near panic, as two track workers pushed him into the gate. The crowd hummed at the spectacle.

I hear ya, buddy.

Sha Tin actually had two tracks, the outer turf, the inner hard-packed dirt. Behind the backstretch was the Shing Mun, the river straightened and narrowed, its sides hemmed by concrete, natural as a bathtub. The Army Corps of Engineers would have been proud. Across the river, more apartment towers, verdant hills behind them.

The track's finish line lay at the northern end of the grandstand and attracted the meat of the crowd. Roberts led Wells to the southern end, which was nearly empty. Wells wondered if they would risk shooting him out here. Maybe. A suppressed pistol, the crowd screaming as the horses came down the stretch. A small-caliber round that rattled inside his skull, leaving no exit wound as it turned his brain to oatmeal. The men would lay Wells on a bench like he was sleeping, mourning another losing bet. They would need only a minute to disappear.

But if they'd planned to kill him, they could have done so with less risk as Wells entered the track, *before* he knew who they were. No. Wells couldn't see it. Anyway, he'd given up his chance to shoot his way out. He would have to trust his instincts, which said that Roberts wasn't an enemy, even if he wasn't a friend, and that these men didn't work for Duberman.

On the backstretch, the jockey and trainers succeeded in steering the big roan into the gate. The crowd held its collective breath as the doors behind the horses clanged shut. The starting bell rang. The front gates flew open and the horses took off, galloping over the lush green turf, beautiful half-ton beasts who levitated with each stride. The crowd hollered as they circled the turf left to right, clockwise, the opposite of American races.

This end of the grandstand had narrow wooden benches, nothing fancy, a place for two-dollar bettors, the men whom luck never touched. They clustered in clumps of three and four, muttering as the horses began their sweep around the turn. Roberts found an open patch, no one within thirty feet, and sat. Wells and the others followed.

"Can I take my hands off my head now?"

"Not a good idea."

The horses were halfway around the turn, the pack spreading out. The crowd at the other end of the grandstand screamed encouragement, and even the men around them perked up. As the horses came around the corner, Wells was not surprised that the big roan was galloping away from the field, his lead lengthening with every stride. He must have been the favorite, because his appearance in the homestretch produced a giant roar of approval.

If it's going to happen, it'll be now —

Now —

Now —

Twenty-five seconds later, the race was over. Wells was still alive.

"Thought we might do you?" Kevin said.

"Crossed my mind."

"Not our style. Not in a former colony, anyway."

Suddenly the pieces locked together. "MI6?" Wells said.

Kevin nodded. "Been asked to find you. Or, as Americans like to say, *tasked.*"

"Not exactly giving it your all. Lose me the first day, haven't sniffed me since."

"We may have underestimated the difficulty. Anyway, these orders came from out of nowhere, a favor for the cousins, not that anyone really calls you that anymore."

"No."

"So we imagined you'd turn up. As you have. Meantime, we had our own ops to run."

"I see."

Wells did, too. The President or Donna Green had asked the British government to help find Wells after his name showed up on the LAX-HKG flight. Since the White House couldn't tell the truth, it would have offered some lame cover story that the Brits would immediately have seen through.

But the Prime Minister wouldn't want to miss the chance to bank a favor. So he agreed, and tossed this particular hot potato to Vauxhall Cross, the headquarters of the

Secret Intelligence Service, a/k/a MI6. In turn, Vauxhall catapulted it into low Earth orbit to Hong Kong. The officers here would have viewed it with distaste. Some would have heard of Wells, even if they didn't know him. Plus they knew that the CIA should be dealing with this mess, whatever it was. Instead, they weren't even allowed to ask their counterparts about it.

But a job from Vauxhall was a job from Vauxhall. They couldn't reject it. Thus, like all good spies, they played both sides. They had no excuse to miss Wells at the airport, so they didn't. They made sure he saw them, and they got pictures. Then they let him run while they went back to real work. *No, sir, nothing new today . . . still looking . . . Of course, sir. Doing all we can.* Their bosses in London understood the game, but didn't interfere. Vauxhall didn't want the hassle of catching Wells, either.

Until Wells killed two guys in the street. Suddenly the station had no choice but to make a serious effort. Its officers knew that Roberts was ex-SAS, so they called him, found him willing to talk. Or maybe Roberts called them, figuring he needed every bit of help from London he could muster if he was about to quit his well-paying job and move home. Either way, they found each

311

other. And once Roberts dangled the cheese, Wells came out of his hole.

"So when you were figuring out how best to trap me, did Roberts tell you the real story, why I'm after Duberman? He tell you that the CIA station here is *helping* me?"

"He told us the story you gave him," Kevin said. "I must say I believe it."

The British. "Must you?"

"Alas, my opinion doesn't matter. We've been asked to find you, we *have* found you, and now we're going to deliver you. Deliver you where, you ask? This very night we're putting you on a ship that will link with an American carrier group in the Pacific. I've been told the journey —"

"You sound like a high-end travel agent —"

"I've been told the journey will take about a week. What your people have planned for you after we hand you over, I have no idea."

"Suppose I say no? You shoot me?"

"I've already told you that's not how we operate. But we will be compelled to hand you to the Hong Kong police and explain your role in that atrocity yesterday. Even if they don't believe us, I'd wager that pistol in your waistband is a perfect ballistics match."

"*Kuss ummak,*" Wells said, a filthy Arabic curse.

"No, your mother's," Kevin said, in English.

"Full of surprises."

"I was in Basra for three years. I may have learned a few expletives."

"Never use a little word when a big one will do, that your motto?"

"Our motto is *semper occultus.* Latin. Translates as 'always secret.' "

This guy.

Wells had three choices but no choice at all. He could try to kill them, but he wouldn't even reach his pistol before they gunned him down. He could call their bluff, but they weren't bluffing. They would turn him over to the Hong Kong police. He didn't have diplomatic immunity. He'd spend the rest of his life in prison here.

Or he could take the deal, figure that Shafer or Duto or even Wright would find him sooner or later. Assuming these guys weren't planning to kill him once they got offshore, dump his body for the sharks. They'd pruned his decision tree to a single branch. What Wells had claimed to want. He didn't feel grateful.

"Don't suppose I get to tell anyone where I'm going."

"You do not."

"Adventure travel on the South China Sea. Let's do it."

■ ■ ■ ■

PART TWO:
(ONE MONTH
LATER)

■ ■ ■ ■

14

MACAO

Cheung Han hadn't expected to come back so quickly. Not after the way the last trip ended.

He had woken up with the worst hangover of his life, nearly as punishing as the fighter crash that ruined his legs. This time, the pain was focused above his neck, as though a malicious surgeon had sliced off his head, wrapped it in plastic, microwaved it, and crudely sewn it on again. Nausea overcame him when he tried to sit against the headboard, sour liquid bubbling up his throat into his mouth. He swallowed the bile, made himself be still.

Around him, a darkness so total that for a few terrifying moments he wondered if he had been buried alive. Or died from the drink, become a hungry ghost, doomed to feed himself for eternity on charred corpses. Then his eyes adjusted, and he recognized the bedroom around him, the forty-second-floor suite reserved for the highest of high rollers. The blackout curtains were drawn, accounting for the darkness. The digital clock beside the bed turned from 6:37 to 6:38. Morning or night? Cheung wasn't sure.

His hand shook as he reached for the light switch beside the bed. He slapped it on, wished he hadn't. He wanted nothing more than to duck beneath a pillow. But he forced himself to stay awake, reconstruct the night. He'd flown to Macao, as he always did. Met Xiao and Jian in the casino basement, the VIP entrance, as he always did.

Then —

Nothing. A blank page where the hours should be. Not blank. Redacted, as the Americans said, blackened with marker, the words there but hidden.

What had happened? Chueng surveyed the gigantic suite. Aside from his suitcase, left at the foot of the bed, it was untouched. He raised the covers, found he still wore the clothes he'd had on the night before.

But someone from 88 Gamma had antici-pated his pain. Water bottles and packets of aspirin sat atop the nightstand. He reached for a bottle. It seemed to dance away from his hand. Finally, he speared it, but his fingers trembled too much for him to grip the cap. He twisted it with his teeth, poured cool liquid down his throat. Another swallow, another, another until the bottle was empty. Then a second. Next, two aspirin tablets, and two more. The effort exhausted him. He closed his eyes, dropped instantly into the black hole of an alcohol coma.

When he woke, the clock read 10:15. His headache had dulled, but now every bone and joint ached. His skin felt like it had been slathered in wax. He stank, too, a whiskey sweat. The ash of fifty cigarettes filled his mouth. His bladder ached like it was stuffed with stone. He was sorely tempted to let loose then and there.

Instead he forced himself up, staggered toward the master bathroom. The suite's size was an absurd luxury when all he wanted was to relieve himself, wash his stench away. The shower proved another ordeal, a dozen showerheads and a touch-screen control. He jabbed at the screen until the water flowed and he could close his eyes and turn over the night in his head. A single link would unlock the memory. Nothing. Nothing. Then he saw the cat on the Beijing airport road, risking his hide for a piece of chicken.

He'd *won.* Won and drunk and drunk and

won. Fifty million dollars? More. And at the end asked for . . . a flower. A fruit still unripe. A girl. Not too young, eleven or twelve. Ten. The thought dried his mouth, sent blood rushing to the little man between his legs. The only part of his body working properly at this moment.

The desire had been in him all along. He'd danced with it for years, pushing the limits further each trip. The whiskey had freed his tongue, nothing more. He'd asked. But what had they said? *Yes, maybe, no, never?* His memories ended like a film cut off too soon. He had a blurry recollection of being steered into the elevator. Then nothing.

But he didn't think anything had happened. He didn't feel like he'd had sex. *A flower.* Part of him believed that he had asked only to see how his hosts would respond. That he wouldn't have gone ahead. His erection said otherwise. And as it drooped, he felt not relief but disappointment.

In the bedroom, Cheung pulled the shades. Night. The casinos of Cotai glimmered outside his windows, a million ways to win and lose. He pulled on a fresh shirt and pants. Upstairs, his shining plaques awaited.

Something more, too. The men who knew his needs. He wasn't ashamed of his desire. Something he wanted, a need as normal as breathing. He had the right. The real mistake had been bottling it.

Nonetheless. He knew very well that his desires were illegal, punishable by prison or even death. His rank wouldn't protect him. The opposite. Xi Jinping, China's president, was making examples at the top of the party. Anyway, Cheung wasn't sure what Xiao would say to him now. Much less Jian and the other hostesses.

Maybe he should bank his winnings, go home. He didn't feel like baccarat, anyway. He had drunk so much that some of the alcohol was still in his system. Experience had taught him that as his liver broke down what was left, depression would overtake him for a day or two, a psychic counterpart to his physical misery. No. Time for him to go back to his work. The vital work that would give China the world's strongest air force.

Back in Beijing, he could keep his wants in check. The state's power hung heavy there. The risks were too obvious. He would wait for another invitation from 88 Gamma. If it came, Cheung would know that the casino accepted him and his wishes. And if not . . . he supposed that in a few months, when the need built up inside him, he'd find a new place to play.

Three weeks passed in Beijing before his phone lit up with the number he'd been waiting to see. "General. It's Xiao." The voice quiet, deferential. "If you have a moment —"

"Speak."

"I wanted to apologize. I missed the chance to say good-bye on your last trip."

"I had to get back to my work, Xiao. The people's work."

"I don't presume to understand, General."

"Which you're interrupting."

"I'm sorry, sir. You know our Sky Tower opens soon. A month or so."

"I hadn't heard." In fact, Cheung was counting the days. The opening would be a natural chance for 88 Gamma to invite him.

"We'd be honored if you'd choose to spend that night with us."

"You want the money you've lost, that's all."

"With your spirit, we're happy to break even going against you. But there's something more. Aaron Duberman invites you to see the Tower *before* the opening."

"For a tour."

"Not only that. You'll be the first person to play in the VIP room. What we call the Sky Casino. The very first. Mr. Duberman himself will watch. A chance to give us a test run."

An honor, truly. To be the first gambler at the world's most lavish casino. Cheung supposed he shouldn't be surprised. They wanted him to give back the money he'd taken. Maybe they figured that the new casino would swallow his luck. Wrong. His heart fluttered. And not only his heart. "I'll check my schedule." Words that meant "yes."

"Of course, sir. Let me know when you're ready."

"As long as you're sure you want to open this way."

"How do you mean, sir?" Xiao's voice quieter than ever.

"With a loss."

A week later, Cheung found himself outside the main entrance of the Sky Tower. The building loomed over him, more than five hundred meters high. Only a few lights shone inside, and the shape was almost negative, a black space blotting out the sky. Cheung leaned his head back, gazed up at the top floor, lit now. The Sky Casino. Wait-

323

ing for him.

"I'm truly the first."

"Yes, sir. This way, please."

Xiao led him to the front doors, the dark space behind them —

And the lights inside flared, revealing a vast lobby, twenty meters high, its walls made of a lustrous metal that changed color by the second, now a swirling red, now blue, now green, a trick that seemed almost magical. Its ceiling was glass, an aquarium overhead, sharks and rays swimming tirelessly. One traditional touch, a huge red dragon in the center. As Cheung walked inside, Aaron Duberman strode from the dragon's open mouth. Duberman wore a black suit, a collarless white shirt, and alligator leather boots that must have cost as much as a car.

"Welcome to the Saloon!" he shouted, with Xiao translating.

"I thought the name was Sky?"

"Yes. Saloon was my first casino, back in Nevada. I used to work the floors just like this. It's good to be back."

"I see." Though Cheung didn't, really.

"So what do you think, General?"

"I won't pretend I'm not impressed."

"The most expensive casino we've ever built. Or anyone else. Twenty-eight billion yuan. My executives told me it was too much, I told them I didn't care, it had to be the best, like nothing else. To make the engineering work, we anchored it with steel cables that run through the Cotai landfill to the seabed. A hundred cables, two hundred meters long each, a meter in diameter. It can withstand a once-in-a-century typhoon, and it hardly sways up top."

"Chinese engineering."

"I'm glad you came, General. The way you left us so fast last time, I worried someone on my staff had offended you."

"Not at all."

"Good. Because nothing matters more to me than the way we treat our clients. Especially men like you. You aren't just players. You're my friends."

If Cheung had been more self-aware, he might have questioned why he merited so much attention from one of the world's richest men. Or the crazy notion that 88 Gamma would open this casino for him and him alone. He was a big player, sure, but not the biggest. If he were more self-aware, he might have recognized where his true value lay.

But then, if Cheung were more self-aware, he wouldn't have believed that he had the right to have sex with a child.

And he did. His desire had risen like a fever since the call from Xiao. On his flight down, he had barely glanced at a report delivered just the previous day from a Chinese spy in Washington, a translated copy of Lockheed Martin's top-secret findings on problems with the software in the F-35 jet. Even the thought of sitting at the baccarat table didn't hold his attention as it usually did. He was already waiting for the end of the night. Yet . . . when the moment came . . . he wondered if he would have the guts to ask for what he wanted. The *courage.* He'd need a few drinks, to steady himself.

"Everything all right, General?" Duberman smiled, and Cheung felt his charm. A gentleman, a man who understood the world. "You seem distracted." Duberman pointed at the aquarium. "I was just saying, we'll bring new sharks through every few weeks so that even our regular players will see something new every time. We have a saying in America, variety is the spice of life. I hate to be bored myself. I hate even more when my customers are bored."

Duberman led Cheung to the check-in desk, empty now, of course. Jian walked out from a door behind the desk, bearing a tray with an unopened bottle of Johnnie Walker

Blue and two glasses. She wore a stark black dress and looked taller and slimmer and more beautiful than ever. For once, Cheung was genuinely surprised to see her. "Jian."

"General. A pleasure."

Cheung went to a knee and kissed her hand, inhaling her scent. Beside him, Duberman poured two whiskies, big drinks, the tumblers half full. Looking at the golden liquid made Cheung's throat ache.

"I'll tell you a secret, General. If you can keep it."

"Naturally."

"What would life be without secrets? I understand that, and so do my employees."

You aren't just players. You're my friends . . . I don't want anyone to get bored . . . What would life be without secrets?

Duberman *knew.* Not only that, he wanted Cheung to know he knew. He must want to be helpful. Maybe he even shared Cheung's tastes. A pleasant vision filled Cheung's mind. *I don't have to . . . and maybe I won't . . .*

But I will.

"What's your secret?" Cheung said.

"We're doubling the maximum up there."

Not what Cheung had expected. "Ten million? A hand?"

"Not just for a hand or two. We'll play all

327

night that way."

A staggering number, enough to turn Cheung's thoughts back to the table. At those stakes, a player could win or lose five hundred million in a night.

"You don't expect me —"

"No. But I hoped you might take some of what you'd won from us last month and start us off with a maximum bet." Duberman smiled, his teeth more perfect than any man's should be. For the first time, Cheung felt uneasy. *Too easy, don't trust him, something's wrong . . .*

But desire overwhelmed the warning, the instinct for self-preservation. "If the maximum is ten million, I'll have to bet fifteen."

Duberman's smile widened. "Do you know why I asked you to be our first guest? My managers said, not Cheung. He's too smart. He won't be so easily impressed. And such a gambler. After what he did to us last month, you want him *back*? I told them, I don't want someone I can buy off with a day at the spa, a fancy dinner. A visit to my mansion. I want the toughest man we can find. We all agreed it was you."

The toughest. Yes. "Be careful what you wish for."

"Isn't that the truth?" Duberman handed Cheung a tumbler and raised his own.

"To the Sky Casino."

"To luck, General. Yours and mine."

"Mine and yours."

The glasses came together with a clink pure as a church bell. Cheung meant to take only one sip, but before he could help himself, the drink flew down his throat. Liquid courage. *Permission.*

"Chou-Lai and I will take good care of you tonight," Duberman said. "Shall we have dinner? Or may I take you straight to the hundred and eighth floor?"

Cheung held up his glass for a refill. "The hundred and eighth."

The VIP salon had walls made of the same strange color-shifting metal as the lobby, though the hues changed more slowly and subtly, so as not to distract the players. For now, the room had no sculpture or paintings, no art, just a single baccarat table. Duberman explained that he had commissioned pieces specifically for the space from Zhang Huan and Zeng Fanzhi, two great modern Chinese artists. They hadn't yet arrived. "The walls will do for now."

Cheung hardly heard him. He couldn't tear his attention from the plaques at the table. His money. And in the dealer's seat, Lin, the man he'd battled a month before.

"General." Lin stood and bowed. Everything as it had been. The night falling into place, a supercharged version of his previous trip. Again Cheung won his first bet, not a natural this time, instead a three-card four that somehow held up to Lin's three aces, in its own way an equally miraculous victory. Cheung saw Duberman flinch as Lin pushed fifteen plaques across the table. Beating the house for fifteen million while the owner watched helplessly.

"My shareholders won't be happy."

"I warned you."

"If this keeps up, we're going to need to come up with a five-million-dollar plaque." Duberman moved to the door. "I have to make some calls. While I'm gone, Chou-Lai will take care of you."

"Is Malcolm here?" Malcolm, the little toady who ran the VIP room at 88 Gamma.

Duberman seemed puzzled. "He's at the main casino. Did you want him?"

"No. Don't trust him." The words mumbled, almost hissed. Cheung had no conscious memory of the way Malcolm had flinched at his demands the month before. Yet he knew that Malcolm was his enemy just as the snake knew the mongoose.

"Then I promise you won't see him again." Duberman wagged a finger at Lin.

"Don't let him win, all right?"

After that first hit, Cheung settled in, sticking to bets of a million dollars a hand, ignoring Lin's gibes that he was playing like a woman to preserve his money. Not so. For the first time, he sat at a baccarat table thinking about something other than the riches he might win.

A couple of hours later, Duberman reappeared to offer Cheung dinner. After Cheung turned him down, he watched for a while, then left again. Cheung drank steadily, but he tried to sip rather than gulp. He didn't want to pass out tonight. Or black out. He wanted to remember every detail, a camera-perfect memory. *Cameras. Of course they're watching, you think they aren't?*

Again he felt uneasy. Again he ignored the alarm. Or, rather, drank it into silence. He emptied his glass and closed his eyes as a dissociative calm spread over him. He was a hundred stories downstairs, watching the sharks swim, but in no danger thanks to the thick glass protecting him.

Cheung opened his eyes to find that Duberman had returned. He watched impassively for a while as the cards and plaques moved back and forth.

"Everything to your liking, General?"

As an answer, Cheung pointed at his

stacks. "A question. Are the suites here ready for business? Or do you plan to bring me back to 88 Gamma?"

"Technically, no one should be here except the construction crews and our own employees. I was planning to take you over there. If that's where you want to go."

"Where else would I want to go?"

"Wherever you like."

"And will you be coming with me?"

As Xiao translated, Cheung focused on Duberman. Would he flinch? But he only nodded. "That's up to you."

Cheung never wore a watch when he played. He didn't want to know how long he'd spent at the table. "What time is it?"

"Three a.m."

Cheung had arrived around 8 p.m. He would have guessed he'd played for three hours, not seven. He counted his plaques. He was still ahead about eight million, but his luck had turned. If not for that first hand, he'd be down. He decided to bet his winnings. If he won, he'd stay at the table, focus on gambling. Back to work. And if he lost . . .

He'd find out if all Duberman's hints meant anything.

He fumbled for the plaques, stacked eight, pushed them forward. "Eight million."

"Finally, some balls," Lin said. He pulled four cards from the shoe, pushed two across the table. Cheung licked his lips as the cards came his way. Did he want to win or lose? He squeezed the cards together, bent low over the table, peeked at the first. A jack. Useless. Zero. *Good.* He pushed it away, peeked at the second card, a seven. For a total of seven. Not quite a natural, but close. A very good hand. He flipped both cards over, trying not to be disappointed.

"Seven. Not bad. Stand on seven." Quickly, Lin turned both of his cards. A five and a three. A natural eight. The winner. "Not as good as this. You lose."

No. I win. Cheung stood, braced himself against the table as the room floated past him. He'd drunk more than he planned. No matter. He had a bottle of Viagra in his pocket. He would take as many as he needed. "Bag it up."

"You're finished for the night? After that? Scared?"

Cheung turned to Chou-Lai. "What we talked about before. The flower."

"The flower, sure."

The moment of truth. "I want it."

Chou-Lai nodded. "Tell him," he said to Xiao. Who said something in English to Duberman. Who gave Cheung the tiniest smile. "If you're sure."

"Yes."

Duberman came around the baccarat table, put an arm around Cheung, waved Xiao over for the translation, a strange three-man huddle. "How old?"

"I don't understand."

"Yes, you do."

A third alarm, blaring this time, yet so far away. "Why do I have to say?"

"I don't want any confusion, that's all." Duberman looked at him almost gently. "I'll say it for you. Fifteen? Sixteen?"

Cheung wanted to scream. To be so close — "No, no. A *flower*."

"I'm sorry, General —"

"Nine. Ten. Eleven at most."

"A girl."

"Do I look like a pansy? Of course a girl!"

Duberman stepped away. He said something in English that Xiao didn't translate and then strode out of the room. A pit a thousand kilometers deep opened in Cheung's stomach. Duberman would kick Cheung out and send him home —

A minute later, Duberman returned. Smiling. He didn't seem angry.

"Everything all right?" Cheung said.

"I have just what you want. Vietnamese.

Beautiful. Ten years old. Let's drink to it. Tequila."

Suddenly Jian was at Cheung's side, a tray with two glasses in her hand, two little shots, one in the middle of the tray, the other at the edge. She handed the one in the middle to Cheung as Duberman took the other. The sequence puzzled Cheung, but he couldn't figure out why. He was too muddled, and too excited.

"Congratulations." Duberman raised his glass and they drank. The tequila was vaguely bitter, chalky on Cheung's tongue. An odd warmth chased it down his throat, into his stomach, and from there spread through him. Not the burn of alcohol. Something deeper and more pleasant. It doubled him over. He would have fallen if Chou-Lai hadn't grabbed his arm.

Duberman stepped away.

"Are you coming?"

Duberman didn't answer, and Chou-Lai steered Cheung toward the door. Cheung wanted to fight but he couldn't. He couldn't make his muscles move. "My money."

"It's fine."

Then Cheung couldn't speak. The tequila must have hit him all at once. No. He didn't feel drunk. Or not just drunk. When he was drunk, he knew what he meant to say even if he couldn't make anyone else understand. Now he couldn't speak even to himself. Something was wrong, he could see the door in front of him, the thing that moved up and down, but he didn't know its name. He knew he should be afraid, but instead he felt the greatest pleasure, *high,* a word he hadn't understood until this moment, a million meters above the earth —

He was outside —

In a car, on a bridge, the lights of a city leaving streaks on his eyes —

Time turned strange. He wasn't blacked out, not entirely, but he couldn't keep up with the world, it was moving so much faster than he was —

Still in the car, slowing now, on a narrow street crammed by dirty concrete apartment blocks. Chou-Lai handed him two blue pills; he felt a bolt of pleasure that he knew them, *Viagra.* He took them without complaint —

Chou-Lai opened a door, a bedroom door; inside a girl lay on a narrow bed, nude, Vietnamese, so young, so beautiful, what he'd wanted all this time — and Chou-Lai shoved him inside and closed the door.

For half a second, Cheung hesitated. He could still leave. Then the girl smiled at him and he stepped toward the bed —

Cheung woke. The pain was so much worse than the month before. Like his body wanted to reject the world. Like he was dying. Like dying would be a relief. He squeezed his eyes shut. He already knew something terrible had happened the night before. That *he* had done something terrible. Though he couldn't remember what.

He wanted to keep his eyes closed forever, hide from the truth, but his body wouldn't let him. His mouth was dry, his thirst overpowering. It was day, it had to be, the light streamed through his closed eyelids. He lay on something painfully hard, not the perfect bed in the high-roller suite. The room around him was hot, no air-conditioning here, and flies buzzed around him, and he knew that when he opened his eyes, he would be somewhere he didn't want to be, looking at something he didn't want to see.

He opened them.

He lay on his back on a concrete floor. Naked. His little bird felt sticky and when he looked down it was covered in brownish dried blood. The blood there didn't scare him. The blood on his hands did.

He moved his head, gently and precisely as a metronome ticking, until he saw the bed. The girl was still on it, one leg dangling, a trace of blood just visible on her thigh. The mattress was bare and a sheet piled on the floor, blood there, too —

Cheung screamed, tried to scream, his voice wavering and thin in his throat.

The night came back to him all at once, Duberman in his boots, the casino, the whiskey, the tequila —

Then nothing. This time, he knew he wouldn't remember no matter how hard he tried. What had they given him? What had he done? He pushed himself up, grabbing the windowsill for balance, ignoring the inferno in his head. The girl lay unmoving, head curled at a strange angle, blood leaking from her mouth —

The door swung open. Two men walked in. *Laowei.* Round-eyes. One not much bigger than Cheung, the other enormous, a mountain of a man. They wore suits and latex gloves. Without a word, they grabbed him, pulled him down a dim hallway. Cheung tried to fight but they were too strong, far too strong.

Thirty meters down, a door on the other side of the hall was open. They threw him inside, pulled the door shut. The room was

338

a mirror image of the other, a single bed, a wooden chair, a dirty window, the smell of sewage, flies buzzing through the open bathroom. One difference. A laptop lay on the bed instead of a girl. The big man pushed him down on the chair as the small one reached for the laptop.

"Watch this." He pushed a button on the laptop and a video played, the image on the screen clearer than the one in Cheung's mind. The Sky Casino. Black plaques sitting on the baccarat table. Him and Duberman.

"How old?"

"I don't understand."

"Yes, you do."

"Why do I have to say?"

"I don't want any confusion, that's all. I'll say it for you. Fifteen? Sixteen?"

Exasperation twisting Cheung's face. *"No, no. A flower."*

"I'm sorry, General —"

"Nine. Ten. Eleven at most."

"A girl."

"Do I look like a pansy? Of course a girl!"

The screen went dark. The big man grabbed Cheung's arm, threw him to the floor. The small one kicked him twice in the back, the pain radiating into his kidneys, up his spine —

"You're disgusting. Get up. Stand."

Cheung pushed himself to all fours.

"Stand."

His legs shook as he stood. "But he agreed, Duberman agreed —"

"I don't think so."

"Play it, you'll see, it comes next."

The man played the video again.

"Do I look like a pansy? Of course a girl!"

On screen, Duberman stepped away, spoke the English words that Xiao hadn't translated.

"You don't know what he's saying."

Cheung shook his head.

"Too bad you studied in Germany and not the U.S. It translates as *'Get out of my casino, you piece of shit. I don't do business with pedophiles.'* "

"But he —"

"He threw you out."

"He *agreed.*" Cheung wasn't sure why he was bothering to argue, the truth hardly mattered, but he wanted to understand. "He gave me a drink —" Cheung could taste it now, feel its strange warmth, the euphoria that followed. Despite everything, his body craved another dose. Not tequila. An opiate. They'd given him those drugs in the hospital after his crash. "Play the rest."

"That's the end. There isn't any more. So he tossed you, you found your way here —"

"That's *not* what happened."

"Tell me, then, how you got here, wound up in that room with that girl."

Cheung had no answer. The whiskey and whatever was in the shot glass had erased his memory. He squeezed his eyes shut, tried to think. A trap. Duberman had *trapped* him —

A slap stung his face, sent him sprawling. From the floor, he looked at his tormentors.

"You think we're done? I have another video for you."

"No, please, no —"

"The one that shows what you did to her."

Bile filled Cheung's mouth as it had the month before. This time, he knew he couldn't control himself. He ran for the bathroom, retched a thin yellow stream of drool and acid into the stinking toilet. He mopped his mouth with the back of his blood-splattered hand and tried to understand how his life had come to this point.

The big man was behind him now, dragging him back, not a moment's peace.

"You don't want to watch?" the other one said. "You put on quite a show."

"Let me go."

"Where? Your clothes aren't there. Nor your phone. Nothing. How far do you think you'll get before someone calls the police to report a naked man covered in blood? What will you tell them when they pick you up?"

"Do you know who I am?"

"I know just who you are. A half man with a thing for little girls." He reached into his pocket, came out with Cheung's air force identification. "General Cheung Han of the People's Liberation Army Air Force. Maybe you should call your friends in Beijing, ask Uncle Xi to cover for you. I'm sure he'll be glad."

Not quite. Xi Jinping and his prosecutors would throw Cheung in a hole for a hundred months. Make him a hungry ghost while he still lived. Then they'd hang him.

Hot tears streamed down his face. *No.* He'd never cried. Not even when he'd woken up in the hospital with every bone in both legs shattered.

"General, you're looking at this backward. The question you ought to be asking is who *we* are."

"Please." He couldn't hide the truth from himself. They'd broken him. He would do whatever they asked, as long as they made this go away.

The round-eye smiled. "Please, you say. Please." He pulled a clean white handkerchief from his pocket, passed it to Cheung.

"Wipe your face. You look terrible."

Cheung mopped at his face. "Who are you?"

"We're the ones who are going to make all this vanish." He made two fists, opened them, *poof.* A magic trick. "And save you."

"Yes?" Cheung hated himself for the hope in his voice.

"But you have to help us first."

15

WESTERN PACIFIC OCEAN,
ABOARD THE USS RONALD REAGAN

Like any city of six thousand, the USS *Ronald Reagan* came equipped with a jail — a brig, in naval lingo. For three weeks, it had held two prisoners: a petty officer caught with six ounces of methamphetamine in his mattress, and Wells.

His MI6 captors had ferried him out of Hong Kong on a trawler, sent him on a ten-day dogleg across the South China Sea. Finally, they transferred him to a gray ship five times their size, the USS *Sampson,* an American destroyer. They gave Wells no fresh clothes, only one shower. By the time he arrived on the *Sampson,* he looked like he belonged in a Mathew Brady daguerreotype of the Civil War, and the crew treated him like he had Ebola. He spent a night locked in an empty storage room before a helicopter brought him to the *Reagan,* a nuclear-powered aircraft carrier a thousand feet long, with a better air force than most countries.

Five petty officers greeted Wells as he stepped onto the carrier's deck, walling him off from the F-18s like he might make a break for them. "Shower, shave, brig," the one nearest Wells said. "Do not pass go, do not collect your hazard pay bonus. Going to make a fuss?"

Not unless it'll pay. After the shower, Wells's captors put him in a blue jumpsuit and brought him to the ship's ninth deck, a warren of low corridors and stale air. His cell occupied the end of the brig, its only connection to the outside world a foot-square Plexiglas window. Its bookshelf was empty but for a single volume, a well-thumbed copy of the *Uniform Code of Military Justice.* Wells settled in to read, though he couldn't decide which section applied. Twenty minutes later, his cell door swung open. Two sailors stepped inside, followed by an officer in a spotless blue uniform with a single gold star and four stripes on each sleeve.

"Mr. Wells," the gold star said. "Captain Devin Barnett. Commander of the *Reagan.*" More than the other services, the Navy was a family business, proud of its

East Coast traditions. Barnett looked the part, with narrow blue eyes, ramrod posture, gray hair trimmed close to his skull.

"You visit all your prisoners?"

"I'm sorry about the circumstances, but I'll do my best to make your stay comfortable." Barnett had a genteel Tidewater Virginia twang. "You'll have fresh clothes, all the books you want, gym access."

"You sound like you're running a La Quinta." Wells was out of patience for false niceties.

The petty officers swarmed him, each grabbing an arm, digging their fingers into his biceps. "You don't speak to our captain that way —"

"Tell Click and Clack to let go before this gets messy." Wells felt his anger rising. The cell was narrow, and the petty officers were crowding him, telegraphing their lack of close-quarters fighting experience. Wells could put them both down, but he'd stain his nice new jumpsuit. *"Please."*

"Go on," Barnett said. "Outside —"

"Captain —"

"And close the door. That's an order."

They went.

"I'm trusting you."

Yeah, with six thousand guys and an ocean on your side. "Wish I could say the same.

346

Why am I here?"

"I've been ordered to hold you —"

"Charges? Authority?"

"You're a material witness in a classified national security investigation."

In other words, the White House couldn't even find a plausible excuse. The material witness label was tissue-thin. No competent federal judge would believe it. But the *Reagan*'s crew didn't include federal judges, competent or otherwise.

"You know who I am, yes?"

"Broadly."

"I'd like to make a phone call."

Barnett shook his head. "Nor email."

"Captain —"

"I don't love it, either, Mr. Wells. But these orders come straight from the White House. I give you my word as the commander of this vessel that as soon we reach American soil, I will personally ensure you speak to counsel of your choosing."

"And when's that?"

Barnett looked at the floor. "We're scheduled to dock in San Diego in eight months."

Eight months. The President might not have the CIA, but he had sidelined Wells nonetheless. Sure, it was only a delaying action, but eight months wasn't bad, considering the President had less than two years left in office. *Justice too long delayed is justice denied,* Martin Luther King had written from a Birmingham jail. Wells could see what King meant. He wondered if he should give Barnett a taste of the truth. But why bother? The guy seemed decent enough, but freethinkers were rarely given aircraft carriers to run.

By now, with Wells out of pocket for ten days, Duto and Shafer would be worried. But they had no threads to follow. Wells hadn't told Shafer about his plans to meet with William Roberts. He'd planned to, sure, but then Shafer hadn't answered his call, and he hadn't left a message —

Stupid. He'd been stupid. Anyway, MI6 had no doubt pulled its own disappearing act for Roberts and his family, given them a paid vacation in the English countryside. Duto would lean on Wright, the Hong Kong station chief. But Wright wouldn't have any idea where to look. The Brits knew, but they weren't about to share. Maybe if Duto went to the top of Vauxhall Cross, maybe not even then. As the weeks stretched into months, Duto and Shafer would assume the worst.

And what about Evan?

"You need to let me call my son. You can monitor it."

"I'm sorry."

"You have children, Captain?"

Barnett grunted.

"What would they think if you vanished? Email him yourself, then. Doesn't have to come from me."

"I wish I could, but the IP addresses from the ship are traceable to someone who knows."

"Then ask somebody at home to set up an anonymous account, I don't care. Not trying to play games. I just want him to know I'm alive." Though Wells figured Evan would pass the message to Shafer and Duto. Give them extra incentive to track him down.

Barnett walked out, left the cell door open. The two petty officers in the brig's corridor shifted leg to leg like they couldn't decide if they wanted Wells to start up. "What's Click and Clack?" From the one nearer Wells.

"Tom and Ray. *Car Talk.*"

"Car what?"

"You never heard of *Car Talk?*" *Man, I'm getting old. Though I could still take you two.*

Barnett returned with a pad and pencil. "Write exactly what you want to say. Nothing cute. If it looks weird, I won't do it."

Wells played it straight: *Evan: Sorry I*

haven't called. I'm safe and healthy but I'll be tough to reach for a while. What I said that last night holds. You're still lucky. Love, Pops.
He gave the sheet back to Barnett.

"What did you tell him the last night?"

"What it says. That he's lucky. Proof of life, as people like you like to say."

"People like me?"

"Kidnappers."

Barnett grimaced. "And he calls you Pops."

"Straight outta Montana."

Barnett folded away the note. "I'll let you know what he says."

A petty officer brought back the note five days later. "The captain asked me to tell you, your son says everything's copacetic."

Copacetic sounded like Evan, all right.

Barnett kept his word about the privileges, too. Every day two sailors brought Wells to the library and the gym and delivered him food from the officers' mess. As a rule, the escorts didn't talk to him, but two weeks on, one blurted out, "I don't get it. Are you a prisoner or a VIP?"

"Ask the captain."

In fact, aside from the lack of sunlight, the cell had certain advantages. Wells had time to read and pray. And he didn't have to worry about seasickness. The *Reagan* was so enormous that even the biggest waves barely moved it. He spent a couple days thinking about his near-failure on Wellington Street, then decided it had nothing to teach him. He could promise himself he wouldn't seize up again, but until the moment arrived, he couldn't be sure. He did decide that if it happened even once more, he would quit. Walk away, regrets or no.

If the next mistake didn't kill him.

Still, captivity grated. Wells had grown up among the twelve-thousand-foot Bitterroot mountains and endless blue sky. He'd spent much of his adult life in the Hindu Kush. He'd always been an outsider, literally and figuratively. Free will might be an illusion, but he treasured it nonetheless. Now he was locked in the belly of a steel whale. Even his sleep was not his own. Though the *Reagan* never shut down entirely, the majority of its officers and crew worked days and slept nights, a standard twenty-four-hour circadian cycle. The brig was no exception. Its lights snapped on each morning precisely at 6 a.m. and turned off at 10 p.m.

The lack of news also frustrated him. He had no idea what had happened to Duberman, or the repercussions of the shooting on Wellington. Did the cops know about

Wells? Were they even now searching for him? Five minutes on the Internet would have answered every question, but his escorts told him that they'd wind up his neighbors in the brig if they let him near the ship's computers.

As the days blended into something approaching pure time, Wells took to marking them off as prisoners always had, a new scratch on the steel wall behind his head just before the lights went out. Eight months. Two hundred and forty days, give or take. An unperson serving unpunishment for an uncrime. At the President's whim. *A government of laws and not of men,* John Adams had written more than two centuries before, but then Adams had never been sent to molder on a floating island.

Night twenty-two. Wells closed his eyes, found himself at the Sha Tin track, watching a dozen huge geese race around the turn. Peretz and Makiv were the two lead jockeys. Peretz stood, waved. *Hey, brother —*

Not your brother. No one's brother — Wells grabbed a pistol and fired —

The pistol let loose a stream of water.

I've heard of silencers, but that's ridiculous — Peretz grinned and raised his own pistol —

The lights snapped on. The track disappeared in the shine of bare steel.

The brig. The Reagan. *Awake.* His subconscious hadn't read the memo about forgetting Wellington Street. Wells rolled to his feet, raised his fists. Good news rarely came this late at night. If Barnett planned to dump him overboard, he'd take as many guys as he could with him. *Six thousand? That all you got?*

The door slung open. Barnett stood alone, unshaven, his eyes tired and narrow. He held Wells's T-shirt and khakis in a freshly folded pile.

"Laundry service, Captain?"

"Get dressed. New orders. Your ride'll be here in fifteen."

"At three a.m.? You want me out of here at this hour, better call for backup."

"Not a trick. I don't get it either, but there's a Greyhound with your name on it."

"A Greyhound?" Wells thought of his cross-country bus trip.

"C-2. Cargo plane. Not the sexiest ride, but it'll take you to Clark Air Base in Manila —"

"I thought the Philippines kicked us out of Clark —"

"Changed their minds. They don't like China either."

"Then where?"

"I don't know."

Anyone could be waiting for Wells in Manila. Assuming he made it there. Wells had the momentary certainty that a crew inside the Greyhound was waiting to toss him at thirty thousand feet, see if he could teach himself to fly on the way down. His clothes were a good sign, unless they weren't. Make him disappear, and his khakis, too.

"This crew brings mail for us all the time. You can trust them."

"Sure I can."

"Look, just tell me who to call. Soon as you take off. I give you my word —"

"As commander of this vessel, yeah yeah yeah."

Barnett pushed Wells's clothes at him. "Forget it, then."

Wells had provoked the reaction he'd hoped to see. Barnett was miffed. Because he genuinely believed that Wells would be safe. Wells wondered what had happened. Had someone else killed Duberman? Had Shafer or Duto figured out where he was, forced the President to let him go? Or —

"Has the President resigned?" Wells said.

Barnett looked baffled. "No. Why would you think that?"

"I put a gypsy curse on him and I wondered if it worked."

"Do me a favor, get dressed."

The Greyhound looked like something from World War II, an ungainly twin-engined bird, snub-nosed and wide, four vertical stabilizers and stubby wings. "This thing flies?" Wells said. "From this deck?"

"Greyhounds have run cargo to carriers for fifty years," Barnett said. "I don't suppose I'll ever get the real story on this."

Not from me. Wells was the plane's only passenger. *Good.* An airman checked his seat belts professionally, but without much interest. Barnett had told the truth. Whatever awaited Wells in Manila, this flight would be safe enough.

The cargo bay door whirred shut. The plane shuddered as the engines spooled up and the props spun. The C-2 taxied into position and rumbled across the deck. It didn't fall into the ocean, so it must have taken off, though Wells couldn't tell exactly when. It seemed to be aviation's equivalent of a four-cylinder Accord: safe, reliable, underpowered.

Aside from a brief patch of turbulence, the three-hour flight passed uneventfully. Somewhere along the way, Wells must have

355

slept, because he opened his eyes to find an airman tapping his shoulder. "Clark Air Base. Outie outie."

Wells followed the airman onto a cracked tarmac. A hangar loomed in the dark, two civilian jets parked just outside. They were CIA specials, both white, both lacking any identification except tail numbers. Two men waited for Wells, the human equivalent of the jets, compact, muscled, and wearing sunglasses around their necks despite the darkness.

The taller paramilitary extended a hand. "Mr. Wells. I'm Mr. Black. This is Mr. Blue."

"Inventive."

"Thank you." The answer was so perfectly deadpan that Wells didn't know at first if Black was in on the joke. "Flight okay?"

"I get antsy when guys like you act polite."

"Makes you feel better, I'm only doing it on orders. This way." Black led Wells toward the larger of the two jets, a G5. Its cockpit and cabin lights were on and a Jetway was already in place. Black waved Wells up the steps.

"Where are we going?"

"I'll tell you when we're airborne."

"Now."

"A stop in Anchorage to refuel. Then Andrews."

Andrews Air Force Base, Maryland. Not for the first time, Wells found himself stunned by the power of the U.S. government. From a cell in the middle of the ocean to the homeland in less than a day, no explanation given, no passport required.

"What's at Andrews?"

"My job is to get you there, full stop."

"Has something happened to Duberman?"

"Who?"

"Your phone."

"Excuse me?"

"I need your phone. To make a call." Wells spoke slowly, being a jerk now, not caring. "No call, no jet."

"How about I do it —"

"Promise, all that gay porn on your browser, your secret's safe with me."

Black fished an iPhone from his pocket.

Shafer picked up on the first ring.

"Ellis."

"John." For a change, Shafer sounded genuinely excited. "Where are you?"

"Just landed in Manila. POTUS had me on an aircraft carrier."

"We would have found you."

Maybe. "I'm here with two guys who want me to get on another plane. They claim we're going home, Andrews. You know

357

anything about it?"

"I do not. But give me the tail number."

Wells did.

"See you soon."

Eighteen hours later, the G5 touched down in Maryland. They had crossed the international date line over the flight, gained twelve hours, so it was around noon, a beautiful late spring day in the mid-Atlantic. Not that the sun did Wells much good. The Gulfstream was nice, but he'd hardly slept. He shuffled like a zombie to the tarmac, where four men in suits waited. Wells pegged them as FBI or Secret Service. They guided him to a black Suburban and set off, emergency lights flashing. Wells didn't bother asking where they were taking him. He was unsurprised when they came up 295 and over the Anacostia and ten minutes later swung onto West Executive Drive, the White House looming.

Duto and Shafer waited in the Oval Office anteroom.

"We have to stop meeting like this," Shafer said.

"How'd they get you out of Hong Kong?" Duto said. "Garry Wright swore up and down he had no idea —"

"He didn't. MI6 picked me up, put me

on a boat, handed me over. Long story."

"Doesn't sound that long."

"I guess not. You have any idea what this is about? I haven't seen a newspaper or a website in a month. Something happen to Duberman?"

The door to the Oval Office opened, and Donna Green waved them in. "Gentlemen."

Again the President sat on the yellow couch in the center of the room. Again a pitcher of water and glasses waited on the center table. But this time, the President's posture felt different to Wells. Not quite defeated, but worn. Like he was done acting. *Good.* Wells couldn't take another *just-trust-me* performance.

"Please, sit."

"That was a neat trick with MI6," Wells said. "Sir."

"You were treated all right?"

"Held illegally, incommunicado, no trial, no hearing. Aside from that, it was fine. Sir."

"You killed Duberman's guards in Hong Kong last month."

"I'm not answering that. Sir. Unless you've suspended the Constitution here, too. Sir."

The repeated *sir*s were provoking a tic around the President's right eye.

"Why are we here?" Shafer said.

The President looked to Green.

"Must be bad if you don't want to tell us yourself," Shafer said.

"The Kremlin has asked for asylum on behalf of Aaron Duberman," Green said.

Shafer cupped a hand to his ear. "*Ring-ring.* Hello? Yes. I see. Cluck you, too. Adios." He pretended to hang up. "Sorry. Those were the chickens."

"Chickens?"

Shafer pointed a finger at Green, though everyone in the room knew it was meant for the President. "Coming home. To roost."

"Do I get to tell you what happened now?" Green explained that Paul Kutsunov, the Russian ambassador to the United States, had called two days before to tell her Duberman was applying for political asylum in Russia. Based on its review, the Kremlin believed he had a well-founded fear of persecution, Kutsunov said.

"I said, 'Well-founded or well-funded?' He didn't think that was funny. I told him we didn't think that Aaron Duberman made a credible political prisoner. Considering he's the biggest donor in the history of American politics. I said I didn't know why he thought Russia would protect him, considering how Russia has treated Jews over the years."

"Not bad," Shafer said.

"He said that if we had contrary evidence, the Kremlin would gladly examine it. But not in private, since as a rule asylum hearings are public in Russia. Which is nonsense. He said Aaron Duberman's human rights were his only concern. He said that even before the Kremlin made a final decision, it had given Duberman preliminary protected diplomatic status —"

"Something else that doesn't exist —" the President said.

"And the Kremlin would view quote-unquote interference with Duberman as equivalent to action against one of its own diplomats. *He will have our full protection.* I told him I hoped Duberman would enjoy the winters in the Moscow. And that was that."

"I guess your first move is to inform the Russians about our friend's role in our little Iranian misadventure," Shafer said. "Let them know who they're dealing with."

"Of course they know —" The President stopped himself, leaned toward Shafer. "I'm tired of your attitude, Ellis."

"Me, I'm tired of you holding people without trial. Was John ever going to see a judge? Or was this a permanent vacation?"

"Eight months," Wells said, "if I didn't get moved to another carrier the night before we landed."

Shafer and the President stared holes in each other until Duto clapped his hands and startled them both.

"I take it we all view this the same way," Duto said. "The Russians know what happened. They've decided to play banker of last resort for our friend. In return, he's letting them use his casinos as honey traps. They figure you won't go public, because you haven't so far. Duberman knows this will end badly, but he doesn't see any other options. Especially with John running around shooting his bodyguards."

"More or less," Green said.

"I further take it that they are correct?" Duto said to the President. "That you *still* won't go public? That you intend to ride this ship all the way down."

The President looked at Wells. "I want you to kill him."

"I'm right *here,*" Duto said. "At least wait until I take a piss to put out the hit."

"Bunch of comedians."

"No, that's Graham Greene," Shafer said.

"Yesterday I was locked up in a floating dungeon because you were protecting your buddy," Wells said. "Now he's gone too far, and the Russians have you scared to use the agency, so you come running. Everybody's favorite off-the-books option. And I'm supposed to pretend we're friends."

"What can I say? I was wrong. I didn't think —"

"That it would leak? That someone would figure out how to use it?"

"I understand how it looks —"

"Just tell me," Wells said. "You ever plan to take care of Duberman?"

The President's silence was the only answer Wells needed.

"You get to clean this one up all by yourself."

"John," Green said. "However we got here, this is what you wanted, right? Nobody in your way. Line him up, take him down however you like. You finally get the guy at the top."

"Not quite." Wells stood, turned for the door.

Green opened her attaché case, came out with a slim file. "I wondered if the Russians really are protecting Duberman or just bluffing. So I asked Garry Wright to check our surveillance on the FSB station over there. Look for an uptick in action, new faces. NSA pulled some files, too."

"I care because —"

Green handed the file to Wells. "Anyone you know?"

She obviously knew the answer, because Wells didn't have to look past the first photo. *Mikhail Buvchenko.* He hadn't even bothered to disguise himself, not that he could. He was big enough to be visible from space. Wells wondered why the Russians were using Buvchenko. He wasn't a real FSB officer. The answer could only be that they knew of his connection to Salome and Wells.

"What happened to the Red Notice?"

"Best guess, they gave him a diplo passport."

"Donna tells me if he'd had his way, you'd be doing time in a Russian prison right now," the President said.

And if you had yours, I'd be doing it in the Pacific Ocean.

"Two for the price of one," Green said.

"Could you lay it on any thicker?" Wells said.

But Green and the President had pulled the winning card from the bottom of the deck. Wells wanted Buvchenko even more than he wanted the President to pay. "I'll think about it." Wells knew as he spoke that he'd already agreed. Like any good whore, he was only arguing over price.

"Take your time."

■ ■ ■ ■

Inevitably, after they left the White House, Shafer dragged Wells back to Shirley's. The bar hadn't improved. In fact, Wells could have sworn that no one in the place had moved in the four months since their last trip. Again they sat at the bar and Shafer ordered a shot for himself and Bud for Wells.

"Do me a favor and don't get sloppy this time," Wells said.

"I wasn't sloppy."

"You practically confessed your love for Orson Nye."

"I only said he smelled good." Shafer sniffed at the shot. "Speaking of, should I be concerned about the faint odor of turpentine I'm picking up out of this?"

"At your age, a preservative is probably helpful."

"The answer I hoped to hear." Shafer put the glass to his lips. "Umm. Wonderfully terrible. So how do we do this?"

"I didn't hear myself agree to anything."

"We all did."

"Don't you ever get tired of being used?"

"Never."

Wells tried to imagine weaknesses in Duberman's security. None came to mind.

"What about Orli?" Shafer said.

"I told you, from what Roberts said, she was on board."

"Was," Shafer said. "Maybe she reconsidered after two guys she knew got shot in the street. If we can find a way to talk to her without him finding out —"

"She'll go running back to him."

"Worst case, that leaves us where we are now."

"Fine. You have any way to reach her?"

Shafer raised his empty glass. "Matter of fact, I do."

16

BEIJING

Duberman had made Buvchenko promise the FSB wouldn't let Cheung hurt any girls. Instead, he and the Russians would trick Cheung into thinking that he'd had sex. The drugs and booze would erase Cheung's memory. As added leverage, Duberman would tape Cheung admitting his pedophilic desires.

You're sure he'll say what he wants, Buvchenko said.

By the time it happens, he'll be blind drunk. Plus he'll think it's just me and him.

Are you sure? You can do this?

Yes.

I hope.

And Duberman had. One week ago this night. He'd badgered Cheung into confessing what he craved, then gave him a shot of tequila spiked with Dilaudid, a powerful opiate. The drug hit Cheung in seconds. He staggered toward the baccarat table, pupils pinprick-tight, tongue lolling like an over-heated dog's. After Chou-Lai led him away, Duberman gave Xiao and Jian a million-dollar plaque each, warned them never to tell anyone what they'd seen.

Then Duberman was alone. And exhausted. The fire stairs smelled of freshly poured concrete as he walked up to the helipad atop the Sky Tower. Only a waist-high wall protected him from the five-hundred-fifty-meter drop. A southerly wind swept away the smog from a thousand Guangdong factories. Beneath Duberman, casinos rose from land that had once been sea. From above they looked strikingly similar, Y-shaped forty-story hotels rising beside flat-roofed sheds big as city blocks. Underneath those sheds, casinos. Even at this hour, thousands of people stood inside them, casting chips on tables. Ants marching, only they were taking food *from* their nests. Above, Duberman, a wingless Icarus. Fitting that all his scheming had brought him here. Without Macao, he would have been just another billionaire.

The territory was a hilly speck of land bordered by the People's Republic on one side, the South China Sea on the others. Portugal had controlled it for hundreds of years before returning it to China in 1999. Under Portuguese rule, a couple of grubby casinos had survived on Hong Kong day-trippers. The Chinese government decided to expand the business. It offered Western casino companies the chance at licenses. But established operators like MGM hesitated. Macao was rundown and corrupt, a distant second fiddle to Hong Kong.

Still, the opportunity intrigued Duberman. Gambling was practically the Chinese national sport. Yet the People's Republic banned casinos within its borders. Macao would give them a chance to bet legally. Duberman saw Macao as a city-sized version of the Sizzlin' Saloon, a dump with potential and a great location. In 2001, he and another Vegas outsider, Sheldon Adelson, grabbed licenses.

The decision was the most lucrative of Duberman's life. Wall Street analysts mocked him when he said Macao might one day be as big as the Las Vegas Strip. He was wrong. Within a decade Macao was far larger. As it exploded, so did 88 Gamma's stock, and Duberman's wealth. By the middle of the aughts, he was worth ten billion dollars. An unthinkable sum.

He had grown up middle-class. After World War II, his parents had emigrated from Shanghai to Atlanta. They were cautious and thrifty, and encouraged the same habits in their kids. At thirteen, Duberman bagged groceries at the local Winn-Dixie for spending money. A wrestling scholarship paid his college tuition. Into his thirties, he lived in a one-bedroom apartment near McCarran Airport. Aside from his appetite for women, he had no vices, no expensive habits. Mainly he worked. He enjoyed casinos, at once the most ethereal and the grittiest of businesses.

What do people buy from us? he asked his new managers every year. *The regulars know they'll walk out poorer than they entered. They should, anyway. They're buying the chance to step out of themselves, live in the moment, risk everything on a card. Then the money runs out, the moment ends. We are the ultimate expression of consumer culture. We sell a product that doesn't exist. They leave with nothing. Yet if we do it right, they leave happy. They're buying* time.

Duberman wanted his customers to leave happy. But part of him hated them, too. For their stupidity. Their greed. Their inability to understand that their desires mattered not at all to the games they played. Math governed his palaces, and math alone would undo the people on the wrong side of the tables. They talked of running hot, but if they stayed too long a chill inevitable as death gripped them. Duberman wished they would see his casinos as places to be entertained for a day or two. On the surveillance cameras, he recognized the ones who had given too much. They trudged out slow as cancer patients, glancing slyly over their shoulders at paradise lost. He took their blood by the gallon. Yet they wished for his grace as desperately as Adam and Eve.

His best customers were fools, and fools were hard to love.

He escaped the contradiction with logistics, making sure visitors had the best possible experience, however they gambled. Each 88 Gamma casino was a giant enclosed city, with malls and Broadway-sized theaters, serving thousands of meals and handling millions of dollars in cash every hour. Duberman learned to lavish attention and money where customers noticed, skimp where they didn't. His obsession with details made his casinos even more popular. Ten billion dollars was only the start. The money flowed to him quick as air.

Inevitably, he picked up the trappings of wealth, mansions and bodyguards, modern art and classic cars. Yet he couldn't escape the idea that somehow God had played a joke on him, giving him so much more money than he could ever spend. He found himself increasingly interested in his Jewish faith. He never forgot that if his parents hadn't fled Vienna, the Nazis would have sent them to the concentration camps, and he would never have been born.

Duberman came to believe that only a powerful Israel could permanently keep Jews safe. He supported right-wing Israeli politicians. He bought mansions in Tel Aviv and Jerusalem and spent months every year in Israel. Then he met Salome. She worked for one of his politicians. Like him, she understood that an Iranian nuclear bomb was the greatest threat to the Jewish state. She proposed that Duberman pay for a plot to frighten the United States into attacking Iran. A false-flag operation, she called it.

The plan was the longest of long shots. It was also treason. Yet Duberman agreed. Without sleeping on the choice, without wondering if Salome was trapping him somehow. As he made all his biggest decisions, borrowing from Jimmy the Roller, risking his fortune on Macao. In this way, he was like his customers, slapdash mystics who waggled their fingers and demanded more cards, whatever the odds. *I just knew a seven was coming.*

Sure you did.

At the time, the decision seemed noble. Necessary, even. In retrospect, Duberman wondered if his fortune had changed him more than he knew. Had he unconsciously grown to believe that he was, if not God, at least a saint, anointed by the almighty dollar? He knew he'd had a harder time imagining his own death as the billions mounted. He couldn't die. Men like him *didn't* die.

Was it not his right to start a war?

With that choice, he'd thrown all the others away.

Orli's modeling shoot in Australia had ended three days after Wells shot Peretz and Makiv. Duberman knew her bodyguards had told her about the killings. But when he called her, she didn't answer or call back. Finally, on the third day, she texted: *Home tomorrow. Face-to-face.* Part of him wondered whether she was returning only to collect the boys and take them to Israel. He showed the text to Gideon.

"Did you say anything? About the Russians?"

"I work for you."

"No half answers, Gideon."

"Not a word. And I won't." Gideon shook his head: *You want to lie to your wife, it's your business. Just don't say I didn't warn you.*

The next morning, Duberman waited at the VIP terminal at HKIA, clutching a fat bouquet of blue orchids. Orli's favorite. She stepped through the frosted glass doors of the immigration checkpoint tan and lean and more beautiful than ever, the sun shining from every strand of her honey-blond hair. No wonder he'd lost his perspective on his place in the universe. He tried to hug her. She raised her arms to fend him off, looked at him clinically, as she had that night in Tel Aviv when the Shin Bet came.

"How was the shoot? Was that little photographer there, the one you don't like?"

"What happened?"

"Let's do this at home."

"What happened?"

"Not here. You'll understand when I tell you the details." He'd bet his fortune that the Chinese security services had this terminal bugged.

The eight-minute helicopter ride from Lantau Island to the Peak felt like a month. She led him straight to their bedroom after they landed. "Now."

"You were never in danger, Orli."

Her face tightened and he knew he'd

made a mistake.

"You think I was *scared*?"

"Of course not —"

"Start again, then. It was Wells?"

"It must have been. It feels like a one-man show, and that's his specialty. And the CIA wouldn't aim for two random bodyguards."

"That's what you call them? Avi and Uri? After how many years?"

For the first time since they'd come to Hong Kong, Duberman felt irritated with her. "You know, I'm the one who had to identify them. The police came here, asked me about it. Wanted to know if I knew who did it."

"Did you tell them about Wells?"

Duberman shook his head, explained how they were caught between the Hong Kong police, Wells, and the President. He didn't mention the FSB.

"So what are you going to do?"

You. Not *we.* He decided he needed to tell her the truth about Cheung. Part of it, anyway. "There's a Chinese general, senior, who's run into trouble at 88 Gamma. A lot of trouble —"

"You're going to spy on the Chinese?"

A Mossad-trained technician swept the mansion for bugs each month. Reflective coatings covered its windows to defeat the laser microphones used by spy services to pick up the vibrations that voices created in glass. Still, Duberman found himself raising a finger to his lips.

"You see why I didn't want to talk about this at the airport."

"This can't work, Aaron."

"I have help."

"From where?"

The letters *FSB* were on his lips. "I can't tell you. Safer for us both. Truly." Though he wanted her to ask again. If she did, he'd tell her, let her decide.

She didn't. "If it works, what then? You trade what you find to the Americans and hope it's enough to buy your freedom?"

"More or less." Duberman wondered as he spoke whether her idea didn't make more sense than Buvchenko's bargain. Maybe he should go directly to the White House. But Wells and Duto would never agree, and Duto controlled the CIA. No. The Russians were all he had.

She looked past him to the city below. "If the police make us leave —"

"They're bluffing, trying to pressure me."

"*If.* I'm taking the boys back to Israel."

"Let's cross that bridge when we come to it." *Or never.* He didn't understand how she could so casually threaten to take away their sons, his sons, after she'd promised to stay with him. No matter, though. Even if the police followed through on their threat, a Russian diplomatic passport would give them new options. London and New York would still be out, but Rio and even Paris might not be. However much she disliked Russia, once he showed her what he'd done, she would see he'd made the right choice.

"Time, Orli. That's all I'm asking."

She came to him, wrapped a hand around his neck. She seemed about to kiss him and her face was the world. She brushed her lips to his ear, whispered: "I'm not the one you have to worry about."

That afternoon, Hargrove Lo, the chief of detectives for the Hong Kong police, came back to the mansion to blush his way through a ten-minute interview with Orli. He followed up the next morning with Duberman, polite but dogged, asking the same questions a dozen different ways. When the interview was done, Lo admitted that his detectives didn't have a suspect. Their inability to make headway made Duberman's own protestations of ignorance more convincing. Still, Duberman knew he needed to do more. He called Geoffrey Crandall, the lawyer handling his residency application.

Crandall was Hong Kong legal royalty. He'd argued more cases before the territory's Court of Final Appeal than anyone else. "Aaron. I understand the police visited again —"

"Can you make a list of the best five or seven charities here? Ones above reproach?"

"Certainly. Tung Wah, Caritas — why, if you don't mind my asking?"

"This week. I'm giving them two hundred million — no, three hundred million HK."

"You want to pledge —"

"Not pledge. *Give.* As in, the money hits as soon as they accept. Split it however you like. Keep my name out of it."

"I should probably hire another lawyer to handle it, then. Our relationship is no secret, and a donation of this size —"

Exactly. "I'd like you to take care of it yourself."

Crandall fell silent.

"I imagine you'd like to do this as quickly as possible," he finally said.

"Correct."

"I'll send a list."

Crandall called back two days later, after Duberman made the donations.

"Aaron. I'm pleased to report that the police have dropped their threat of immediate deportation. However, you and your family still have to apply for a visa when the hundred-eighty-day waiver expires." Duberman's American passport gave him an automatic 180-day exemption from Hong Kong's visa rules. The countdown had started when he arrived from Israel. "And the police plan to recommend that the immigration department reject that application. Of course, if circumstances change, their position might as well."

Three hundred million dollars had bought him less than three months in the territory. An expensive rental. Luckily, he could afford it.

Now Duberman had some time. Too bad he couldn't have helped the police find Wells even if he'd wanted to. The man had vanished. Maybe he feared that the cops were closing on him and had left Hong Kong. Maybe he was lying low and waiting for another chance.

William Roberts was gone, too. He'd quit before they could put him on leave, disappearing from the mansion on the afternoon Peretz and Makiv were shot and never coming back. After four days, Duberman sent

Gideon and his men to Roberts's apartment. They found it cleaned out, his family gone. The disappearance had to be related to Wells, but Duberman couldn't see how. He wondered if Roberts was helping Wells plan an attack on the mansion. But with each day, that explanation became less plausible.

In any case, Duberman had bigger problems. The Russians wouldn't protect him until he delivered Cheung. He needed to convince Cheung to come down. To be sure that that ninny Malcolm Garten didn't hear about the trip. And to be sure that the Chinese security services didn't stumble on Cheung.

Ten days after the shootings, Duberman helicoptered to Macao to meet Buvchenko. As he flew in, he saw his new casino towering over Cotai, its structural work finished months before, ready to open as soon as the workers installed beds and furniture and of course the baccarat tables. He realized he was looking at the perfect four-billion-dollar excuse.

Cheung had bitten. Now Duberman stood on the roof of the Sky, looking at the bridges that connected Cotai with the old Macao. Cheung was out there, an 88 Gamma limousine delivering him to an apartment north of the city center. Duberman had already sent Buvchenko the video of Cheung demanding *nine, ten, eleven at most.* Past that, he didn't know and didn't want to know what the Russians had planned.

He stepped onto the concrete wall at the edge of the roof, peeked down the glass cliff. A third of a mile straight down. From this height, the avenues and bridges below were as tiny and perfect as the veins in his palm. To jump, unthinkable. Duberman thought back to his high school physics class, the acceleration of gravity, nine-point-eight meters per second. Sixteen feet the first second, almost fifty the second . . . he couldn't do the math. Ten seconds of free fall, more, accelerating the whole way. Yet at the World Trade Center that day, dozens of men and women had smashed windows and chosen air over fire.

Unthinkable? Nothing was unthinkable when the inferno came.

The wind picked up, caught him in a gust, pushed him to the edge of the wall, his alligator boots scuffing the concrete. He windmilled his arms as desperately as a cartoon character, heart thumping madly, eighteen hundred feet —

Not now —

The gust died and he turned and stepped onto the roof. He went to a knee and stared up into the sky. The light pollution from the casinos occluded the stars, and he could see only a few unnaturally bright specks that had to be satellites. So far from God, so close to the FSB. If he escaped this trap, he would make good on all his promises. He would find a hundred worthy charities. He would spend more time with his sons. He would, he would.

He heard his helicopter before he saw its lights. He looked around, not realizing at first that it was flying *below* the casino's roofline. Finally, he spotted it, a Bell 429, rising toward him in the dark. Its spotlight flicked on and it approached the giant encircled *H* painted in white on the roof and set down with an odd balletic grace. He dodged the rotor wash and ran for it. For Hong Kong and his family.

As the helicopter leapt into the sky, Duberman knew he'd beaten fate once again.

Or not.

He met Buvchenko the next day in a two-room Kowloon office rented by an 88 Gamma subsidiary. Gideon waited outside with the two FSB officers who chaperoned Buvchenko everywhere.

Buvchenko put his palms together, offered a mocking bow. "Sensei."

"It went all right?"

"Perfect."

"And the girl?"

"We killed her."

Duberman tried to speak, couldn't. The room's sour air seemed to choke him.

"You think we could leave her to cry to the police after what that pig did to her? Anyway, she was just a whore. She's better off. Trust me."

"Mikhail —"

Buvchenko squeezed his shoulder. *Buddies.* "Don't look so shocked. I'm joking. She's hundred percent good. Back in Vietnam where she belongs. Nothing happened."

"If I wanted to see her —"

"Go to Hanoi."

"Hanoi has ten million people."

"We're partners now, Aaron. We have to trust. I tell you the girl is fine, she's fine."

Duberman made himself ignore the voice in his head: *She's dead. You know she's dead.*

"Our turn to keep our promise. Our ambassador calls the White House today, makes sure they understand, you are one of us."

One of us. *I'm one of* you *now.* "It can't be that easy."

"Let them complain. It means nothing. Just like Ukraine."

"Wells?"

Buvchenko waved Wells away. "We'll take care of him, too, if he's dumb enough to try. Bonus for you. Smile, Aaron. You're free."

"Arbeit macht frei."

Buvchenko reached into a paper bag, came out with a high-necked bottle of Grey Goose, two shot glasses. Buvchenko handed Duberman the bottle, held up the glasses. "Why Grey Goose, not Smirnoff, Stoli? Because Smirnoff is *dermo,* and Stoli I couldn't find."

Duberman poured two glasses.

"Budem zdoroby," Buvchenko said. "To our health."

They clinked and drank. Buvchenko took the bottle, poured two more. "We have a saying, between the first toast and the second, a bullet doesn't pass."

"It's a stupid saying." Duberman raised his glass. *"L'chaim."*

"First the German, now the Hebrew. Be glad Nikolai and Sergei don't hear you talk like a Yid."

"Not everyone is as cosmopolitan as you,

Mikhail."

Again they drank.

"You'll let me know what the White House says?" Duberman set his empty glass down, turned for the door. And felt Buvchenko's hand on his shoulder.

"Aaron. Before you leave. One request. You go to Beijing in, let's say, a week."

"I don't —"

"No *don't*, no *can't*, you *can* and you *will*. The general expects you."

Duberman closed his eyes. Why had he expected anything else? *A nightmare, I just need to wake up.* When he opened them again, nothing had changed. "What's my excuse?"

"88 Gamma wants new planes. With so many of your best customers Chinese, what better way to show your respect than to buy this new Chinese plane —"

"The average Chinese billionaire would rather ride a Gulfstream."

"You are *investing* in the *community.*" Buvchenko grinned, the smile that said, *I'm smarter than I look. But not quite smart enough to keep that fact to myself.* "Anyway, it's just an excuse for you to meet. You give him something, take something back —"

"They catch me, they'll kill me."

"No one catches you. No one even looks.

Everyone likes your casinos, and besides, you're richer than they are. All they care about, the Chinese. The famous Aaron Duberman, the thirty-billion-dollar man. You have a nice meeting with Cheung, he takes you up in one of those stupid planes, you give him this." Buvchenko tossed Duberman a thumb drive, gray and anonymous. "He gives you the same thing, that's it. I probably don't need to tell you this, but don't open them, please. Or lose them. When you're back, you call me."

A nice meeting.

"How do I look him in the eye after what happened? And vice versa?"

"Chinese, you barely see their eyes, anyway." Buvchenko grinned. "Probably don't talk about his last little trip to Macao. Don't worry, he won't, either. The past is for God, the future is for the tsars." He poured himself another shot and drank it down.

"You're full of advice today."

Buvchenko shrugged.

"Tell me again about the girl." Duberman knew he sounded like a child asking for reassurance.

"The girl's fine. Promise."

An answer Duberman chose to accept. Because, truly, what else could he do?

He walked out to find Gideon standing as

far from the Russians as the room would allow. "Everything all right, *boss*?" An unsubtle emphasis on the last word. The distance between them widening by the day. The FSB hadn't destroyed him, not yet, but it had destroyed their friendship. The lies and elisions were corroding his life with Orli, too.

What happened with the general? she'd asked, as they lay in bed after he came back from Macao.

It'll need a few days to sort out, but it worked.

You sure you know what you're doing?

He'd nodded and she'd reached for him. But he couldn't help feeling that for the first time in his life, he was about to be the recipient of pity sex.

What would he tell her now? Nothing. He'd tell her nothing.

Beijing. He'd never liked the city, choked with smog and traffic and twenty million Chinese. Yet here he was, to pick up secrets for the FSB. From a man who had probably raped a ten-year-old girl. Gideon wasn't coming, his excuse that he needed to travel with Orli. Her agents had called two days before with the surprising news that a director who wasn't Michael Bay wanted her to come to Tokyo to talk about a part.

She hadn't wanted to leave the boys again on short notice, but decided that she couldn't miss the chance. Anyway, Tokyo was only about five hours from Hong Kong. She could be there and back in less than a day. He'd encouraged her. She needed the distraction.

As Duberman walked down the Jetway, Cheung stepped out of a waiting Mercedes limousine. He wore full dress uniform, a general's stars and wings on his shoulder boards. He was composed, relaxed, nothing like the madman Duberman had seen the week before. He extended a hand. Duberman tried to imagine that he felt skin and not scales as they shook.

"Mr. Duberman, I've heard so much about you," Cheung said, through the interpreter beside him.

"Call me Aaron."

"Aaron, then. You know I've been to your casinos. It's a pleasure to meet you at last."

Smoothwind's factory was clean as a three-star kitchen. Duberman found to his mild surprise that Cheung had a professional presentation prepared for him on the jet, mocked-up cabins and 3-D renderings. The Smoothwind was thirty percent cheaper than the Gulfstream it copied, with better fuel efficiency. For a few minutes, Duberman immersed himself in the presentation and forgot the thumb drive that lay in his pocket like a cyanide capsule.

"Have I convinced you?"

"I like what I see. But none of this matters until we fly it."

"I hoped you'd say that." Cheung stood. "Please, come with me."

Outside, the jet waited, long and sleek and painted a shocking red. "Not the usual color, but we wanted to make a statement."

The interpreter bowed to Duberman. "The general asks me to stay here. He says that if you have any questions, save them for later. For now, he wants you to relax and focus on the flight experience."

"The flight experience. Yes."

They sat side by side in the Smoothwind's brown leather seats. As the jet rolled down the runway, Duberman couldn't shake the feeling that it would crash. A fitting end. But it rose easily. As it leveled off, Cheung extracted a gray thumb drive and placed it on the armrest between them as carefully as an addict chopping a line. Duberman fumbled in his pocket, handed over his own drive.

They passed the rest of the flight in silence. Duberman had a thousand questions, but wouldn't have asked a single one even if Cheung spoke perfect English. The answers no longer mattered. All he and the man beside him needed to know was that they had both chosen the same master.

17

Orli couldn't help feeling disloyal. But she was glad to escape. From Hong Kong, from the mansion, from her husband most of all. Three months ago, when he'd told her, the giddiness she'd felt had surprised her. He'd tried to start a war. Spectacular insanity. What no one understood about Aaron was that for all his calculation, at heart he was a dreamer. Greedy dreams, but then weren't the best dreams greedy? *I want riches beyond measure, a beautiful woman half my age, the sun never to set on my empire . . .*

So they had to leave Israel. For a while. It would take them back. After all, Aaron had done what he'd done to *save* it. Meantime, they would be the world's richest refugees. No overloaded ships or internment camps for them. They would live in splendor, an army of bodyguards watching over them.

391

But in the month since Wells had shot Uri and Avi, the reality of her new life had set in. Even a thirty-room mansion could be a prison. She wasn't scared, not exactly. But she woke in the deep of the night wondering what Wells or the Americans or the police would do next. The Chinese, too, now that Aaron was making them his enemy. His and hers and their sons. She didn't care what happened to her, as long as the boys were safe.

Aaron had always carried himself like a stallion who'd just won the Kentucky Derby, head high, eyes bright. Now a shadow shaded his face, mold inching into an abandoned house. He no longer strode. He walked. Slowly. For the first time, he seemed *old*. He hadn't given up, she knew. He was still fighting. But he seemed to fear that his struggling was only tightening the knots that bound him. He was lying to her, too, or, if not lying, not telling the whole truth. She wondered if he had already made a deal with the Chinese or the Americans.

They hadn't had sex much lately, but a couple days before, she'd felt nauseated and wondered if she might be pregnant. When she saw the single line on the stick — *not pregnant* — she felt nothing but relief.

Why not leave, then? Take the twins, go

home to Tel Aviv? But she couldn't abandon Aaron yet. She'd never told him, or anyone, but during those last months with Jamie, she'd started to use. To keep up, to stay cool — *cool* being the ultimate prize for any rocker not named Chris Martin. Needles scared her, thank God. Even so, by the end, she'd been more than dabbling. She had her own stash.

Then Aaron came along, with his energy and cars and *money,* yes, all that money. The whole getting-high-and-lying-in-a-dark-hotel-room thing seemed ridiculous as it was. Plus he was the best lover she'd had in years, unashamed, almost gleeful for the pleasure they had. She knew he'd been around, but all that sex seemed to have taken him past cynicism to an innocence of sorts: *We're here, we're doing this, might as well enjoy it.*

She'd flushed the Baggies down the toilet after their first time together. A bad few days, and then the itch faded. After a couple of months, she hardly thought about the stuff. When she did, she tried to remember it like the most terrible flight she'd ever had, London to Rio in July, suffering through hour after hour of mid-Atlantic turbulence so terrible she couldn't believe the 747 would survive. *Thank God I got through.*

Still, she feared the pull of the drug enough to turn down an epidural when she delivered the twins. Aaron didn't deserve the credit for her quitting. He hadn't even known. Yet she gave it to him, anyway. She worried that leaving him might open the door to a relapse. Stupid. She hadn't been a mother back then. Children changed everything.

Knowing the fear didn't make sense didn't help her shake it.

So she stayed. But with each day, the negatives grew more obvious, the positives harder to see. The scale had nearly tipped. Under the circumstances, the call from CAA had come as a godsend, a clean excuse to get away for a day. A Spanish director who went by a single name, Inaguyo, wanted to talk to her about a sci-fi adventure he would be shooting later in the year. Even better, he was in Tokyo promoting his *Godzilla* remake. She wouldn't have to go across the Pacific.

"Can you send me a script?" she asked her agent, who had the only-in-Hollywood name of Tiffany DeBeers. Orli had never asked if it was real.

"You have to meet him first. If he likes you, he'll show you some pages, ask you to read."

"Sketchy."

"I promise you, whatever he's got will be a big step up from *Grown Ups 2*. Look, he'll only be in Tokyo until the end of the week —"

Now here she was, at the Park Hyatt Tokyo, the hotel Sofia Coppola made famous in *Lost in Translation,* one of her all-time favorites. A good sign, surely. Even better, Inaguyo had the Presidential Suite, where Bill Murray and Scarlett Johansson had flopped around without ever having sex. Orli looked forward to seeing the room, though she knew that even the most luxurious hotels couldn't offer anything she didn't have already. One of the hidden disappointments of the billionaire's life.

The meeting was scheduled for 8 p.m. Good timing. She spent the morning with the twins before putting them down for their after-lunch nap and heading for Tokyo.

Normally, she traveled with two bodyguards. This time, Gideon had insisted on coming, too, instead of sticking with Aaron, who was flying to Beijing to meet the general he was trying to trap.

How can you be sure this guy won't lock you up? Orli had asked him the night before.

I have something on him he can't beat.

Three months ago, even a month, she would have demanded details. Instead she rolled away and tried to sleep.

At the Hyatt, she followed Gideon off the elevator. The suite's door was propped open with a black binder with a white label on which the single word INTERGALACTIC was written. Orli picked up the binder, found it empty. Strange. Gideon knocked, led her inside.

The living room was ten meters long and nearly as wide, and featured dark wooden floors and a spectacular view over central Tokyo, the city's neon coming alive as the day ended. Water bottles sat on a coffee table near the windows. The room was empty, the doors to the bedrooms closed.

"Inaguyo? Mr. Inaguyo?" Orli hoped she was pronouncing his name right.

"Be right out. Make yourself comfortable." He sounded American to Orli, no trace of a Spanish accent.

"This is wrong," Gideon said. He pulled his pistol, stepped between Orli and the bedroom door as it opened and a man in a white shirt and jeans stepped out.

"Easy," he said, in Hebrew. "We just want to talk." Another man followed him, a little guy, older than Aaron, nearly bald. The bags under his eyes made Orli want to call her makeup artist.

Behind them, two more men walked into the suite. Now her other guards drew their pistols, too. Gideon put an arm around Orli, backed her toward the door. "Let's go."

"Orli, I promise you'll want to hear what we have to say," the old man said.

She did. Whoever these men were, she was sure they didn't plan to shoot her in the Park Hyatt Tokyo Presidential Suite. "Put the gun away, Gideon." He hesitated. "Now."

Gideon holstered his pistol. The door to the second bedroom opened. A man stepped out, tall, broad-shouldered, handsome, the faintest touch of gray in his brown hair.

"Wells," Gideon said, the single word conveying an encyclopedia's worth of disgust.

"Chai-chai." Wells and the old guy sat down. Orli took the couch across from theirs, with Gideon standing behind her.

"I'm sorry we lied." Wells sounded like a cowboy at a campfire, his voice low, almost guttural. She had to lean in to hear. Wells was responsible for all their trouble. He'd killed Uri and Avi. She'd expected to hate him on sight. But she didn't. He looked at her almost shyly, like an old friend who didn't want to break bad news.

"For what it's worth, we hear Inaguyo's a jerk," the old man said. "Handsy type. I'm Ellis Shafer. I work for the agency."

The first agency that came to mind was CAA. Then she realized he meant the one with the *I* in the middle. "Did Tiffany know?" She couldn't believe her agent would lie to her this way. Though why not? Agents lied all the time.

"We told her we needed a safe way to contact you without your husband finding out."

"This is crazy. You make up this story, drag me to Tokyo, why?" Maybe she'd have the chance to act in this room after all. She prepared to be surprised when they told her about the Iran plot.

"We know you know," Shafer said.

"I know *what*?"

"It's okay," Wells said.

"I'm telling you I have no idea —"

"William Roberts —"

"Who?"

"Now you're just being stupid," Shafer said, and a flare bloomed in her stomach. People so often assumed she was dumb because of the way she looked. "Of course you know Roberts. Your head of security in Hong Kong until he stopped coming to work."

"Sure."

"Roberts told me you said I was stalking you," Wells said.

"I've never even met you —"

"Exactly," Shafer said. "So we know you know. Otherwise, why say something so stupid?" He emphasized the last word, and she knew he was baiting her. "You knew the real reason that John was after your husband and wanted to give Roberts a halfway decent excuse for all the extra security."

Gideon started yammering in Hebrew at the mention of Roberts's name. "Quiet," she said. "Give me a minute." The interruption gave her a chance to regroup, but she couldn't imagine how to explain what she'd told Roberts.

"It's a lie." The lamest possible excuse.

"We'll call him," Shafer said. "You two can discuss."

They weren't guessing. They *knew.*

"Okay, you got me, Aaron gave Roberts that story and I went with it." Not a quiver in her face. After so many years in front of a camera, she could control every muscle. She wasn't going to show weakness. Or ask forgiveness. Even if that was what they wanted. Especially if that was they wanted.

"Why?"

She'd known what the world thought

when she married Aaron. And her friends. *How long's the prenup? Bet you already have a divorce lawyer picked out . . .* She didn't care, they were wrong, she meant her vows. To betray him now —

But truth seemed the only option. "What you said. He told me what he'd done, the whole plot, told me you might come after him."

"When was that?"

She had an odd impulse to plead guilty, though she was innocent. If not for the twins, maybe she would have. Just to see how they'd respond. "If you're asking if I knew before, the answer's no. This was after. The Prime Minister met him, said we had to leave Israel."

"He told you, and you went with him to Hong Kong anyway."

"I wanted my boys to be close to their father."

Wells craned his head at those words like a dog who'd heard a whistle meant only for him.

"Life lessons for the kiddies?" Shafer said. "How to start a war in three easy steps."

Wells reached into the binder, slid a picture to her. "You know him?"

Inside, surveillance photos of a man who was almost cartoonishly large. He had Slavic

features, cruel eyes and thin lips. *Russian.*
She couldn't be sure how she knew, she'd
never seen him before, but she did. Her
parents had fled men like him. Maybe the
revulsion that she felt was in her genes.

"Mikhail Buvchenko," Shafer said.

"Nice guy," Wells said. "Likes shooting
horses."

"Mikhail works for the FSB," Shafer said.
"For the last month or so, he's been in
Hong Kong. He and his buddies have
something going with your husband."

A lie, surely. Yet for the first time, she
wondered if she had misjudged Aaron. "Not
the Russians, Aaron knows what I think of
them —" She looked over her shoulder at
Gideon. He wouldn't meet her eye.

"Something else you don't know. Last
week the Russian ambassador to the U.S.
told the White House that one Aaron Duberman has applied for political asylum in
Russia —"

"That's not possible —"

"Not possible, certain. It happened. Don't
believe me, ask your husband. For him, his
loving wife, kids, too. The Kremlin's already
warning us not to interfere. So how about
that, the twins speaking Russian, going back
to the homeland? Back in the USSR, you
don't know how lucky you are —"

401

A low grunt escaped her. Surprise that sounded like pleasure and came from the same root, *I didn't know I could feel this way.* To think that a minute before, she'd blamed herself for betraying Aaron.

At least now she understood why he was so sure that he could use whatever the Chinese general gave him. She stood, looked at Gideon. "Is it true?" He didn't answer, and she knew. She knew, and still she wanted him to say so. "Is it?" Her voice rose, echoed off the windows.

"I warned him," Gideon said. "I told him, when Buvchenko came, he wouldn't listen —"

"This man came to our *house*? And you didn't tell me."

"You know what I owe him." His voice a whisper.

"Go. *Go.*"

"He should stay," Shafer said. "We have questions for him."

She wanted to argue, but what difference did Gideon make, anyway? He was no one. Not after this. She sat down again. Wells slid across more photos.

"More Russians?" She didn't know them, either.

"Correct. We figure your husband and the FSB made a deal, protection in return for

402

access to the people who come to his casinos," Shafer said. "Gideon, know anything about that?" The third American, the one who spoke Hebrew, translated.

Gideon didn't answer.

"You can't save him now, it's over," Shafer said.

Orli heard these words in a strange stereo, English and then Hebrew, as if some cruel god wanted to pound the truth into her —

"Tell him." Speaking to Gideon in Hebrew, but looking at Wells. "Whatever you know, tell him."

Then all at once she felt motion behind her. Wells put his hands up. She turned to see that Gideon had pulled his pistol on Wells. Meanwhile, the two other Americans by the door had drawn their own guns on Gideon, and *her* guards on the Americans. She imagined bullets stretching the air, winking at each other as they passed. She knew she should be afraid, but she was only annoyed. Men. Any excuse to whip out their guns.

Everyone in the room was itchy and wide-eyed except for Gideon and Wells, who stared at each other like two bucks about to lower their heads and charge. Wells had nothing in his hands, but he didn't seem to care.

"This what you want?" he said. "Gunfight at the Hyatt."

"Tell me why I shouldn't. For Avi, Uri, Adina, and all the others —" Gideon spoke Hebrew to Wells's English. They couldn't possibly have understood each other, but they did all the same.

"They paid their money, they took the ride." The words not cruel, but matter-of-fact. For the first time, Orli saw the steel under Wells's skin, saw why Gideon, who didn't fear anyone, feared him.

"You think you're going to live forever?" Gideon said. "That you won't be judged —"

"Enough," Orli said. "Put that little thing back in your pants before I get up and take it from you. Then tell them what you know."

"You don't want to hear what I know." An ironic smile curled Gideon's lips. She knew he was right, she would regret whatever he had to say. But they had all gone much too far to turn back.

"Now."

"Yes, Mrs. Duberman. Whatever you like." Gideon stuffed the pistol inside his waistband. After a moment, the other men nodded at one another and holstered their weapons, their faces half embarrassed, half relieved.

Gideon sat next to Orli, leaned toward Shafer. "You're right. Buvchenko came to us, offered this bargain, Aaron took it. He's already delivered his first fish. A Chinese air force general, Cheung is his name, Cheung Han, very senior —"

"He turned a PLAAF general?" Shafer said, after the other American translated. "In a month? How?"

"Cheung likes little girls —"

"You misunderstood." Orli's voice sounded strange in her own ears. "He wouldn't." Speaking not of Cheung, but her husband. "He's a good father —"

"I'm sorry, Orli, it's true. He brought Cheung to the new casino, the VIP room."

"It's not even open."

"Exactly. Brought him where no one could see and convinced him to admit what he wanted and gave him to the FSB. What happened after that, I don't know, but it must have worked or the Russians wouldn't be protecting him."

"How little?"

"What?"

Gideon was silent. "The girls, how little?"

"Gideon, I'm not sure exactly. Not, you know, developed." The shame made his voice a whisper.

"Prepubescent, you mean. *Children.*"

405

"It was only one —"

"Oh, good. Only one. And Aaron gave her to this general?" What had he said to her after he helicoptered back from Macao that night? *It worked.*

"Orli, I swear, I don't know what happened exactly. I didn't want to be part of it. That's why I wouldn't go to Beijing with him today."

What had her husband become? One step, another, the next . . . a man looked in the mirror and a wolf looked back. Now the tears came, and she was crying, not for herself but for him, the choices he'd made, the life he'd thrown away.

Yet beneath the sadness, fury. Aaron had no right to do this, betray her after what she'd told him about that day in Paris, make himself a criminal . . . to throw away the billions that belonged to their children. She hated thinking of the money so soon, but how could she not? It was overwhelming.

Though it hadn't saved her husband.

She was finished with him. She wiped the tears, knew she wouldn't cry again.

"I'm sorry," Wells said. "People go crazy when they're cornered."

"Go to hell."

The room was quiet for a moment.

Then Shafer stood. "Now that we've all

had a chance to *tell* each other how we *feel*
—"

"You, too, old man —"

"Gideon, when was the last time Aaron met Buvchenko?"

Gideon waited for the translation. Then: "A few days ago. Four or five."

"After Macao."

"Correct. That was when Buvchenko told him to go to Beijing."

"Do they have a contact number, a regular drop, anything like that?"

"I don't think so. Buvchenko came to the mansion the first time, but that wasn't set up, Aaron didn't know he was coming. Since then, Aaron calls him or he calls Aaron. They saw each other a few times in Macao to arrange this thing with Cheung. Last time, at an office Aaron has in Kowloon."

"You go every time?"

"So far. Two other FSB guys come to the meetings, too." Gideon picked out two photos from the stack that Wells had shown Orli. "These two. Nikolai and Sergei. Nikolai's the boss."

"But Buvchenko handles Aaron?"

Gideon nodded.

"Do you have Buvchenko's number, his email? Or the others'?"

"No. Probably on Aaron's phone, but I'm not sure. Maybe he memorizes it."

"If you asked him for it —"

"He'd wonder. He knows what I think of Buvchenko. You don't have eyes on the Russians already? You have these pictures —"

Shafer ignored the question. "What about you?" To Orli. "Can you get his phone?"

"Sure. I know his passcode. No secrets in our family." A smile died on her lips.

"Could he have a burner? A spare phone?"

"I don't think so."

"So will you?"

"Will I *what*?"

Shafer looked away from her. His exasperation might have been real, she couldn't tell.

"Get his phone for us. At least tell us if you hear him call Buvchenko."

She wanted to be out of this room, away from this man Shafer, his obnoxious questions, his demands.

"What if I don't?"

"We can help you, too," Wells said. "Protect you."

"How long? A month? Six months? I betray my husband, betray the Russians. You forget about what I've done soon enough. They never do."

"You don't want to help us, don't," Shafer said. "Either way, it might be best if you took your children to Israel as soon as possible."

"And you kill Aaron?"

"We won't be inviting him to any Fourth of July parties."

She shook her head: *Answer me.*

"It's a long shot, but if we can find a way to work with him we will," Wells said.

"Use him against the Russians and the Chinese, you mean." She was surprised how little she cared. "Something I don't get. My husband told me you used to work for the CIA, but you don't anymore."

"You can assume we speak for the government," Shafer said.

Now she saw. "The President wants to kill him without making the Russians mad."

"The President prizes flexibility."

"And nobody's more flexible than we are," Wells said.

She stood. "I'm going home, to talk to my husband —"

"That's a mistake."

"You're afraid he'll tell me you're lying?"

"I'm afraid you'll start something you can't stop."

"You can't seriously expect I'll desert him without talking to him."

"I thought he was in Beijing to meet the general, anyway," Shafer said to Gideon.

"Yes," Gideon said, after the translation. "But not staying over. Home tonight. He might be back already." He looked at Orli. "I'll pick up the boys. You go to Tel Aviv."

"You're a bigger fool than he is if you think I'd trust you after this." Anyway, she wanted to hear what Aaron had to say for herself. After five years and two kids, she owed him that much. Maybe Shafer and Wells had lied.

Though she knew they hadn't.

"When you decide what to do —" Shafer handed her a card, two mobile numbers, two email addresses. "Friendly advice. Sooner is better than later."

"For me or my husband?" She walked out without waiting for the answer.

After she left, Shafer dismissed the other Americans, grabbed his phone.

"I need a report on a Chinese general named Cheung Han, PLAAF, yes . . . Glad you've heard of him, that's your job. I'd like everything we have. In one hour . . . Yes, an hour. Pull your thumb out of your ass." He hung up without waiting for an answer.

"Channeling Duto?" Though Wells couldn't entirely blame Shafer for the attitude. After so many years on the margins, they finally had the full weight of the agency behind them. They'd had seven operatives on this floor, and they could have had more. They would leave Narita just after midnight on an agency charter, clear HKIA in the morning with clean passports — and, even more impressive, clean fingertips.

The Hong Kong immigration checkpoints had fingerprint scanners, of course. But the agency's Directorate of Science and Technology had found a way to beat the scanners, millimeter-thick molds made of a combination of silicon and gelatin. The molds carried real prints from the FBI's fingerprint database. The agency used prints only from people who had died before 2000, a ghoulish but effective way to be certain that the prints weren't already in immigration databases.

The agency's engineers vacuum-packed the molds in sterile plastic containers about the size used to store contact lenses. They could be carried in a diplomatic pouch or even mailed and stored at room temperature for years. The molds were single-use, but the agency made dozens of copies of each unique print. That way an operative could clear immigration repeatedly with the same print and thus the same passport and identity.

Because the molds were so thin, they easily warmed to human body temperature, and the gelatin had conductive properties similar to human skin. The combination meant that they could easily fool even third-generation fingerprint scanners that measured temperature and electrical resistance — though most airports still relied on basic devices that did little more than photograph prints and check their whorls and ridges against their databases.

With more and more immigration agencies deploying scanners, the molds had proven incredibly useful. Every station now carried them. Best of all, an operative who ran into border trouble for some other reason could simply put finger to tongue. The gelatin and silicone dissolved within seconds and left no trace. Of course, he'd then be stuck with his real fingerprints.

Wells had tested the molds at Langley before coming to Tokyo. As far as he could tell they were foolproof. And as much as working for the agency had frustrated him, he had to admit that its technical wizardry made life in the field easier.

In the morning, they would meet with Garry Wright, who was even now trying to find Buvchenko. Unfortunately, the Russian seemed to have gone to ground. As always, language skills remained a problem for the agency, and Hong Kong station had only three field officers who spoke Cantonese. They were watching the Russian consulate in downtown Hong Kong, but they hadn't spotted Buvchenko in a week. Another technical problem, this one easily solvable if they could convince Gideon or Orli to give them Buvchenko's phone number. The NSA's ability to track mobile signals was astonishing, and the FSB was using rudimentary techniques to communicate with Duberman. Maybe because it didn't expect him to last long.

But of course Shafer had alienated Orli, their best lead.

"You didn't need to push her that way," Wells said.

"She wasn't exactly jumping to help us."

"Maybe if you hadn't been such a jerk."

"You and your supermodel crushes. He told her what he'd done and she got on a plane and went halfway around the world with him. Don't give me that kids-need-Daddy crap. She thought they were untouchable."

"She doesn't think that anymore."

"Yeah, and she's not the only one. Gideon's awful twitchy for a pro. Get the feeling he's had it with the boss man?"

"Wonder what he meant about owing him."

Shafer reached for his phone. "I'll ask the geniuses if they can find anything."

"We shouldn't have let her go, Ellis. She's in way over her head."

"She's free, white, and twenty-one, she can do what she likes."

"Think she'll call?"

"No way she goes down with him. But maybe she just takes the kids and goes back to Israel on her own, says to hell with all of us."

"I don't have any problem with that."

"Don't get too hooked, John. We may need to squeeze her yet."

18

Orli spent the flight from Tokyo turning over what that ridiculous little man Shafer had told her, trying and failing to find some answer for her husband's behavior. She landed at 6 a.m., seeing spots from exhaustion, not sure how she could face him, knowing she had no choice. "You should have told me," she said to Gideon, as he led her onto the helicopter that would bring them to the Peak.

"Try not to judge him. He was desperate."

As if desperation absolved her husband's sins. His betrayal. *We're partners,* she'd told him in Tel Aviv. All she'd asked, in return for running across the globe with him. Instead he'd turned to the Russians. Though he knew she hated them.

Then the girl.

She didn't understand how he could have

betrayed her so completely. Or how she could have known so little about him.

Another storm was forming off the coast and the winds shoved their helicopter sideways as it flew over the bay and toward the Peak. As they bounced, Orli thought of a model she'd known, Renee. A surfer's body, short spiky hair, real muscles. She worked mostly for alternative brands that specialized in girl power. They didn't compete for the same jobs, no jealousy, so they were real friends, rare in the business. They got married within a month of each other, tried to get pregnant around the same time, too. A friendly competition.

A few weeks after Orli found out she was pregnant, Renee called. *Ever get dizzy and fall down the first couple of weeks?* She was waking up with night sweats, too. Nothing like that had happened to Orli. *Go see your gyno.* Who checked her out, sent her to a clinic for scans. *Routine, but let's do it today just to be sure.*

By dinner, Renee had her diagnosis: a glioblastoma multiforme, an inoperable brain tumor.

Orli saw her the next day for coffee, which quickly became cocktails, because why not. Renee told Orli the story tightly, coolly, not a single tear, like she was talking about someone else, someone she didn't know all that well. The cosmic unfairness seemed impossible. Orli instinctively focused on the practicalities, finding an answer.

"Is there anything? There must be something —"

"We all pretend the world doesn't have teeth, Orli. That it never wants a sacrifice."

"How's Jake taking it?" Her husband.

"Haven't told him."

For once, Orli's face betrayed her. "I know it'll tear him up, but you need to tell him."

"You think it's for *him* I'm not saying?" Renee laughed. "If I don't" — her voice shrank, the humor gone now — "then it's not real. You see?"

She was dead eight months later.

Now Orli was the one staring into the world's maw. Now she understood why Renee had wanted to stay silent, to erase the truth by ignoring it. The logic of a child sticking her fingers in her ears as a tornado shrieked close.

The mansion was silent as she walked through the family quarters. For the first time, the absolute mechanical perfection of the place struck her, the walls skim-coated with nontoxic paint, floors radiant-heated, the air filtered and allergen-free. Everything just so. Did Aaron see her the same way? Another perfect accessory? Did he even know why he wanted her?

The twins slept down the hall from the master suite. She had insisted that they live in the same room. They'd been together inside her, and she wanted to keep them together as long as she could. They lay side by side in their little cedar beds, handcrafted in Sweden for twelve thousand dollars each.

Her life had turned absurd without her notice.

As they often did, the boys had turned in the night to face each other. They were a beautiful pair. Boaz took after her, blond, blue-eyed, snub-nosed, verging on pretty. Rafael was his father's son, brown eyes, curly hair, even Aaron's square chin. She kissed them, tasting the faintest sweat on their foreheads. They were all that mattered. She backed silently out of the room before they woke.

She was almost surprised to find Aaron in bed and asleep, not pretending, his breathing steady and even. She edged between the thousand-count cotton sheets, put a hand on his naked hip, slipped her fingers around him, felt him stir.

Whatever desire she had for him was long

gone. She squeezed him hard, nothing erotic in the motion, and he yelped, sat up, grabbed for her arm. She slipped out of bed, stood above him, watched without mercy as he tried to gather himself. His skin was looser than she remembered, his hair grayer.

"Is it true?"

"Is *what* true?" He sat up. The steroids and the workouts gave him a younger man's muscles, but they couldn't change his sagging skin. He tried to stare her into submission, but she was used to men staring at her. "I don't know what Gideon told you —"

All the answer she needed. "It wasn't Gideon."

"Just tell me." He'd never spoken to her this way before, clipped, angry, like she was an employee who'd screwed up.

"That meeting in Tokyo, the Americans set it, Wells and that other one, Shafer, they told me about you and the FSB."

She realized her mistake as the words left her lips. Better to let Aaron believe Gideon had told her. Now he knew the Americans were moving against him.

"You went to meet *Wells*?"

"I didn't know he'd be there, I thought the meeting was real, they set it up."

"He told you a story and you believed him?"

"Why wouldn't I? Gideon agreed."

"No, no, no." As if she and Gideon had betrayed him rather than the reverse. He padded across the bedroom to his walk-in closet.

"Tell me," she said to his back, quietly. Though what could he tell her that she didn't already know? Her anger was fading more quickly than she could have imagined. The poets were wrong. The opposite of love wasn't hate. It was the absence of hate, and every emotion.

The opposite of love was death.

"You know I saw Cheung yesterday." He stepped out of the closet wearing a gray T-shirt and the silk boxers he favored. How had he ever seemed anything but ridiculous to her? "He wants to help us."

"Us, you and the Russians?"

"I don't know exactly what Wells told you. But yes. I've talked to the Russians." He sounded almost bored, like she was wasting his time. "They've offered us citizenship."

So Wells and Shafer had told the truth. But Aaron's confirmation made the prospect less real instead of more. Like a camera crew was about to jump out of the closet shouting *Surprise!*

"Live in Siberia?"

"Diplomatic passports. We could live anywhere."

"You think the Americans will respect that? If they know you're working for the FSB?"

"This isn't the Americans. It's Wells and his friends —"

"They said they're working officially this time, Aaron."

"They're lying."

Orli thought of all the men she'd seen in Tokyo, the hotel suite, the way they'd convinced her agent to play along. Tiffany was no fool, she would have insisted on talking to someone at CIA headquarters before agreeing. "I don't think so."

"Either way, they can't do anything about it, not unless the President is ready go public with everything. If he was going to do that, he would have already. I'm not worried about the Americans. The FSB can handle them."

"When were you going to tell me? When we landed in Moscow?" Like she was a child. She'd believed he respected her for more than her looks. Maybe he'd believed it, too. They'd been wrong, both of them.

"Don't you see? It would solve everything."

What she saw was that he'd lost his mind, caught himself in a fantasy world, pretending as always he could push reality aside by sheer force of will. Not this time. This time, reality wasn't going anywhere.

"You think you can dream the Russians away?"

"What are you talking about, Orli? Let me play this out, it's *working* —"

"Sure. Anything else you want to tell me?"

He looked at her in apparent sincerity. "I don't think so."

"The girl? The one you gave Cheung."

"There wasn't any girl. I mean, yes, but she was a decoy. Nothing happened to her —"

"How old? Gideon called her a child."

"Gideon never saw her, and I didn't, either. That's the truth, Orli. Never even met her. She was Vietnamese, she's already back in Hanoi. We worked out a plan, they promised —"

"Oh, they *promised*. What was her name?"

He reached for her. She raised her hands.

"Tell me you know her name, Aaron."

"I made the best choice I could, Orli. For us."

"I'm taking Boaz and Rafael to Tel Aviv."

"Not now."

The certainty in his voice unsettled her.

He was telling, not asking.

"The boys need a father. A man in their lives. And we need to be together."

"Remember. When this started. You said I could leave anytime?" No. She didn't need permission. She tried again. "Keep the prenup, the money —" His billions didn't matter, they were as tainted as everything else. "We're going home. Where we belong."

"We belong *together,* Orli, we're a family. You're not thinking clearly. Buvchenko will tell you himself, how it's going to work. The Russians need me, they need me as much as I need them. We're in this together."

"So we're all partners, you and me and Buvchenko?"

"Mamma! Mamma!" A cry from down the hall. Rafael. He usually woke first.

"Go check on our son, give me five minutes." He grabbed her forearm, hard enough to hurt, hard enough to remind her that even at twice her age he was far stronger than she. He pushed her toward the door, slammed it closed.

She wanted to believe she was still on the plane, sleeping. But the finger-shaped welts already rising on her arm said otherwise, the cause-and-effect peculiar to reality.

Both boys were stirring now. Seeing them,

she realized she'd been a fool for fearing she'd ever use again. Heroin had been a cheap and bright and ultimately useless pleasure. Her love for these two brought her joy without end. She didn't want to take them from Aaron, but he couldn't undo what he'd done. He would understand.

Even if he didn't, he couldn't keep her, this was Hong Kong, not Saudi Arabia, she wasn't a prisoner, she wasn't his property. Maybe he wouldn't let her use the Dreamliner, maybe she and the twins would fly commercial for a change. The thought made her smile, and Rafael sensed the change in her mood.

"Mamma." He blinked open his wide brown eyes. "Mamma."

"Raffy." She scooped him up, thinking now about how she could get out of Hong Kong, what to leave and take —

Aaron walked in, iPhone in hand.

"Mikhail Buvchenko would like to speak to you."

She took the handset, ended the call, threw the phone past him into the hall as hard as she could. It smacked the wall and her husband looked at her dead-eyed, as her agent had that day in Paris.

"We're going."

"You're going nowhere." He stood in the

doorway. In her arms, Rafael screamed *"Mamma! Mamma!"* with big gasping sobs.

She tried to push past. He didn't move. "You want to desert me, I can't stop you, Orli. The boys, they stay."

She reached for Boaz. The boys were big now, but she could carry them both —

"Have fun trying to get them out of Hong Kong without passports."

She stopped moving like a cartoon character mid-frame, one foot in the air. Even infants couldn't travel without passports. The twins had had theirs since they were three months old. Rafael's photo made even the crustiest immigration officers smile, he was curly-haired and wide-eyed and grinning toothlessly like a little old man.

She put him down in his Swedish bed, pushed past Aaron, ran for their bedroom. She kept the passports in her nightstand with her own, they'd been there the day before when she went to Tokyo. She was sure, she'd seen them when she grabbed hers.

Gone.

She rifled through the drawer, pulled it out and tipped it over, a thief in a hurry, scattering change and phone chargers and a dusty spare tampon. Down the hall, Rafael screamed, and now Boaz had picked up the chant, *Mammamammamamma* —

She ran to them. She felt fear beneath her rage, like she had stepped off a forest path into a hidden swamp, the ground soft, sucking at her shoes, tugging them off. She was alone, no one to throw her a rope or a branch, she needed to slow down, no panic, or before she knew it, the mud would take her, a strange slow-motion death —

Instead of hitting her husband, her first instinct, she reached for Rafael and picked him up. She turned for Boaz, but Aaron grabbed him first. They stood on either side of the beds, patting their sobbing children, a temporary truce. Holding Boaz seemed to soothe both son and father. Aaron had always been a good dad in an old-school way, not much of a diaper-changer or a bottle feeder, but he loved the kids and they loved him.

The stress is making him crazy, that's all. He's afraid to lose them. She wanted to ask about the passports, but challenging him wouldn't help. Anyway, she knew where they had to be. Besides the vault in the panic room, he had a safe in his walk-in closet. He must have hidden them when she was in here with Rafael.

Every beautiful woman had experience dealing with irrational men. "Let's figure this out." She made her voice quiet, soothing. "Together."

"Everything's going to be okay." His voice mirrored hers, soft now, almost tender.

"I just think, wouldn't it be better to wait for you in Israel. You'll be a hero when you come back —" She stopped, knowing she was laying the honey on too thick.

"We left together and it's better if we come home that way. Besides, you can't expect me to trust my kids to a junkie."

One word, and the quicksand was waist-deep. She didn't know what to say, what he knew, *how* he knew. No one knew.

"You think I didn't check you out before I proposed? Your little habit."

"I don't have a *habit*, Aaron. Never did."

"I worried about it. But the psychiatrist I talked to, she said she thought it was thrill-seeking. *Environmental,* I think that was the word. A fancy shrink word for you being bored, hanging out with idiots with more money than sense."

More money than sense. He'd actually just said that. Oh, the irony. She held her tongue.

"You were so beautiful, I liked you so much, I figured it was worth the chance. You know me, I like to gamble. Anyway, I started paying your dealer so that if you ever called him again, I'd know."

I started paying your dealer? He'd gone mad, she saw. From fear or the wish to escape what he'd done, the choices he'd made, or some insistence that he couldn't lose, or all three. Or maybe he'd always been mad and she hadn't known. Either way, the conversation had turned inside out. They couldn't talk about how he was holding their kids hostage, or spying on China for the Russian government, or *had played pimp for a ten-year-old girl,* because he had out of nowhere made her years-old drug use the issue.

"I know you're scared, Orli, but we're all right. I'm not going to tell you these Russians are nice people, but they need me now."

"Let me just take the kids to Tel Aviv, Aaron." She put a hand on his shoulder, an obvious trick, but one that had worked for her before. She stroked his arm, tried to remember what she'd liked about him. "You're right, I'm scared. I'll feel better there."

His phone rang. He shook her off and hurried into the hall.

"No, Mikhail, sorry. She's right here." He came back, pushed the phone on her. The phone's screen was broken, spiderweb-shattered like a bad-luck mirror. Nevertheless, she took it. Let Aaron believe she was listening. Being reasonable, as he would say. She would accept the humiliation if it calmed him down, brought an end to this bizarro world where she was an addict and he was the defender of their realm. Then maybe she could find a way out. Maybe the Israeli consulate could issue replacement passports secretly. Maybe she could ask the Hong Kong police for protection. At least they knew part of the truth.

"Orli. Your husband says you're upset." Buvchenko's English was better than she expected, accented but understandable. He made the word *upset* seem ridiculous, a euphemism for *premenstrual.* "May we meet?" Like he was a barista offering a free refill.

"No, thanks."

"You don't have to go anywhere, I'll come to you —"

She couldn't listen any longer, and she feared what Aaron might do if she hung up again. She passed the phone back to her husband. "Yes . . . Fine . . . We'll wait. I think that makes sense for everyone, too." He hung up. "He'll be here in twenty minutes."

"Aaron, you can't be serious."

"We should get ready."

■ ■ ■ ■

The minutes passed in something like a trance. She was awake, conscious. Yet her will was gone. She watched herself pull on her clothes, tell the nannies to give Boaz and Rafael breakfast. She remembered the feeling from her heroin days. But the drug's detachment came with euphoria, like her brain was too busy enjoying itself to work. This morning she felt only dread.

She wondered if she should call Wells, but her phone had vanished. Probably in the closet safe with the passports. Anyway, what she'd told Wells the night before still held. She couldn't count on the Americans. They would use her to get to Aaron. Once she gave him up, they'd discard her. She couldn't trust Gideon, either. If he hated what Aaron had done so much, why hadn't he told her? Some leftover loyalty to her husband.

In the end, the fear of making another bad choice overwhelmed her. In what seemed like no time at all, she found herself standing next to Aaron in the mansion's driveway as a white van rolled inside, one of the tall ones that tradesmen used. The two gate guards stood a few meters behind them. She didn't know where Gideon was. She suspected Aaron had given him an errand, sent him outside the mansion for a few minutes so he wouldn't be here when these men came.

The van made a quick U-turn so its nose faced the gate. Even before it stopped, its back doors swung open. Three men were inside, Buvchenko and the two FSB operatives whose photos Wells had shown her. The FSB men squatted on their heels like monkeys, monkeys with pistols. Buvchenko sat on the edge of the van's cargo compartment and waved them closer, deeper into the quicksand.

"Aaron. I believe you have something for me."

Aaron pulled a gray thumb drive from his pocket, gave it to Buvchenko. In turn, Buvchenko passed it to the Russian squatting to his left, then handed Aaron a thumb drive of his own. "For your next meeting." He looked at Orli. "My God. As beautiful as your pictures."

She cursed at him, softly, in Hebrew.

"Let me tell you that Aaron is doing excellent work for us and we intend to keep our bargain. However, if you insist on interfering, I can't guarantee the safety of your family."

There it was. "These are your partners?" she said to Aaron. "Threatening my *children*?"

"If you hadn't interfered —"

He even used the same words as Buvchenko now. "Please go away." She wasn't sure if she was talking to the man beside her or the one in the van. "Go away, please." Maybe if she moved the words around enough, they'd hear.

"A better idea," Buvchenko said. "Come with us. Your husband can send your children back to Tel Aviv to stay with your family until it's settled —"

As if the thought had just occurred to him, as if it wasn't the reason he'd come here.

"Settled, what's settled? You'll never stop."

"This is temporary."

She knew he was lying, of course he was lying. Yet she wanted to believe. She'd visited the Holocaust Museum on school trips, part of the curriculum for every Israeli child. Now she saw for herself how the Nazis had convinced her people to shuffle without argument into the gas chambers. *It's only a shower, you'll be fine, all of you, clean after the train . . .* Lies that everyone knew were lies, so many had died already. Yet the words papered over the panic, offered escape from the truth of extinguishment.

"You don't need me." But of course they did. She was the one who could blow up whatever they were planning. Aaron was no threat. They already owned Aaron.

"Don't take her," he said. "I'll go." She looked at him and saw *him* again, afraid, trying to be brave, as if the threat to Boaz and Rafael had shocked him to reality —

"Generous, but you're doing such important work. You stay. Don't worry, we'll give her back soon enough, we just need you to meet the general again."

"I can pay, whatever you like —"

Buvchenko no longer pretended to listen to her husband. He flashed his hand sideways, enough. "Orli, we don't have much time. Decide now, *now.*"

"You think people won't notice I'm gone?"

"It won't be long."

She believed that much, anyway. The Russians couldn't be thinking more than a few days ahead. The game was moving faster than the players. Wells had warned her. *I'm afraid you'll start something you can't stop.*

"Don't," Aaron whispered in Hebrew.

"Why did you bring me out here, then?"

He had no answer. She turned to Buvchenko. "I don't care what you do to me

433

as long as you don't hurt my boys." The best way, the only way, she saw now. Maybe she'd live.

Maybe those underground chambers really were showers.

"Then let's go." Buvchenko reached out a hand.

A moment later, Aaron grabbed for her. She stepped toward him until they were not even an arm's length apart and grabbed the outside of his shoulders to brace herself and brought up her left knee between his legs as hard as she could, no hesitation, the Krav Maga training taking over, driving the softness there up and into his hips. He groaned and crumpled.

Behind her, the guards raised their assault rifles and then lowered them and ran for her. She turned toward Buvchenko and grabbed his titanic hand, big as a bear's paw. He tossed her over his shoulder and into the van. The FSB man next to him yelled in Russian and the driver gunned the engine. The gate began to close, but too late, the van was through. Buvchenko reached for the doors and pulled them shut. Her last glimpse was her husband, still writhing on the ground.

The van turned left and sped east along

Lugard Road and then left again, down the switchbacks etched into the side of the Peak. The Russians barked at one another, their language fast and harsh, vaguely like Hebrew. She caught the English word *drone* a couple of times, it popped out of the Russian like a cork.

At a light near the bottom of the road, Buvchenko turned to her. "Is it true, what your husband told me? That the Americans are coming?"

"Yes." She felt oddly relaxed. She'd made her choice, and the boys would be safe. She was proud of herself, too, though she knew thinking those words cheapened what she'd done.

"Wells?"

She decided to pull his chain. "You're scared of him, too. I wouldn't have guessed."

"Go ahead." Buvchenko's eyes slipped half closed, like he was burrowing into himself, a memory he'd never share. "If thinking that makes you feel better."

The van crawled through the crowded streets near the harbor, skyscrapers on every side.

"Anyway, whatever you're doing, you don't have long. Wells will kill Aaron now, he doesn't care."

"*Da.*" The prospect didn't seem to ruffle

Buvchenko.

"So that's it? All this effort for one general?"

"Cheung knows everything there is to know about the Chinese air force."

"But when the Chinese figure out what you've done, they'll be furious with you."

"You're an expert on international politics?"

She bit back the curse on her lips.

"No, actually you make a good point. I wasn't going to tell you, but why not? Our little secret." He ran his hand down her arm, a proprietary touch, a wordless reminder that she belonged to these men now. "The general thinks he's working for the Americans."

For the first time in a long, long time, maybe since that afternoon in Paris, she felt naïve. A child in a grown-up world. "I don't —"

"When we came to Cheung in Macao, after the girl, we told him we were CIA."

"He believed you?"

"He doesn't speak English, he doesn't know where he is, what he's done, we could have told him we were from Mars and he would have believed us. And why would Cheung think your husband would work for Russia? He's American."

"So when the Chinese find out what Aaron did with Cheung —"

"They'll blame the Americans for spying on them. You're right, they'll be furious. Not with us."

"But the Americans are trying to *kill* Aaron. Why would they kill their own spy?"

"You think they're going to admit they did it if they kill him?"

"Even so, they'll deny they recruited Cheung. They'll tell the Chinese —"

"What? Some crazy story about Aaron Duberman wanting to become a Russian? Who would believe that?"

Nobody. Especially since her husband wouldn't be around to explain the truth. The FSB would kill him if the Americans didn't. The fact that Buvchenko was blabbing to her didn't say much for her own life expectancy. Or maybe he knew that if the Russians ever let her go, she'd be smart enough to keep her mouth shut forever.

The plan's boldness amazed her. "No wonder you don't care what happens to him."

"Who knows what the Chinese will do to retaliate? And in the future, every American company in China, the government will wonder if they're working for the CIA. So, yes, it would have been nice to have longer with Aaron, pick up some more Chinamen, but this works fine."

The van turned into a parking garage, swung down a level, stopped. Buvchenko pushed open the back doors, tugged her out. He was so big that he could move her without having to hurt her. Fighting him would have been like trying to stand up to a tidal wave.

A BMW sedan waited, engine running, trunk lid up. Buvchenko led her to the back of the sedan. "Inside." The trunk was lined with the soft sound-dampening acoustic foam she recognized from Jamie's studio; too late she understood why he'd talked to her as they drove through the city: He hadn't wanted her to scream or bang on the walls of the van, which weren't deadened. People were so much crueler than animals. At least animals didn't lie to their prey —

"No way."

"A little while."

She couldn't help herself, she screamed.

His face changed, they weren't friends anymore. He picked her up like she was made of straw, covered her mouth with his hand. "You remind me of my sister." The words made no sense. At first Orli thought she'd misheard. She was still trying to understand when he threw her into the trunk, slammed the lid. The darkness was total, and the panic rose in her as the car rolled away. She couldn't help herself, her nerve broke, and she put her fingers in her ears and told herself, *This isn't real this isn't real.*

19

Wells cleared Hong Kong immigration without a second look from the officer at the diplomatic/VIP station. Whatever happened with this mission, he was taking home boxes of finger molds as souvenirs. But the lift of successful tradecraft lasted only until Wells saw Wright in the arrivals hall. The station chief's arms were folded and his nose wrinkled like he'd just stepped on a cow patty. He might as well have worn a sandwich board reading *Bad news!*

Shafer and Wright exchanged the shortest handshake in history before Wright led them to a black SUV at the curb.

"Sure she wasn't playing you?" Wright said without preamble, as soon as the doors were closed.

"Absolutely."

"An hour ago, our drone caught her taking a ride with your Russian friends."

"Voluntarily?"

"You know the security at that place. They opened the gates, a van came in, she got in, they left. It's even weirder than that, you'll see —"

"Where'd they go?"

"Down the hill. Had to let them go after that. Too many skyscrapers, too much weather."

"You lost her?"

"Did I stutter?" Wright passed them the laptop. "See for yourself."

Clouds blurred the footage, but Wells recognized Orli and Duberman standing near the mansion's gate as the van arrived. The back doors opened, revealing a man who could only have been Buvchenko. The three spoke for about ninety seconds, according to the drone's timer. Then Duberman reached for Orli, who turned to him —

And kneed him in the crotch. Not lethal, but no fun, either. She grabbed Buvchenko's hand and jumped into the van as her husband fell. The van sped off before the gates could close. The guards milled around their fallen master and didn't pursue. Wells replayed the crucial seconds on slow motion, then super-slow. He had to agree with Wright. Orli had left on her own.

"They threatened her. No way was she

working with them. If you'd seen her yesterday —"

"Never say never," Shafer said. "Any au-
dio?"

"From six hundred feet up?" Wright said.

The feed continued as the drone followed
the van down the side of the Peak and into
the skyscraper canyons below. It lost altitude
as it tried to keep the van in sight, then
abruptly turned around —

"You didn't lose her. You left her." Wells
found himself unaccountably angry. Maybe
Shafer was right about his supermodel
crushes.

"Easy, killer. We only had the one bird up
and maybe you've forgotten, Daddy's the
one we want. We have no static surveillance
up there, it's impossible. I didn't want him
to disappear, too."

"She's not part of this."

"Funny, not how I see it. For what it's
worth, I have guys watching the consulate
in case they show there."

"You should have stuck with her," Shafer
said. "Not for her, for Buvchenko. But
forget it now. Here's what doesn't make
sense. Say she went voluntarily, she's working for the FSB —"

"She went voluntarily."

"Enough, Garry."

Wells still wasn't used to hearing that throat-slitting tone from Shafer.

"Again. Say she did. If she's working for them, when she got home, she would have told Duberman and the Russians what we told her. The other scenario is that they coerced her somehow. But even then, he only would have let them take her if she got mad and blurted everything out. Either way, he knows we met her."

"Point?" Wright said.

"Point is he has to know we're after him. Which means the FSB must know, too. So what's the play? Why take her? All she does is add to the mess."

"Aside from her obvious charms." Wright smirked.

But Wells didn't take the bait. As usual, Shafer had cut to the most important question. If the Russians knew the United States was actively chasing Duberman, then they knew that their plan to turn 88 Gamma into a worldwide honey pot had backfired. Why bother to take Orli?

"Point two," Shafer said. "This was predictable."

" 'This' meaning what?"

"Meaning all of it. Why waste so much effort on something that was likely to blow up this fast? They had to know, once they told us they were giving Duberman diplomatic protection, we would have to come back at them. Unless, after the way they've pushed us around in the Ukraine and Syria, they think they can do whatever they want and the White House won't respond."

"Maybe that *was* the point," Wright said. "See how far they can shove it down the President's throat before he finally gags."

"Or maybe they have a game we aren't seeing."

"Anyway, it's not like they didn't get anything. Cheung's a four-star general —"

"I'd be happy to run him, too, but he's not Uncle Xi. Not even a minister. And the FSB couldn't have counted on getting someone at his level right away, they couldn't know Duberman had him lined up. Something's missing."

Outside, the rain that the clouds had promised all morning began to fall, tentative drops and then without warning a downpour, a classic subtropical drenching. Wells stared into the thick gray sky. Duberman was hidden up there somewhere.

"You aren't so dumb, Ellis," Wright said.

"Tell my wife."

"What next, then? Go up the hill, see the man himself?"

"And offer him what for his cooperation?

A one-way ticket to the Supermax?"

"Better than a bullet."

"He may feel different."

The idea of confronting Duberman carried more than a little appeal. Except for the dozen squads of Hong Kong police who would no doubt come scrambling up the mountain. Even so . . . Wells felt the space low on his back where a pistol ought to be. "Before we do anything else, we need to get strapped." He expected pushback, but Wright nodded.

"Truer words were never spoke."

On the other side of the harbor, Duberman sat in his kitchen, a bag of ice clamped between his legs. He'd dismissed his guards. He didn't want them seeing him this way. He reached for his phone, called Buvchenko, got no answer. He even wasn't sure why he was calling, what he'd say if the Russian picked up. *Let her go, I'll do what you say?* Like he wasn't already. Anyway, why did he want Orli back? She'd shown her colors this morning, threatening to take the boys from him. His sons. His heirs. After everything he'd given her. She should have trusted him, understood he'd done what he'd done for their family. Still, disloyal as she'd been, he didn't want the Russians to hurt her.

Life can only be understood backwards, but it must be lived forwards, Kierkegaard had said. But he was exactly wrong. Duberman had understood every one of his choices while he made them. Only in retrospect did he question them. His life was a bridge, falling away behind him as he walked. The regrets came from looking back. So no more looking back. He would escape this mess. With or without his wife.

His phone's cracked screen lit up. A blocked number.

"Aaron." Buvchenko, of course.

"Where is she? What have you done with her?"

The words sounded absurd as they came out of his mouth. Buvchenko apparently agreed. "Don't pretend to be something you're not. Just listen. You need to meet our friend again."

The word *friend* was so incongruous that Duberman didn't understand straightaway. Then he did: *Cheung.* "When?"

"Tonight. Very late. One in the morning, say."

"I only got back last night. He won't possibly agree."

"Have your man call him, the one who set it up last time. Tell him whatever you like, that you've decided to finalize your order and you'd like him to visit. The new casino again."

"I'm not sure he'll want that —"

"Worry about yourself, not him. You hand him something, he hands you something, same as before."

"Then he goes."

"Not right away. Play cards for a while. Four a.m., he goes back to Beijing."

"After you meet us? You have a message for him?"

Buvchenko didn't answer, as if the question was beneath him. In the silence Duberman heard a muffled *thump* behind Buvchenko, the sound of something heavy hitting the ground.

"I need to know my children are safe."

"Of course."

"You don't need to keep her, Mikhail, I can handle her —"

"One last thing. If the Americans call you, try to meet, you tell me immediately. Yes?"

"Are they here?"

"Keep your heart strong and nothing will stop you."

This last bit of motivational advice was too much. Luckily, Buvchenko hung up before Duberman had to answer.

Yet, ultimately, he didn't blame the Russians for his fall. They were doing what they did, pouncing on weakness. He didn't even blame Orli. She was a stupid girl who'd panicked, as stupid girls did. No, the villain here was the same man as always. John Wells. Wells had undone Duberman's plans from the very start. He had made a mission of destroying Duberman's life, and Duberman had let him.

Now Duberman heard Gideon, coming out of the garage, shouting, "Aaron! Aaron!"

"In here, Chai."

A week before, Duberman had hired a lawyer to arrange a forty-million-dollar credit line at Two Typhoon Finance, a Kowloon bank with a shady reputation. Money-laundering experts joked that the initials *TTF* stood for The Triads' Favorite. In place of the usual guarantees, the line was secured by fifty million dollars in gold ingots deposited at Two Typhoon's headquarters. Thus the bank happily extended the line even though its only named beneficiary was a company called Reddie Super PLC, which existed only in a Kowloon post office box.

This morning, with Buvchenko on his way up the Peak, Duberman had sent Gideon with a letter instructing Two Typhoon to draw the line for Reddie Super and wire all forty million to an account in the Cayman Islands, a payment for "services rendered." Through a series of prearranged commodities trades, three-quarters of the money would make its way to a Panamanian front company that Duberman controlled. Thirty million dollars. Enough money to disappear. Yes, fleeing would be the ultimate act of desperation, what he'd promised himself he'd never do. But he needed to keep his options open.

In any case, the letter provided the excuse he needed to make sure Gideon wasn't around when the Russians came.

Gideon walked into the kitchen. He wore his usual suit, and to a casual observer would have looked like a middle-aged lawyer. Only the way his eyes roved the kitchen betrayed his agitation. Like he was on enemy territory. "Eric" — the head gate guard — "said Orli —"

"Did you do as I asked?"

"They gave me this." Gideon pulled an envelope from his suit.

Inside, a confirmation of the transfer. "Orli's gone. Buvchenko came and she went with him. I tried to stop her, but she kicked me —" Duberman held up the ice bag — "and ran."

"Why?"

"He threatened to kill the kids if she didn't go." Duberman would rather have lied, but he couldn't come up with anything plausible.

"You sent me away because you knew he was coming."

"I worried you wouldn't control yourself around him, yes. After that show in the garage."

"You wanted them to take her."

"*You're* the one who didn't tell the truth, Gideon, not me. She told me what happened in Tokyo, how you saw Wells."

Gideon sagged slightly, and yet his lips tightened. Shame and defiance.

"You were in the same room with him and you didn't do anything, after all he's done to us —"

"It was impossible, Aaron. He had men there, too. Anyway, I was more concerned with Orli."

"You want to know about this morning? She insisted on meeting the Russians, hear for herself about what I was doing with them. When Buvchenko came, she got mad. He threatened the kids and she panicked. I told her to trust me, but she wouldn't —" Duberman found himself believing his own words. The story was hardly a lie, merely a revision of the truth.

"I can't imagine why."

Forget Orli. She's gone. Wells, Wells is the problem we have to solve. But Gideon wouldn't agree, and Gideon was no longer accepting his orders without question. The ingrate.

Suddenly the lie, no, the solution, jumped to Duberman's mind.

"I haven't told you the rest. Buvchenko just called me. He promises he'll give Orli back. But he has errands for both of us first. He's ordered me to meet Cheung in Macao tonight. One a.m."

"And what does he want from me?"

"I'm not sure if what he's asking is FSB business or personal. I suspect the latter."

"What, Aaron?"

Duberman paused, letting Gideon's curiosity build. Even now he understood how to work an audience. "Did Wells give you a way to reach him?"

Gideon nodded.

"Buvchenko wants you to set a meeting. And kill him."

Gideon clasped his hands, sank into himself. Duberman wasn't sure how to read the pose.

"Mikhail Buvchenko asked for this. In return for Orli."

"This and Cheung, yes. I thought you'd

want this."

Gideon stepped so close that they were almost touching. "What's the endgame, Aaron?" His voice was a whisper, yet every syllable of Hebrew was clear. Duberman could see him, thirty years ago, more, a young sniper in South Lebanon, whispering to the soldiers around him as he lined up his next kill.

"I don't know." The right answer. Gideon would think him either a liar or a fool if he promised anything more. "But I'll bet they don't want to keep her, either. They're holding her for leverage. Let's give it to them. Then maybe I disappear, leave her and the kids." He forced out the words, though he knew that after this morning, he would never, ever leave his children for *her* to raise alone. He wouldn't let her win that way.

"I still don't see —"

"Tell you what. Consider this your chance to repay whatever it is you owe me. When it's done, we'll go our own ways. What the Russians do to me won't be your problem."

Gideon reached into his suit, his eyes unreadable. Almost sleepy. For a half second, Duberman wondered if he might be pulling his pistol. But, no, his phone. "If you say so."

452

■ ■ ■ ■

Wells felt his phone buzz just as he followed Shafer and Wright into the one-room apartment in Mong Kok, Wright's safe house.

"Hello?" The word carried a thick Hebrew accent. *Gideon,* he mouthed to Shafer.

"This is John."

"Are you in Hong Kong?"

"Yes."

Wells listened. "When? All right. I'll be there."

He ended the call. "That was Gideon. He says Orli wants to meet at noon at the International Commerce Centre." Another of the landmarks that Wells had memorized before coming to Hong Kong, the territory's tallest skyscraper, more than fifteen hundred feet high. It was on the Kowloon side of the harbor, not the island.

"So Orli wants to meet?" Shafer said. "He mention her field trip with the Russians?"

"He did not. Maybe he didn't think I'd come unless he dangled her."

"Or maybe he'll shoot you in the head as soon as he sees you."

"What's the point? They have bigger problems."

"Doesn't have to be a point, John. He

knows they're all circling the drain. Maybe he just wants to take you down, too."

Shafer might be right. Gideon had been on a hair trigger in Tokyo, and he was almost certainly lying about Orli. The Russians had taken her only a couple of hours before. Why would they have given her back already?

Still, Wells had to go.

"You just supposed to go floor by floor until you find her?" Wright said.

"He said there's an ice rink."

"Yeah, there's a mall next to the tower and it has a rink. I've never been, but it was a big deal when it opened." Wright glanced at his watch. "Forty-five minutes. Not much time to get a team together."

"He said no teams. Just me and him and Orli."

"Did he?" Shafer said. "I'm shocked."

20

Shafer and Wright insisted on backstopping Wells. He didn't argue. If Gideon only wanted to talk, he'd understand why Wells had protected himself. And if not . . .

A check online revealed that the mall next to the rink was called Elements and had a vaguely naturalistic theme, a way to distinguish it from every other luxury shopping center in Hong Kong. "Guessing you don't spend much time there," Wells said to Wright.

"Sadly, no. Though I have been to the bar on top of the ICC. Crazy views."

The rink had its own entrance at the southeastern end of the mall, the opposite side from the International Commerce Centre's lobby. Wells, Shafer, and Wright quickly sketched a plan. Wright would enter on the rink side, see if Gideon had a team in place. Wells would come in from the skyscraper end, make his own surveillance-detection run. The mall was relatively long and narrow and had multiple levels, an unusual footprint that had probably come from the need to build around the massive infrastructure supporting the skyscraper, MTR line, and highways around it. The setup had dozens of good places to hide, ideal for watchers, tough for countersurveillance. Still, Wells had to try. Shafer would give Wells a five-minute head start before following from the skyscraper side.

Wright didn't have tac radios at the safe house. They were stuck with their phones. They decided Wright would text *555* if he saw Orli or Gideon, *000* if he didn't spot anyone, *911* and then the number of guys if he made a surveillance team. Wells wouldn't text unless he decided to abort, in which case he'd go with *999*.

"Call Duto?" Wright asked, when they'd finished the plan.

"No."

"Good luck, then. See you there." Wright adjusted his holster and left.

"He's not bad," Shafer said, once Wright's footsteps were gone. The guy going in first was usually at the greatest risk, but Wright had taken the job without complaint.

"Yeah." *Not bad* summed Wright up nicely. Wells still didn't understand the Muslim

456

John joke from a month earlier. Maybe he never would. That hiccup aside, he couldn't complain. He gave Wright three minutes, headed out, hailed a cab. He felt calm, ready for action. This journey, so much longer and stranger than he had expected, would soon be over.

The taxi dropped him at the skyscraper's entrance at ten minutes to noon, and he trotted down the escalator to Elements, passing from Water to Metal on his way to the Fire zone, which weirdly enough was home to the rink. Each zone carried its own perfunctory decorations to invoke the theme. Otherwise, the mall was simply another marble-floored tribute to the Western luxury brands that the Chinese loved, and mostly empty on a weekday morning.

Wells ducked into stores at random and stopped in an oddly sweet-smelling bathroom for about ninety seconds. He wasn't trying to lose any watchers. They knew where he was going in any case. But if he could surprise or frustrate even one into showing himself, he'd be ahead.

No one jumped out, but as Wells passed the Prada store, a man drew his attention, a trim curly-haired guy in a suit. The guy was either one of Gideon's team or an investment banker on a coffee break. Wells pretended to be interested in a three-thousand-dollar jacket as the guy picked up a bag that could be described only as a male purse. He poked at the seams, ignored the price tag. An operative would have checked. So, banker.

Probably.

Wells moved back down the hallway, felt his phone buzz. He pulled it, found a message from Wright: *000.* He tucked the phone away, looked up — and saw Gideon staring at him. The Israeli had materialized a hundred feet away, four stores down, at the Y-junction of three corridors. His right hand was tucked beneath the left flap of his suit coat. The Sig Sauer P238 that he favored was small enough to hide there without attracting attention.

The problem with using phones instead of radios. By accident or design, Gideon had stepped into the hall in the seconds when Wells dropped his eyes to check the text. Now Wells was in a tough spot. He couldn't look over his shoulder to see if he'd been wrong about the Prada banker, or if anyone else was coming. If he reached for his pistol, Gideon would get off a half-dozen shots before Wells fired one. Gideon was probably a better shot than Wells, anyway. At a hundred feet, Wells had barely a one in four chance of putting a round center mass.

Gideon nodded to Wells, *Come on, come on.* Instead Wells raised a hand, crooked his fingers, *No, you.* Then ran like the ball-hogging linebacker he'd been at Dartmouth, not away from Gideon but *toward* him. His only play, a way for Wells to change the angles without turning his back. A safe move, if Gideon was enough of a pro to understand it. Wells couldn't reach behind his back for his pistol while he was sprinting. In motion, he was no threat to Gideon. Of course, if Gideon did mean to shoot him, then Wells was making his life easier by shrinking the distance. But even then, Wells had an out. If Gideon pulled his right hand, Wells would dive for the nearest store entrance, out of the line of fire.

Wells ate the floor with long strides, just conscious of the shops on either side, mannequins promising three-hundred-dollar T-shirts as a path to happiness. Gideon kept his hands steady under his suit. After two seconds, fifty feet, Wells stopped himself, trying not to slide on the slippery polished marble. All along, he kept his eyes on Gideon's right arm and readied himself to jump if it started to move. His heart thumped, fast and steady, ready for action. Wells had believed Gideon would see they were on the same side now. But if he was wrong —

A second passed. Another. Instead of pulling his pistol, Gideon made an oddly precise quarter turn to his left, so he was no longer facing Wells. Accepting the ceasefire without a word before either man had even shown his weapon.

Gideon looked across his body at Wells. "All right?"

"All right." Wells brought his palms together prayerfully in front of his chest. Another de-escalation. The sequence would no doubt have seemed bizarre to any sales clerks who might have happened to be watching it, the language open and secret at once. Like lovers exchanging pleasantries at a dinner party, their spouses beside them. *What have you been up to? Oh, keeping busy.*

"You have men?" Gideon called.

Wells held up two fingers.

"None for me." Gideon reached up with his right hand inside his suit and holstered the pistol under his left armpit.

"We walking now?"

Gideon turned and they came toward each other, slow, almost ceremonial steps.

"All right," Gideon said again, when they were face-to-face.

"This'll go quicker once the translator

shows." They'd brought the guy they'd used in Tokyo. Young, mid-twenties, a CIA contract employee named Ben. He spoke English, Spanish, Arabic, and Hebrew flawlessly.

Five minutes later, Wells, Gideon, and Ben sat in the food court. Shafer and Wright were at the other end of the room.

"Where's Orli?" The crucial question. If Gideon lied, Wells couldn't trust anything else he said.

"She's not coming."

"You said —"

"The Russians have her. I didn't know if you'd come to meet only me."

The right answer. The truth. "But she only came home this morning."

"Seven a.m., Aaron sent me to a bank in Mong Kok. When I got back, Orli was gone. Our guards said Buvchenko came in a van, she and Aaron talked with him, not for long, she kicked Aaron and they left."

Exactly what the video had shown. "What were you doing at the bank?"

"Aaron gave me a letter for them. I think he's moving money. Maybe going to run."

"He can't think —"

"I don't know what he thinks anymore."

"You've worked for him a long time."

Gideon explained how Duberman had

461

saved his son, news to Wells, a story the agency hadn't cracked. "After it happened I pledged my life to him. And still I would. But something's come loose in him."

"He tell you why Orli went with Buvchenko?"

"He says because the Russians threatened the kids. But there must have been something else, too, Aaron did something and she decided she couldn't trust him anymore. When I saw him he told me Buvchenko gave him two conditions to give back Orli, one that I kill you. I didn't argue, but why would the Russians care about you? Aaron's the one who wants you dead, he's obsessed, blames you for everything. Like if he kills you, it'll all go back to the way it was."

"Magical thinking." The same reason gamblers came to Duberman's palaces.

"But in a way, he's right. You're responsible for Orli at least. She didn't know the risks."

"You heard us last night. We tried to explain. We told her we'd protect her."

"You knew she wouldn't believe you. Or maybe you didn't, but he did." Gideon slid his eyes to Shafer. "If you cared, you would have pulled her and the kids out, found some pretext, held them until this was done. Even if she didn't want to go."

How could Wells argue? Wright had pulled the drone off Orli this morning. *Daddy's the one we want.* He and Shafer were playing a different game than he was.

"Men like you and me, we're not even the guns," Gideon said. "We're the bullets."

"What was Buvchenko's other condition?"

"He told Aaron to meet Cheung again in Macao. Tonight. Tomorrow morning, really. One a.m."

Barely thirteen hours away. And why? *Because the Russians know they're out of time.* The FSB's ultimate play almost didn't matter at this point. They were rolling the op.

"You need to help me find her," Gideon said.

Wells understood. Buvchenko wouldn't have much use for Orli after he squeezed what he could from Duberman. The FSB would have no problem murdering them both in a semi-plausible accident. A plane crash, maybe, or, even more plausibly, a helicopter. Even billionaires' helicopters weren't immune from the weather. *Casino magnate Aaron Duberman and his wife Orli died today when their helicopter slammed into the South China Sea in heavy rain on what is normally a routine fifteen-minute flight from Hong Kong to Macao . . .*

"We'll find her. If you haven't noticed,

463

she's hard to miss. And Hong Kong's not that big." Though Wells knew firsthand that if the Russians managed to put her on a ship, the task would be far tougher.

"Nor that small. Do your people know where to find Buvchenko?"

"No. If we can get his phone —"

"I couldn't find a way to ask Aaron the number this morning."

Wells considered. "Give me Aaron's number. Maybe we can trace it from there."

Maybe. Buvchenko no doubt knew the risk that the NSA could back-trace him and was using single-use burners and Internet telephony to call Duberman. Still, he couldn't avoid having one semipermanent number, a way for Duberman to reach him on short notice. That incoming phone would be their best chance.

Gideon gave Wells Duberman's number. "Now what?"

"Go back to the mansion, tell Duberman I didn't show, I got nervous. He'll like that. First priority is Buvchenko's number."

Gideon pushed back from the table. Wells raised a hand.

"Also. Your front gate must have cameras. Can you get the video, the make and model and plate of the van?"

"Yes."

"What about last month, when Buvchenko came the first time? Was that the same van?"

When he heard the translation, Gideon smiled. "A BMW. Nice. Blue. We should have that also. The video's saved a year at least."

"Get us that, maybe we'll pull a rabbit out of the technical hat." Wells knew he should end the conversation there, but he couldn't help himself. "Are we good? What's done is done?"

Gideon hesitated after he heard the translation. He looked at the tabletop, seemed to consider a half-dozen answers. "If I'd wanted to shoot you, I would have already," he said finally. "Let's get Orli."

He pushed back, walked out without a word to Shafer or Wright. He still had the limp.

21

BEIJING

Cheung sat alone in his office, trying to focus on a report on the problems with the air-to-air missiles for the J-31, when his phone rattled. Somehow he knew even before he looked at the screen who was calling. He picked up the handset with his fingertips, like an archaeologist pulling a cursed relic from a tomb.

When he saw the number, a wish-prayer came to him: *Erase what I've done.* The most selfish and juvenile of pleas. He wasn't asking for the girl, only for himself. Anyway, even the most powerful god couldn't make time run backward.

Cheung sent the call to voice mail and pushed the phone into his top desk drawer. Hide the relic, hide the curse. Irrefutable logic. Inside the drawer, it rattled again. Cheung felt his panic slide into something else, a sick eagerness. *Do it to me already,*

466

whatever it *is. Finish it.* He grabbed the phone.

"General."

Xiao. For some reason Cheung had expected Duberman. But Duberman didn't speak Chinese.

"My employer would like to extend another invitation for a visit."

Cheung laughed now, the sound backfiring in his throat. Was this how it felt to go mad? Each individual word made sense but together they added to less than nothing.

"He would, would he?"

"Tonight. One a.m., to be precise."

"Not possible."

"He can send his own plane if you'd like. If that would be more convenient."

"Did you hear me, Xiao? I said no."

"He says your friends insist. That they have questions they need answered, and soon."

Xiao's voice was as small and deferential as ever, yet the words turned the phone to lava in Cheung's hand. Questions, indeed. His friends, indeed. The thumb drive that Duberman had passed to him the day before asked for detailed technical specs on the J-31 and the next-generation ballistic missile program that the Chinese were secretly designing. Cheung had imagined the Americans would start slowly and build, but they seemed intent on grabbing all the information they could right away. What would they want next time? Every drone program?

Typical American impatience.

"Also if you'd like, he can promise you more entertainment like last week."

Now Cheung knew he was going mad. Doubly so, because despite everything, he felt himself stir. They'd slapped him, and now they were offering him a plate of dates. A treat. He still couldn't remember what had happened the week before.

Didn't he deserve a time that he remembered? Next time he'd remember.

No. There would be no next time.

To silence the voices in his head, he snapped at Xiao. "Does he think I'm some functionary? That I drop everything and come south whenever he asks —"

"I understand your importance, I promise. So does he. I can tell you that he intends to give you a very good excuse for meeting on such short notice."

"What's that?"

"The plane order he plans to place with you."

Duberman had that much right. No one would question Cheung's visit if he came back to Beijing with a launch order for the Smoothwind. Anyway, Cheung knew he couldn't say no. "All right. Tell him I'll be there. Maybe I'll even come early, so I have some time to gamble." The last words escaped Cheung's lips before he could stop himself.

Mad, truly.

22

HONG KONG

Wells's frustration rose after Gideon disappeared into the mall's recesses. They had barely a half day to find Orli and disrupt the FSB's game. Yet they couldn't go straight at Duberman, and they had no obvious way to find Buvchenko unless the NSA came through.

So he and Shafer headed back to the American consulate and the CIA station there. The consulate was on Garden Road on Hong Kong Island, the lower slopes of the Peak, only blocks from the restaurant where Wells had killed Peretz and Makiv. The Chinese security services watched everyone who entered. The FSB might well be trying to monitor it, too. But Wells and Shafer had to risk the surveillance if they wanted help from the NSA.

The CIA and NSA knew only too well that the Chinese and Russians trawled the public Internet as aggressively as they did. So, at a cost of twenty-two billion dollars, the NSA had built its own worldwide fiber-optic network, physically separate from the privately owned cables that carried data over the Internet. The agency used the network for what it called routine-classified cables, anything at the For Official Use Only, Secret, or Top Secret levels. For more important transmissions, such as discussions of ongoing operations, the CIA depended on the satellite network that the NSA had launched during the Cold War and been updating ever since. The satellites had less capacity than the fiber lines, but they were effectively impossible to hack. The Pentagon shared some traffic and the multibillion-dollar annual cost of maintaining both networks.

In the wake of Edward Snowden's leaks, NSA had tightened its security further, especially for stations inside or bordering China and Russia. It simply would not respond to requests that weren't sent through the American-controlled networks. Operatives who didn't have their own portable sat connection or couldn't get to a station had to call Langley and route the request through a desk officer, as Shafer had done for Wells more than once. That move didn't improve security, but it did save the NSA from responsibility if something went wrong. But with Shafer in Hong Kong, they were stuck with the NSA's rules.

Wright set them up in a coms room two doors down from his office, the usual windowless acoustically baffled electromagnetically shielded if-the-world-ends-you'll-read-about-it-now-but-you-won't-feel-it-until-tomorrow cubbyhole. A pleasant enough place to spend an afternoon. From there, Shafer called the senior duty officer at Fort Meade to ask for a trace on Duberman's number.

The time difference meant that they were making the request in the early morning in Washington. But the NSA operated on a true twenty-four-hour timetable, a necessity since most of its targets lived in Africa, the Middle East, and Central Asia. Considering the simplicity of the request, Wells figured the agency would have an answer for them in an hour at most.

Nope. The problem that had plagued them since the start of this mission popped up yet again. Duberman was an American citizen, and for better or worse, the NSA no longer treated requests to tap or trace American phones as cavalierly as it once had. Before Snowden, the agency could have "self-certified," a polite phrase for breaking the law today, telling Congress in six months. Now it demanded court preauthorization in all cases, unless the person making the request would confirm in writing that the information was needed to stop an imminent terrorist attack on United States soil.

Wells heard this explanation firsthand, as Shafer put the duty officer on speaker ten seconds into what turned into a three-minute speech. Along the way, Wells watched Shafer go through all five stages of telephonic bureaucratic grief: head-shaking, eye-rolling, forehead-slapping, twin-middle-finger-raising, and finally finger-pistol-to-temple mock suicide.

"We need this now," Shafer said, when the guy was done. "We're looking at a major intelligence operation involving the FSB, the PRC. With a meeting in less than twelve hours."

"Unfortunately, that doesn't meet the benchmark I've outlined."

"Subsection 3A or 5B?

"I'm sorry, Mr. Shafer." His tone suggested otherwise.

"I can ask Vinny Duto to call, if that'll help."

"The standards are the same for everyone. Even the President."

Shafer cradled a pretend assault rifle and opened up on the phone, *rat-a-tat-tat*. "Fine. What happens next? You call one of your lawyers, tell them to take it to FISA?" The Foreign Intelligence Surveillance Act court, the special federal judges who oversaw the NSA.

"Correct. Then our attorney decides whether the request merits waking a FISA judge tonight or if it can wait for a regular emergency hearing in the morning."

Even Wells saw the duty officer had just told them they'd be waiting.

"And how will this paragon of legal excellence decide?" Shafer said.

"If it gives us a chance at an HLT" — high-level target — "in ISIS, AQ, or some other designated group, we'll call tonight."

"Vladimir Putin. You may have heard of him."

"Waking the judges is a last resort."

"Tell me you're joking."

"Mr. Shafer, I promise we will get that emergency hearing when the court opens. Then it's up to the judge. Assuming he signs off, we'll trace two levels down, every number for the last ninety days. We find anything you want us to follow, and it doesn't belong to a U.S. citizen, we'll run it

474

immediately. I assume we're looking for Russian or Chinese numbers of suspicious origin as a first priority."

"Correct." Shafer was resigned to defeat, Wells saw. "So when will we have that first trace?"

"If the judge okays it, I'd guess noon." Meaning midnight Hong Kong time. Ten hours away. An hour before the meeting between Cheung and Duberman.

"That's not even close to good enough."

"It's the best I can do."

"One more question. If I call you back with a Russian number, or numbers —"

"That we should be able to do right away."

With that minor win, Shafer ended the call.

"All of a sudden, they're dotting every *i*?" Wells said. Irony that smelled like sewage, so thick Wells needed to pinch his nostrils. This emphasis on legal procedure had been nowhere to be found when the President locked him on the *Reagan.*

"The judge'll give it to us."

"Orli could be anywhere in ten hours."

"She could be anywhere now. If it's any consolation, it doesn't matter whether they run the trace in ten minutes or ten days. No way Buvchenko is dumb enough to let us catch him on an incoming call. Better hope your buddy Gideon comes through before he goes to Macao with his boss tonight."

Shafer's mention of Macao gave Wells a fresh idea. "Why don't we ask the White House for help with that?"

"You mean hit the meet, send in a Delta team to pick up Cheung and Duberman? Hypothetically speaking, assuming we lock down the location and we're confident we can do it without civ casualties?"

"Sure." Black Hawks skimming over the South China Sea.

"First off, you know DoD hates ops with no notice, no prep. Second, who knows what we even have in the area? Probably the closest teams are in Mindanao —" The island where the United States helped the Philippine military fight Islamist terrorists.

"So put the team on a plane."

"Think it through, John. Going at the FSB is one thing. They started this when they offered asylum to Duberman. The Chinese, that's different. No way can we put American soldiers into PRC airspace to grab a four-star PLAAF general. Especially when we don't know exactly what the guy's done."

Shafer was right. The President would never agree. If the Chinese caught American soldiers trying to kidnap a senior PRC general, the repercussions would be unfathomable. As in World War III unfathomable.

"I mean, if you want, I'll call Duto, ask him to ask."

"Forget it. What if I go in myself? Ask Wright to helicopter me in?"

"You're forgetting something."

"What's that? Security? I doubt Duberman or Cheung will want witnesses for this —"

"What you're going to do when you get there. It won't exactly be a clean grab. Probably they'll die before they let you put them on a helicopter."

"I'll burn that bridge when I come to it."

"As a rule, I admire your can-do spirit, but you're going to need more than that this time."

"Why am I the only one who cares what's happening here?"

"If there were an easy answer, we would already have found it, John." Shafer flipped open his laptop. "While we wait for Gideon, let's see what we have on the FSB here. Never know if it'll come in handy."

Wells figured Shafer was trying to distract him. But he had nothing else to propose. So the afternoon shrank as they looked through the station's records on the FSB. But the CIA's top priority in Hong Kong was

China, not Russia. The files didn't have much, though they did include photos of nine local FSB case officers, including Sergei and Nikolai, who was believed to be the most senior operative. The station estimated the Russians had at least a dozen officers in Hong Kong, plus twenty or so logistics, support, and administrative staff. The FSB's core mission in Hong Kong was assessed as economic espionage, with a secondary focus on monitoring China's naval moves in the South China Sea. Russia didn't have a direct stake in the body of water, but its ally Vietnam did. The information was all interesting enough in an academic way, but it brought them no closer to finding Buvchenko or Orli.

"See what we've learned, John?" Shafer said, after two hours.

"That you're content to waste the afternoon because you think she's expendable."

"Let's say I have a different view than you as to what we owe her."

Wells was saved from answering when one of his burners buzzed. He grabbed it, found a text from Gideon. Not a phone number, but photos of two license plates, one noted as "van," the other as "BMW." Neither was a diplomatic plate, good news. Diplo plates would have meant the cars were openly registered to the Russian consulate, a dead lead.

Wells pushed the phone at Shafer.

"Don't think of it as saving her. Think of it as blowing up whatever Oleg Nemtsov" — the Director General of the FSB — "has going."

"When you put it that way."

Even the coms rooms didn't provide access to the most highly classified data at Langley — raw images of stolen documents, for example. Those could be viewed only from what the CIA called Loop Zero, the networks inside the Langley campus itself.

Still, they could reach into almost two hundred CIA databases that collectively held a staggering amount of information. Some of the databases, like the white pages, were publicly available to anyone with an Internet connection. Some had been bought from third-party providers like Dun & Bradstreet. And the rest had been stolen by the NSA. Like, for example, automobile, property, and corporate records from all over the world, including Hong Kong.

Within five minutes, Shafer had found registration and ownership records for the BMW and the van, translated from the original Chinese filings. After another five minutes he began to purr like a cat waiting outside a hole where a mouse was trapped. Wells was content to let Shafer work, knowing he was as good as these hunts as anyone in the world. Forty-five minutes later, he pushed his laptop to Wells.

"Check it out." The registration records showed that a Hong Kong company called Kowloon East West PLC owned both cars. The filings for the company showed that its address was a post office box in Tsim Sha Tsui. No employees, no sales, all records care of a Kowloon law firm.

"So a shell owns the cars? That helps us how?"

"Good back-office tradecraft, you set up a new company for every registration or ownership record. Ideally, you go a step past that, use lots of different lawyers for the filings so there's no pattern even at the nominee level. No connections. Unnecessary connections are sloppy tradecraft. But that's expensive and hard work. People get lazy, especially if they think no one's ever going to look. So now we know the cars are linked."

"Which we already did."

"Yeah, so what are the odds that those are the only two cars that company owns? I reversed the search, went from the corporate side." Shafer tapped the keyboard, pulled up three more auto registrations.

"Good, now we know they own more cars."

"Now you're being intentionally difficult." Shafer closed four ownership records, left one open. "Okay, if you look, you'll see they transferred the title of this fifth one last year to another shell company" — called 839653 Ltd. and registered to an apartment in Kowloon. "Six presumably random digits. Now, that's tradecraft."

"I'm glad you approve. So, good, the Russians decided to sell one of their cars."

"To another shell company. And that wasn't just any car. It was a Mercedes AMG sedan, barely two years old. The big souped-up one. Runs more than a hundred thousand dollars in the U.S., a million-plus HK?" Shafer pointed at the screen. "Check out the recorded transfer price, which our friends at the Hong Kong Transport Department were good enough to provide."

Fifty thousand Hong Kong.

"Five percent of what it was worth," Shafer said. "I'll bet you all Duberman's money that the person behind 839653 Ltd. is an FSB case officer."

Finally, Wells understood. "Stripping assets." Many of Russia's richest men had built their fortunes just this way. They used other people's money to take control of companies or government-owned property. Then, secretly, they sold themselves valuable pieces for pennies on the dollar.

"If the guys at the top can steal a billion barrels of oil, you think an FSB officer doesn't think he's entitled to a Mercedes courtesy of the Russian taxpayer?"

"Not bad, Ellis."

"Somebody's sloppy, somebody else is greedy, we have a trail."

"We still don't have a name."

"No, we have something better. An address. Twelfth floor, 231 Ki Lung Street, in the Prince Edward neighborhood. North of Mong Kok." Shafer pulled up a satellite shot of the building, which looked like every other concrete apartment mid-rise in Kowloon, fifteen or so stories of shabbily painted concrete festooned with air-conditioning units. At street level, a storefront whose dirty windows revealed shelves filled with trays of junk. *Kwon Pang Watch Repair,* the store's sign read. A break for Wells. A watch store should close by six p.m., fewer people to watch the building's front door.

"Do yourself a favor. Don't forget that number. It may be handy."

"839 . . ."

"839653."

"839653. Even if you're right, we don't know the apartment is Nikolai's, just FSB."

"You think the senior ops guy at the station lets somebody else have the AMG?"

The door opened, and Wright entered. Shafer explained what they'd found.

"We can put up a drone, watch the apartment while you keep tracing," Wright said.

A sensible idea. But it spiked an instant fever in Wells. No more robot eyes in the sky, especially ones that could look but not touch. It was now past 5 p.m. By the time he got to West Kowloon, it would be six at least. This time of year, the sun set in Hong Kong around seven, so it would be nearly dusk, one of the safest times for a break-in. After nightfall, people naturally increased their suspicion of strangers. But at sunset their instincts hadn't fully kicked in. If anything, they relaxed as the workday finished and they headed home. Anyway, Wells couldn't afford to wait past dark. Cheung and Duberman were set to meet in less than eight hours, and this apartment was more likely to be a lead than the end of the trail.

"No drone," Wells said. "You have another bike for me?"

"If you must."

"I must."

23

Wells rode northwest on Ki Lung Street, looking for the watch store that marked 231. There. He pulled the Honda to the curb for a peek. Up close the building had all the charm of an air-raid shelter, a thousand water stains flecking its pale yellow paint. Its entrance was beside the watch store, a narrow glass door protected by steel bars. Behind it, a vestibule ended in a second barred door, a good sign. Some buildings around here had night watchmen, but the ones that did rarely bothered with double security doors.

Above the doors, windows glowed in the gathering dusk. The building had more than a hundred apartments. Hundreds of potential witnesses, hundreds of innocent bystanders. Not the place for a gun battle, especially with a police station only blocks away on Prince Edward Road.

Wells kicked the bike into gear and rolled

off. A block down, he parked in an alley, tucking his helmet beside the front wheel. The bike was a Honda CB600F, the same model he'd used when he'd shot Peretz and Makiv, down to the year and color. Shafer wouldn't approve. The police could easily connect two identical bikes. But Wells appreciated the familiarity. This time, he carried two pistols, one loose in his backpack with a suppressor already screwed on, the second hidden in his waistband. *Sometimes you feel like a nut . . .*

The traffic from Hong Kong Island had been light. Wells was a couple minutes ahead of schedule. He wanted to rush inside and so made himself do the opposite. He sat sidesaddle, listened to the neighborhood, truck engines thrumming and kids shouting, pigeons cooing and chickens squawking. Despite the very real dangers of avian flu, more than a few Hong Kongers still raised poultry in their apartments. Strange city, its modernity skyscraper tall, an inch deep.

More distantly Wells heard a muezzin sound the call to the *maghrib.* He wanted to begin his ablutions, join the prayer. He fought the impulse, knowing he couldn't afford the attention or the time. He slipped off the bike, tucked a baseball cap low over his forehead. In his backpack he felt the comforting weight of the pistol and the black calfskin gloves beside it. He was alone tonight. Wright had offered backup, but Wells said no, and Wright didn't push. The agency and the FSB kept each other at arm's length for obvious and good reason. No station chief looked forward to the prospect of tit-for-tat assassinations, officers shot in the street. Anyway, Wells didn't mind running without backup. On a fast, simple op, going in alone could be safer than working with a partner you didn't know and hadn't learned to trust.

A hundred dinners hung in the dusk, the sweet, heavy smells of grease and onions and garlic and chicken frying. For once Hong Kong seemed something more than a petri dish for loneliness. Wells was calm as he walked. Aware. *Awake.* Near the building's front door, he pulled his autopick, a cigarette-lighter-sized tool that could beat any civilian lock in seconds. Wells had always considered it the most useful device the agency had ever invented, though the fake fingerprints were about to take that prize.

He stepped to the door — and a commotion from the street turned his head. A boy, no more than four, zigzagged across the pavement toward Wells as the kid's father hollered and gave chase. Wells stuffed the autopick away and ran for the kid. Fortunately no cars were coming, and he scooped up the boy a moment before the father reached him. The dad was panting, out of shape, potbelly poking from his working-man's white T-shirt.

"Thank you," the father said. "He sees you, want to say hi."

The guy seemed to be blaming him, like Wells was the Peter Pan of jaywalking. "Sorry." Wells turned away, hoping to end the conversation quickly.

"It okay. We live here, anyway." The father nodded at the entrance to 231. A bad break. Dad would remember him if the police came knocking. The kid pointed at Wells, jabbering, "He says you have backpack, too. Like him." The kid was wearing a tiny Snoopy pack.

"Observant little guy, isn't he?" Wells resisted the urge to substitute another word for *guy*. Now the kid was taking off his pack, holding it for Wells. Bad to worse.

"He says, can he see what's in your pack?" Dad said. "Trade. I'm so sorry —"

Sure. I'll just unscrew the suppressor so junior can hang on to the nine more easily. "I wish I could, but I have to go."

The dad translated, and the kid screamed like Wells had stuck a knife in him. Wells stuck out his hand to shake, but the kid yelled even louder. Wells backed away quickly, the kid shouting the whole time. What no one explained about real-world fieldwork, what Hollywood always misunderstood, was that success or failure on an op could come down to a break as trivial as a child's outstretched finger.

At the corner Wells turned left, walked into the first store he saw, a no-name minimarket. He bought a Coke, made himself nurse it for ten minutes, giving the kid and his dad a chance to go inside. Like sand through the hourglass. Finally, with the dusk settling into night, he returned to the building, making sure that this time he had the entrance to himself.

The autopick solved the outer and inner locks as quickly as a key. Inside, Wells found a dirty beige-tiled hallway and rows of mailboxes scratched with indecipherable graffiti. He wondered why the Russians had chosen the place. The neighborhood was hardly glamorous, and almost one hundred percent Chinese. Though probably they'd come here for the same reason Wells and Wright had picked Mong Kok. The neighbors might notice a white face, but they would hardly ask questions. The building offered a break from endless surveillance, too. Only one CCTV camera watched the hallway and it dangled from its mounting bracket in a way that suggested it hadn't worked in a while. Still, Wells couldn't imagine that the Russians had brought Orli here. She would have attracted too much attention, and if she'd fought, the whole neighborhood would have heard.

The fire stairs were at the back of the hall. Wells pulled on his gloves, made his way up. On the sixth-floor landing, he picked up faint voices above. He stopped, inched his hand back toward his pistol. The voices quieted, then picked up. A boy speaking Cantonese, a girl laughing. Probably on the roof, or the top landing. Teen lovers didn't have many chances to be alone in this city. Wells walked on.

At twelve, he left the stairs and found himself in a narrow hallway lit by shaky fluorescents that gave it a faintly haunted feeling. He counted twelve apartment doors, more than he'd hoped to see since he didn't have an apartment number, only the floor. Still, the process of elimination was quick. Kids' voices, no way. Dinner wafting out, unlikely. Cantonese-language television, probably not. The Russians might understand the language, but Wells didn't see why they would subject themselves to it. He checked off nine apartments, left himself with three. He heard an elevator rattling up, knew he needed to decide. He went for the door with the most security, two deadbolts instead of one, no lights visible under the door. As soon as he chose, he was sure he was right.

He pulled the autopick, put it to the top lock. It clicked through, snapped back the bolt. The lower lock was tougher, with a flat metal frame around the lock itself. Wells was just putting pick to keyhole when the elevator stopped. He had no choice but to duck back into the fire staircase. From the landing, Wells heard the chime of the elevator's electronic bell. Footsteps came toward the back of the hallway. Wells pulled his pistol. If the Russians found the top lock undone —

In the hall a man muttered softly in Cantonese. A woman answered. A door opened and closed. Then silence. *Friends? Lovers?* Wells had guessed at a thousand lives over the years. He counted ten, holstered his pistol, crept into the hall. Empty again. This time, he took the time to examine the apartment door for simple tripwires, like a piece of Scotch tape stuck to the frame and the door. He didn't see any, a surprise. Intrusion monitoring was basic tradecraft. Maybe he'd chosen the wrong apartment. Still, he had already picked one lock. No reason not to take a look. He pulled his autopick, lined it up with the lower lock, set it to work.

When it was done, Wells put an ear to the door to listen for rustling inside the apartment, whispers in Russian. Nothing. He flattened himself beside the door, reached across it to twist the knob, pushed the door open slowly with his left hand, in case someone had set a shotgun or other trap inside. Wells silently answering Evan, seven thousand miles away, *Starting to wonder how you make it out there.*

As the door opened, Wells heard not a shotgun blast but an alarm's insistent beep. Just inside he saw a control panel, its numbers now glowing orange. No wonder the Russians hadn't bothered with Scotch tape. Wells looked inside. The room was dark, blackout shades drawn. Entry was the most dangerous moment of any break-in. Wells would be silhouetted against the open doorway, giving anyone inside an easy shot. He stepped through, flipped on the light switch beside the alarm, spun to cover the room, closed the door behind him.

He found himself in what looked to be the combined living area and kitchen for a two-room apartment. The place seemed empty, but the alarm screeched a warning and its control panel flashed orange. Wells stared at the panel, wondering how he could possibly decipher the code —

Then he knew. The six-digit "name" of the shell company, the one Shafer had told him to remember. Only he couldn't. *839 . . .* the first three digits were right, he was sure. He keyed them in, stopped, hesitantly tried *536,* knowing he was close but wrong, Julia for Juliette wrong. He punched enter. The alarm beeped three times fast, a decisive rejection.

839 . . . 563 . . . enter. Again three fast beeps, and the backlighting for the panel's numbers went from orange to red, he must be almost out of time —

839 . . . 653 . . . enter.

The alarm quieted and the backlighting on the panel turned green. Shafer was a pain in the ass, but his instincts were gold. Wells stepped back, took in the room. Oddly, silver cylinders about the size of soda cans were attached to the front door's hinges. Motors, Wells guessed. He wondered if the alarm included a trigger to turn them on, force the door shut, trap would-be

493

thieves inside.

The room had surveillance, too, golf-ball-sized cameras mounted in the corners. Wells assumed that they weren't routinely monitored and instead checked only if the alarm went off. No spy agency on earth had enough men to watch empty safe houses. Still, the cameras were another good reason for Wells not to linger. Wherever Orli might be, she wasn't here. The alarm and the strange automatic hinges made the apartment feel more like a stash house than a safe house, a hiding place for money and weapons rather than people.

The room where Wells stood was about fifteen feet square, with functional furniture. A week-old copy of the *South China Morning Post* lay on the coffee table, along with a stack of Cyrillic-language magazines. So the place was in active use. Someone had been here a week ago, or less.

The room had no rugs, pictures, or bookcases, no obvious hiding spaces. Wells turned to the galley kitchen, pulled open cabinets and drawers, found nothing of interest. The fridge held a takeout box of chicken tikka masala, a six-pack of Tsingtao, a bottle of Grey Goose vodka. Wells put the chicken to his nose. It didn't smell, so it could be no more than a couple of days old.

Which only increased the odds that someone would be back soon.

Wells peeked at his watch, found he'd
been in the room almost two minutes
already, on the twelfth floor for five. The
odds of being caught increased exponen-
tially with time on target. Two minutes was
ideal, five acceptable. Anything past ten was
worse than amateurish. He hurried into the
inner room, found a sloppily made queen-
sized bed, a closet that was open to reveal
men's shirts and jeans, a steel desk with a
Wi-Fi router on top. No laptop. No surveillance cameras in here, at least none Wells
could see. Beside the closet another door
led to what had to be a bathroom.

Then he saw a two-drawer filing cabinet
tucked under the desk. Both drawers were
reinforced with steel and closed with dial
combination locks that would be immune
to the autopick. Wells holstered his first
pistol, pulled the one with the suppressor
from his backpack. He squatted down,
sighted, shot both locks at their weakest
point, where the steel bolt entered the lock's
housing. The suppressor quieted the pistol,
but the metal ping of round against lock
was louder than Wells would have liked. At
least the ricocheting rounds didn't catch
him in the face.

The bottom drawer stuck when he pulled on it. When he finally muscled it open, he saw why. Thick rubber-banded stacks of hundred-dollar bills filled it nearly to the top. Maybe two million dollars in all, Wells guessed. On top of the stacks, a plastic bag a couple inches square that held a half-dozen shiny stones. Diamonds. Big ones. Worth a few hundred dollars if they were fake, a few million if they were real; only a jeweler would know. Finally, one more bag, this one a standard Ziploc, filled with a white powder that wasn't baking soda. Wells resisted the impulse to steal it all, just to piss off the FSB. None of it would help him find Orli.

He closed the lower drawer, pulled open the top. He found a less lucrative but more promising stash. A pair of Makarov 9-millimeter pistols sat atop a thick stack of papers. Wells thumbed through the stack. Statements in English from a half-dozen banks, corporate records in Cyrillic, a rubber-banded sheaf of documents in Chinese that seemed to be related to a property development. Wells grabbed everything, including the pistols, stuffed it all in his backpack. He had no idea what might matter. Let Shafer sort through it back at the consulate. Anyway, Makarovs had been his preferred pistol until Anne had shamed him into going with Glocks, far more reliable.

A wastebasket was tucked beside the cabinet. Wells peeked inside, found nothing but a crumpled receipt from Calcutta Best Indian Restaurant, presumably the source of the tikka masala in the fridge. He shifted his attention to the desk's only drawer. It was unlocked. Inside, pens, business cards in Chinese and English and Cyrillic, blank invoices from what appeared to be a local car repair shop, a burner phone with a cracked screen and a charger still attached to its body, a roll of condoms, and the apartment's sole personal note, a picture of Nikolai with his arm around a pretty Slavic woman. Wells took everything but the condoms.

He was torn between wanting to leave and checking the closet and bathroom for more. He returned to the living area, listened for anything in the hall, any signs that the neighbors had noticed the ricocheting shots. But he heard nothing except ordinary sounds, televisions and families talking.

One more minute, two at most.

In the closet, he found that the jeans and shirts were very expensive and very large. The combination suggested they belonged to Buvchenko. An AK was propped against the back corner, a half-dozen spare magazines stacked beside it. Wells pulled the rifle, found it oiled and clean, no signs that it had been fired recently. Its presence slightly surprised Wells, but then the agency had its own assault rifles in the consulate. He hoped he'd find an old laptop or two stowed in the closet, where retired computers often ended up, but no.

He started to check the pockets of Buvchenko's clothes, changed his mind. No time. In the bathroom he found a half-dozen pill bottles on the sink, along with vials of clear liquid with hand-lettered Cyrillic labels. Buvchenko's steroid regimen, probably. Wells grabbed the pills and vials, a pointless but satisfying thumb in Buvchenko's eye, and walked out through the bedroom, one last look. He had found as much as he could have hoped, short of a laptop or a real phone rather than a burner. Buvchenko was meeting Cheung in not even six hours, and Wells didn't know if Shafer could tease out anything meaningful soon enough to matter, but at least they had a chance.

In the living room, Wells reached for the alarm panel, wondered why he was bothering. Buvchenko and Nikolai would know the place had been hit soon as they saw the cabinet. Then Wells had another idea, a way to wrong-foot the Russians. What if he set the alarm off intentionally, waited on the stairs, ambushed whoever responded?

But he didn't know how fast the FSB would come or how many men would show. He couldn't waste an hour, much less half the night, hanging out on the landing. And the alarm would cost him his greatest advantage, the fact that the Russians didn't know he'd found this place and was closing in. Best to go. He reached for the door —

And heard the chime of the elevator as its doors opened. Then footsteps. Two sets. But no voices. Men who wanted to be quiet. Could they have seen him here? Of course, if they'd checked the cameras. In fact, if the cameras were Internet-enabled, whoever was in the hallway could be looking at Wells right now, and know exactly where he stood. Even if they *hadn't* checked the cameras, and this visit was a simple coincidence, they would know something was wrong as soon as they reached the door, because it was unlocked. Wells had left it that way after he'd turned off the alarm, he'd seen no reason to lock himself in. Now he couldn't, the sound of the deadbolts would be obvious.

The footsteps edged closer. Now the room was a trap. They could toss in a CS grenade to smoke him out or even a frag if they wanted to play nasty —

One move. Wells raised the pistol with his right hand, went to the door, pulled it open with his left. He stepped into the doorway, his finger pressuring the trigger, ready to shoot as soon as he had an angle.

He found himself looking not at Buvchenko or any Russian but at two Chinese men walking hand-in-hand down the hall. He put the pistol on first one and then the other. The men only shook their heads. They both wore T-shirts and jeans, tight, no room to hide a pistol. Coming home quietly for reasons of their own, and Wells had almost killed them. He put a finger to his lips and nodded. They glanced sidelong at each other, nodded back. Wells lowered the pistol, pulled the apartment door shut, backed away to the fire stairs, and ran for the street.

Life was full of surprises.

24

Duberman paged through his closet, looking for the right suit, the suit that would settle the night. He had a hundred and thirty, all made-to-measure in Milan, none quite the same, subtle gradations of blue and gray and black, tiny variations in piping, stitching, buttons, and fit.

Tonight he wanted something stylish. Raffish, even. A throwback to the Sizzlin' Saloon. He found it at the end of the rack. Gray, wide lapels, broad white stripes, big shoulders, narrow waist. Practically a zoot. He paired it with a gray silk shirt, a white tie, patent black shoes. For a watch, instead of his usual Patek Philippe, a platinum Rolex with diamonds and sapphires.

He checked himself out in his three-way full-length mirror. A speakeasy vibe. Cheung wouldn't understand. But Duberman wasn't dressing for that slavering Chinese pedophile.

The pièce de résistance, the Kahr Arms P380 in his closet safe. The Kahr weighed barely a half pound unloaded and was not even five inches long, four inches high. Smaller than some smartphones, small enough to fit easily in the suit's breast pocket.

Duberman had bought his first pistol, a Smith & Wesson, after that dinner with Jimmy the Roller at the Mirage. He'd taken shooting seriously back then, seriously enough to sit through a safety course and fill out the paperwork for a Nevada concealed-carry license. Over the years, he had added a dozen different pistols to his collection, ranging from the Kahr to an old-school .44 Magnum. Still, he had stopped carrying any of them long ago.

Why bother, with Gideon to protect him?

He pushed aside a shoe rack to reveal a wall safe. He spun the dial, pulled it open. Besides the pistol, it held fifty thousand dollars in hundreds and twenties, and a handful of sex toys that he'd used with girlfriends before Orli. He'd never had the guts to ask her to try them. The thought turned his lips, a grim smile. *That* ship had sailed.

And this morning's additions to the safe, Orli's iPhone and the boys' passports. They stared at him, silently accusing him. Though he knew he'd done nothing wrong. Duberman had never been much of a reader. But at the University of Georgia, four decades ago, he'd found time for one English class, *Introduction to Southern Literature.* Inevitably the reading list included *All the King's Men,* the Robert Penn Warren classic. The other novels bored him. Faulkner tried too hard. Everybody else was stuck on slavery and race. But Warren's novel captivated him from first page to last. Power and ambition, secrets and lies. Not just the lies men told one another, but the ones they told themselves.

He flipped through the twins' passports. So many stamps. His sons had traveled more in their first two years than most people did in their entire lives. He'd given them so much already, and he wanted to give them so much more. Unbidden and unwanted, the climax of *All the King's Men* came to Duberman then, Willie Stark in his hospital bed. The governor. The boss. Shot and dying, his friend and errand boy and finally nemesis Jack Burden at his side. The boss insisting to Burden, *It might have been all different, Jack. You got to believe that.*

Jack, he'd pretended to agree. But he hadn't believed anything of the sort, had he?

Duberman felt an unexpected wetness against his cheeks. No. Men didn't cry. *He* didn't cry, that was certain. He dropped the passports back in the safe like they'd burned his fingers. He scooped the pistol, checked the magazine and the safety, which wasn't on the frame but an internal trigger block. He popped in the mag, slipped the Kahr into his inside breast pocket. *Say hello to my little friend.* That fast, his fear vanished. He examined himself in the mirror. Perfect. The Kahr left only a tiny bulge, and the suit was gaudy enough to distract even a close observer.

Past nine p.m. now, sun gone, thick tropical clouds like a cap on the sky, reflecting a million colors from the skyscrapers. Hong Kong was at its most otherworldly in this weather, a sci-fi colony that happened to be on earth. Duberman had brought engineers and metallurgists to the mansion on a night like this, told them, *I want the new casino to have walls like these clouds.* Impossible. Only it wasn't; they'd made his vision real.

Down the hall, the twins slept. Rafael's little fists were curled up. Boaz was muttering anxiously. Children shouldn't see their parents fight. Duberman kissed them on their foreheads, and they seemed to relax.

At least they weren't worried about Orli, not yet. She'd left them before for photo shoots. Duberman didn't know what he'd tell them tomorrow, the next day, the next. He'd think of something. They were adorable children. Everyone around them loved them. They'd be fine.

He found Gideon in the kitchen, quiet, sitting on a barstool and sipping mineral water.

"Boys okay?"

The question pleased Duberman. Gideon was leaving his misplaced anger behind. "For now. Anything from Wells?"

Gideon shook his head. "His phone's off now."

"So, to Macao." Duberman kept his tone light, like he was suggesting they go out for pizza.

"Shouldn't I stay? He still might bite."

"I want to get there early. In case Cheung's planning something. Or even Buvchenko."

"Have you heard anything more from either of them?"

Duberman shook his head. He had texted the Russian to tell him the meeting was set, got the single word *Da* in response. He still didn't know whether Buvchenko or the other Russians planned to come to the meeting, or what they would tell him and Cheung if they did.

"Maybe you should call Buvchenko. See what he wants before you go over."

Duberman didn't know why Gideon was pushing the point. "After. When we have good news."

Question anything about Aaron Duberman, but not his taste. He had a closetful of ten-thousand-dollar bespoke suits he could have worn tonight. So Gideon understood that Duberman had made himself look ridiculous intentionally. What he didn't understand was *why.* He wondered whether the suit was a cloak, a way for Duberman to tell himself, *This is not who I am.*

"All dressed up," Gideon said.

"You didn't know me when I had just the one place in Reno. I'd come in like a cowboy one night, a rocker the next."

This would have been the early eighties, Gideon figured. While Duberman worked his casino floor in a ten-gallon hat and a cap pistol, Gideon was in Lebanon killing anyone foolish enough to step into his crosshairs. Soldiers? Maybe. The men he'd shot had rifles. But most of them hadn't worn uniforms. The IDF's rules of engagement were clear: *Any males of fighting age carrying weapons may be considered enemy soldiers and targeted without warning.* Fighting age was not defined. Some of Gideon's kills hadn't been old enough to shave.

"Never thought of you as the nostalgic type, Aaron."

Duberman pulled on his lapels, straightened out his suit. "Good or bad, amazing how fast it goes. Like it never even happened."

Saying good-bye. He knows. Even if he doesn't, he does. Gideon felt an unexpected rip in his heart for Duberman, a wish to protect him even now. For Tal, if no one else. *Kill for you. Or die for you.* Whatever Duberman thought, Gideon hadn't forgotten his promise. Maybe together they could find some way to finesse Duberman out of the grave that he had dug himself.

Besides, Gideon had heard nothing from Wells since sending over the license plates hours before. Enough waiting. "Ready when you are."

"Great." Duberman's tone was suddenly brisk, businesslike, and Gideon wondered if he'd been fooling himself. Was the man truly scared? Or did he take whatever pose he needed to bend the people around him? After so many years working for Duberman, Gideon ought to know. But he didn't.

Maybe that uncertainty *was* all the answer he needed.

The uncertainty, and the fact that Duberman hadn't mentioned Orli once.

"She'll be back." Like he was reading Gideon's mind. "We'll work things out."

Gideon felt his phone buzz. A text from Wells, auto-translated from English into Hebrew. *Ready to meet. Star Ferry HK term ASAP.*

"What's up?" Duberman said.

"Wells." Gideon turned the screen for Duberman to see. Wells had been smart enough to keep the text vague, make it seem as if this meeting would be their first of the day, making up for the one he supposedly had missed before.

"Go. Take care of him. There'll be a helicopter waiting for you when you're done."

So Duberman's hate for Wells trumped everything, even his fears of a trap.

"You still want me to kill him? If I can?" Gideon deliberately substituted *you* for *Buvchenko,* wondering if Duberman would slip, admit he and not the Russian was the one who wanted Wells dead.

"Nothing's changed."

Gideon slipped off his barstool, stepped close to Duberman.

"You think anyone ever believes they're going to die, Aaron? Really believes it?"

"You're the sniper."

"Good luck, boss."

Duberman grinned, like the word itself was a joke. He reached out, squeezed Gideon's arm. "Do what you have to do. I'll see you at the top of the Sky."

25

Gideon had left the fancy iron up the hill. The SUV that sped toward the Star Ferry taxi stand where Wells and Ben the translator waited was a midsize Toyota four-door with tinted windows. Wells tossed his suitcase in back, slipped in beside Gideon. As they pulled the doors shut, Gideon sped off, downshifted into a hard left turn, the Toyota's tires squealing on the wet pavement.

"You don't want to get pulled over," Wells said through Ben. "Not with what's in back." The suitcase held a pair of Heckler & Koch 416s, the preferred automatic weapon for the agency's special operations group. As a rule, Wells preferred pistols over automatic weapons, which were hard to silence and impossible to hide. If he needed an H&K's firepower, the operation had probably already gone south. Nonetheless, when Wright opened the station's safe, Wells

510

took them, along with CS grenades, a Taser, a stack of flex-cuffs, and other goodies.

Gideon slammed the brakes, jamming Wells against the seat belt. "You found her."

"Maybe."

"You bring me here for maybe? I was going to Macao with Aaron."

The words implied that Gideon was still protecting Duberman. Wells decided not to push the issue. Orli, then Duberman.

"First things first. He's not staying." Wells nodded at Ben. "He's here so I can tell you what I know, you decide if you're in, we drop him off."

"Then what? You and me and the FSB? Yelling at each other in two languages while we spray and pray."

"Up to you, Chai."

"Why me? Why not one of yours?"

"Station chief won't risk it with the FSB. Not when we don't even know what happened to her."

"I told you, she never goes with them on her own."

Hope you're right, or we'll both feel dumb. "When we find her, we can ask."

An hour before, Wells had ditched the motorcycle a half block from the consulate and run to the front security gate, backpack jangling from his shoulders. No time for subtlety. The Marine guards were expecting him and waved him through the metal detectors that the Makarovs in the backpack set off. Two minutes later, Wells unlocked the biometrically controlled entrance to the station and stepped into the conference room where Shafer waited. He dumped out the pack. The pistols bounced across the conference table and nearly slid off.

"Seriously, John?"

Wells grabbed the Makarovs and the steroid vials, stuffed them back in the pack.

"Where'd you find it all?"

"Mostly, a locked file cabinet in the bedroom."

"Place was live?"

"I think Buvchenko's sleeping there." Wells decided not to tell Shafer about the code for the alarm. The man's ego was out of control already.

Shafer pushed aside property records and corporate documents, focused on bank records.

"I'll get someone who reads Mandarin," Wells said.

"Sure, but it won't matter. This looks like a prospectus from a Chinese developer. An apartment complex someplace like Shenzhen." Shenzhen was a Chinese city on Hong Kong's northern border. In 1980, it had barely existed. Now it had ten million people. The ultimate Chinese economic miracle.

"Why would the FSB buy property in China?"

"Maybe they have money stuck there. Anyway, it's a dead lead. No way would they try to sneak her across the border. She's here or on a boat. Let me look at the bank stuff, you check the phone."

Wells wanted to be annoyed, but the division of labor made sense. He tried to turn on the burner. It stayed dark behind its broken screen. He plugged in its charger. Still nothing.

"Tech support —" Shafer said, without looking up.

"Thank you, Ellis."

The station's tech officer was a twenty-something named Regina. Wells had met her earlier in the day. She had an intuitive millennial familiarity with electronic gadgets — and a bachelor's in computer science from Carnegie Mellon. Her office was windowless, its floor bare concrete, three safes against its back wall. Not exactly cozy, but necessary. Regina had access to more classified information than anyone in the station except Wright. Maybe anyone including Wright.

"Mr. Wells —"

"Hoping you can help me with this." Wells held up the phone and charger.

"If it's not completely fried." She reached for it. "Give me five minutes."

"If only bringing everything back from the dead were so easy."

She didn't smile.

"I'll be in Wright's conference room." Wells eased out, found a case officer who could read Chinese, and asked her to look over the property documents. She agreed immediately. Wright had told his officers to do whatever Wells and Shafer asked. No one was complaining about working late.

Wright had put the station's street operatives out, too, posting one to watch the safe house that Wells had just hit, two to monitor the Russian consulate, and the fourth to Hong Kong International in case the Russians tried to bring Orli through the main terminal there. But those moves were long shots. Shafer was right. The Russians must have had Orli in a safe house that they hadn't found yet. Their inability to generate leads gnawed at Wells. Why hadn't Gideon delivered Buvchenko's number?

On the other hand, what if he and Shafer were wrong about the ticking clock? What if the FSB didn't plan to roll up the operation for days, even weeks? In that case, Wells should have left the safe house untouched. They should be waiting rather than chasing.

Guess upon guess. They wouldn't have answers until they found Orli and asked her.

While Shafer sorted through the bank records, Wells checked the business cards from the drawer, looking for a pattern, not finding it. A travel agent in Moscow, a partner at an accounting firm in Macao, two real estate brokers in Guangzhou, the managing director of a British private security company in Kowloon. Wells pushed the last to Shafer. "Worth a visit?"

Shafer picked up the card. "James Neill, Special Situations and Services PLC. If we can't come up with anything better."

"Just because you didn't find it —"

"Important business cards don't get stuffed in drawers. They stay in your wallet. Or if they're really vital, you put the info in your phone so you can't lose it, then throw them away."

Something about what Shafer had said itched at Wells. A clue they'd missed.

Regina knocked, stepped inside, a legal pad in her hands. "Good news or bad news first?"

"Get to it," Shafer said.

"I don't know what happened to that phone but it's dead, pretty much. Those cheap burners store texts, call records, whatever junk photos they take in their own flash memory. That's all fried. Only Langley has any hope of bringing it back."

"So it's gone —"

Regina raised a hand: *Let me finish.* "One nice thing about burners, they run on portable SIMs. Which don't store much, but they do have the core directory, meaning any phone numbers anyone's bothered to save. I guess the logic is that you want those even if you ditch everything else on the old phone. Anyway, I swapped the SIM into another burner shell, turned it on. Came up with four numbers, all Hong Kong country code."

"Where's the phone?"

"The new burner? Charging."

"Have you checked any of these?"

"Just in local public databases. Three came up blank. But the first two share a prefix with a public number for the Russian consulate, so I'm guessing they'll route there. The third didn't go anywhere."

"The fourth?"

"The fourth is for an Indian restaurant in Prince Edward." Regina gave Wells the pad with the numbers. "I'll be back with the phone in a few minutes, sooner if I find anything else —" She disappeared.

An Indian restaurant. The receipt in the wastebasket. Wells realized what was bothering him. The blank invoices from the car shop. Why keep so many of them? Why have them at all?

He found them under the pile of Russian corporate records. They were old-fashioned repair invoices, twin carbon-copy sheets with a box above for estimates, space below for the actual charges. The company's name and address were printed in black at the top in Chinese and English: *Dah Chong Excellent Automotive, 51 Hip Tong Street, Wong Chuk Hang, Hong Kong: SERVICE ALL MAKES, ALL MODELS.*

Wells grabbed a pencil, lightly scrubbed across the paper, hoping for a phone number, an address, a name. Nothing. He handed the sheet to the case officer translating the property records. "Where's this?"

"Wong Chuk Hang? South coast of the island. Near Aberdeen. Nothing place. The police academy is down there. And Ocean Park — that was the biggest amusement park here until Disneyland came."

Wells pushed the second invoice at Shafer. "Can you think of any good reason why I would find blank receipts for a garage on

Hong Kong Island in a safe house in Kowloon?"

Shafer pulled open his laptop, typed so hard that Wells worried he'd break the keys. Three minutes later, he turned the screen toward Wells. Fifty-one Hip Tong Street was the corporate address for Dah Chong Auto PLC. Along with another company, this one with a name that was a six-digit number, just like the one that owned the apartment Wells had raided in Kowloon.

"Try too hard to be anonymous, leave a pattern," Shafer said. He pulled up a fresh window on the laptop. Hip Tong was a dead-end street built into the southern slopes of the mountain range that ran across Hong Kong Island. A ground-level view revealed a narrow road pinched by cracked gray concrete mid-rises, a mix of parking garages and light manufacturing. Even by Hong Kong standards, the street was ugly and hyperfunctional.

"Fifty-one," Shafer said. The subject property, as real estate brokers liked to say, stood five stories, with rows of narrow balconies that fronted shuttered blinds. Wells guessed the upper floors held a sweatshop. Hong Kong still had some. Wells didn't see any signs for the garage, though the building did have a steel garage door at

518

its east end and a green Castrol sign.

"Not exactly a quiet spot for a hide," Wells said.

"Seen many of those around? Plus keeping her on the island makes sense for them, if they're not sure about her. They don't risk bringing her through the harbor tunnels. And" — Shafer clicked back until the screen revealed Hong Kong Island's south coast from Aberdeen to Stanley — "Lots of places to land a go-fast" — a motorboat — "pick her up for a three-hour tour."

If Shafer was right, the FSB had picked a tough spot to hit. The garage had only one street-side entrance. Drone surveillance would be difficult, and the dead-end street meant that anyone casing the place would be obvious to the people inside. Attacking from behind the building would mean crossing onto the mountain several hundred feet up and angling down. Or coming in low, following an alley hemmed by buildings on one side, the mountain on the other. If the Russians had anyone watching the back, the alley would be a deathtrap. And gunfire would attract a quick response from the cops bunked at the Police Academy, not even a mile away.

Still, Wells knew he had no choice. He reached for his phone. Time to text Gideon.

■ ■ ■ ■

By the time Wells finished explaining the situation to Gideon, the Toyota was approaching the southern exit of the Aberdeen Tunnel, which ran under Mount Cameron and was the fastest route between Hong Kong Island's north and south coasts.

"You think this is the place because of a piece of paper," Gideon said.

"A piece of paper I found in an FSB safe house. You want to be sure? Should have gotten Duberman to give you Buvchenko's number."

Gideon pulled off at the first exit after the tunnel. To the south, Wells saw an Ocean Park cable car gliding through the night, full of Hong Kongers on their way home. It was nearly 10 p.m. Duberman and Cheung were supposed to meet in three hours.

"You have pictures of the place? A map?"

Wells handed them over.

"Impossible."

"Let's say tactically complex."

"Let's say suicide."

"Look, we launched a drone maybe fifteen minutes before you picked me up. From the mainland side, so I'm not sure it's overhead yet. And even if it is, we can't expect much.

The angles are terrible and this one doesn't have the kind of radar that would let us see through walls. Still, we can let it spin, hope they move her, see if anyone comes out the front. We can wait all night." And miss any chance at Duberman's meeting.

"Say it's the right place. We don't even know how many men are in there."

"It's only ever been Buvchenko and the two FSB, right?"

"Right."

"Why would that change?"

As an answer, Gideon put the Toyota in gear, swung back onto Highway 1. After less than a mile, he exited to a service road parallel to the highway, turned onto Hip Tong. The street looked even shorter and narrower than it had in the photos. It dead-ended without even a cul-de-sac to make U-turns easier. It was clearly intended only for deliveries, garbage pickup, and ambulances, not random private vehicles. The good news was that it was empty, not another car or truck on it, much less pedestrians. Even if the Russians did have surveillance cams watching the garage entrance, a single pass ought to be safe.

Gideon drove to the end of the street, turned the Toyota around, drove slowly back down. This time, Wells was on the garage side. He felt his senses freshening, his blood quickening. He held his pistol in his lap, twisted his head to stare at 51. Like a tourist on safari trying to spot a lion in the bush.

The garage door was down but not padlocked. A dim line of light snuck out under it. To its left, a security door, its glass cobwebbed with steel. Above, twin security cameras. Wells looked up, for anyone who might be in the balconies, but they seemed to be empty.

"Any ideas?" Gideon said.

"Got to have a back door. I think I come in the front, noisy, you go in the back. You saw the lights. Somebody's in there."

"Can I ask a question?" Ben said. "Why not call the cops from a burner? Report a kidnapped woman. Let them do the work."

A superficially smart play that Wells had already rejected. "None of us speak Cantonese —"

"Someone at the station can do it."

"More important. The Hong Kong police, they won't send in a SWAT team. Most likely, they think it's a prank. Those calls are usually pranks. And this isn't exactly Juarez. They send a car out, two cops, guys who maybe see five robberies a year. They knock on the door. Buvchenko answers, says no problem, come on in. Then he shoots

522

them both and takes off. Maybe he takes Orli, or maybe he shoots her, too."

"He'd ambush the cops."

"You think he's coming out with his hands up? *You got me, boys. Well played.*"

Gideon barked in Hebrew at Ben. "He wants to know what we're talking about."

"Tell him."

After a back-and-forth in Hebrew, Ben turned to Wells. "He says you're right."

Of course. He knows. Wells leaned over to Gideon. "We going in? Or hanging out, hoping they move her?"

Gideon grimaced like he was having a Tourette's attack and finally nodded. He parked on the service road beside Highway 1 while they came up with the barest plan. They would park the Toyota twenty yards down from Hip Tong, on the steep short road that ran between it and the highway. Wells would give Gideon a one-minute head start to navigate the alley behind the buildings. Then Wells would move in from the front. Ideally, Gideon would reach the back of the garage just after Wells came to the front door.

"You're sure there's a way in back there," Gideon said.

"Has to be a fire door, at least a window."

"Maybe it's locked."

"Then shoot your way in." Wells had only one autopick and he needed it himself.

Wells would start with the pistol, try to be quiet, but if he ran into resistance, he would open up with the H&K. As soon as Gideon heard shooting, he would come in from the back.

Ideally, they would pin the Russians between them. If not, Wells would have to deal with them as they tried to escape to the street. Either way, they should count on being finished two minutes after Wells started shooting. One would be better. Automatic weapons drew cops like nothing else.

"You think we get her away that fast?" Gideon said.

"I don't care if we get her away. We handle the Russians, she's safe with the cops."

"Speaking of safe," Ben said. "I'll stay. I can drive."

"It's okay." The guy was nice enough, but Wells didn't think he'd ever been in the field.

"What if one of you gets hit, you need help getting to the car —"

Maybe having a wheelman wouldn't hurt. And Wells didn't have time to argue. "Fine. But you stay with the car unless you hear one of us yelling for you."

Ben grinned like a peewee who'd been picked for the varsity. Wells wondered if he'd made a mistake.

"Ready?" Gideon said. "Or you want to keep talking?"

"Let's go."

26

Buvchenko and the FSB guys had talked about raping Orli most of the day.

When Buvchenko pulled her out of the BMW, she kicked and punched wildly, banging her hand on the underside of the trunk lid. He looked down on her curiously. Like she was a noisy but unthreatening animal, a squirrel or fawn, that had somehow found her way into his house. She screamed, and he put a giant hand over her mouth and nose and squeezed until she stopped. He slapped duct tape across her lips, and he and Sergei taped her to a cheap but sturdy metal chair and shoved her in an oily back corner of the garage.

"It'll be all right," Buvchenko said. She stared at the ceiling.

The afternoon ticked by. For an hour or so, they played Durak, a Russian card game. Then they shifted to chess, Nikolai playing Sergei and Buvchenko at once. The garage was airless, stifling, and they were as bored as campers on a rainy day. They couldn't even call anyone or use the Internet. Nikolai had made them turn their phones off. The call from the station was supposed to come through the garage's landline.

Sergei's first suggestion was sly, almost off hand. It came after Nikolai had demolished him for the third straight chess match. He wandered over to the corner and stared at Orli with all the subtlety of a dog eying a T-bone.

"Quit it?" Buvchenko said after a couple of minutes.

"Look at her. We'll never have another chance at a piece like this. I'll bet she's tired of that old Yid and his limp dick, anyway. Let's show her how real men do it."

"Let's just get her to the boat," Nikolai said.

"Can I play some games on my phone, at least?" Sergei said. Like rape and video games were interchangeable substitutes for each other.

"As long as it's on airplane mode."

Sergei distracted himself for a while pretending to be a dragon. Or maybe a guy who hunted dragons with a machine gun. Then he disappeared into the room at the back of the garage that served as an office

527

and kitchen area. When he emerged, he was holding two dusty bottles of Smirnoff.

"Look what I found."

So they drank. They drank to the success of the operation, which had already yielded the best intelligence on the Chinese air force in the FSB's history. They drank to Russia. And for their third drink, Sergei raised his glass and said, "Let's teach that thing in the chair a lesson. Something she won't forget."

This time, Nikolai didn't argue. He smirked.

The more shots of Smirnoff they did, the more graphic Sergei's suggestions became. "She's stronger than she looks," Buvchenko said. "She'll make trouble."

"You can't hold her, Mikhail? She probably weighs fifty-five kilos. If you're not man enough, I'll do it myself. Twist her arms behind her back until she knows not to fight."

"Say you break them."

"Then I break them. The boss can go first, then my turn. You last. Give her a kiss before you start, you're romantic."

"Nemtsov won't be happy."

"You think we're sending her back to Tel Aviv? All these excuses. Worried about your *khuy,* Mikhail? Take a Viagra. I know you have them." He looked at Nikolai. "Come on, boss. I've wanted one like this my whole life."

Buvchenko wasn't even sure why he was trying to protect Orli. Maybe just because Sergei annoyed him so much. It wasn't as if he'd never forced himself on a woman. In a village outside Gronzy, his squad, eight men, had once had their way with a mother and daughter. But the mother had tried to blow them up with a suicide vest, only it hadn't gone off. Then the daughter had grabbed a knife and cut his sergeant in the arm. She was fifteen, maybe fourteen, who could tell with the Chechens? Anyway, they'd deserved their punishment. When his last soldier was done with them, Buvchenko shot them both. Give the mother the martyrdom she wanted. As for the daughter, he was saving her from misery.

Orli was different. She'd come on her own, to protect her children. Yes, Nemtsov was probably going to tell them to dump her in the ocean along with her idiot husband, but they didn't have to rape her first.

Orli didn't speak Russian, but Buvchenko could tell she knew what they were saying. She shrank in her chair whenever Sergei approached. As they got into the second

Smirnoff bottle, he took off his shirt, revealing pecs as big as hubcaps, and waxed so they shined under the garage's fluorescents.

He poured cups of vodka, no more shots, dirty plastic cups with Honda logos, and pushed them on Nikolai and Buvchenko. Buvchenko choked the stuff down, he knew Sergei would be watching. Nikolai's eyes had turned hard and stony. His hand strayed to his crotch every time he looked at Orli, the motion smooth, unconscious.

Nikolai went into the back to piss, and Sergei poured a fresh glass.

"Let this one settle," Buvchenko said.

"Stupid. For her. Loosen her up." He walked toward her and shook the cup, pantomimed drinking. She nodded. Sergei reached for the duct tape.

Buvchenko pulled him back. "You want her to scream?"

"Of course I do." He reached over, tore Orli's shirt neatly in half down the middle as she shook her head almost diffidently.

Buvchenko couldn't help but look. She wore a simple white bra, lace at the edges, almost modest. Her skin was tan all over, no evidence of bikini lines, her stomach flat and smooth, as if she'd never had a baby. The word *beautiful* didn't begin to describe her. She made him think of a line from his sister's Bible: *The Word became flesh and dwelt among us.*

Nikolai came back. "Oh," he said. He trotted to the chair, knelt beside it, looked at Orli like she was a prize puppy he was thinking about buying. He put his hands on the edges of her bra, pulled them back to expose her nipples, and gently brushed them with the back of his hands. She held herself rigid and stared at Buvchenko. She'd evidently decided that he was as close to a protector as she had in this room.

Buvchenko wondered whether they would do it right then. But Orli's eyes turned wide and panicked and she flung her head back and forth. Nikolai let go of her bra, kissed the tops of her breasts. He stood and walked out again. Buvchenko understood. Nikolai was married and had a daughter of his own. Still, Buvchenko knew Nikolai would overcome his reluctance soon enough. In an hour, maybe less, depending how quickly he drank, how cannily Sergei encouraged him.

Buvchenko couldn't stop the wolves. They'd have her.

He might as well, too.

27

As Gideon disappeared toward the alley behind Hip Tong, Wells called Shafer.

"Anything new?"

"Phones quiet."

"We're going in."

"That quick?"

"That quick."

"Macao after?"

"Thanks for the vote of confidence, but let's find her first."

"Talked to your Israeli friend about what happens when you do?"

"Not yet." Gideon seemed to have made the same calculation as Wells, best friends forever, for the next five minutes.

"Might want to figure that out. Anyway. We have a helicopter chartered."

"Thankee. Got to go." Gideon's head start was almost gone. Wells clicked off, grabbed an oversized black shopping bag, the H&K and the suppressed pistol inside.

"Remember, you stay here."

Ben nodded. Wells stepped out of the Toyota. He wore a black long-sleeved nylon athletic shirt, black jeans, motorcycle boots, black gloves. All he needed was a bumper sticker: TROUBLE: STAY BACK 100 FEET. Though no one was around to see anyway.

He turned left onto Hip Tong, keeping to the south side of the street, opposite the garage, looking for an angle. He had wrapped the pistol in black gauze so it wouldn't rattle against the H&K inside the pack. The street's silence surprised Wells, no televisions playing or apartment dwellers chatting, only a distant mechanical banging, metal on metal.

Then a scream. A woman's voice, pitched to shatter glass, echoing between the apartments —

Gone, no more than two seconds, no follow-through, like someone had flipped a switch, the silence more frightening than the sound itself —

Wells pulled the H&K from the bag, slung it across his chest. He grabbed the suppressed pistol, dropped the bag in the street, ran for the front of the garage, watching the steel door, ready to shoot at any movement. The street was too narrow to offer cover. If the Russians knew he was here, they might be setting a trap, forcing Orli to scream to lure Wells close so they could drop him.

At the edge of the garage door, Wells stopped to listen. He heard low male voices speaking Russian, arguing, maybe. No woman, no sounds of movement, no signs that anyone knew that he and Gideon were closing. He crept to the concrete wall that separated the garage door and the front door, reached for the front door's dull steel knob.

It turned.

Wells gave himself five seconds to think through the layout inside. From his position, he could see only the wall on the far side of the door. He didn't know whether the door opened directly into the main garage bay or whether the building's thick concrete support pillars walled it off. He hoped for an open bay. He could pull the door wide, get low, open up with the H&K. A pillar would block his angles, make him an easy target for anyone watching the front.

No matter. He couldn't wait. He knew, too, that on the far side of the building, Gideon must have heard the scream. Wells wanted to get in first. He put a hand on the knob, opened the door fractionally, eased it the rest of the way with his right foot, peeked inside.

As he'd feared, the door didn't open directly into the bay. A support pillar inside formed a short corridor. Behind the pillar, the garage opened up. The light inside revealed racks of equipment stacked against the wall to Wells's left. Behind them, a card table with three metal chairs. Beside it, a 250cc motorcycle. At the far end, maybe fifty feet away, Wells saw a brighter square of light, a doorway that he guessed led to the garage's back office.

The voices started again. Then a low rip, fabric tearing.

Wells left the H&K against his chest, lifted the suppressed pistol. He stepped inside, peeked around the pillar. A BMW sedan was parked in the front of the garage, nose out. Behind it, in the back right corner of the garage, a huge man faced away from Wells, naked except for a pair of tight black boxers. Wells couldn't be sure because he couldn't see the guy's face, but he didn't think the man was Buvchenko. Beside the giant, a second, smaller man squatted beside Orli's splayed legs. As Wells watched, he pushed them together, reached for her waist, grabbed her white panties and pulled them off.

Wells still didn't know where Buvchenko was, if he and more guys might be in the

535

back. Didn't know and didn't care. He came around the column so he had an open take. No hesitation, no second thoughts, he lifted the pistol at the standing man, aiming center mass. The guy was so big he could hardly miss, he pulled the trigger, once, twice, three times, the pistol hummed its notes —

Three rounds struck true, the guy's back arched. But he didn't go down, not right away. He roared like a bear that had been hit with a too-small tranquilizer. No matter, Wells could finish him in a few seconds. Wells put the pistol on the second Russian, who was standing and turning in response to the shots. As Wells had hoped. By moving up and away from Orli, the guy was giving Wells a clean high shot, one that wouldn't kill her if Wells missed. He fired twice. The angle was tougher than he thought, he heard one shot slap the corner of the garage, he wasn't sure about the other, he pulled the trigger again —

When to his right, peripherally, he glimpsed motion —

Buvchenko, coming through the doorway from the back office. He was shirtless, a blurred blue-black tattoo covering his massive pecs. He'd seen Wells already and was reaching for a pistol on a table beside the doorway. Wells spun toward him, knowing he was too late, Buvchenko had him covered and would get shots off, but he had no choice, he had to try, hope Buvchenko missed —

Buvchenko grabbed the pistol and in one motion *flung* it at Wells, a hard forearm strike. Wells realized he wasn't looking at a pistol at all, he'd misunderstood, the thing was a wrench, a foot of steel. It came out of Buvchenko's hand with incredible speed. The guy was a beast. It spun sideways at Wells's head, and Wells ducked and raised his arm, bailing out like a batter caught wrong-footed by a hundred-mile-an-hour fastball, trying to, anyway, but he was spinning *into* its path —

The wrench caught Wells on the right shoulder and temple, the shoulder, mostly. Better than a straight strike to the head, but not much, because the blow opened his right hand as neatly as if he'd willed it, some accident of nerves. Wells dropped the pistol. He stumbled backward, already feeling the blood streaming down his face. Darkness inked his eyes. He would have gone down, but the building's pillar caught him.

He leaned against it, blinked the black away, made himself lift his head as Buvchenko ran for him, *charged* him, obviously planning to finish him with his hands rather than going for his pistol, wherever it was. Wells looked for his own pistol. It had skidded halfway under the BMW, out of reach. He grabbed for the H&K on his chest, tried to lift it. Too late. Buvchenko was on him —

Wells turtled, ducked low. Buvchenko turned a shoulder and slammed Wells into the concrete and hit him on the side of the head above the ear with a sledgehammer right hand. Wells had never been punched so hard before, again, again, a hurricane, the Russian was so strong —

Wells tried to hit back, but he had no leverage, couldn't even raise his hands —

He felt himself slipping, the black rising. He knew that if he went under he'd never wake up, Buvchenko would put him on his back and choke him out —

The concealed carry —

The pistol on his back, Wells remembered it now, no way was Buvchenko expecting it, no way would Buvchenko figure Wells for another pistol on top of the one he'd dropped and the H&K, only he couldn't get to it, Buvchenko had him against the wall and he had no room —

Wells made his left hand a claw and scratched at Buvchenko's face, tearing at the Russian's skin with his nails, grabbing for eyes and mouth, a move so cheap and desperate that Buvchenko stopped punching him long enough to grab his wrist and bend it back. The pain was enormous, enough to clear the cobwebs the wrench had left. Wells wondered if Buvchenko was strong enough to break his wrist with one hand. Probably.

"The famous John Wells." Buvchenko smiled. "This is all you have? Dress like a ninja, fight like a bitch."

"Fuck you, Mikhail." Not exactly the strongest comeback, but — *Just lay off for a second, give me one second to come off this wall* — Wells tugged his arm ineffectually, wriggled sideways like all he cared about was freeing his arm. "All the Viagra in the world won't fix your two-inch *khuy.*"

"Fight like a bitch, bleed like a bitch. When I'm done with you, you'll beg like a bitch." Buvchenko gurgled and spat on Wells's face. He forced Wells's wrist back, focused on the arm, staring at it, watching it bend. Wells turned his hips sideways like they were the world's two worst dancers and scraped his back away from the concrete and reached for the pistol in his waistband with his right hand —

Buvchenko pulled harder, and Wells's

wrist gave, snapped like an oak branch cracking. The pain soared into Wells, a miracle of agony, but he was ready, he'd known, he'd made himself ready, this was the only way, and he had the pistol in his hand. He screamed and jammed it into Buvchenko's side and pulled the trigger —

The unsilenced shot echoed in the garage and skin and muscle sprayed off Buvchenko's side and his back, two holes, entry and exit. The Russian's eyes went wide and his mouth sagged. He grabbed at Wells's broken wrist like he didn't know what else to do. Wells pulled the trigger again, and this time Buvchenko stepped back and sagged like he'd tried to squat with too much weight. He went to one knee and braced himself against the ground. *"Blyad,"* he said. *"Blyad, blyad, blyad."*

Wells kept the pistol on him and watched the life spurting out of the holes in Buvchenko's side and back, the blood coming slow and steady, a red stream washing his waist. The wounds were a couple inches above the waist, below the diaphragm. Wells guessed he'd hit Buvchenko's liver or kidney but missed the big arteries, the wounds devastating but probably survivable if he got to the hospital quickly enough.

"Yebat menya," Buvchenko whispered, his

540

eyes flat and empty as ever. And in English, "You shot me." Like he still couldn't believe it.

Wells looked at his hand, hanging limply off his arm like a flag on a windless day. It felt even worse than it looked. The pain made him gag. He heard steps at the back of the garage now, Gideon shouting in Hebrew.

The other two Russians lay in the corner. The smaller one was crumpled, unmoving. Wells had caught him with a shot under the armpit, through the heart. Better to be lucky than good. The big one was dead, too. He'd bled out while Wells was busy with Buvchenko. Orli was awake. She turned her head slowly, like her brain didn't believe what her eyes were telling her. A shiner was rising from her right eye. Her panties lay beside her like a flag of surrender.

As Wells ran to her, she covered herself, one hand over her sex and the other across her breasts like she thought he was going to hurt her. Duct tape covered her mouth. He pulled it off as gently as he could.

"I guess I should say thank you," Orli said.

"You should put your clothes on."

She lifted her hands, exposing herself completely. Wells turned away.

"No, look at me. It's my body, not theirs,

and I want you to see."

His face must have betrayed his confusion.

"You earned it. Your *arm,* man." He turned to her, and she stood, raised her arms, pirouetted. Wells couldn't take his eyes from her.

"Something else you should know," she said when she was finished. "About what they were doing."

Finally, shots from the back of the building, glass breaking. Gideon, one minute late. And in the distance, the first sirens. "Tell me later." Time to go. But first, Buvchenko. Wells turned to him.

"Prisoner now, treat me nice." Buvchenko's skin was sallow now, his breathing labored. Still, he smirked. "Go to the hospital together."

The laws of war made surrender an absolute right. But as he crossed the room, Wells thought of that winter day outside Volgograd when Buvchenko had shot a horse in front of him, cut down the animal to prove he could.

Buvchenko never blinked, but as Wells raised the pistol and put the tip beside his temple, he opened his mouth. *"Ny—"* Wells squeezed the trigger and blew off Buvchenko's head. Nothing pithy, no last words. The

Russian's body slammed down. Wells forced his left arm against his chest and turned for the front door. He didn't like leaving Orli, she was obviously in shock, but he didn't have a choice. The sirens were louder every second.

Outside, a welcome surprise, the Toyota waiting, engine running, facing east. Wells slipped inside. "Go."

"Gideon?"

"Go." Too bad. One minute late. Wells owed him nothing.

They rolled off. "What happened to your hand?"

"Just drive."

"I think there's a hospital in Aberdeen."

We're going to Mong Kok." Going to the consulate again would be pushing his luck. He'd meet Wright and Shafer at Wright's safe house. Wright might know a friendly doctor. At the least, he could bring the consulate's Marine medic. Wells just needed his wrist to be stable enough to survive a helicopter ride over the Pearl River Delta.

He had a date in Macao.

28

The medic, a skinny black guy named Beach, deftly palpated Wells's wrist. "I want you to know, this is at the edge of what I do. Hospital'd be better."

Wells shook his head.

"You say so." Beach unrolled a quick-set bandage and gently wrapped Wells's wrist and hand. "That'll stabilize it," he said, when he was done. "But you need a real doctor in the morning. Clean out the bone fragments. Put in a pin so that it heals quicker, nothing slips around."

"That bad?"

"See how blue your fingers are? Something in there is blocking nerves, blood vessels. I can't fix that. You don't get to someone who can in the next twenty-four hours, you might lose those piggies."

All that work to rehab his foot, and now this. Wells laughed.

"You think I'm joking?"

"I'm like one of those highways that as soon as the crews get done paving, they have to start all over again at the other side, they never really fix it."

"Whatever. I shouldn't give you this, I've seen twenty-year-old privates with more sense, but you're gonna need it." Beach dug into his kit, came up with a morphine ampule.

As badly as he wanted the relief, Wells shook his head. "You have Advil? Tylenol? I gotta stay sharp."

Beach gave Wells four of each. "In my professional opinion, they won't do jack."

"A little suffering is good for the soul." Wells dry-swallowed the pills.

"Then yours is gonna be in great shape tonight."

Wells told Wright and Shafer everything, everything except the way Orli had spun for him at the end.

"Give us a sec?" Shafer said when Wells had finished. Not the response he'd expected. Shafer and Wright left, closed the apartment's door. Wells heard them murmuring in the hallway. A couple minutes passed, long enough to annoy him. It was almost midnight. He'd have to hurry to be in Macao in time to catch Duberman and

Cheung together. Wells was about to go outside after them when Shafer walked back in. Alone. He stood close to the door, like he was afraid Wells would take off.

"Any chance Gideon got away?" Shafer said. "Media hasn't mentioned anything about anyone being arrested."

"I don't see how. He's not our problem, anyway."

"Unless he gives you up."

"Not his style."

"What about Orli?"

He couldn't help himself, her name brought him back to the garage, not only how she'd looked but what she'd said, *I want you to see.* A diamond's beauty, a diamond's hardness. "No. They push her, she'll say she was in shock, she can't remember."

"And you don't know what she wanted to tell you at the end?"

Wells shook his head. "About that helicopter, Ellis."

"I think we should focus on getting you out of here. Charter to Japan or if HKIA's no good, a ship to the Philippines."

"Without Gideon or Orli, no way the cops make me. Not in time to matter, anyway. We were on the highway by the time we saw anyone coming. And that Toyota isn't even ours."

"FSB's going to be looking, too."

"I'm not suggesting I buy a place here. I'll be gone tomorrow morning at the latest. They won't come back that fast." Wells didn't understand Shafer's sudden caution. He stood from Wright's ugly yellow couch. "Let me put on a shirt that isn't covered in Russian blood and get out of here."

Shafer raised his hand like a traffic cop. A flicker in his eyes Wells couldn't read.

"This coming from the White House, Ellis? President change his mind again?"

"I just want to be sure we're thinking it through."

"Done thinking. You won't give me the helicopter, I'll take a ferry." Though Wells would much rather fly. A ship wouldn't arrive in time. And a copter would set him on the roof of Duberman's new casino, save him from the pesky immigration officers at the Macao Ferry Terminal. Even if an air traffic controller noticed it landing at the casino rather than the terminal, the Chinese air force would hardly scramble. Macao's airspace was low priority, chasing down a gambler who wanted to skip immigration even lower.

"Duberman's not going anywhere, John. It's all over but the shouting. You've done enough for one night. Give somebody else a chance."

Inside the cast, Wells's wrist throbbed. Suddenly he understood. "This is about Buchenko." Wells stepped toward the door, stared at Shafer until the smaller man blinked, looked away. "If anyone in the world had that coming —"

"It's not about who he is. It's about who we are. And it's not just what you did. It's the way you're talking about it."

"Get that from a Hallmark card?"

"Murder with special circumstances." A phrase prosecutors used when they intended to seek the death penalty for heinous crimes.

"That what I am to you?"

"You need to get some sleep."

"Go back to Langley. You don't belong out here."

Shafer shook his head: *Maybe you don't, either. Not anymore.*

"This conversation's done, Ellis. Give me a ride or I find one myself."

Shafer folded his arms across his chest and looked up at Wells, and Wells wondered what he would do if Shafer didn't move.

Finally, Shafer ducked his head in surrender. "Okay, John. One condition."

Wells waited.

"Whatever happens over there, tonight's done, you rest."

29

MACAO

The helicopter pilot was Wells's age, a bald-headed white guy who wore brown fingerless leather driving gloves. *He's good,* Wright had said, his last words before Wells walked out of the apartment. *Just don't ask his name.* Wright seemed less bothered than Shafer by the way Wells had executed Buvchenko. Maybe Wright understood better.

Or maybe he just didn't care about Wells.

The Bell 206 was a single-pilot, four-passenger bird, reliable, used by police departments all over the world. The pilot flew beneath the cloud cover into an easterly wind that kept them under a hundred knots and sent whitecaps scudding over the South China Sea nine hundred feet below.

Ten minutes after they left Hong Kong, Wells caught his first glimpse of Macao, a neon smudge beneath the clouds. Minute by minute, the territory took shape, the city's hills to the north, the artificial island of Cotai to the south. The top of Duberman's new tower was at the southern end of the island, lost in the mist.

When they were close enough to see the marquees of each individual casino, the pilot pushed the Bell southwest, giving a wide berth to the ferry terminal and its immigration officers. A few seconds later, the radio squawked in Chinese. The pilot ignored it.

Below, the sea's flat gray waters gave way to Cotai's engineered borders. Dead ahead, the Sky loomed. The tower was not just extraordinarily tall, but wide and deep, a glass-sheathed mountain. A quarter mile from it, the pilot pushed the cyclic stick between his legs to the right while raising the collective lever at his left side. The twin maneuvers put the Bell into a rising, declining-radius loop around the tower, like the helicopter was wrapping it in Scotch tape.

A couple of hundred feet up, the clouds began, lacy, then thicker, swirling around the building, blurring its edges. Four loops brought them over the top of the tower. The pilot maneuvered them until the Bell hovered directly above the roof, a hundred feet or so up, though the clouds were thick enough that Wells couldn't be sure. Spotlights on the building's corners tunneled through the mist.

"You got this?"

"Easy." The pilot flicked on the helicopter's own spotlight and lowered the collective.

The clouds cleared enough for Wells to glimpse a white circle with an *H* at its center. The pilot feathered the pedals to control yaw while gently working the collective. The Bell came down as smoothly as an elevator and Wells wondered why he'd worried —

Ten feet above the roof, the wind shifted, drove them west, left, toward a concrete block topped with steel brackets, an anchor for window-washing risers. The pilot saw the danger, raised the collective, pushed the cyclic right. But the helicopter didn't respond right away. The wind drove the Bell toward the concrete. The block was at least ten feet long, six or seven feet high, fifteen feet back from the edge of the roof. Wells wondered if it was big enough to tip them sideways, spin them down the side of the building —

Finally, the helicopter responded, bit into the wind, pulled up and away, its left skid just scraping the block, leaving a jagged black line of paint on the concrete. Three hundred feet above the roof, the pilot cut the spotlight and put the Bell into a slow loop. The clouds parted and Wells saw the whole massive roof, nearly two hundred feet on each side, vents and window-washing equipment and pipes and fire exits surrounding the helipad. Wells wondered where Duberman's chopper was, realized he had probably set down at his other casino and driven over rather than risking a landing here.

"That's easy, hate to see hard."

"Ready for another try or you need fresh underwear?"

The pilot came to a hover and again began to bring them down. For a while, they barely descended. Wells figured the pilot was trying to get a sense for the frequency and rhythm of the wind gusts. About two hundred feet up, a big one caught them, but this time the pilot was ready and the helicopter recovered much more quickly.

"Not by the book, but I'm putting us down quick this time." He lowered the collective and Bell dropped fast toward the very center of the *H*. "Brace for landing," he said, when they were maybe thirty feet up. Wells folded his right arm over the sling that held his left and leaned forward. The helicopter banged hard against the pad, bounced, landed again, both skids down now. The jolt tore at Wells's wrist and set his arm aflame.

"Good times," the pilot said.

Wells unbuckled himself, leaned forward, swiped his fingers over the butt of his pistol like a lucky charm. "I'm not back in ten, get out of here."

The pilot grinned: *You think I needed you to tell me that?*

Wells stepped onto the pad, turned for the nearest fire stairs, about thirty feet from the edge of the north wall of the roof. Before he reached them —

The door swung open. Duberman stepped out. After him, Cheung. They must have been in the casino that was just below the roof, heard the helicopter, come up.

Cheung was a small man, his face red and flushed. Duberman wore a pin-striped gray gangster suit, white chalk stripes and wide lapels. All he needed was a big cigar and a pinky ring. He stopped so fast when he saw Wells that Cheung banged into him, a cheap vaudeville act, the Chinaman and the Pimp.

Behind them, Gideon.

Gideon?

The wet wind sang. For three, four, five seconds, Wells and Duberman stared at each other. Wells had last seen Duberman four months and six thousand miles away, stepping off a plane in Saudi Arabia. They'd both believed at that moment that Duberman had won, the United States was going to attack Iran.

Instead, Duberman had lost, first his war and then everything else. He stepped forward. "John Wells. I missed you." He made a cross with his fingers. "That work on you?"

"Everything ravaged, everything burned," Wells said.

Duberman looked back to Gideon, barked a question in Hebrew. *Why is he here? Didn't you say you couldn't find him?* Something like that, Wells imagined.

So Gideon had escaped the garage. How? Wells flashed on the motorcycle against the wall and knew. Then Gideon outraced Wells to Macao in a helicopter of his own. But why? To protect Duberman? Tell him Orli was safe? Beg him to surrender?

Gideon stepped out from behind Duberman now, giving himself an angle on Wells. *I draw on your boss, what do you do?* Wells needed Hebrew. And telepathy.

"Don't tell me you're working with Buvchenko?" Duberman said.

554

"Buvchenko's dead."

"Lying."

"I killed him myself."

Duberman stared at the sky as if the clouds could confirm the news. "What about Orli?"

Thought you'd never ask. "She's fine. Safe. Come on. Let's go home."

"So they put me a cage until it's time for the needle." Duberman shook his head. Wells stepped toward him, but he turned away, strode to the edge of the tower, pulling the other three with him.

"You've got the best lawyers in the world, Aaron." Wells wasn't sure why he was arguing. Maybe after what Shafer had said, he wanted to give Duberman every chance.

"You don't mind, I'll show myself out." Duberman backed up until he just a couple of feet from the edge of the parapet —

"Don't —"

"I think we both know the game's over. But before I go, I have something you might want." He reached into his suit pocket —

Wells understood a half second too late, Duberman was carrying, a lousy little pocket pistol, a popgun, so small it hadn't even ruffled his suit. He came out with it as Wells reached under his shirt for his own pistol and felt it snag, the hard landing had caught it in the holster —

Duberman brought the pistol up and locked eyes with Wells, and Wells saw the truth there — *one for you and one for me* — and finally Wells freed his own pistol and brought it forward, but he had no chance now, the ball was still in his hand and the horn had sounded —

He heard two quick *pops* somewhere behind him —

Two neat holes in Duberman's suit —

Duberman looked down at his chest. His mouth opened and the pistol came out of his hand and clattered on the roof of the four-billion-dollar monument he had built to himself. Wells looked back, saw Gideon in a shooting stance, of course Gideon, in the end the scales had tipped, he'd chosen Wells over the man who'd saved his son —

Duberman went to his knees and Gideon ran for him, they were murmuring in Hebrew. Wells stayed back, let them speak. Too soon, Duberman tipped forward. Gideon caught him and put him on his back. By the time Wells reached them, Duberman was gone, staring at the sky with eyes that didn't see.

Wells closed them. "Thank you," he said to Gideon.

"For her." Gideon knelt beside Wells and

prayed over Duberman, a quiet stream of Hebrew.

Wells heard footsteps scraping the concrete, raised his head. Cheung was coming. Wells raised his own pistol, thinking Cheung might go for the pistol Duberman had dropped. But Cheung trudged past like a sleepwalker. At the edge of the parapet, he reached into his pocket and came out with a shiny black plaque Wells had never seen before.

Cheung looked at it for a moment, spun it out into the night, a backhand Frisbee flip, like he wanted to be sure gravity still worked. Then he stepped onto the parapet and took one final stride. No hesitation. As if the clouds themselves could hold him. An emperor of the air. He didn't scream or whisper. Not a sound. When Wells reached the edge and looked over, Cheung was gone, not even a speck in the night.

Gideon finished praying, walked to the helicopter. Apparently he didn't plan to let Wells ditch him this time. Then Wells was alone with Duberman. What was left of him, which was nothing, two hundred pounds of well-groomed meat.

Wells had won. Yet he wanted more. He

had a thousand questions for Duberman, beginning and ending with the simplest, the most important: *Why?* But the man had taken the answers with him.

Maybe there were no answers. Maybe human beings never understood themselves, much less anyone else. Wells looked up from the corpse just as the wind blew apart the clouds and opened the sky to the moon.

His voice rose in his throat, a scream. A howl.

EPILOGUE

Wells wanted to see the President.

The feeling wasn't mutual.

Wells didn't care. And he had the whip.

So once again he found himself in the Oval Office anteroom. He'd landed at Dulles four hours before, just enough time to have his wrist properly set, shower, and shave. He hadn't brought Shafer or Duto. This conversation belonged to him alone.

The first stories hit the wires an hour after Wells's United 777 left Hong Kong. Police in Macao had identified the body of a "senior Chinese official" outside the Sky casino and found Duberman shot to death on the roof. A few minutes later, the *South China Morning Post* reported that the woman police had found in a garage the night before was Duberman's wife. *We normally do not identify possible victims of sexual*

559

abuse without their consent, but given the importance of this case . . .

For once, Wells was glad to have an airborne Internet connection. The conspiracy theories grew wilder by the minute, though even the craziest couldn't touch the truth. Wells wasn't sure if the Chinese would figure out what had happened. The FSB would, but Nemtsov and his masters in the Kremlin might be predisposed to write off their dead officers as the cost of doing business and move on.

Might.

No matter. Wells didn't feel like worrying about who might come after him tomorrow, or the next day. After this meeting, he would disappear. Maybe he'd see Evan again, though he feared he might be pushing his luck with the kid. Maybe Orli, to hear what she had to tell him about Buvchenko and the Russians. He wasn't quite willing to admit he had other reasons to visit.

No matter what he did, where he went, he had to spend some time alone with himself, see what he'd become, if Shafer was right. Find his own answer to the question he'd asked Duberman: *Why?*

The President kept him waiting an hour. Pulling rank to show his irritation with this visit. But ultimately he had no choice, and Donna Green opened the door, waved Wells inside.

The President sat behind his massive desk. He didn't stand as Wells walked close. Didn't say hello or put out a hand or ask about Wells's arm. No courtesies today, false or otherwise.

Wells sat in the chair on the right, and they looked at each other until the President snapped his fingers. "You wanted to talk. So talk."

But the words Wells had planned to say choked him. He wished he'd let Shafer come. Shafer would have enjoyed this moment. Wells turned to Green instead. "Four months ago, you promised to be the truthteller, right? Tell him the truth."

"What truth?"

"He needs to resign."

"Here," the President said. He leaned across the desk, his eyes dark. "You have something to say, say it to me."

Wells thought of Cheung, stepping off the building. At last he found his voice.

"It's over. Sir."

"Who made you king?"

"Say whatever you like. Terminally ill, whatever."

"When I don't die?"

"Miracles never cease."

A flicker of a smile crossed the President's face. "I'm not going anywhere. The country needs me."

Glenn Mason, Salome, Duberman, now this man. One after the next, they'd fallen to the curse that no gypsy bothered to cast. They stared so hard at their own lies that they could no longer see the truth.

"Your biggest donor winds up dead with a Chinese four-star at his front door. You don't think somebody's going to ask questions about what he's been doing, make the connection to Iran?"

"Ask, maybe. Answer, not so much."

Wells had anticipated sadness. A valedictory moment. Not this brazen insistence. He felt his temper coming loose. "You're wrong. But either way, you're not going to have the chance. I'm not letting you."

"You got what you wanted."

"We both know I'd still be in that brig if the Russians hadn't gotten involved. Four months ago, this room, you gave me and Shafer your word about Duberman. You had the chance to keep it. You didn't."

The President stood, turned away from Wells and his desk. He stared out at the Rose Garden, immaculate and perfect. A view not available at any price. "So you punish me. Show off. Petty revenge and the whole country pays. The whole world."

"I'm doing now what we should have had the guts to do then." *This time, the guy at the top doesn't skate.* Wells stood, joined the President at the windows. He didn't understand this compulsion to hang on to power. But then he'd always been outside looking in. "Announce it in the next forty-eight hours. Or I will. Sir."

"Public won't be so great for you, either. How many murder raps?"

"Guess I'll have to take that chance."

Wells turned away, walked to the door, ready to leave the Oval Office, the White House, Washington, all of it. He couldn't remember when he'd felt so free. Maybe he couldn't escape, but he could pretend. For a while. "I've always been the survivor type."

ACKNOWLEDGMENTS

Neil, Ivan, Karen, and the rest of the team at Putnam — those books wouldn't exist without you.

Bob and Deneen — thanks for the wise counsel.

Jackie, Lucy, and Ezra — you make it all worthwhile. Family is the ultimate blessing.

And to all of you, whether you've been with John from the beginning or just found him now, thanks for spending your time with us. Without you, John wouldn't exist. I always appreciate feedback — email me at alexberensonauthor@gmail.com and let me know what you think. If you want more frequent updates, follow me at Facebook .com/alexberensonauthor or twitter.com/alexberenson.

See you next year!

ABOUT THE AUTHOR

As a reporter for *The New York Times*, **Alex Berenson** covered topics ranging from the occupation of Iraq to the flooding of New Orleans to the financial crimes of Bernie Madoff. His John Wells novels include Edgar Award-winner *The Faithful Spy*, and *The Ghost War*, *The Silent Man*, *The Midnight House*, *The Secret Soldier*, *The Shadow Patrol*, *The Night Ranger*, *The Counterfeit Agent*, and *Twelve Days*. He lives with his family in Garrison, New York.